THE HIGH PRIESTESS

KATIE CROSS

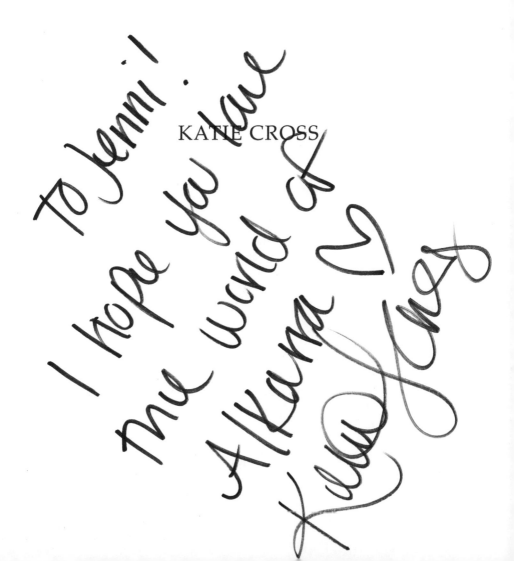

To Jenni!
I hope you love
the world of
Alkana ♥
Katie Cross

The High Priestess

YA Fantasy

Fiction

CONTENTS

To my little Warrior Princess.
May you always know that your power comes from within.
You are power.
You are strength.
You are ability.
And you will change the world.

INDEX OF ILESE WORDS

allo—hello, common greeting

andrea—caretaker of a property

ederra—beautiful

eliza—church

Griseo Petra—Hole of the First Life. The place where landowners believe the soul flies through after death on the way to their next existence.

jauna—master of a property

lavanda—laundry

maltea—friend

masuna—my love

pastanda—protector

poena—arena / the agony

sa—expression of respect, meant to be given on first meeting someone of status

titi—mouse

ultima—final day, last day of the week

ultima mort—last death

vinsela—special prison in the Saltu Jungle

wa—yes

GIVERS

La Principessa—Giver of Hope. Prayed to by all covens.

La Christianna—Giver of Courage. Prayed to by the East End Coven.

La Tourrere— Giver of Peace. Prayed to by the Necce Coven.

La Immanuella—Giver of Strength. Prayed to by the Samsa Coven.

La Salvatorra—Giver of Justice. Prayed to by the Mayfair Coven.

Castaneda Family

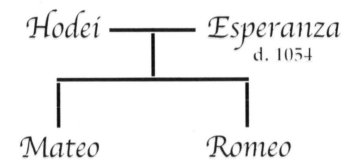

Hodei ——— Esperanza
d. 1054

Mateo   Romeo

Guita Family

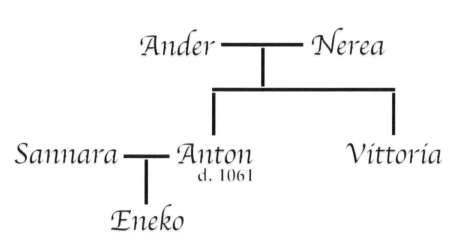

Ander —— Nerea

Sannara —— Anton
d. 1061

Eneko

Vittoria

HISTORICAL NOTE

If you've read any of my other books in the world of Alkarra, you may have noticed that I never gave specific dates or timelines, specifically concerning the year.

That's partially because I didn't want people to equate a year in Alkarra to a year in our world. (The two are *quite* different on many levels.) And partially because I had no clue just how many book ideas I'd come up with for Alkarra.

Now that I've settled in, I think I'll stay awhile.

But as I've proceeded into the Historical Collection as a series based on historical events mentioned in my other books . . . I can see how a firmer timeline is desperately needed.

If you're a new reader, read on! Vittoria awaits.

If you've previously read *the Network Series* or *the Dragonmaster Trilogy*, then let me help you place this in history a bit.

The High Priestess takes place starting in the year 1065, during the Castaneda Dynasty. You may recognize the name *Castaneda* because they were toppled by the *Aldanas* a few hundred years before you meet Diego and Niko Aldana in the third book in the Network Series, *The High Priest's Daughter.*

So, this story takes place around five hundred years before *The Dragonmaster Trilogy* and six hundred years before *The Network Series*.

Hope that helps. ;)

—Katie

1

VITTORIA

An elegant silk dress, the color of blood, spilled across Vittoria's palms.

Her hands trembled as she stared at the bottom hem. The thick edge of cream-colored lace was torn at the front of the dress. When she looked more closely, she found the tear ran all the way through the expensive silk, almost to the knee. She let out a long, slow breath, and the little hairs of silk rippled. The torn fabric sent a glacial chill down her spine.

"By the Givers," she whispered. "They'll take all my food."

Her empty stomach grumbled a worried assent.

She picked up the small scrub brush used specifically for lace and dropped it into a bowl of tepid water. Then she frantically surveyed the rest of the elaborate garment—no small feat, with nine layers of fabric beneath the silk. No other tears.

But no way to repair it.

Late summer air drifted into the room from an open window, cooling her hot skin. Water boiled in a cauldron over a crackling fire, which sent more humidity into an already-damp room. Outside, witches passed by in a quiet background murmur that softened the utter silence of the basement *lavanda*. Occasional calls rang out from the dressmaker above her.

This dressmaker was well-known among the elite landowners in her city, Necce. To lose this job would cripple Vittoria's chance of buying breathing medicine for Pere or a meal for her five-year-old nephew, Eneko.

A loud *thud* overhead drew her back to the present. Vittoria straightened her shoulders and mentally pulled herself together. She was a *lavanda* maid, not a seamstress. She cleaned laundry, didn't fix it. Still, she had to figure something out.

Maybe the *andrea* wouldn't notice the tear when she came down to check?

No chance of that. Of course the *andrea* would notice it. If the dress was already promised to a landowner's daughter for an upcoming ball, the girl would demand retribution for the offense. Silk this elegant came only from the Southern Network. It cost more currency than Vittoria would see in her lifetime.

An itchy suspicion nagged at her. This *andrea* had been sneaky in the past. She may have planted that tear so she could blame Vittoria and not pay her for cleaning both complicated dresses. The mauve dress had fifteen different layers that required attention. The *andrea* had an older seamstress she'd make fix it with magic, most likely.

Vittoria dismissed the suspicion. She wouldn't accuse the woman before she knew for certain. Best to get the work done and deal with it later, though she silently cursed herself for not checking each dress for damage before the *andrea* went back to work.

At twenty-one years old, she should have known better.

Vittoria shoved a lock of black hair out of her face. She could leave and get no pay—nor ever be able to work here again—or she could clean the dresses and hope for half a food bucket in pay.

For the next hour, she focused on her work. The correct potion on the silk. Wet heat from a boiling cauldron.

Scrub, scrub, scrub.

What felt like an eternity later, Vittoria slipped the shoulders of the crimson dress onto a wooden hanger as the upper door creaked. Sweat trickled down her back. All the windows were already open, but the stone basement kept heat like an oven. She hung the hanger on a hook in the stone wall and straightened the mauve dress with a few tugs. The footfalls of a heavyset woman sounded on the stairs just as Vittoria spun around.

Seconds later, a squat woman with perpetually slitted eyes appeared. She wore a gray dress that matched her hair, both flat and neat as a pin, and a pair of cloth shoes. A bolt of panic slipped through Vittoria like lightning.

Shoes!

She'd taken her wooden shoes off an hour ago. The heavy, awkward things made *lavanda* work impossible. If the *andrea* saw her barefoot . . . Vittoria edged to the left, where a bucket might hide her bare toes. Then she bowed her head.

"*Andrea*," she murmured.

The woman ignored her and approached the dresses with an outstretched hand. First, she touched the mauve silk, running her fingers down the sleeve and inspecting the lace around the neck. Vittoria had cleaned away all the specks of dirt and stray strings. Even the hem was clear, the lace cleaned by hand with her small brush and a special potion made just for light-colored material. Vittoria clamped her hands behind her back. The caustic soap had reddened the skin over her knuckles, but the dress practically glowed.

The *andrea* turned away from that one after studying each of the fifteen underlayers. Each perfect, as always.

"Humph."

Vittoria held her breath as the *andrea* moved on. The front of the crimson dress faced the stone wall. Perhaps she wouldn't—

"What," the *andrea* muttered coldly, "is this?"

She'd noticed the issue unusually fast. As if she'd been looking for it. The woman flipped the dress around and motioned to the tear.

Vittoria drew in a breath. "It was there when I began, *andrea*. Before I even took it off the hook."

"It wasn't."

"When I went to clean the lace on the hem, I noticed it."

The *andrea*'s beady eyes tapered until they became mere lines. "You expect me to believe that?"

"Why would I tear it? *How* would I tear it? There's nothing sharp down here."

"Laziness?" the *andrea* cried. "Foolishness? You stepped on it? You're nothing but a *lavanda* maid, so what do you know?"

Vittoria hid a flinch. "*Andrea,* I assure you I didn't cause that tear. My work is sound, and it always has been. I've worked here many times in the past. Your dresses are otherwise perfectly laundered and prepared for presentation to your buyers."

"No food for you today." The *andrea* waved a hand. "Go. Don't come back. You're not welcome here anymore."

"But I did the work you conscripted me to do today. Please, just cut the amount of food if you're upset. I should at least get payment for the mauve—"

"Go!" the woman shouted, a strand of hair falling from her thick bun.

Vittoria longed to shout back. Her throat ached with it. She'd spent six hours on the mauve dress. Six hours she'd never get back. Six hours of stolen time, and what could she do about it? Vittoria clenched her fists. Eneko's tiny, smudged face floated through her mind. He would go hungry again tonight. Pere would cough and moan in his sleep.

All of this was for nothing.

Vittoria hesitated a moment, then opened her mouth to counter again. Warmth wrapped around her throat, silencing her like a strangling hand. Magic. The *andrea* had used a silencing spell on her.

Rage simmered deep under the surface of Vittoria's mind.

"Not. A. Word," the woman said through gritted teeth. "Or I'll have your tongue cut out. Go."

The *andrea* gathered both dresses and turned to go up the stairs, but not before casting a suspicious look over her shoulders, as if Vittoria would chase after her. Vittoria wanted to throw the brush at her, but refrained out of fear. The landowners lived out on a peninsula near the ocean, among elaborate homes, shops, and gardens made of bleached stone, but they had shops in Necce. Both in Necce and on the peninsula, Guardians roamed the cobblestone streets. One move against the *andrea*, and she'd be sent to prison to waste away and die. If she were conscripted to a house, which she never had been, they'd sew her mouth shut for talking back. A favorite punishment among the noble elite.

Then Pere would die.

Eneko would starve.

No, Mere and Pere had already lost one child. She couldn't abandon them out of frustration at a worthless *andrea* who stole her time and used magic against her. Other workers had endured far worse.

Vittoria closed her eyes, stuffed her rage into a little corner in the back of her mind, and turned to find her wooden shoes. Tears made her vision hot and blurry, but she blinked them back. No, she wouldn't waste any tears on such a wretched witch. With any luck, La Salvatorra, the Giver of Justice, would come and shred those dresses to ribbons in the night.

She sighed.

If only the Givers were real . . .

When she crouched to pick up her clogs, she stopped. Sitting next to her shoes, near the back door, was a wooden bucket with a metal handle. The interior of the bucket was heaped with flat *pitta* bread, linen bags the size of her palm, shiny apples, and what appeared to be slices of smoked eel. A bright-blue symbol the size of her palm hovered over it, conjured by magic. It was an intricate, woven design, like hundreds of braids tied together.

The sign of La Salvatorra.

Her breath caught as the sign faded. Hadn't she just thought of La Salvatorra? Had she somehow summoned him here?

No, that was insane.

The tears she'd valiantly fought disappeared as she touched the food. The bread was pillowy and warm. The seeds in the small linen bags were crisp. Even the apples smelled fresh, as if they'd come straight from the orchards that ringed the northern outskirts of Necce.

She looked around, but of course, the *lavanda* was empty. There was nothing here but potion bottles on the wall and barrels of fresh water, as usual. Of course he wasn't here. La Salvatorra was a reputed Giver and famously powerful with magic, but she imagined he was little more than a bored landowner who liked to help others.

How did he know?

She glanced at the windows. He'd overheard, perhaps. Did La Salvatorra prowl around the city to find workers to help, or had he happened on her?

Vittoria shook herself. It didn't matter. For a moment, she could almost believe La Salvatorra was real. That Givers—magical witches sent by the goddess of the sea—actually watched over workers. Listened to their prayers. Brought justice, hope, courage, or strength. But the Givers were myths. Tales. Legends that workers told each other in the dark, miserable, hungry nights while the landowners took their food.

La Salvatorra—or, rather, the witch who had been offering gifts to workers under the symbol of La Salvatorra, spurring on rumors of a Giver in the streets—was likely a charitable landowner. A rogue, for no one knew him. He hid behind his magic, but served the workers. Yet the workers believed him to be endowed with power from Prana, here to dispense justice on their behalf.

And somehow he'd heard of her plight just now.

Eneko would not go hungry today. A feeling of sheepishness crawled over Vittoria. La Salvatorra was the Giver of the Mayfair Coven, to which she belonged. Surely, Mere would count this as proof of the Giver's existence.

"He has watched over us!" she would say. "The Givers see all."

Skeptical but still grateful, Vittoria grabbed five *pittas*, five apples, and several smoked eels. One for each of them at the house. She stuffed them into the deep pockets Mere had sewn into her dress. They weighed her dress down, but the folds of her skirt managed to hide them. Only a fool carried their food for others to steal.

More food remained in the bucket, of course. Vittoria gathered the rest in her hands, then stepped out of the basement *lavanda* with relief.

A warm wind brushed over her skin as she stood in the crowded Necce alley. The back entrance kept her separated from the landowners on the cobblestone roads. Only workers flowed through the alleys back here.

The castle divided Necce into two sections. The landowners' homes occupied all of the peninsula on the southern edge of the city. The castle and all its resplendent magnolia trees and gardens stood like a gleaming sentinel to the north of the peninsula. Beyond the castle lay north Necce, where landowners shopped and managed their trades, and where the workers lived.

Not three steps into the alley, a figure huddled in the shadows. Vittoria stopped, crouched down, and peered into the face of a female witch. A gaping red eye socket stared back at her. Dried blood drained down a gaunt cheek. The other eye was a warm chocolate brown, bloodshot from tears. This injury was recent and clearly still painful.

"*Allo,*" Vittoria whispered. She passed a piece of *pitta* bread over. "For you, *maltea.*"

A wrinkled, trembling hand reached out from the folds of filthy clothes. The witch's lips formed the words *thank you* as she pulled the bread to wrinkled lips. A mouth full of teeth meant she must be young, though it was hard to tell. Was she caught looking at something a landowner believed she shouldn't? Falsely accused of something else?

Did it matter?

Vittoria squeezed her hand and shuffled to the next hungry soul on the street.

"Here, *maltea,*" she murmured to a one-armed beggar.

"You call me your friend?" he asked in a shaky voice as he snatched the food. He growled, but it was confusion, not anger.

Vittoria smiled. "All workers should be friends, shouldn't we? Have some food. May La Principessa bless you."

A charcoal drawing decorated the alley wall nearby—a picture of a woman with long hair, her hands held out at her sides. Despite streaked dirt and what appeared to be dried blood on her feet, a shockingly white magnolia flower rested on the woman's chest, unmarred by filth and time.

Vittoria slowed, let out a deep breath, and touched the foot of the drawing. She murmured the salutation to La Principessa, Giver of Hope, before she gave away the last of the food.

La Salvatorra had blessed her today. She might not believe in the Givers, but at least she knew that.

The ocean chanted softly near the pier as Vittoria slipped through the streets of the Mayfair Coven early the next morning. Shouts from navy ships, the scurrying of rats, and the quiet illumination of candles in the windows enveloped her as she left her coven and headed toward south Necce to find a landowner home in need of a *lavanda* maid.

She'd gotten a late start after a coughing fit sent Pere into spasms. Mere left for her conscripted job as a cook in the Moretti household well before the sun came up, which left Vittoria to care for Pere. Settling him had taken longer than she'd expected. A late *lavanda* maid was a hungry one.

Minutes later, she winced as a third wooden door slammed in her face. "No work!" the *andrea* of a restaurant called through the door. "Come back next week."

"Well." Vittoria scowled. "I didn't want to work for you, either."

With a sigh, she started down the alley again. Dawn lightened the far horizon as she headed for an inn she'd worked in before. It was the second day of a six-day week, which meant there would still be leftover laundry from the weekend. Landowners always traveled from the country to the city on the weekends.

The advantage of having *two* houses.

Her stomach growled even though it was satisfied by the food La Salvatorra had given her the night before. As she passed a lone statue of La Christianna, Giver of Courage, her fingertips trailed along the bottom of the statue. La Christianna always had bare feet. She was worshiped in the East End Coven, but all workers appreciated her statue. Every worker needed courage.

Her mind wandered back to La Salvatorra as she walked. She'd heard of the mysterious Giver who showed himself in person, but she'd ignored the tales until now. How did he find witches who needed him? That wouldn't be hard in Necce. Did he use magic to be invisible? She shuddered at the thought.

The use of magic, she'd long ago decided, was quite rude.

While her mind wandered, she approached another inn. Before she could knock, she caught sight of another *lavanda* maid through the window. The maid waved to Vittoria with an apologetic grin. Vittoria smiled, waved back, and continued on.

"Givers," she muttered.

Another five locations yielded no work. Desperate, she abandoned the landowners to check the less-wealthy places in north Necce. She found herself in the narrow, dank alleys of the Necce Coven. With a shiver, she continued north, toward friendlier covens. The Necce Coven was thick with rebels who attacked the landowners in riots and ignored the High Priest's edicts. They were always trying to recruit more workers into their dangerous ranks.

They also had their heads cut off by Guardians and placed on pikes in the alleys.

The Giver of Peace, La Tourrere, peered down at Vittoria as she scurried past, his face stern with hidden rebuke. Odd that a man who gave peace would appear so annoyed all the time. Vittoria sighed. Another hour of searching and she'd be firmly out of a job for the day. Perhaps her luck had run out with La Salvatorra aiding her yesterday.

With hope, Vittoria knocked on the basement door of a brothel. Another *lavanda* maid opened it, then shook her head. She had the same black hair and dark eyes as Vittoria—as all the witches in the Eastern Network.

"I'm sorry, Vittoria," she said quietly. "Not today."

Vittoria smiled. "Thank you. Have a good day."

The girl closed the door, her wooden shoes loud on the stone floor as she walked away. Vittoria let out a long breath. Home, then. She'd head back to Mayfair Coven, care for Pere. Take care of Eneko. Her neighbor, Alona, had injured herself yesterday. Vittoria could visit her.

She spun around with a sigh, then came to an abrupt stop. A food bucket hovered in the air right in front of her. La Salvatorra's mark glowed above it. Startled, she simply stared at it for a moment.

Another food bucket?

The sign began to dissipate into clouds. Vittoria reached out. As soon as she touched the bucket, the magic holding it in the air vanished, and it sank into her hands. This couldn't be a mere stroke of luck this time. No.

Had he followed her?

Been following her?

"*Allo*?" she called.

The alley yielded nothing but wet stone walls, wisps of receding fog, and the refuse dumped out of windows. She stepped further into the shadows.

"La Salvatorra?"

No witches peered down on her from windows. She craned her head back. None on the rooftops that she could see. His ability to do magic gave him all the advantage, because he could be standing next to her for all she knew. The High Priest, Hodei, had passed an edict over twenty years ago that prevented workers from receiving any education. No reading. No writing. No magic.

Vittoria stared at the food in breathless surprise. A tumult of emotions filled her. Relief. Elation. Disbelief. Was she lucky? Did she have a hidden savior?

Realizing that she was standing in the middle of an alley with a full bucket of food, she quickly stuffed some into her pockets. *Pitta* bread again. Cheese this time, yellow and thick with a hard red rind.

What luxury! She broke off a piece and carefully placed it in her pocket. Five *pittas*, a hearty chunk of cheese, and two bags of seeds later, she still had over half a bucket. That would feed her, Eneko, Mere, and Pere for another day. There would even be enough for Sannara—Eneko's mother—if she happened to come home today. Mere's food rations from her work as a cook in the Moretti house would buy more medicine for Pere that they could store.

If she saved it, they could buy extra potions. Or have two meals today.

The call of a beggar in the street pierced her ears. "La Tourrere! Hear my plea!"

Vittoria sighed. No, she wouldn't have two meals today. They'd have one, like always, and she'd give the rest away. Luck—or La Salvatorra—had happened on her twice. She should share the goodness.

"Well." She cast her gaze around her again. Though she spoke to the air, she had a feeling that someone was listening. "Then I'll share it if you're going to be so generous. There are many injured who go to the *eliza* of the Giver La Principessa. I shall share this with them there. Th—thank you."

She couldn't be sure, but she thought she heard a soft, masculine chuckle as she left the alley.

∾

"Tori!"

A happy shriek greeted Vittoria when she returned to their home a few hours later. A mop of unruly hair crashed into her legs.

She staggered backward, laughing. "*Allo, Eneko.*"

Eneko tilted his head back and stared at her with wide eyes. Like his pere, her brother Anton, he had dusky skin and a fast smile. His youthful, still-bright grin pulled at her heartstrings. Today, wrinkles on his forehead betrayed his concern.

"You're back?" he asked, puzzlement in his voice.

"I am."

"But no work means . . ."

Vittoria smiled and crouched next to him. "Today, I have a special surprise. La Salvatorra has visited me again!"

His eyes widened. "Food?"

"More food." She reached into her pocket and gave him the largest piece of round *pitta* bread. "Here."

Eneko snatched it out of her hands and stuffed a quarter of it in his face in seconds.

Vittoria pulled it away. "Take your time," she chided gently. "You'll become sick. Enjoy your food, Eneko. You're impetuous, like your pere." She tapped his nose. "Cheeky."

He grinned, and her heart melted. "Mere says that Pere smiled just like me," he said around a mouthful of bread.

"He did."

Eneko widened his smile, then grabbed a stick that had fallen to the ground. "Thank you, Tori. I love having so much food! La Salvatorra should come every day."

She ruffled his hair and straightened up. "Do me a favor, *masuna?* Go next door and check on Alona."

He grimaced. "She was hurt, Tori. Her arm has blood on it."

"I know. I saved some food for her. Tell her I'll be there in a few minutes, then wait for me there? She loves talking to you. You can tell her stories and brighten her day."

"About La Immanuella!" He jumped, wielding his stick like a sword. "I'm La Immanuella, and I'm strong!"

Vittoria laughed as he parried an unseen foe and spun around so quickly he fell on his rump.

"Go, Giver of Strength." She nudged him back to the door. "I will be there in a moment."

Eneko disappeared outside with another cry, waving his stick against invisible invaders. Vittoria shut the creaky door behind her, expression placid as she moved to the rickety table in the middle of their square home. She unloaded the food on a flat, wooden tray there, grateful to see it so full for a second day in a row.

They lived at the bottom of a three-story building in the Mayfair Coven. Years ago, maybe a hundred, it used to be a landowner's house. After the great divide between classes, decades before Vittoria's birth, the owner had dashed to the peninsula and abandoned this building.

Vittoria's family lived in a room on the bottom floor—five witches in a square space meant as more of a storage closet. Charcoal drawings of Givers populated the walls of the home. Mere redrew them every week, worried that if they forgot one, the Giver would be upset.

A wet, wheezy cough issued from Pere's chest. He beckoned her with a wave.

"La Salvatorra again today?" he asked.

"Yes."

She handed him a *pitta*, but he waved it back with a warm smile. He placed a hand on her cheek. "Later, *masuna*. We eat as a family, always."

Vittoria put her hand over his. Shocks of white streaked his thin black hair. She imagined, if he were a landowner, it would be thick and full. A scraggly beard covered his face now, hiding his gaunt cheeks. His eyes used to dance—Pere always loved to tell amusing stories on the farm—but now they were glazed with pain.

She put a hand on a knobby knee beneath his blanket.

"And your legs?" she asked.

He shrugged, but one hand rubbed his right thigh, which was little more than bone, lying inert beneath the blanket. All the muscle had wasted away. Six years ago, Vittoria and her family had lived on the farms far outside Necce. A cow had trampled Pere, slamming a hoof onto his back and breaking it. Unable to walk or work, he faced execution by the landowner. Vittoria, Anton, and Mere had carried him away in the night.

Eventually, they took refuge in Mayfair Coven to scrounge for work in Necce.

That was years ago, when her brother Anton still lived and things weren't quite so frightening. Now, Pere lived on a mattress on the floor. Infections plagued his lungs while the rest of them scrambled to earn food every day. Vittoria had been fifteen when they arrived in Necce. Most girls were conscripted and assigned to a trade by age six. Pere's intermittent sicknesses and, eventually, Eneko's birth meant someone had to be home to care for them.

Vittoria worked as a *lavanda* maid so she didn't have to show up to a conscripted service every day, like Mere. On the days when Pere and Eneko needed someone at their side, Vittoria was there.

"There is more potion for your pain." Vittoria stood to reach for the glass bottle of light-yellow potion that sat on a counter far out of Eneko's reach. "It's fresh, Pere, from last night. Why don't you have some?"

"No, no. It's too soon. We shouldn't use it too much. I'm fine. Sannara left a little while ago."

"Sannara was here? We haven't seen her in weeks."

"She didn't stay long. Eneko didn't even see her."

Vittoria tensed. Sannara, her brother's widow, moved like a fog most days. She was twenty-one, like Vittoria, and had birthed Eneko at the young age of sixteen. She came home with food or supplies every now and then, but never told them how she found it. Pere assumed she sold herself to desperate men, and he said in vulnerable moments how he hated the circumstances that drove her to it. But Sannara had never confirmed any of their questions.

Sannara did Sannara's business.

"Alona," Pere continued with a yawn. "She's fevering now."

"I'll go see her."

Vittoria pulled a thin blanket from her cloth hanging bed and tucked it over him. He smiled at her from a mattress filled with old straw on the floor. They'd need to change it soon. When she looked at Pere, she thought of her dead brother, Anton, with a pang that never seemed to fade.

"These food buckets." Pere tilted his head back to stare at the ceiling, hands folded over his stomach.

Vittoria grabbed a stick with twigs tied at the bottom and swept their hard-packed dirt floor. "What about the buckets?" she asked.

"Do you think La Salvatorra is giving them to you for a reason?"

"He's only given me two, Pere."

He made a sound in his throat. "But twice means he's followed you. Twice means . . . something."

"Two isn't a pattern."

"Not yet."

She frowned. Did it mean something? Maybe La Salvatorra had stumbled on her twice. Though, that wasn't very likely. Pere had a point. One she didn't like. Had La Salvatorra followed her? Did he want something in return?

Pere broke into her thoughts. "Then again, who are we to question the Givers?"

She hid a scowl as she pulled a few wooden sticks off the floor and set them on their table for Eneko to find again later.

"La Salvatorra is a witch, Pere. A landowner, likely, and as much our enemy as he is a savior. He's called La Salvatorra by the workers, but that doesn't make him a Giver."

Pere chuckled. "Ah, Vittoria. You are so serious-minded for such a young woman." His expression sobered into melancholy. "I'm sorry that your life has required you to face such truths so soon. Of course the Givers are stories, but they do work, don't you think? Do we not feel more hope when we pray to La Principessa? More courage when we speak to La Christianna?"

Her response caught in her throat. "Pere . . ."

He waved her off. "No, I understand. You don't have to believe, Vittoria. The Givers will bless you anyway." His eyes drifted closed with another yawn as he readjusted his body farther into the mattress. "Just don't tell your mere."

Vittoria watched him fade into sleep as she set the broom back in the corner. Then she grabbed a *pitta* bread, pinched off a chunk of cheese, and headed over to Alona's with La Salvatorra on her mind.

2
MATEO

S lick cobblestones hushed Mateo's boots as he slipped down a darkened road in the heart of Necce, the old city by the sea.

He clung to the buildings to stay out of sight. Only the occasional torchlight from a porch or the sad flicker of a candle softened the air. The stars overhead illuminated the night sky. It was the third month of summer. Fall would be here soon, and more desperate days would follow. He stopped, stared at the sky for a breath or two, and kept going.

Vittoria was walking home from a *lavanda* job at a men's tailoring shop. Like all workers, her wooden shoes thumped on the ground and she walked with a metal pipe in her left hand. Her eyes darted around, wisely watchful, but she didn't seem frightened. Her neck was taut, but without panic.

Here was a woman used to the violent streets.

Good. With a graceful neck like that, she needed to be aware.

Mateo kept an eye on her as she curved around to check her back. He was hidden behind a spell and wouldn't be noticed. She stopped on the left side of the road, near several broken crates and a pile of decayed food. Landowners didn't come this far, so the utilitarian cleanliness of the streets had waned.

Mateo paused.

She rapped on a wooden door leading to a ramshackle two-story building built for a small family of four. Most buildings in this part of Necce had been abandoned and left to die. But the workers had filled them quickly. Instead of four, it likely housed fifteen. Maybe fewer now that witches seemed to be disappearing off the streets, fleeing to the protection of the rebels more than ever.

He stilled, breath held. Her white-knuckled grip on the pipe hadn't eased as she waited for someone to answer her summons.

Clearly, Vittoria was distracted by something. He didn't like that. It wasn't safe, particularly not in the Necce Coven, even with the watchful gaze of La Tourrere overhead. A woman as beautiful as Vittoria couldn't afford a single lapse of attention in a world like this.

A young girl answered the timid knock. The two of them murmured back and forth for a minute. Keeping his eyes on the shadows across the road, Mateo used a simple spell that made it easier to hear the conversation.

"Any work?" Vittoria asked.

"Not tomorrow. Maybe the next day."

A sigh. "Do you know of any other places that need help?"

"No. The rebel riots against the landowner shops near the Samsa Coven have left many women upended. *Lavanda* maids are so available that some have offered to work for half portions of food."

Mateo frowned. Troublesome. The rebels had been escalating their insurgency tactics against the landowners for weeks now. Riots made their situation worse in most ways, although he could understand the burning need to be heard at any cost. But the fractured rebel groups weren't working together anymore. Not that he could tell, anyway.

Unfortunately, innocents like Vittoria bore the brunt of the consequences.

"Thank you," Vittoria said. "Do you have enough to eat? I . . . stumbled into some extras. I would be happy to share."

Mateo's head cocked to the side.

How had she made it to this age with such a disposition? There was no room for softness as a worker. Four days ago, he'd walked by a dress shop and heard her argument with a notoriously difficult *andrea*. The food bucket had been easy to send. What startled him was seeing her, not five minutes after he'd used a spell to put the bucket there, giving over half of it away. Nothing could have shocked him more.

So he'd followed her. Watched her go home, attend to a neighbor, play with a little boy. She was quiet, lovely grace.

And that's when he'd had the best idea of his life.

It had taken all night to truly contemplate the idea. To think to the end of it and back. The ramifications. The negatives. He'd driven his men mad as he paced, talked it out, and dreamed up the ending.

Now, four days later, he'd given her four buckets.

And every day she'd done the same thing—kept half, given the rest away.

The other girl accepted Vittoria's offer of food with a grateful smile. "Thank you, *maltea*. We did not have work today. May La Principessa bless you."

They exchanged a kiss of each cheek, and Vittoria stepped back. She pulled a shawl more closely round her shoulders, glanced around, and kept walking. If he'd counted correctly, she'd just given away the last of the food. Her shoulders sank a bit lower now. Dejection about the lack of work, perhaps? He studied her as he followed, intrigued beyond words.

A shadow moved out of an alley just as Vittoria passed. Male, if the broad shoulders meant anything. There was a bit of swagger in his steps as he stumbled closer to her. Laid off, likely. The talentless died in their own wallow these days. Even on a busy side road—which this one wasn't— Vittoria could get pulled away. The alleys of Necce were dark and plentiful. Most workers didn't bother to listen or help anymore. Too entrenched in their own misery.

Two quick strides, and Mateo caught up to the witch. A hand on the back of his neck, a growl of warning, and a flick of his wrist left the attacker lying in a pile of dank, molding rubbish. The witch groaned and then passed out.

Vittoria, knuckles white on her metal pipe, glanced over her shoulder in the vague direction of the witch. Seeing nothing of concern, she turned warily back around.

She headed away from the city center and toward the Mayfair Coven. It was quieter there, more residential, with fewer hidden ipsum taverns and less desperation. But it was on the other side of the city. The farther away from the landowner shops, the less the Guardians patrolled. In the outer rings of Necce, refugees from the farms and country were forced to work and live in close quarters. Chaos abounded.

For the fourth time, he followed her . . . just in case.

Rats peeked out of the refuse, scurrying boldly over piles of excrement and slipping into the walls. Vittoria kept her pipe at the ready. Fifteen minutes later, she slowed in front of a door, glanced around, and slipped inside.

Her house.

He paused a moment, made sure she remained safe inside, then transported to a different part of Necce. Wind brushed against his face as he stood high facing Samsa Coven, on top of the *eliza* of the Giver La Principessa. Lights from Magnolia Castle flickered to the south. Beyond, the ocean curled in blue waves. Screams, laughter, and sobs alternated from below, threaded with cries of, "La Principessa!"

La Principessa, indeed.

Mateo's thoughts churned over Vittoria as he stared at the city. A shuffle of feet, and the sound of someone else breathing, joined him. Mateo removed his invisibility spell and looked to his left.

A tall, broad-shouldered man appeared. He had dark hair shorn close to his head and a goatee around his lips. Muscles rippled along his arms, intensifying the serious expression on his pockmarked face. He was fifty-something years old—ancient for a worker, with the wrinkles to prove it.

"Benat," Mateo said.

"Majesty."

Mateo rolled his eyes, but said nothing.

"Your night with the young woman was successful?" Benat asked. With hamlike fingers, he gripped the railing that encircled the top of the *eliza*. Magnolia flowers cascaded off the top of the wall, their smell lightening the air. They were spells. Flowers enchanted to live through anything. Mere had put them there a decade ago, at least.

Mateo nodded. "Another bucket given, another bucket distributed."

"She's consistent."

"So far. The question is whether she'll continue to share what we give her. And if she does, for how long? If we give her resources for a long time, maybe she'll start to hoard. Maybe she'll get comfortable and stop sharing. Maybe..."

He let his own thoughts trail off.

Benat grunted. "You don't have forever to play this game."

"I don't need forever. Just a few months of her doing what she clearly does so naturally. Pere is ill, but not yet dying. If Vittoria proves to be the right witch, we have a real chance."

"Your plan is wild."

Mateo laughed. "It is. And it's the only way. The only thing that neither Pere nor Romeo would anticipate."

"She's a *lavanda* maid."

"No one better."

Sobs came from below again, so Mateo initiated his favorite magic—Sarteran—which was still unknown among Hodei's magic-seeking Guardians. Using magic that the Guardians weren't trained to feel, hear, or sense gave them ample opportunity to help workers but remain undetected.

It was time to get to work.

"Your men are in place, I presume?"

Benat straightened, clearly eager to get to their nightly rounds. "Yes, Majesty. They wait below."

"Then let us give justice in the name of La Salvatorra tonight. Tomorrow, I speak with my pere and Romeo," he said brightly, "and who knows if I'll even live through it?"

Benat snorted. "For honor," he said with a thump on his chest.

Mateo grinned.

"For honor."

Three days later, Mateo regarded a bloody slash across his forearm with a narrowed gaze. It was deep enough to bleed, but shouldn't need to be stitched closed. High chance of infection, though.

Perfect.

Twilight fell around him. He stood on the outskirts of the landowner coven and carefully watched the basement windows of the *lavanda* in a bustling house. This landowner, Moretti, was famous for his elegant hospitality and extravagant parties. Landowners all over the Eastern Network came to his mansion in Necce for his lavish balls and dinners. So many witches meant big crowds. Big crowds meant a lot of bed linens, tablecloths, servants' clothes, and silk napkins to launder.

Which meant Vittoria was fast at work today.

She'd been up earlier than usual this morning, before the first hint of dawn. Her mere worked at the Moretti house in some capacity he hadn't figured out yet, which was likely how Vittoria had known there'd be work today. They'd walked here together, and Vittoria had arrived minutes before a rush of other *lavanda* maids desperate for food. Since *lavanda* maids weren't conscripted, they had to grope for work every day. Brutal.

He'd spent the last three days invisibly walking Vittoria to and from work to ensure her safety. Word had spread rapidly regarding her generosity. A few witches watched for her now, this elegant witch in a hopeless world. She gave food, laughter, or help to everyone.

Today, he'd finally speak with her.

She wouldn't know him. Not yet, anyway. He wanted to introduce himself as La Salvatorra, the witch who had given her food buckets for the last seven days, but now wasn't the time. He had to prove her out still.

Could she actually change the world?

His face warmed again, then slowly cooled. His belly grew in girth, his shirt tightening around him. The rotating transformative magic that he used as La Salvatorra shifted every few minutes, changing his appearance from head to toe, which made him impossible to track in a crowd.

He stopped the magic, an ancient one he'd found in a century-old grimoire. Kakkans, or something like that. Obsessed with transforming themselves and the mortal enemies of the Cudans. Didn't matter, because the magic wasn't inert, despite being out of use. No one else knew of it, which was an edge he needed against landowners obsessed with honor and magic.

Instead, he issued a basic transformation spell. His usually wide shoulders narrowed, and his towering height shrank so he'd be no taller than Vittoria. The thick black hair that fell to his shoulders shortened. His hazel eyes turned muddy brown, and his face rounded out slightly.

Thankfully, the magic didn't hurt. Was mere illusion. Over time, it did drain his energy to maintain. Like a muscle, magical power could be built and strengthened. He'd become quite powerful with magic over the years, thanks to his constant use of it as La Salvatorra.

Once the transformation was complete, he stepped into the street.

Landowner streets were wider, built with cobblestones and made to last, unlike the dirt roads in the covens of Necce. On either side of the streets were lawns and gardens and the elegant mansions that lay behind them. Every landowner house had one side that backed up to a less-conspicuous street to allow the workers quiet access. No Givers adorned the walls here, making this coven less visually cluttered than those in north Necce, where workers sketched their Givers with charcoal on every surface.

Mateo crossed the road and knocked on the *lavanda* door. Seconds later, it creaked open. Vittoria peered out, her hazel eyes reserved. She wore a cream-colored dress underneath an emerald overlayer that protected her clothes from potions. Her hair was pulled away from her face in a loose braid, although a few tendrils escaped.

She took his breath away every time.

Up close was no different, with her heart-shaped face, pert nose, and full lips. She was thin, but not yet deathly so. Somehow, her family seemed to work together and eke out a living in a world where many dwindled in their own despair. That despair was why La Principessa was considered the most powerful Giver of all. She offered hope.

"*Sa.*" He dropped his head slightly. "I have heard you are a healer."

She straightened. "I'm a *lavanda* maid, not a healer."

"But you have a reputation for helping workers, and I need help. No apothecary would see a worker with such an incision as mine." He lifted his arm. "Infection will set in soon if it's not cleaned."

Her teeth sank into her bottom lip. She glanced behind her, then back at him. She didn't even flinch at his gash, just studied it, then finally opened the door.

"Quickly."

He stepped into the room, and she closed the door behind her. Then she slipped past him, barefoot, and motioned to a bench. "Have a seat."

"Thank you. I can pay you for your help."

She waved that off. "Save the food for your family."

He lifted an eyebrow. He'd expected something so selfless from her after all he'd seen her give away on the streets, but it still startled him to hear it.

"You are . . . very giving."

Vittoria didn't look at him again, but a half smile lingered on her lips. She moved toward a basket filled with discarded linens.

"When I can be, I like to be. I can't promise you'll be healed." She cast a quick glance at his arm. "Workers come to me because I have access to soap, hot water, and old cloths, which is rare enough, but not because I can heal anything. I know no healing incantations or magic."

"But you help."

Their eyes met for a moment, then she turned away. He felt her gaze all the way to the bottom of his toes. For the last week, she'd unknowingly commanded all his attention. He couldn't stop thinking about her. He'd given thousands of food buckets away over the last ten years, and never had someone shared so much of what they received. They took it home and ate it over several days or tried to eat it all at once and made themselves sick.

But Vittoria was different.

Tonight, she'd receive her seventh bucket, but this one would refill itself at least three times. Zuri had all the food ready for him to transport into the bucket with a spell, because not even landowners could conjure food that satisfied hunger and nourished the body.

He had little doubt Vittoria would reserve some for her family, then give away all the rest. Still, he'd test her. Because if she started to keep it—and who could blame her?—then he'd know she wasn't the one.

But oh, how he wanted her to be.

Vittoria worked steadily as she prepped a few old rags and grabbed a potion from a glass bottle over a hearth.

"Your name is Vittoria, yes?" he asked.

She nodded.

"You are becoming known for your charity. There were two witches outside waiting for you to finish your work here."

To his surprise, a wry smile filled her face. "Yes, they are my friends. I've known them for many years. They're hungry and unable to work. Who can blame them for waiting?" She motioned to his cut as she approached. "This potion will sting."

He shrugged. "Where do you get the food to be so generous?" he asked.

She hesitated. "A . . . kind landowner."

It required all his considerable concentration not to react. *A kind landowner*? He was the legendary La Salvatorra! To the workers, a Giver come to life, and to the landowners, a pesky gnat that needed swatting. She knew what his sign was and who gave her the food. She thanked him for it every day.

A *landowner*?

He fought off the initial insult with a smile. "How fortunate."

Her gaze darted to him, then back to his wound as she dribbled a little potion over it. Had she sensed some tension in his voice?

"It's not like that," she snapped. "I don't sell my body to him."

"I never imagined that."

The potion frothed over the blood, so she quickly put a wet, warm cloth over the top of it and applied a little pressure with the weight of her hand. The cut stung for a moment.

"Well." She chewed on her bottom lip. "To be truthful, it's . . . it's La Salvatorra that leaves the buckets. He has been leaving them for me for over a week now, and I don't need all that food. So I share."

"Ah!" His face lit up. "Who else? He's a very good man."

She rolled her eyes.

He fought not to choke. Had she just rolled her eyes? "You . . . you do not like the legendary Giver?" he asked in a strangled voice, failing to affect a casual air.

She had the moxie to appear amused. Call him arrogant, but he'd earned at least a little recognition after all the years sacrificing his food, his safety, and his name to the streets. Mateo lived in a weird in-between. Born of nobility, living among workers. He claimed neither side, because how could he? He straddled the middle because at least the middle would have him.

When he was La Salvatorra, he felt all that slide away.

"La Salvatorra is not a bad witch," she said slowly. "A bored landowner, I would imagine, with wealth and time to spare. At least he has a conscience . . . or maybe he just loves danger."

"He *does* something, at least."

Her nose wrinkled. She shrugged with one shoulder. "Maybe . . . but he's not very effective, is he?"

Mateo swallowed hard. This girl and her opinions! "Effective?" he cried. "Think of the lives he's saved!"

"You are a friend of his?"

He grinned. "I could only be so blessed."

Her eyes rolled again.

"I'm amazed!" he said, unable to hide his astonishment. "He gives you food to spare and you speak badly of him?"

"No." She unwrapped the bandage. "Not badly. I am grateful for the food he's given to me, my parents, and my nephew. But . . ."

She trailed off, clearly lost in thought as she obtained another bandage, soaked it in a cauldron of steaming water, and returned. When she mopped up his arm, she frowned.

"Yes?" he prodded.

"I just think that La Salvatorra is a bandage over a festering wound. He hands out food to witches who will just need more the next day. We are still hungry. We are still workers. We are still uneducated."

Mateo let out a long breath.

She winced. "Does it hurt a lot?"

"No, it's fine," he croaked. He couldn't even feel the cut, but his pride stung. Never in the last decade had he ever stumbled on a worker who didn't love La Salvatorra. He didn't need to be thought of as an almost-god —Givers were the next-closest thing. But all the other workers held his name in reverence. Vittoria? She'd cast it out with the wash water if she could.

There must be some explanation.

"Do you believe in the Givers?" he asked.

She hesitated. "Ah . . ."

It was his turn to sound amused. "I take that as a no."

"It's not so simple as that. Givers are supposed to be more powerful than witches. They're supposed to be benevolent and watchful over workers. But La Salvatorra has not given justice. Not truly. Because we are still oppressed." She shrugged. "How can the Givers be real if not even La Salvatorra has saved us? La Salvatorra, if he is a Giver, is a disappointment. Which means the Givers can't be real. That means that La Salvatorra is a landowner with a conscience."

Astonished, Mateo could only stare at the floor. Of all the things he'd expected her to say today, none of it was *that*. His mind spun.

What could be said?

Vittoria had made several points. Good points. Points that he'd never heard or considered before.

"Fair," he said, his voice barely moderated. She didn't worship the Givers, at least. That was one point in her favor regarding his whole plan. But could she be trusted? That's what he'd set out to prove.

For some reason, he felt he could trust her more than ever now.

She softened her words with a gentle smile as she wrapped a white bandage around his arm. She looped it back around, then tied the two ends together.

With a nod, she motioned to the door. "You may go."

He stood. Should he reveal himself to her earlier than planned? In spite of her attitude toward La Salvatorra—or perhaps because of it—he decided it was time, after all. "Thank you for your help," he said warmly. "May I give you some food?"

"No, save it for yourself or your family, or give it to one of the witches outside. But thank you."

"No, I must insist."

A bucket appeared on the floor, this one with a lighter color and wider girth than normal. Twice as much food as he'd ever given her filled it. There wouldn't be room enough in her pockets. She'd have to carry the bucket, which is what he wanted. Witches needed to see her with it. Her eyes widened as he whispered the ancient spell for the sign of La Salvatorra. His symbol appeared seconds later.

Vittoria gasped. Then she glared at him.

"You!" she cried. "You are La Salvatorra?"

He reinitiated the rotating magic so his appearance would change. As his features eased into something else, she took a step backward until her back collided with a table. Her face had gone pale.

He held up a hand. "Don't worry, Vittoria, I won't hurt you."

Her spine snapped straight, shoulders back. "I'm not afraid," she said. "I'm annoyed!"

She meant it. She didn't appear to be scared.

Instead, she looked livid.

"You let me speak so . . . openly about you!" she hissed. "What, are you spying? Following me around? Why are you giving me buckets? I . . ." She faltered, then softened. "I didn't mean to disrespect your work, but I won't take back what I said."

He grinned, truly amused now. "You made fair points, Vittoria. I wouldn't want you to take it back. I need the truth. It did surprise me," he added candidly with a wink. "No one has ever hated me before."

She bristled. "I never said I hated you."

Mateo smiled, but she recoiled a little. What must his expression look like? He'd grown slightly in stature, and a thick belly protruded beneath his shirt. Great. She'd be highly impressed with this. Mateo brushed that off.

"Would you continue to distribute the food buckets? For the last seven days, I've hoped and assumed you would. But I realize perhaps we would both benefit from an agreement." He let out a long breath. "What you're doing is possibly the most important work I've ever done."

Her mouth bobbed open and closed. "You want me to keep giving away your food?"

"Yes."

"Why?"

Mateo hesitated. There would come a day when he would lay the whole plan at her feet, but not yet. Not until time proved out his theory. Not until all the workers in Necce recognized her face.

"Because I fight for justice," he said quietly. "Even if it doesn't seem like it. You're right—the system is broken. La Salvatorra was never meant to save, but to . . . to help. The reputation created itself. But know that I *am* working for more. To change things, I mean. Will you trust me, Vittoria? I have set things into motion that will set workers free if you will help me with it. All you have to do is what you're doing now."

Her voice faltered only a moment more before she nodded. "Yes," she said. "I will distribute your food."

"And I will keep you safe in return. You won't see me, but I'll escort you to and from your jobs and as you seek work. That's it. I will not be stalking, watching, or following. Just protecting."

Her shoulders relaxed. When her eyes darted over his face, then his chest, he realized the magic had changed him again.

Understanding dawned on her face. "I will never know you, will I?"

"Never," he murmured, "is a long time. Soon, Vittoria, I'll reach out again. Until that time, distribute the food and help wherever you can. Somehow, we'll find ways to get you what is needed. Food. Medicine. Bandages. Blankets. We have access to all of that at least some of the time. I'll be protecting you, so if you need something, just be obvious about it somehow."

A thousand questions seemed to fill her gaze, then, but Mateo nodded once and transported away before she could ask them. For now, he needed her focus and her face. The rest of the plan could be set in motion behind the scenes.

For the first time in years, Mateo felt hope.

∽

Two Months Later

Mateo's transportation spell delivered him to the beach. Only a second passed before he regathered his wits—transporting had always been disorienting—and took in the scene before him.

Ocean waves crashed with a gentle hiss. Two men stood a few paces away, staring at him. Mateo's stomach lurched. He hadn't spoken directly to them in years. So why had they called him here today? They knew his plans. Ignored him as he flittered around Necce, speaking to landowners and workers alike. Acted as if he didn't visit the farms, the orchards, the balls in landowner houses that would welcome the estranged son.

In the distance loomed Magnolia Castle, the jewel of the Eastern Network.

They'd chosen a spot north of Necce and not far from the Saltu Jungle, where neither workers nor landowners ventured. A giant rock stood in the middle of the ocean like a gray thumb. Wind had worn a hole through the middle of it that the landowners called the *Griseo Petra*, the Hole of the First Life. They believed that souls who departed the Eastern Network with honor left for their next life through that hole.

A wizened old man with a back and shoulders hooked like a question mark glared at Mateo. His beady black eyes cut as sharp as diamonds.

"Pere," Mateo said with a brittle smile.

He wanted to rub the sleep out of his bloodshot eyes, but didn't dare. A rebel riot had kept Mateo, Benat, and his men out in Necce for longer than usual. Vittoria had also left for her job early, which had prevented him from getting any sleep before this meeting.

"Mateo," said Pere in a gravelly voice. Pere, the High Priest Hodei, once stood at a strapping height comparable to Mateo's. Now he was hunched over to half his usual height.

Power, Mere had once said. *Hodei is embodied power.*

Time had dealt Hodei a cruel hand. The old man's eyes didn't contain any less venom despite having to glare up at everyone, his neck kinked at an awkward angle. He had long, white hair tied away from his face and cold brown eyes. If such a thing were possible, his deteriorating health had only made him more wrathful.

"I'm dying," Hodei declared.

The words issued from his mouth like a blighter. Mateo blinked once. His gaze slipped to his younger brother, who stood at Hodei's side. Romeo was gentler in features than Hodei, but not by much. Romeo said nothing.

Hodei's declaration wasn't entirely shocking. His health had been in decline for years.

But still . . .

Mateo schooled his expression. "*Allo* to you as well, Pere."

"The apothecary says I have no more than three months." Hodei pressed his lips together and tried to draw in a deep breath, but failed. His health had forced others to take over much of his work. Romeo. Balta. Others on the Council. Though once a man of power, he was now little more than an old man waiting to die.

"And what do you think?" Mateo asked. "Are you dying?"

Hodei's gaze pierced him. "I have long enough to make sure you don't succeed me."

Mateo smiled. "The third assassination attempt made it clear you don't want me on the throne. No need to reiterate."

Hodei scowled, no doubt still peeved about the foiled plots.

"Pere." Romeo used a spell to conjure a padded wooden chair. "Your seat."

There was no warmth in Romeo's care, and there never had been. Though Mateo and Romeo shared a sour distaste for Hodei, they'd spoken only intermittently over the last ten years. Mere's death when Mateo was fourteen and Romeo eleven had fractured whatever brotherhood they once had.

Romeo resembled their deceased mere, Esperanza. Brown velvet eyes, thin shoulders, and a once-bright smile. Mirth certainly didn't follow Romeo, but prosperity did. He resembled a gentle rabbit, not a hardened leader. He had the same broad stance as Mateo, though he stood several hands shorter. He wasn't outgoing or confident in the same way, but held a stern intensity that Mateo appreciated.

Romeo had always been a hidden surprise. With his sharp mind, he would make a perfect Head of Guardians, but Romeo wanted more than that.

Romeo wanted to be High Priest. He wanted to take over Hodei's position, negotiate a long-term peace with the other Networks, make no changes to the social structure, and protect the precious landowners who stood behind him.

At any cost.

Mateo, on the other hand, filled a doorway with just his shoulders, like Pere once had. He was quicker to engage with people and fast with strategy. He smiled at the right times, and then a little bit more, so witches reluctantly liked him. Even landowners. He wanted to change everything about the social structure and already protected the workers who'd started to rally behind him.

The two had always been different.

"Mateo," Romeo said as Hodei settled into the chair. "*Allo.*"

"*Allo,* brother," Mateo murmured. "It's good to see you."

And he meant it. Once upon a time, he'd adored Romeo as his little brother. They'd caught frogs and wreaked chaos together.

"I assume you've heard the rumor about me invoking the Law of Rights now that Pere is dying," Romeo said. He held Mateo's gaze without a sign of remorse.

There was no rumor, of course. But Romeo always loved throwing witches off. He loved control, just like Hodei.

At the words *Law of Rights,* Mateo's stomach clenched again. He kept his face impassive.

As the eldest son of the High Priest, Mateo should rule by law when Hodei died. Except no landowner wanted the *wild son*—who was sympathetic to workers and banned from the castle—to ascend to power. No, they wanted the son Hodei had chosen. They wanted Romeo, the son they knew because Hodei had flaunted him, trained him, possessed him for the last ten years. The son who wanted to dutifully follow in Hodei's bloody footsteps.

Except for that pesky law that Romeo couldn't just *have* it while Mateo was still alive.

Romeo, the beloved of both their parents, could contest Mateo's ascension through the Law of Rights. Once it was invoked, Mateo and Romeo would have to survive a series of tests. The winner—the only one alive at the end—gained the throne. The Law of Rights meant Mateo would have to kill Romeo to win.

Something Mateo had never been okay with.

Of course, High Priests had overturned old laws before, but this was one Hodei couldn't erase. Just enough landowners on the Council insisted it be upheld, as a matter of future security. And they loved their entertainment and bloodshed.

If there was anything the Law of Rights guaranteed, it was bloodshed.

Mateo was mostly unknown in the landowners' world. Some of them knew him. Some of them had him over for dinner and tolerated him and his progressive ideas. In their thinking, Romeo was beloved, like a god. Mateo had no chance of winning. So why erase the law?

He'd prove them wrong.

"The Law of Rights, yes." Mateo's lips twitched in a half smile. "So you threaten to invoke it."

"It's not a threat."

"I assumed not."

"I plan to initiate it shortly."

"It's your right."

Romeo studied him with an openly curious gaze.

"You'll never win, Mateo," Hodei said. He peered up and tried to straighten his spine, then grimaced and gave up.

"Your faith in me is appreciated, Pere."

"I'll give you this last chance to back down and keep your honor," Romeo said. "Are you still determined to ascend to the throne?"

"Yes."

Romeo ignored him. "We'll set you up with a house, a stipend, and as many witches as you desire to keep you company. You'd want for nothing. Just sign the throne over to me, and save yourself from the tests."

When Romeo invoked the Law of Rights, he would initiate a series of three tests. The Test of Courage. The Test of Magic. And a fight to the death against each other—with no weapons or magic. Fists and hands only. Last one standing took the kingdom. Each test was spaced apart by several weeks to allow recovery—if the participants survived at all.

"I'm not afraid of the tests," Mateo said.

"You will die, Mateo," Romeo replied coldly. "Not to mention how poorly prepared you are for leadership. The rebels are on the verge of anarchy. They want to destroy every member of our family, kill the Council and all male landowners, and install their own leader. The Central Network threatens the border. So, what is your plan? To liberate the workers and break the spine of our country? What if the Central Network attacks? What if the rebels take over Necce? How could you possibly know what you're doing?"

Mateo hid a flinch. He didn't hate Romeo for invoking the Law of Rights against him. When Pere took Romeo away, Mateo knew this day would come. Mateo would have invoked it, too, were he in his brother's position.

But he did hate Romeo for assuming so little of him.

No, he hadn't been wasting the eleven years since Mere died. He'd worked harder than Romeo ever had to. He learned the same magic, read the same books, fought the same fights, traveled the same roads—only he did it alone. He'd survived in the streets even though Hodei had cut him off.

In that time, Mateo had learned the grimoires. The laws. The ancient texts. He'd visited every coven in the Network, met the High Witches, and discussed their needs. He found landowners, dined with them. Talked politics. Attended a very few social events with the landowners who lived on the fringes of society—the ones that most didn't care about.

Romeo knew all of that.

Still, he discounted him.

"I have no plans to die, Romeo. Your concern is appreciated."

Romeo said nothing, but his stony silence gave him away. Whenever he'd been annoyed as a little boy, he'd tightened down like a clam and then exploded later. Was it the same way now? Mateo's thoughts spun out, but he curbed them. He could think of Romeo later.

"Even if, by some miracle, you kill me in the match," Romeo continued, "there's the question of whether the landowners will follow you."

"If they have no choice, they'll do it gladly."

Romeo scoffed. "So you'll incite civil war to satisfy your need for power? You'll turn against the landowners who control this Network?"

"You think the landowners could fight?" Mateo scoffed. "They can't even do their own laundry."

"You underestimate their magic," Romeo muttered.

Mateo hesitated for the first time. That was the weak spot, wasn't it? With an adequate magical defense, the landowners could potentially hold out for a while. Try to form a splinter government and rule themselves. But for how long? They needed the workers.

Mateo could outlast them.

"There is no way you can win them." Romeo waved an arrogant hand, as if that ended the conversation. As if there wasn't *so much more* to this situation that he just kept ignoring. The gesture was so like Hodei that Mateo's throat tightened.

"I suppose being banned from Magnolia Castle after Mere's death had something to do with that," Mateo muttered, unable to keep the steel from his voice. "I still can't go near it unless invited."

Romeo acted like he hadn't said anything. "You're too much of a wild card. Too sympathetic to the workers. You'll do nothing but destabilize what we've built."

Mateo clenched his teeth. He didn't want the Law of Rights. Didn't want to fight Romeo. But he also didn't want Romeo on that throne. Somehow, he'd have to come to terms with what he had to do.

"When you invoke the Law of Rights," Mateo said softly, "then I will accept it. But know that I'm willing to discuss other paths. I don't want to take your life, Romeo. But if I have to, then I will."

Hodei laughed—a wheezy, crinkling sound, like tearing onion skin. "Oh, Mateo. How you will fall in this world. Foolish boy. I'm ashamed to call you mine. No more discussion. You had an opportunity to retreat and rejected it. Your death is your own, and you will die without honor."

Mateo ignored him, but couldn't stop the twinge in his chest. The words were nothing new. The sentiment was as common as the sea air. But still . . . the reality stung. Pere would never approve. He'd chosen Romeo as the son to groom for the High Priest's throne because Mateo thought for himself and couldn't be controlled. Hodei didn't like anything he didn't control.

Fortunately, Mateo wasn't planning to reform the Network for Hodei's benefit, but for everyone.

Even for Romeo, though he'd never understand.

Mateo clenched his fists at his side, fighting the sudden thrum of rage that slipped through him. Judgment, cool and crisp, filled his brother's eyes. His brother, who had lived in the lap of luxury. Who had the approval of their only remaining parent.

"You can expect my announcement shortly," Romeo said.

Mateo nodded. Understanding the patterns of Romeo's mind had never been his strength. Unfortunate, but true. Hodei hacked a cough, jolting Mateo from his thoughts.

When Hodei calmed, he looked at Mateo and said nothing.

"Then I shall go," Mateo said.

Romeo cast one last, pointed look at his brother before he transported away. Hodei left without a word. Mateo stared at the sand where they'd disappeared, the gentle hiss of the ocean at his back.

Questions swirled through his mind. Was Romeo *truly* in Pere's lap? Had the years with such a hard man not jaded him? Romeo would have seen Hodei's constant deceptions and manipulations, while Mateo saw the oppression of the workers. Had Romeo shut off his compassionate, loving side over the years with Hodei? Those couldn't have been easy years. Mateo had wished daily that he could have saved Romeo from their pere.

He didn't think he misunderstood the quiet hatred he felt from Romeo —for Mateo and for Hodei. Romeo hated Hodei just as much as he did. At least they had that in common. But Mateo would be a fool if he didn't assume Romeo affirmed Hodei's vision for the Network. Romeo loved the landowners. Had a strange affection for Necce and all its quirks. He'd protect his witches, even at the expense of the workers, just like Hodei wanted him to.

Mateo would at least be willing to try to help *both* landowners and workers.

His mind fluttered back to Vittoria. So far, his plan the last two months had worked quietly and smoothly. Workers had come to anticipate Vittoria. To know her in the streets. To call to her, flock to her. Mateo drew in a cleansing breath, letting his thoughts run for a minute.

Release. A sensation of letting go slipped through his body, easing his tense back and arms. He thought of Romeo's lack of belief in him. His skepticism.

Release.

With another sharp breath, Mateo rolled out his shoulders. Time to get some sleep. Then he'd accept Romeo's invitation to compete under the Law of Rights.

And prepare himself to kill his brother.

3

VITTORIA

Footsteps thudded across the floor above Vittoria's head, sprinkling dust on a freshly pressed towel as she folded it. Motes lingered to form the vague shape of a magnolia flower before they dispersed. She gritted her teeth. The *andrea* would come down soon. Unfortunately, it was the same dressmaker who had denied her food months before by pretending Vittoria had caused a tear.

That would *not* happen again today. She'd done thorough inspections of each garment right in front of the *andrea*.

Shrieks issued from a new riot outside. Flashes of fire. Screaming horses galloping down too-thin roads, the hooves hammering the cobblestones like thunder. Vittoria shuddered. The High Priest must have announced a new edict or something.

She turned back to the laundry line stretched near the fire and plucked a hand towel off the thick twine. Behind it, a winding stone staircase led to the upper floors of the shop.

Steam thickened the air, and sweat dribbled down her spine. She hummed Eneko's favorite song as she stacked the towel in a basket on top of several new chemises. One hour before Eneko's bedtime. Just enough time to finish, receive her food, and make it back to their home to feed him.

Sannara hadn't been seen in over six weeks now. He'd stopped asking about her and clung to Vittoria at night instead.

At the top of the stairs, a thin doorway slammed against the wall.

"*Lavanda* maid!" the *andrea* cried. "You have five minutes."

"Yes, *andrea*. They shall be done."

The door slammed shut.

"Eneko," Vittoria said under her breath. "Think of Eneko."

She grabbed the basket of laundered clothes. Every slip, chemise, and towel was perfectly folded. They all smelled fresh. She slipped up the stairs, set the basket at the top, and disappeared just as the door creaked open again. Silence reigned for several seconds while the *andrea* inspected the clothes.

"Fifteen minutes," the *andrea* called. "The sheets are due next."

Vittoria's stomach went cold. "Sheets?" she called. "What sheets?"

A moment of silence filled the air. "The sheets in the corner, you idiot girl. Why else would they be sitting there?"

Across the room, in the back corner, was a crumpled linen bag she hadn't noticed. The grayish color gave it away—it held sheets from home, she'd bet. Her nostrils flared. Many *andreas* tried to slip their own laundry into the piles the *lavanda* maids cared for. Most shopkeepers didn't want to employ *lavanda* maids on their own, or wash their own clothes, so they snuck clothes in.

This *andrea* had fooled her again. If Vittoria didn't clean the sheets, she'd lose her food. The *andrea* would simply slip them in tomorrow for the next *lavanda* maid, or try to fool that *lavanda* maid as well.

Laundry for free, yet again.

"You have fifteen minutes if you want your food tonight," the *andrea* called. The door slammed shut.

With a groan, Vittoria closed her eyes. Fifteen minutes wouldn't even give her time to heat the water, not to mention dry, press, and fold the sheets. Not without magic, at any rate, and that wasn't an option.

With a new batch of Pere's medicine fresh on her mind, she resolved to try. Perhaps the *andrea* would show mercy if she scrubbed them in cold water and had them drying before the fire. She stood to grab the bag.

Then glass shattered.

She ducked behind a steaming wooden bucket with a cry. Glass shards flew across the room. A muffled curse followed. When she peeked back out from behind the bucket, she saw a slight male figure on the floor near the window.

"Givers," she murmured. "Who are you?"

No one tumbled in after him, but the sounds of the riot grew louder outside. Running feet. Shouts. Then the noise from the alley disappeared, leaving an odd silence.

Vittoria peered at the figure on the floor. Stubby eyelashes. Dark hair. Dirty face. Half of a beard on his sharp jaw. He was short, smaller even than her.

Was he dead?

She should call the *andrea* right away . . .

"*Allo?*" she called. "Are you . . . hurt?"

A groan responded.

She advanced. Something inside her wanted to see the man's expression change. His hair darken further. His eyes swap colors. Because then he'd be La Salvatorra, that vague figure who protected her every day, fed her family, and haunted her dreams. She looked for him everywhere but saw him nowhere. His voice, however, remained in her mind. A solid, husky echo. Although she had no reason to believe it, she suspected his voice had been his own. Sultry. Deep.

"Can I help you?" she asked.

Another groan, this one more like a growl. She picked up a fire poker with a glowing red tip and swung it in front of her, just in case. Her brother, Anton, had given her enough self-defense lessons that she felt the confidence to step forward.

"Are you injured?" she asked.

"Yes."

The response came like a roll of thunder. The man on the ground gained his feet all at once, as if he hadn't just fallen through a window. The sudden movement forced her to leap back, poker ready. The man pressed the heel of his hand against his head and blinked rapidly.

"You'll have to pay for that window," she said.

"Of course."

She'd expected him to protest. Her eyebrows rose. "What?"

"I will pay."

"You will?"

"I broke it, didn't I?"

There was a warm quip to his tone. Something familiar about his voice. He was . . . oddly affable for someone who had just plunged down a hole and through a window. She peered at him more closely, something like hope building in her chest. She knew that voice. Had tried to replay it in her mind countless times over the last two months. To hear a hint of it in the streets while she distributed food.

He stared back at her.

Where had his beard gone?

"Forgive me," she murmured. "But did you have a beard just now?"

His once-stubbled face appeared clean-shaven now. She hadn't imagined it, had she? A trick of the light, perhaps. But hope filled her. Was this La Salvatorra? Had he returned?

He scrubbed a hand over his face, but didn't elaborate. Instead, another wince racked his features. "Yes."

"La Salvatorra?" she dared to ask.

He grimaced as he reached back. "Yes. I'm sorry—I didn't mean to make an entrance like that. The horses—"

Her heart fluttered for a second. Words filled her throat, then stopped as his features changed again. She lowered the poker.

"You're hurt."

"In my back. Glass, maybe?"

"Turn around."

He lifted one eyebrow, but obeyed.

In all the weeks that had passed since he'd made himself known to her, she hadn't spoken to him again. Blankets, buckets, and medicine appeared at some point in her day. She gave it away to the needy, the bucket would disappear, and then she returned home, safe every time. In her mind, he was an elusive figure. An idea. A hope. A protector.

La Salvatorra was safety.

Now, he wore the loose white shirt of any worker on the street. Dust and soot marred the back. A shard of glass stuck out from his right shoulder blade, and a crimson stain spread across the material. A second stain bloomed just below it. He was a normal witch, just as she'd always assumed. With blood and sinew and pain, just like her. But still . . . her mind had built him up as more.

"There's glass in your back," she said.

"By honor," he muttered. "Of course there is."

By honor. A landowner phrase. Their belief system revolved around the vague idea of honor as a guiding, governing force. They lived for honor. Tried to die with it. It decided whether they advanced to their next life. Which should, if they had honor in their current life, be a better one.

His shoulders had grown while her thoughts raced. Why would he maintain the changing magic with her? Didn't they know each other? Although they never interacted, she felt as if they were . . . friends. Had she made it up? Likely, he saw her as a worker and nothing more. An asset to protect, perhaps. Setting aside a flash of disappointment at the thought, she set the poker down and motioned to a stool.

"Have a seat. I need to pull those out."

He obeyed without hesitation. "Thank you, Vittoria."

The sound of his deep voice speaking her name made her stomach shiver. She fought back a smile and nodded instead. He might change his appearance, but his voice was the same rolling velvet. He sent a rueful glance at the broken window. Glass glittered on the floor like castaway diamonds.

"Fix the window, please?" she asked crisply.

"Of course."

Seconds later, glimmering windowpanes filled the space. They appeared new, not weathered by time and dust. The glass on the ground glittered away until not a speck remained. Stunned, she stared at it for a full five seconds before shaking her head and turning her attention back to the task at hand. Magic.

What a powerful ability.

Focus, she told herself. *You must heal La Salvatorra.*

Again.

She stepped up to his back, where the bloodstain formed a teardrop pattern. His hair had darkened into a deep ebony. Bronze skin, unblemished, flowed from beneath the white shirt now.

Vittoria reached under a table and grabbed an old bucket filled with torn fabric scraps. She searched for long, thin ones, her tongue utterly tied now. What could they talk about? Nothing, maybe. What should she say? *Thanks for the food* sounded trite. Too weak. *So, how is that grand plan to save the workers coming along?* Too searching. Too . . . awkward.

All of this was awkward.

She studied the glass in his back as she tore a long strip of fabric in half with a vengeance. The sound of thudding feet overhead momentarily distracted her. She moved faster.

"Forgive me if this is too presumptuous," he murmured, breaking the silence, "but why are you a *lavanda* maid? I've wondered for the last several months why you're not conscripted into a trade. With your lovely face, you should be working within a landowner's house with steady food."

Vittoria bit back her reply, even if she was grateful for something other than the silence. *Lovely face* sent a little thrill through her.

"I have no desire to work in a wealthy house."

He lifted an amused eyebrow. "You don't want to eat?"

"I didn't say that."

The glass fragments embedded in his back would be easy to pull out. No doubt he had a spell to heal quickly, assuming no shards were left behind. The benefits of magic. He didn't even suck in a sharp breath when she probed the edges of one of the wounds. The squishy flesh trickled blood, which stained the glass a translucent red.

"Is it because of your nephew?" he asked.

She hesitated. How much should she reveal to him? There was little in her life to hide, and nothing he probably hadn't observed by seeing her home.

"And Pere," she said.

He made a sound in his throat.

"Tell me honestly," he whispered with a raw sincerity that caught her stomach. His mannerisms were more intense tonight. Less affable and breezy, as if something weighed on him. "Do you still think La Salvatorra is a disappointment?"

Vittoria let out a long breath. There was a touch of longing in his tone. Did such a man want *her* approval? The thought almost made her laugh.

"Are you concerned about your reputation?" she asked lightly. "Or do you worry about the welfare of the workers who so deeply respect you?"

"Workers."

She wrenched the shards free, one after the other. He only grunted when she shoved the cloth onto his bleeding back, forcing his spine to arch. She'd deliberately chosen that moment to remove the glass. She wanted to think about his response. She tossed the bloody strips and glass into the fire, then made short work of wrapping the linen around his ribs, her heart thumping in her chest when the door upstairs flew open.

"*Lavanda* maid!"

Vittoria froze, her hands midair over his back. A flush of cold surged through her body so quickly she felt certain he'd feel it in her fingertips. His gaze snapped toward her, his breath held.

"Yes, *andrea*?" she called.

The *andrea* didn't respond, but instead barked at someone else upstairs. With a growl and a stamp of her feet, the *andrea* disappeared with a slam of a door. Presumably to deal with something else. Vittoria had minutes, if that.

Vittoria finished tying off the bandage and stepped back. She gestured to the doorway that led to the alley.

"You are free to go," she said.

He stood slowly. "Not yet," he murmured.

Relief filled her. She didn't want him to leave yet. It was like she'd captured sunshine, and she wanted him to stay with her for a few more minutes and warm her day. She motioned to the bag in the corner.

"Any chance your magic can clean some sheets? The *andrea* brought her own bedclothes and sprung them on me. Likely so she wouldn't have to pay again."

He grinned without mirth, the pain still apparent in his gaze.

"For you?" he murmured. "Anything."

Vittoria's stomach flipped at the warmth in his words. His hair lightened from his roots into a stark white, like new cotton. Did he ever show himself in the cycle of transformative magic?

The bag flew to her, surely under a spell, and she dumped it out. He whispered something, and the rumpled sheets underwent a transformation. The faded gray cotton changed back to a subtle white. Stains faded. He worked cautiously so the clothes appeared cleaned, not transformed. Otherwise, the *andrea* would accuse her of magic and she'd be piked within hours.

Sheets, pressed and folded, stacked themselves in her arms.

"Thank you," she said.

"Fortunately, I learned simple household spells years ago." He winked. "It's my pleasure."

His deep voice belied the young man he now appeared to be. Why did the magic rotate so quickly tonight? Some of his personas lasted only ten seconds now, where before it had been minutes. She gave a nervous smile, then set the clothes in a basket, dashed up the stairs, and left it there. When she came back, he stood near the door holding the usual bucket of food. She slipped on her wooden shoes, then accepted it.

"Thank you."

"Thank you for healing me again," he said with amusement.

"Always."

His expression softened. Their fingers lingered for half a breath before he released the bucket to her hand. His face sharpened with intensity.

"May I walk you home?" he asked quietly.

"Don't you always?"

He smiled. "Indeed, but this time I was going to go with you visibly."

"Yes, of course." She motioned up the stairs. "But, first, the *andrea*."

"Forget her." He scoffed. "There is enough food for you in the bucket."

"I was going to buy Pere's medicine again with the food from today."

His brow ruffled. He had small eyes and a wide nose now, but wasn't unkind in appearance. "I can supply you with medicine."

"Yes, of course. But that could go to someone else in pain. Why would I cast this food aside when others could benefit from even the smallest amount? Besides, I worked hard for it. We receive so little . . ."

His forehead smoothed out. "You're extraordinary, Vittoria."

She blushed as the door opened at the top of the stairs, then held her breath at the sound of shuffling sheets. For several long moments, the *andrea* said nothing, as if she couldn't quite figure it out. Vittoria's heart beat faster. The *andrea* could still accuse her of magic.

Finally, the *andrea* muttered, "Food is in the bucket," and slammed the door.

Vittoria's lips twitched. "One moment."

She slipped over to the stairs. Being away from him for a breath or two gave her a chance to collect her wits. She ascended the stairs slowly and tried to empty her mind. A few stale *pittas* and a crock of leftover soft cheese waited inside. She collected it, pushed it into her pocket, and returned with a slightly clearer mind.

La Salvatorra opened the door as she approached, but stood in her path. "I have something I'd like to ask you," he said. "After you're done with your usual distribution."

The magic had stopped rotating. None of his features changed now. He was a thin-shouldered, middle-aged man with dark hair and eyes and a beard that could have made him anyone. She imagined that the changing magic might draw more attention in some situations, which is why he'd paused it now.

Was this him? Unlikely. Why ever reveal himself to anyone? It would be too great a risk.

She felt breathless when she said, "Yes."

He smiled, and it brightened his eyes.

"Then let's go."

4

MATEO

M ateo watched Vittoria from the corner of his eye as she slipped down a street toward the Mayfair Coven. The space between her shoulder blades was tense again.

After they first met months before, she'd acted the same way. Her shoulders would tighten every morning when she left her house. She'd gaze around, as if searching for him. She studied lingering witches more than usual, regarded faces. Over time, she seemed to forget he would be there. That's when she relaxed.

Today, her shoulders were tight as a harp string, and her hair seemed to shiver at an occasional breeze off the ocean. As a worker, she was sturdy beneath her thin clothes, but too slender. No holes in her garments, which meant she carefully maintained what she had.

In a word, she was as lovely as ever.

They walked into Necce in an easy silence, headed toward her favorite haunt at the *eliza* of the Giver La Principessa. She bent near witches that waited for her, offering food, greetings, even invocations from various Givers. A crowd of ten followed her around daily now. They searched for her in *lavanda* windows and sang praises to La Salvatorra with blessings on her head. Vittoria always deferred their praise, too busy asking them about their own lives.

Whether due to her nerves or circumstances, the food bucket emptied quickly. As soon as the food ran out, the bucket disappeared. She brushed the crumbs off her palms and straightened.

"You're a natural with witches, you know," he said. "They seem drawn to you."

Her lips twitched with what should have been a smile. "Thank you." Her penchant to blush drew his gaze, but he forced his focus to stay on the neighborhood. Tension laced the air tonight, and trouble loomed ahead.

Her hazel eyes, like endless velvet, finally registered a fracas he'd been watching for minutes now.

Witches amassed at the end of a road, near an *eliza* for the Giver La Tourrere in the Necce Coven. Shouts arose from the growing crowd. Romeo had issued the official announcement regarding the Law of Rights less than an hour ago. A discarded newsbook shuffled in a light breeze as they walked by.

LAW OF RIGHTS ACCEPTED, it read.

"A riot?" she murmured. She edged a little closer to him. Pleased by her instinctive move toward him, he closed the gap until their arms brushed.

"Potentially."

Chants rang through the street, just perceptible to the ear.

Mateo! Mateo!

Such sentiment sent a mixture of relief and fear through him. Leadership was always a battle between terror and confidence. To hear them chant his name bolstered his courage—he wanted to help them and they *wanted* his help. It gave him confidence with every word.

It also terrified him.

Was he leader enough? Could he be the witch they wanted him to be?

Vittoria drew his thoughts away, her forehead wrinkled. "Mateo?" she said. "Why do they chant his name?"

"The heir to the throne."

She waved that off. "Yes, of course, but why are they chanting his name?"

Mateo filed that away for later. She knew of him. That certainly helped a little and gave him an unusual sense of relief. Why he wanted her to know about him, he couldn't say. Not all workers knew of him, even though he ventured into Necce as himself often. He'd lived among workers for years, on and off in different buildings. Had spoken with High Witches in all the covens. Attempted to meet rebel leaders, even though they didn't allow that anymore.

"Mateo has just accepted the Law of Rights challenge from his brother," Mateo said. "Romeo issued it this morning. I believe those witches are celebrating because they support him and want him to be High Priest."

She blanched. "Oh."

Curiosity drove him to ask, "You have heard of the Law of Rights?"

"Pere speaks of it now and then." She swallowed, scuttling past the alley that led to the growing crowd. A witch called out to her. She smiled, waved, and continued on. But the uncertainty hadn't left her gaze yet.

"Are you frightened by it?" he asked, focusing on the wrinkles between her eyebrows.

"No," she said quickly. "It is nothing to me. Except that I would want Mateo to win, of course."

He nearly sighed. La Salvatorra might be a disappointment to her, but Mateo hadn't been yet. Merging the two would be . . . interesting.

"Perhaps he'll also disappoint you?" he said with a sly smile.

"Are you jealous?" she quipped with a saucy grin.

He smiled. "Who wouldn't be?"

Vittoria chuckled. The farther they moved from Necce Coven, the quieter the alleys and streets became. Vittoria drew in a breath, her shoulders expanding, then asked, "What did you wish to speak to me about?"

He frowned. The middle of the street wasn't the best place to have this conversation. She likely wouldn't feel safe if he transported her anywhere. While he had seen her twice a day for the last several months, she had not seen him. Such an amount of time might explain his uncanny draw to her.

Still, if they didn't talk about it here, where else? He searched the street with a quick glance. Not many witches out. Perhaps this would be private enough.

But how to say it?

He cleared his throat as he felt her apprehension grow.

"I have appreciated all your help the past few weeks," he began, then stopped.

"It's been an honor," she said slowly. Her eyes grew wide. "Are you done, then? Has this . . . has this ceased?"

Her attempt to stifle her fear was pitiful. Every ounce of her voice betrayed her. He put a hand on her arm.

"No, not at all."

She relaxed under his touch.

"You distributing food buckets to workers is all part of a plan that I've come up with to try to help workers. To get all of you out of this mess. But the time has come to go to the next step of the plan, and I want to see if you'd be willing to help me."

Vittoria hesitated, gaze cloudy with concern. She met his gaze but stepped to the right to put a little space between them. He wondered if she was even aware of it.

"What is your plan?" she asked.

"First, I must reveal a few things to you. My identity, for one. My true identity." He drew in a breath. Better to just get it done than linger. His voice dropped until only she could hear him. "I am Mateo, son of Hodei, of the Castaneda line."

She stopped in the middle of the street. Eyes watched them from the alleys, and most of them wouldn't be friendly. Moving targets were harder to hit than still ones, so he hooked an arm around her waist and gently tugged her along with him. It felt like escorting a board. She followed, but her steps were halting.

"I am twenty-five years old," he continued quietly as he jovially smiled at a passing witch. His tone remained low. "Pere is dying, which is why Romeo has invoked the Law of Rights and I have accepted. In one week, I face the Test of Courage. Two weeks after that, I'll go into the Test of Magic. When I pass both, and if Romeo does also, we will meet in a fight to the death. When I win that fight, I will inherit the throne and can truly change things for workers. But to do that, I need help."

All the blood seemed to have left her face. Her legs moved, but her gaze was fixed straight ahead as they crossed into the Mayfair Coven. These streets were more peaceable, but not by much. Tension boiled everywhere, no doubt driven by the rebels. The rebels would want to take advantage of this announcement. They'd provoke riots. Incite frustration against landowners. Even though the rebels didn't want Mateo in power, either, they'd use him for their own gains.

Mateo tightened his hold on her when her steps faltered.

"Vittoria?"

"Mateo," she whispered. "You are . . ."

She trailed off again, blinking. He kept them moving, past witches with suspicious gazes and gaunt expressions. Mateo glared the witches with aggressive postures back to the shadows. They averted their gazes, weapons hidden.

"Give it a second to sink in," he murmured.

They walked without speaking for another full minute. The color came back to her face. In those moments, she seemed to pull herself back together. The fear faded, and puzzlement seemed to follow.

Eventually, she extracted herself from his grip to walk on her own. He kept a wary eye on her. She seemed . . . confused, but not angry. Still, she wouldn't look at him. The thought that she might be afraid of him cut to the bone. That was the last thing he'd want.

For what felt like an eternity, she processed the unbridled truth.

"Mateo," she said again, this time with more strength. "You are . . . Givers, but the next High Priest has been following me every day."

He rolled his lips to school a bark of laughter. That was certainly one way to look at it. He quietly appreciated her apparent trust in his ability to *become* the next High Priest.

She studied him with uncertainty for a moment, her thin shawl hanging over both arms. A breeze whispered by, brushing them with the fresh scent of clean linen. The gentle smell among the refuse of the streets made his head swim. But wasn't that Vittoria? A breath of fresh air.

Finally, she stopped. She craned her head back. "It makes sense," she declared. She laughed, but there was no humor in it. She shook her head, pulled her shawl over her shoulders, and wrapped it tightly around her. She kept going. Mateo followed.

"La Salvatorra is obviously wealthy, for one," she said, her tone moderated. "Wealthy enough to share food without suspicion. Any other landowner who had buckets of food go missing every day would be under scrutiny. The son of the High Priest would have a guaranteed food bucket all his life, and probably without question."

"Romeo, perhaps," he muttered wryly. "I am a different matter."

"Your brother is favored?"

A mirthless grin twisted his features. "Very much so."

Vittoria continued on, unloading her thoughts now. "Regardless, you conjure what appears to be very strong magic, which indicates extensive education. There's something different about your voice. The accent isn't quite right. You haven't lived just a landowner's life. I worked the farms until I was fifteen. You have hints of a country accent, but nothing definite."

"Perceptive," he said, gratified by it.

She snorted. "Aren't you afraid you'll be found out?"

"I've never spoken with any beneficiary of La Salvatorra as extensively as you, so no." He cast a sidelong glance at her. "Are you disappointed?"

To his relief, she smiled. "No."

"A hard-won opinion."

She faltered, that heavy concern creasing her brow. "I don't know you at all, La—Mateo. You . . . are a stranger to me. So, why did you pick me? Why are you telling me this?"

The words hurt him, for some reason, and he fought not to wince. They were absolutely true, but he didn't want them to be. A stranger to Vittoria? It felt so . . . strange.

Mateo sighed. "That brings me to the next thing I wanted to tell you. I . . . I need you in the next part of my plan."

She slowed, and he realized that they were at her house. The street here was quiet. No one else stirred, not even inside.

"And what could a *lavanda* maid do to save the workers?" she asked.

"Everything," he whispered.

With her arms folded over her middle, Vittoria waited for him to explain. She leaned back against a wall. He wanted to reach out and touch her, but held himself back.

"Do you want your family to eat every day?" he asked.

"Of course."

"Do you want them to be safe?"

Her head tilted to the side. "Who wouldn't?" she drawled.

"Do you want better for Eneko?"

"More than anything."

"If I ascend to the throne, the battle is only half-won. Maybe only a third. Once I have the throne, I must keep it. I must lead all witches, which means I need to understand the world of the landowner and the world of the worker. They must be brought together. We're already on the verge of civil war. If I upend the class system, the landowners may turn on me. On the workers, who out of desperation join the rebels. The rebels may try to kill me to take the throne and put their own High Priest there. No matter who wins—me or Romeo—someone will strike. They'll strike hard and fast."

He heard the starkness of his own voice. The underlying sense of desperation in the words. Until he'd said it out loud, he hadn't compre-hended how bleak this had all truly become. The worry reflected in Vitto-ria's eyes only made it feel more real.

"But what does that have to do with me?" she asked.

So many things. He put a hand under her chin and nudged her so she had to look up at him.

"I need someone at my side who the workers will trust. Someone the workers will see as a sign that I won't be Romeo or Pere. That workers will have a voice in the new Network. Then, when I win against Romeo, we have a chance of preventing civil war between the landowners and the rebels."

Vittoria leaned back, her face pale. "Me?" she whispered again. "You trust *me*? A *lavanda* maid?"

"With my life."

"But why?"

"Because you are selfless. Constantly selfless. You fought to get your food tonight so you could save all the rest for other workers. Don't think I didn't notice that you kept the food from the *andrea*, the food of poorer quality. Vittoria, you care. You speak to witches. You see the witch behind the facade. You are the only one who can do this. I can't tell you more than that. Not until I know your answer."

At that, she only blinked. She stared at the ground. In a hollow tone, she asked, "How? How would this happen?"

Mateo swallowed hard. Of course she'd jumped to the weakest part of this whole plan. "I would ask you to be my High Priestess."

A hand went to her suddenly ashen face. "High Priestess?" she whispered.

Mateo ran a hand through his hair. He didn't enjoy the uncertainty or shock in her face. But could he blame her? Not at all. There was no way to soften the truth or offer something else. They *must* be handfasted. There could be no way for her to back out of the handfasting later. The Network needed them to be steady and strong.

"Yes," he finally said. "My High Priestess."

"But the High Priestess is the wife of the High Priest," she croaked.

He nodded.

She staggered for several moments, then laughed. Her expression cleared, eyes brightening. "Surely, you're kidding. An elaborate joke?" Her amusement faded. "Something?" she whispered.

"Never," he said soberly.

"La—Mateo," she hissed in frustration. "Your world is a different place." She grabbed helplessly at her limp dress. "I could never . . . can you imagine me in the castle? Talking to landowners? The landowners who nearly massacred me and my family? I . . . a High Priestess!"

"I would be with you every step of the way."

"I can't even read!"

"I'll hire a tutor."

"Magic?"

"My friend Zuri has already volunteered to teach you if you agree."

She scowled and turned away.

"I'll feed your family for the rest of your lives," he continued. "We'll give them a new house, a safe one. My apothecary friend will personally see to your pere and his pain. Magic may be able to help, somehow. Your family will want for nothing, and neither will you. I can guarantee Eneko a better life, even if I don't survive."

Her expression softened again, this time with a sense of disbelief. She searched his eyes, as if he bore the truth there.

"The landowners will try to kill me."

"They would have to kill me and my man, Benat, first," he said quietly.

"Pere has sent assassins out three times to kill me and clearly hasn't been successful. We're stubborn men and hard to kill."

She put a hand to her forehead and laughed. "You're a fool, Mateo. To bring a *lavanda* maid into the castle? To rule? The landowners will hate you. They'll think we're both a joke and would never take us seriously. You would lose everything, and I would lose my head."

"They already know we're on the brink of civil war. For that reason alone, some have already started to listen to me. Maybe even enough of them will side with us to prevent war. And Benat will always keep you safe. If things turn for the worse, you and your family will be protected."

"And you?"

"We'll have to let fate decide that."

He sealed his lips. He couldn't give more away. The last ten years of his work had finally started to culminate, and now timing was everything. She stared at him as if he had two heads, her mouth bobbing open and closed.

Finally, she shook her head. "You ask too much."

He nodded. "I know, but with it comes a chance to change the world. With it comes safety for your family. This is an offer of a position of power. I don't know what else you might want. Whatever it is, I will give it."

"And if I say no?"

On top of the north wall, an image of La Principessa drew his eye. The charcoal had started to smudge and flake off, a casualty of the fog that rolled through in the mornings. In the image, La Principessa knelt, hand over her heart and head bowed.

"Then you say no," he said. "And you will return to your life as you know it. Benat and I will find another plan."

He stepped back to give her space. Her shoulders visibly relaxed when he moved away from her.

"Don't decide tonight," he murmured. "I will return in the morning. I'm sorry, but I can't give you more time than that."

Vittoria hesitated, then nodded once. Her dubious expression gave him little hope.

"I'll think about it," she whispered.

Mateo disappeared into a transportation spell because he couldn't stand another moment. The last thing he saw was the image of a magnolia flower falling from La Principessa's hands.

5

VITTORIA

Vittoria sat on the ground in her home and stared at the moonbeams that spilled onto the floor. If she listened very, very hard, she swore she could hear the churn of the ocean.

Eneko's head lay in her lap, his chest steady with the rhythmic rise and fall of his breaths. She ran her fingers through his hair, comforted by the movement. Memories of Anton slipped through her aching mind. Calm, clear nights like tonight made her miss him. Long for his steady confidence and quick smile. He'd been their saving grace when they fled the farms. Things seemed to come so easily to him. This house. Mere's job at the Morettis, which he'd found for her when they were days away from starving.

Thoughts of Anton led to Mateo, and her mind shifted again.

La Salvatorra.

Mateo.

High Priestess.

She couldn't stop thinking about Mateo and his outrageous request. No matter the order she tried, she couldn't puzzle the pieces of his wild declaration together. Not in a satisfactory way that made any sense.

Mere sat next to her, wearing a deep frown. Mere shared Vittoria's same heart-shaped face and too-slender body. Wrinkles around her eyes and streaks of gray in her raven-black hair aged her, but she still had grace. Food stained the front of her apron, which she hadn't taken off. Her lips moved silently. Nightly prayers to the Givers.

"High Priestess," Mere whispered all of a sudden. "It doesn't seem real."

Vittoria just shook her head. Her homespun dress lay limp against her legs, stained gray from all the washings. She stared at her knobby knees. Could she imagine her dress full like the landowners'? Heavy? Layered until it was hardly wearable? She'd laundered landowner dresses for years now. Secretly despised their waste of massive amounts of material. As High Priestess, she'd have to wear them, surely.

Wouldn't she?

Would Mateo make his own rules? What roles or customs would survive?

"And if he dies?" Mere asked, voice pinched. "What would happen to you if Mateo died?"

"Then I die?" Vittoria shrugged. "He mentioned someone who could save us before that happened, but . . ."

Mere scowled. "We never wait for other witches to save us, do we? No, you'd have to be ready with a plan yourself. What if there is retribution against the family? The landowners may find us. Hold us hostage. Eneko would be a prize to bargain with."

Unfortunately, the wild idea wasn't outside the realm of possibility. Not these days. The thought of it sickened her.

"I don't know, Mere."

From a nearby roof, someone bellowed out threats against the High Priest. A rebel recruitment meeting, no doubt. They'd scuttle soon, when Guardians caught a whiff and came on patrol to investigate. Though they came so rarely out here, they might not even show up. Vittoria wondered where Mateo was, then forced the thought away.

Mere reached up to close the window, but Vittoria stopped her. The stuffy room smelled like unwashed little boy and felt too close and confining. She longed for open, quiet spaces. A beach, perhaps.

"A few more minutes of fresh air," she pleaded. "Just until we sleep?"

Mere relented with a nod.

"Food for the rest of your life," Vittoria said a minute later. Her gaze lingered on Eneko as she brushed a lock of hair out of his face. "Safety for Eneko. Medicine for Pere. You could quit the Moretti house and cook for only your family."

Mere smiled. "A dream indeed."

"Not a dream," Vittoria replied. "A reality. Isn't it? Isn't that what Mateo offers? A better life for all of you. How could I turn that down? It would be so selfish! Maybe Sannara would come home to stay. Eneko would know his *real* mere."

"At what cost?" Mere raised her eyebrows. "You being High Priestess? It's a prison, Tori. An elegant, beautiful cage. You'll be the object of ridicule of the landowners. They'll hate you. Maybe try to kill you. The workers would say you sold out to the landowners for a better life. There would be no respect from either side. Is food worth freedom?"

Vittoria reached over and grabbed her arm. "Yes," she whispered with tears in her eyes, "if it guarantees food and health for my family."

Mere's nostrils flared. "It is too much," she whispered and waved her hand. "I have lost my son. I cannot lose my daughter."

"So you will lose Eneko to starvation? Pere to infection? Is one life more important than another?"

Mere opened her mouth to reply, but closed it again.

Vittoria swallowed a lump in her throat. Pere burst into a coughing fit, and Mere stood and crossed the room. With a sweet murmur, she helped him sit up to have a drink. Vittoria watched them, grateful for a break from Mere's intense emotional waves.

Watching Mere and Pere together swept in a fresh round of concerns. Mateo wanted them to handfast. They'd spend the rest of their lives together. Would she and Mateo share the same affection as her parents if they handfasted? Would she be able to look on him with the same tenderness in twenty-five years? Would they be alive?

Was love a possibility?

Her stomach burned at the thought. She didn't even know what he looked like. He could be horrendous, for all she knew. A regular troll.

She doubted it. Besides, that didn't matter anyway. Food mattered. Safety. Kindness. Affection rather than rage. In Vittoria's world, frustrated husbands often committed violence. She would not be a beaten wife like so many others. Mateo, she felt, would not be like that.

But did she *know* that?

Vittoria crooned a soft word to Eneko when he stirred. He settled back against her, his face tucked into a fold of her skirt. Her heart cracked at the thought of not seeing him every day. Could she endure the pain of him growing and changing and learning without her?

Mere returned. "Sannara sent a message with a boy. Said she'd try to visit in a few days. She included some more medicine for Pere."

"No idea where she is?"

Mere shook her head. Vittoria pushed aside a pang of worry for Sannara. She was so secretive, but helped supply food or medicine or something for Eneko. Pere had two new bottles of medicine. Several leftover *pittas* were hidden up high. Where she received such treasures, Vittoria had no idea.

At least, she didn't want to know.

"Givers bless her," Mere said with a *tsk*.

They fell back into silence. In her mind, Vittoria replayed the conversation with Mateo for a fourth time. Why did he believe in her? A *lavanda* maid. Could he see something in her that she didn't see in herself?

"He said he would teach you reading?" Mere asked. Her jaw was tight, her hands folded in front of her.

"And magic."

Mere hummed a reply. "I've hated myself for not teaching you," she whispered. Her voice was thick with emotion. "I can read. Know my letters. But it seemed too frightening to give them to you. Too great a risk. If we were caught, you could be piked."

Vittoria squeezed Mere's arm with a comforting touch. "I never wanted you to, Mere. The risk was too great. I don't blame you."

Mere's sparkling eyes turned to face her. "Would we ever see you again?"

"I would demand it."

"How would he keep you safe?"

"I'm not sure, Mere. Magic, probably."

"You must learn it, too." Mere poked her arm with a sniffle. "Though you don't care for it, you must try. Can you imagine the safety you could give yourself? Invisibility. Transportation. You could see us whenever you wanted. See Eneko whenever you wanted!"

Mere threw her hands in the air and quieted her exclamation. Pere had fallen back into a restless sleep. Vittoria watched him with a wary eye. He breathed so shallowly tonight, his ribs barely moving under his too-loose linen shirt.

"Perhaps the workers will follow Mateo," Vittoria whispered. "Perhaps they will see a protector in him already and everything will be fine."

"Perhaps."

"And I would live in a castle," Vittoria whispered. "Even if it were just a cage, knowing you were fed and cared for? That you had a home? It's . . . it's all I could ever ask. I would go to the grave in peace at the end of my life."

Mere lifted her hands. "We have a home. Home is where the witches you love are, Vittoria. Not things."

Vittoria glanced around the almost-empty room and silently disagreed. Dirt floors. Scratched walls with a single window that faced an alley. Rats scurrying around at night. Eneko slept on a mat not far from the hearth. Pere on a straw mattress. Mere and Vittoria in hammocks suspended from the ceiling. They tucked the beds up during the day and pulled them down to sleep.

This was a hovel, not a home.

Outside, the street lay quiet and dark. A nearby torch had burned out and smoked gently. Her thoughts drifted just like the ash falling from the burnt wood.

Maybe home *was* with the witches you loved, but the security of food and a good neighborhood was important too. They did have a home. But though quiet for the most part, it still wasn't safe. Wouldn't *be* safe if things spiraled into a civil war. She shuddered as she imagined flames licking up the walls, consuming the house. So many rebel riots had ended with the destruction of the buildings that housed rebels or workers.

Why not here?

Her gaze dropped to Eneko. He stirred when she ran the backs of her knuckles against his cheek. The sharp shadows of night did nothing to hide his gauntness. His thin fingers twitched. Beneath the old shirt lay ribs, easily countable.

If she accepted Mateo's offer, he'd give them all food. Medicine. A home. A real home, not a hovel. Eneko would have dimples in his elbows like landowner children and so much energy to run.

If she said no, she'd remain here. She'd work as a *lavanda* maid while the days passed. Every day she would wonder if she'd made a mistake as the same sun traveled through the same sky while they did the same work.

Day after day after day.

This endless cycle, did it never change? Would this be what Eneko and his children and their children knew? Vittoria stared at the shadows on the wall. Her mind unraveled, the tangled web suddenly unsupported. Her thoughts fell. They lay in gossamer strands at her feet, as if they'd lost all power.

Her resistance crumbled like stone on a dying wall. All arguments faded into the background of her insecurity and doubt. Of course she would be Mateo's High Priestess. Provide for her family. Change her Network.

For her family.

For Eneko.

For every desperate witch.

She shook her head with a humorless laugh. A *lavanda* maid among the nobility. A High Priestess.

The absurdity.

The sleepless night passed in vague shadows and waking dreams. Just before dawn, Vittoria wrapped herself in her shawl and slipped outside. She tilted her head back to stare at a changing sky that bled from inky black to a bruised gray. A chill crept in from all angles, but she didn't move because she knew he would come.

He arrived minutes later.

"You must be cold."

One moment she was alone, the next he stood at her side. The warmth of a heavy cloak covered her shoulders, its hem so long it rested on the ground. His smell, sand and salt, was reassurance without words. Embrace without touch.

"I'll do it."

The declaration flew out of her all at once.

Mateo paused, little more than a shadow next to her. The sun easing into the sky offered enough light that she could just make out dark, disheveled hair. This version of him towered hands above her. She tilted her head back to see into his eyes. His broad shoulders would span the widest barrel.

His hand brushed her face, the whisper of his fingertips against her cheek. "Are you sure?"

"Yes."

"What has convinced you?"

"My family." She tilted her head toward the window. "Eneko. If I can provide a new home, safety, food . . . I . . . I must."

His hand dropped away. She swayed toward it for half a second, wanting to call back its warmth. The growing light revealed a little more. Full lips. Dark eyes. Thick lashes. Hair as black as the night dropped to his shoulders. A handsome profile, at the very least.

Mateo lifted a hand to his face and scrubbed the fatigue from his eyes. "Then we must act immediately to announce it." His expression darkened. "I have never done this before. No one has ever done this before. I can't tell you what to expect. The landowners may be harsh. Cutting. Cold. The rebels may try to attack. All of them may threaten you, but I will always keep you safe."

"No member of the nobility has ever handfasted a *lavanda* maid, you mean?" she quipped with a smirk.

He grinned. "Not in the Castaneda line."

Vittoria sucked in a full breath, amusement gone. "I have one condition."

"Anything."

"Reveal yourself to me without magic."

His hands spread out to his sides. "As you see me now."

As if the sun had conspired with him, the first beams of full light broke over the eastern sky and illuminated the world. She studied his deep-bronze skin and endless eyes shadowed by heavy lashes. His gaze was soft, but his muscles and features were hardened like a chisel.

His confident stance and the regal bearing of authority in his unwavering gaze was an otherworldly strength that spoke of more than physical prowess. Her hand reached out to touch his chest, as if to affirm that he was real. Her fingers trembled against his shirt for only a moment before she pulled her hand back. Heat burned on her fingertips. For some reason, it *felt* real. He stood before her as the protector she'd always wanted. The one who had lived in her dreams.

He was also far more handsome than she'd ever anticipated. He swept her breath away with his intensely concerned gaze.

"Mateo," she whispered.

Mateo was more warrior than vigilante. She wanted to laugh. The snively, ratlike characters he'd occasionally disguised himself as had hidden all *this*?

Deep magic, indeed.

"Thank you," he said softly, and so much lingered in the words. "Thank you for your trust. I must go now. There is . . . much to prepare. We must move quickly. Benat, my friend and protector, will come soon. He'll transport you to my house, where you'll be safe. Shortly after that, more witches will come to take your family to safety."

"How quickly?" she asked, breathless as he took a step back. She didn't want him to go. Oddly, she wanted to follow him right then, to throw herself into the path of her future. But she didn't, because there was still Eneko. Her family.

The space between them gave her opportunity to breathe. A bucket appeared in his hand, overflowing with food. He extended it to her, as serious as ever.

"For your family. Your pere's medicine is inside, enough for a week. We announce our betrothal tonight." He winked. "Don't fear, Vittoria. For I am always at your side. We go into this new life together."

6

VITTORIA

A well-dressed man arrived two hours later. Benat's short black hair framed his kind eyes. His square face was indistinguishable from his thick neck, and his clothes had neither stench nor stain. A deep intensity belied his gentle smile.

"*Sa*, Lady. I am Benat," he said to Vittoria with a slight bow.

"Vittoria." She bowed her head with a smile. "Thank you for coming. It's good to meet you, Benat."

Mere sat next to Pere on his mattress, and Eneko watched Benat from the other side of the room, clutching a few wooden blocks Mateo had sent with a magical spell. Concern marred Eneko's features beneath the hints of soft sugar along the edge of his lips. Hidden within the toys had been several delicious treats. Eneko had never had such a sugary treat before. He'd gobbled them so quickly his stomach hurt.

Apprehension filled Vittoria's core as Benat stepped toward her.

"I'm here to bring you to Mateo's," he said.

The fear of this first step could overwhelm her if she let it. She'd never been away from her family for more than a day. But she wouldn't allow it to overpower her, because she'd chosen. Still, it eroded her courage. Tugged at her to stay. To put away this madness and remain in the safety of her family.

"Are you ready?" he asked.

"Yes." She swallowed hard, and felt more courage for the agreement. "Yes, I'm ready. I have nothing to bring with me."

"Mateo will provide everything. Zuri is already preparing the house for you. You've never transported before?"

"No, I have never transported."

"I will transport you."

She grimaced. Pere used to do small spells when she was a little girl, but hadn't worked any magic since Hodei had trained Guardians to seek out magic users among the workers, then put the lawbreakers' heads on pikes in the street. The severed heads dripped blood and brains for weeks before the ravens ate their eyes, hair, and skin. Old skulls still rattled in the farthest reaches of the East End Coven.

Magic made her apprehensive.

"Is there any other way?" she asked.

"My men are outside watching. They'll come in as soon as we leave and take your family to safety."

Eneko darted up to her side and pressed his shoulder into her leg. She wrapped her arm around him, holding him firmly.

"When will I see them again?" she asked Benat.

He shot a quick wink at Eneko. "Tomorrow, if you wish."

Her shoulders relaxed. So soon? Of course. Mateo had been nothing if not kind. "Thank you," she said. "That helps."

"It's almost impossible that anyone would know about you or this plan, but we won't take any risks, I assure you."

"We?" she asked. "Who else is there?"

He smiled. "I'm Mateo's . . . Guardian, for lack of a better word. I have a team of ten men who help me and Mateo in his work as La Salvatorra. My men and I keep Mateo and La Salvatorra safe. Now we'll keep you safe."

"That's a relief," Mere muttered.

"You are loyal to him?" Pere asked.

Benat nodded to them. "He is like a son to me. I have no family but him and my men. I'd give my life for all of them. For your daughter as well."

Pere nodded once. When he looked at Vittoria, his soul showed in his teary eyes. Tears clouded her eyes in response.

Benat held out a hand. "I can transport both of us, but I'll need to have a hold of your arm to do it. You can expect darkness and pressure. Count or do something in the back of your mind—it helps. Transportation is not painful, but it is rather uncomfortable."

Vittoria nodded. "Just one moment?"

"Of course."

Vittoria hurried to Pere. She lay her head in his lap, eyes squeezed shut. Eneko ran over with a cry and snuggled into her side. With a little peep of emotion, Mere clutched all of them in a massive embrace.

Pere stroked Vittoria's hair.

"Pere?" she whispered

"Yes, *masuna*?"

"Have I made a terrible mistake?"

"No," he murmured. "You have accepted your destiny from the Givers like a brave soul. You will change the world."

Vittoria pulled away, tears hot in her eyes.

"I am so proud of you," Pere said. He pressed a shaky hand to her cheek. "Your courage is remarkable. La Immanuella will give you the strength you need to see this through."

She clutched Eneko to her. He didn't cry, but he held her so tight her ribs hurt. "Tori," Eneko whispered. "You're leaving us?"

Her reply choked her.

"Please." Mere grabbed Vittoria's hand and one of Pere's. "Let us plead to all Givers on your behalf today."

Mere's voice dropped into a quiet, steady intonation as she whispered a blessing, invoking it on Vittoria's head on behalf of all the Givers. Vittoria closed her eyes and listened, heart in her throat. When Mere finished, she pressed a kiss to Vittoria's hand.

"You can do this, *masuna*." Tears collected in Mere's eyes. "We love you."

Vittoria squeezed her fingers as Eneko let out a little cry.

"Tori, don't go! I love you."

Hearing the emotion in his voice was too much. She hugged him, pressed a kiss to his hair, and whispered, "I love you. I will see you tomorrow." He tried to cling to her when she stood and turned to Benat, but Mere peeled him away.

"Please," she begged. "Transport me away now while I still can."

Benat grabbed her arm and sought her silent permission with a questioning gaze. When she gave it with a nod, something cool trickled through her body, then whisked her into a thick darkness and away from Eneko's terrified howls.

7

MATEO

Late that afternoon, when the sun inched toward the far horizon, sand melted beneath Mateo's feet.

His transportation spell ended with a misstep that almost tripped him. He shook his head. His eagerness to check on Vittoria had almost broken his concentration. A dangerous misstep in that sort of magic.

The briny scent of the ocean brought him back to the present. He stopped, pulled in a deep breath, and closed his eyes. The ocean sighed in response.

The tension from sparring with Benat at the quarry calmed, though it left traces of pain in its wake. Sore muscles. A tight back. A rolled ankle. They'd fought with wooden sticks to prepare Mateo for the upcoming Test of Courage. But the pain would all fade. Even with all there was to do for Vittoria, he couldn't forget the tests.

A thousand things assaulted his thoughts when he opened his eyes again, but he brushed those aside. Right now, his sole focus was Vittoria. She'd been at his house with Zuri all day. He'd check on her, they'd transport to make the betrothal announcement, and he'd bring her back home. After she was settled, he'd venture back out to the covens with Benat and his men to listen to the talk among the workers.

Rumors of Romeo's rigorous training schedule, the preparation of the battle arena, and a potential skirmish on the Central Network border would have to wait until morning.

Five days, he reminded himself. *Five days until the first test.*

With renewed focus, he strode toward a small, pale house hidden against the sandy beach on the distant outskirts of Necce proper. Far enough from the city to avoid detection. Close enough to keep track of what happened there.

The exterior of the house was square and simple—and deceptive. The true house hid behind magical incantations he'd found in a grimoire near the southern edge of the Eastern Network. The book had been an abandoned old thing that had turned out to be worth its weight in gold—it held a plethora of spells related to disguises.

From here, the building looked like an abandoned shed. A ridge of sand and rock hid it from passersby. Magic made it easily defensible for now, assuming no one attacked from the sea.

The wind blew at Mateo's back as he approached, urging him inside. The door opened ahead of him with a quick outpouring of magic. A sprawling, comfortable home awaited him, decorated with floor-to-ceiling windows, cushions on the floor to sit on, and wooden window sconces every few paces along the wall. Half-melted candles lay cold, waiting for night.

Zuri, the woman he'd hired with the specific goal of preparing Vittoria for this new world, rushed up to him. Her hair was cropped short, just below her ears. Only a few months ago, her husband had died in a rebel riot. In the way of most workers, she'd shorn her precious hair to mourn him. Sadness lingered in her warm eyes, but her new employment seemed to have given her purpose again.

"Majesty." She inclined her head. "I—"

"Zuri, I've told you. Until Hodei passes, you cannot give me his title. For now, I am simply the master of this house. *Jauna* is fine, but I'd prefer Mateo."

Zuri propped a hand on her rounded hip and raised an eyebrow. "And I have told you that I don't care what you tell me, I shall call you Majesty. I have lived most of my life being told what to do, and now that I'm free, I'm doing whatever I want. Dare you to argue with me, Majesty. I'm a raging-mad widow who not even La Christianna would come near. You want to try?"

She held out both hands in an invitation.

He laughed. "You win, of course. Say what you like."

Zuri motioned to the back of the house with a tilt of her head. "That's better. Now, your betrothed has locked herself in your room."

Mateo frowned. "Locked?"

"Well, she's asked to be left alone. *Locked* is a bit dramatic."

"Why?"

Zuri shrugged. "Great question. She was . . . resistant to my fashion suggestions. Anticipating that might be the case, I offered only a few of them so she wasn't overwhelmed. They were mild, too. Hardly any skirts and no hooped sleeves. But she wouldn't be swayed. She's been asking for you."

Mateo's concern deepened. "Thank you, Zuri. I'll speak with her."

Zuri faded back toward the stone hearth on the opposite side of the room. Open windows welcomed in the rumble of the ocean as Mateo strode to the back of the house. He paused outside his room, ear canted. No sound came from within.

With a quick rap of his knuckles, he called out, "Vittoria? It's Mateo."

There was a soft shuffle, then the door opened. He slipped inside.

The room was dimming with the sunset. The double doors that faced the ocean had been thrown open, admitting breezy air. Mateo turned to find Vittoria, half-expecting to see her trembling in the corner or throwing something.

Instead, she stood in the middle of the room with her shoulders back, hands at her sides, regarding him with a stoic expression. Was that a challenge in her gaze? He hoped so. He enjoyed it when she pushed back.

Her hair, freshly washed and dried, shone in the light. The black strands lay on her shoulders in lazy curls. Her body looked as clean as a fresh bar of soap. Even her nails had been buffed and trimmed, no longer ragged and broken. Zuri had dressed her in a simple ivory shift with sleeves to the elbows and a high neckline. The dress fell to the floor in only a few layers, if that. The layers shifted in the breeze.

Such a dress wasn't high fashion. At least he'd never seen a landowner's wife wear anything like it. The dresses of wealthy women were billowing and huge, kept that way by massive hoops. They took up an awkward amount of space around their arms and made the simplest tasks almost impossible.

But Zuri had accomplished the most important things, at any rate.

"Are you all right?" he asked.

Vittoria nodded. Her voice was stiff when she said, "Fine."

"Zuri is . . . concerned."

"She's kind, but she's also . . ."

"Insistent?"

"Yes."

Mateo relaxed, hands at his sides. He smiled. "*Insistent* is certainly one word for her. She was raised to help landowner wives prepare for the social events that come with their duties. She's quite confident in that world. I brought her here to ease your transition."

"I am not a landowner's wife."

"No, you're not."

Vittoria gestured to the edge of a bed that hung from the ceiling with thick sea ropes. It was stuffed with a feather mattress and graced by several blankets. The bed swayed in the breeze, the wooden box that supported the mattress creaking. Several dresses fluttered off its edge, mostly silk, it seemed, but a few other fabrics he didn't recognize. All of them were bright and full, with numerous layers. Zuri would have gotten them as castoffs from dressmakers. Dresses with tears or odd hems or inconsistent coloring. She must have repaired them, for they seemed perfect.

"She presented those to me," she said, swallowing. Her chin lifted. "To try on to pick one to wear to the betrothal announcement tonight. Said that first impressions are important. I have refused them."

"All right."

The simple scalloped neckline and high waist of Vittoria's gown made him think of . . . well . . . a clean worker. Simple. Unadorned. No color, just straightforward. Anticlimactic, but oddly perfect.

He felt like a fool for not seeing this before.

Her tone increased in pitch. "And the charcoal and the lip color and the fake eyelashes. I've refused those as well. She cannot change my face, Mateo. I won't do it. I won't do incantations that make my skin look flawless. It's a lie. I will *not* be a lie."

"All right."

Her hands spread down the length of her, and her jaw tightened. "I plan to be presented to the witches just like this when we announce the betrothal."

Mateo nodded. "I think you're compassionate, perfect, and lovely."

Vittoria's clenched fingers visibly relaxed. Her expression shifted to one of confusion. "You're . . . you're not upset?"

"Why would I be?"

"Zuri says I won't look like nobility. She's concerned the landowners may be offended. As if I'm insulting them by presenting myself as I am. A *lavanda* maid."

"You probably will offend them."

She blinked.

He sighed and ran a hand through his hair. "No matter what you do, Vittoria, they will be offended. If you wear their fashion? They'll be offended. If you don't? They'll be offended. You can't please them no matter how hard you try. You may as well do what feels best to you. You and I are here for the workers *and* the landowners. Be yourself, and let the rest go."

Her entire body softened. "Oh." She swallowed. "Thank you. I'm . . . I'm not sure what I'm supposed to be worried about here. This is all very over-whelming. Lovely." She glanced at the room with a wry look and a half smile. "But overwhelming."

Mateo closed the space between them and rested his hands on her shoulders. She tilted her head back to look at him. He studied her, his stomach smoldering like a hot coal. Vittoria didn't need any of the accou-trements that came with landowner life. She had a natural softness about her. Inherent courage, he imagined. As he stared at her, he couldn't help his hope.

By the Givers, but they had an actual chance at this.

"*You* are who I'm presenting, Vittoria. Not a noble witch. Not anyone else. You shall appear as you feel most comfortable. My trust in you is implicit. Whatever you decide, that is what we'll do. And gladly. What can I do for you that will give you courage for tonight?"

She pulled in a deep breath as she wrenched herself back together. He admired her deeply for it.

Seeming better, she said, "I feel as ready as I can be. I don't know what to expect."

"Neither do I," he said with a soft smile. "I do have one thing I would ask you to wear tonight, if you will?"

He opened his palm and conjured a curling, creamy magnolia flower. Its rusty-pink interior bled into the delicate leaves with a gentle blush. It sprawled across his hand, overtaking it in size. He held it out, gesturing to her shoulder.

"If I may?"

She nodded once. He slipped a long pin out of the stem, his fingers delicately sliding under her neckline near her left shoulder, where he pinned the flower. Then he stepped back. She fingered the bloom awkwardly.

"Is it too much?" she asked.

"It's lovely, just as you are. All witches will see it."

"Thank you, Mateo." Her fingers ran over the smooth texture of the petals. "I . . . already feel better."

"Good, because we must be on our way now. Benat's men have been spreading word via my messengers into all of the nearby covens. Other cities and the most remote covens will hear the message later, from Benat's men."

"Now?" she whispered. Her expression paled.

He nodded. "The time is now. Witches gather as we speak to hear an announcement from the very elusive Mateo." He offered her his arm with a quick smile. "Rumor has it that even La Salvatorra will be in attendance."

Vittoria stood next to Mateo with her shoulders pulled back, eyes trained on the horizon, in a show of supreme regalness. Tonight's goal was easy enough. Announce her. Get her to safety.

Yet so much could go wrong.

They stood on the rooftop of the *eliza* of the Giver La Principessa. It lay in the heart of Necce, on the interior edge of every coven. Every road in the city funneled right to the *eliza* like spokes on a wheel. The holy building, erected over two decades ago by the hands of volunteer workers, was made of different types of stone. Most of the stones had been scraps from local quarries or rubble from fallen buildings that landowners had destroyed to make way for something new. The workers, so desperate for a haven, had even used quarry dust to create mortar to hold up their *eliza*.

The faces of the workers, Mere had once said, fingers on her face, expression slack with memory. *They were always covered in dust. Always gaunt. Always desperate. The Givers will avenge their sacrifice. Justice, no matter how long it takes, will come to our witches, Mateo. La Salvatorra will see to it.*

Mateo jerked out of the thought, unwinding himself from Mere's voice and back to the present. Conjured magnolia flowers, the symbol of La Principessa, graced every archway of the *eliza*—every floor, every doorway, every window. Their pungent aroma lingered in the air. Mere, years ago, had cast the incantation that kept the magnolia flowers perpetually alive. Powerful magic to live so long, but that was Mere.

Hidden power in a landowner dress.

The *eliza* was little more than a facade of stone and hope, and the only place landowners never ventured. Not even Romeo with his unusual attachment to the city of Necce. The *eliza* of the Giver La Principessa was the only sanctuary workers sought.

Which made it the perfect place for Mateo to declare his choice of High Priestess.

Hundreds of witches awaited, amassing near the front doors and boiling out onto the streets, stretching down alleyways. Every minute, more came. There were four entrances to the *eliza*. Benat's men blocked each entrance, eight men in all. Four visible, four hidden. They would admit no one while he and Vittoria stood on top. Two more roamed the gathering crowd to listen to its murmurs. Benat's men were once workers they rescued from the streets, trained by Benat himself. They had sharp eyes and listening ears and undying loyalty.

Benat met Mateo's studious gaze and nodded once.

All clear so far.

"So many witches," Vittoria said. "How will they all hear you?"

"Magic."

The wry expression on her face said, *Of course.*

"When?"

His gaze flickered to the large clock on the tower outside the market. "In two minutes, on the hour."

She pulled in another deep breath. Mateo reached for her hand, clasping her cold, trembling fingers in his own. She didn't pull away. An eternity seemed to pass while the number of workers swelled below. Mateo reviewed his speech in his head. He hadn't written it out. He kept ideas strung loosely together and trusted himself to know what to say in the moment. For now, he kept a wary eye out and listened to the lonely whine of wind in his ear.

What better moment for Romeo to strike against him than this one? Of course, Romeo didn't officially know about Vittoria yet, although he had spies everywhere. Word of a gathering had surely reached the castle by now.

Vittoria, seemingly oblivious to the danger, kept her chin high. Finally, when the hand ticked to the hour, Mateo cast an incantation to expand his voice. He tried to slow his thumping heart with a deep breath.

"*Allo*, my fellow witches," he called. "It is my pleasure to stand before you tonight as Mateo, son of Hodei. Your future High Priest by right, fate, and honor."

His voice traveled through Necce in a gentle roll. It drifted down alleys to whisper to the most-distant regions. The farms. The quarry. All the way to the heart of the covens just beyond bustling Necce. A slight echo rang back. Such an use of magic would tire him before he ventured out as La Salvatorra. By the end of the night, he'd be exhausted. But it was worth it because such use built up his power and tolerance. And these workers needed to know.

Cheers rose from the boiling mass below.

Mateo. Mateo.

He lifted two hands, and silence fell. The power of all those eyes felt heavy in the air. Vittoria didn't waver at his side, although her knees shook.

Splashes of color interrupted the generally dismal sea of clothes as landowners and their wives left the shops and transported away from the unexpected crush of workers. Never in all his life had he seen such a sight of gathered workers. Neither had the landowners, which was precisely the point.

Yes, Mateo thought. *See their numbers? They are more powerful than you think.*

"I, Mateo, have accepted the challenge under the Law of Rights issued by my brother, Romeo. I have no fear, for I will win the throne and represent all witches—worker and landowner alike—well."

He paused, allowing that to roll through the crowd and the covens. More cheers. The sound bolstered him. Vittoria gripped his hand, her fingers so small in his. A few witches attempted to run into the *eliza.* His guards stopped them. Vittoria's magnolia glowed on her chest, brightened by a spell.

"But I cannot do it alone," he continued. "Tonight, I seek your approval. If we are to forge change, a High Priestess must be at my side. A High Priestess of grace, equality, and honor. Without her, I am nothing to you."

The low-level hum quieted.

"For that reason, I present my betrothed, Vittoria Nerea Antoinetta Guita, daughter of Nerea Antoinetta Isabella Sal and Ander San Guita of the Mayfair Coven."

A ripple of astonishment spread through the city and swelled in a great crush of sound. Vittoria sucked in a sharp breath through her nose. Mateo gripped her fingers tighter. Up so high and unable to see their expressions, he couldn't tell if the workers were astonished or excited.

He pressed forward, determined to believe the best.

"You already know her, don't you? She is a *lavanda* maid. You have seen her generosity. Seen how much she cares for workers. With Vittoria, I seek to restore equilibrium to a failing Network structure," he continued, "and *all* of its witches. Workers and landowners. I care for all of you. You are all important. With Vittoria at my side, I know it is possible to bridge the gap and create equality for all."

The suspense built as Mateo turned, gazing down every road. Assessing every shadow. Every sound in the cacophony. The last several months of work came down to this.

Never mind that the moment he made this announcement, most of the landowners would gladly murder him and Vittoria. By making this declaration, he was stepping wholeheartedly onto a path that would most likely kill him before it ever saved anyone.

"Workers, what do you say?" he called, thunder in his voice. "Will you accept Vittoria as your High Priestess?"

8

VITTORIA

Vittoria's heart threatened to pound out of her chest as she stared at all those eyes. All those witches fixated on *her*.

A *lavanda* maid.

No, a future High Priestess.

Mateo stood like a fearless sentinel beside her. He seemingly had no qualms. No sense of terror at the enormity of what he strove to do. She understood little of this political game, but she did know that asking the workers for their opinion on anything was a fast shot to death at the hands of landowners.

Up until this very moment, Vittoria had felt as if this were all a vague dream. Perhaps some half-baked joke that would end as soon as someone jumped out and laughed at her for going along with it.

You? they would say. *A* lavanda *maid? How could you possibly be the High Priestess?*

But Mateo was so clever. He had made sure the workers had seen her face. Known her for her generosity. The last several months suddenly made sense. How could they reject her? It was an oddly reassuring realization.

Mateo reached out, a hand on her arm. He stood at the edge still, gazing out on the crowd. His brow had wrinkled.

"Mateo?" she murmured, startled by the strange expression on his face.

"Look."

When she followed his gaze, a breeze ruffled the magnolia flower strapped over her heart. The crowd below shifted, starting from the front. The movement rippled backward, one witch at a time. Once she comprehended what was happening, her breath whooshed out of her all at once.

The witches were kneeling.

Workers in every street dropped to one knee, heads tilted back to face her. They held a hand over their left shoulder in the gesture of approval. A hushed reverence fell over the city, punctuated only by occasional murmurs until every witch in sight had knelt.

Hot, scalding tears filled Vittoria's eyes.

"Your witches," he said gently, "approve."

Swallowing hard, Vittoria dropped to one knee, hand over her left shoulder in return. A blast of sound broke out when she stood back to her feet. Witches stood, calling out with indiscernible words. The ruckus of approval rose even louder than Mateo's deep voice. He pulled her into his side with a heavy arm, and she felt anchored to his strength with gratitude.

They stood there for a full minute, the sound rolling like thunder.

No backing out now.

Nor would she wish to. Eneko lived bright in her mind as she faced those thousands of witches.

There was an eruption of sound, and several shrill screams came from the ground on the right. Vittoria whirled to see what had happened just as Mateo pushed her toward Benat.

"Come, Lady," said Benat. "I will see you safe. Witches are starting to act out below."

"Go," Mateo added with a nod. "I'll be there soon."

Vittoria turned away with Benat, then stopped. Standing on the rooftop of a neighboring building was a bent-over old man. His white hair stood in sharp contrast to the sooty roof tiles behind him, and his cold eyes pierced hers with a chill.

High Priest Hodei.

Vittoria paused to regard him for only a moment before Benat guided her down the stairs and into an enclosed room where they could transport away without being followed.

She shivered in the wake of those cold eyes.

The next morning, wind brushed across Vittoria's cheeks. She stood in the sunshine, eyes closed. The touch of sunlight tingled on her skin. She soaked up the bright air with a sense of relief.

She had the luxury of standing in sunshine instead of a *lavanda* hovel. Open sea air. A lovely breeze. There would be no sneaky *andreas* to boss her around, no scrubbing fabrics in hot water, no caustic potions on her hands.

Nothing but . . . this.

The thought that she might never return to the *lavanda* life both thrilled and terrified her. What if she had to go back? How could this plan ever work? She felt nearly unable to comprehend a life where she didn't have to scrub her vitality away.

The sound of singing swords came from behind her. She half-spun to see Benat and Mateo locked in a tangle of weapons and spraying sand. Advance. Retreat. Clang. Parry. Grunt. The animalistic side of Mateo startled her. Until now, she'd only seen his gentle gaze. Quick smile. Kind eyes. Witty laugh. This was entirely new, almost primal. His strength seemed all but unfailing in the dazzle of sun on sword.

In the far distance, she could just make out Magnolia Castle through the haze of the ocean. It cut an odd figure in the mist. She turned away from it. There would be time enough for considering her place in that world, Givers willing.

Two of Benat's men guarded the perimeter of the house. One watched over the ridge of sand, stone, and scrub that hid them. The other strode around, eyes darting here and there. When he passed her, he nodded but remained silent. Their broad shoulders and thick thighs, unusually strong for workers, made them prowl more like predators than Guardians. She wondered where Mateo had found them.

He'd need them, no doubt.

Her stomach dropped as she thought of what lay ahead. She'd avoided thinking about the inevitable tests last night—she'd just tried to get through the betrothal. It felt strange to open her thoughts to it so wholly now, because the tests were the next step.

The Test of Courage came in four days. The Test of Magic would follow two weeks later. Then the battle against Romeo after two more weeks. Less than five weeks in all. That's all she knew. Their handfasting at some point, perhaps? She couldn't imagine handfasting with the Law of Rights in the background. Would it be better to handfast him before the final battle, or after?

What if there *was* no after?

Vittoria turned her thoughts from that path. Of course Mateo could die, but why focus on it? If they handfasted after he succeeded, her family could be safely invited. Would he allow her a simple ceremony? Must it happen in the castle? She smiled as she thought of Eneko dressed up. They'd buy him new clothes. He wouldn't be so gaunt or pale . . .

Assuming Mateo defeated Romeo, they'd likely move into the castle. No leader would live in a shack, surely, even one so luxurious as this. That meant landowners would be part of her daily life. She'd have to play hostess, deal with the political process, and maybe have children.

Vittoria blanched. Givers, she hadn't thought of that.

Her mind barreled down the path of the future, despite every attempt to stop it, leading to her greatest fear of all.

How was she to be High Priestess in this brand-new world?

The workers who knelt before her last night had effectively committed treason against the High Priest, protected only by their sheer numbers and the threat of rebel retaliation. Those workers now had expectations of her as their future High Priestess. They wanted her to lead them to a better life.

All the elation of yesterday faded to an uncertain whisper of doubt.

How can I do this?

Despite how little she knew Mateo, her growing sense of respect for him was real enough. They would be friends, if not lovers. More than she might have expected as a *lavanda* maid—many girls handfasted out of desperation or loneliness. Though she'd be a fool if she didn't admit she felt something for Mateo. Stirrings. Hope. A confused sense of safety, maybe.

Was it more than that?

Vittoria suppressed the urge to watch him, shirtless and sweaty in the sand. He'd protect her and her family. She knew that, if nothing else. The thought bolstered her. She was here for them, wasn't she? For them, she could do anything.

Even be High Priestess. Particularly to such a handsome High Priest.

For now, it was enough.

Vittoria sighed and glanced around. A wall of stone and sand lay behind the tricky little house. Mateo's sprawling home looked as small as a *titi* hovel, a nest for a mouse, from the outside. More of an old shed than anything else. Within, however, was a sprawling, comfortable home with windows, doors, and so much natural light. It was five times larger than anything she'd ever known, though still humble by landowner standards.

Breakfast, prepared by Zuri, waited on a tray inside. Vittoria regarded it again, head tilted. She'd never eaten in the morning because they always ate all their food at dinner as a family. Landowners did, though. It seemed an . . . odd luxury.

Would she need to?

With the song of swords in the background, she slipped back inside and stripped to her chemise. Then she bustled around the room that Zuri had said was her own.

"Majesty says to make yourself comfortable," Zuri had said with a warm smile. "It would be his room, but he prefers to sleep outside. Men are strange that way. Although, this close to the sea, it is tempting."

To keep her absolute terror at bay, Vittoria rearranged the room. She slipped all the books and parchments into a box that she tucked into the corner. She couldn't read yet, so why look at them? She stripped a sheet off the bed and moved things around until the whole room looked as if a storm had blown through it.

Ten minutes later, she stepped back to regard her creation.

In the far corner, up against the wall and the floor-length window that overlooked the beach, she'd shoved the most comfortable chair. Then she'd taken sheets and tucked their corners into two hanging pots. The result was a screen that hid the chair, a pillow, and a large chunk of ocean and sky.

It would be her space. Bare. Empty. Small. Minimal. Just like home. A mirror, an armoire, a hanging bed, and an actual painting of La Principessa remained behind. She'd only seen paintings from a distance before.

In this one, La Principessa knelt near a small child and his crying mother, a gentle glow of light around her hands. Here, La Principessa's features were quite young. Not much older than Vittoria's, in fact. The boy looked like Eneko, which stilled her aching, swollen heart. He held a magnolia flower, presumably gifted to him by La Principessa.

Vittoria sat in her hiding spot, her back pressed to the wall, and breathed. The chill of the wall permeated through her ribs, into her body. It centered her like a shot of gravity. Her mind calmed. The edges of ragged panic settled into something not unlike curiosity. Maybe terror. There was a fine line between them.

"Vittoria?"

The booming voice came from behind her closed door. Vittoria's eyes popped open. Mateo, not Zuri as she'd expected. A gentle knock followed the sound of her name.

"I'm here," she called from behind the sheet.

Mateo entered the room with quiet footfalls. He paused, then advanced to her hiding spot. The curtain slowly parted to reveal his face. He was sweaty, still dressed in a white shirt unbuttoned to the center of his chest. Thick brown breeches hugged his legs to the floor, where he wore leather shoes. His chest still heaved a little from the exertion.

"You are well?" he asked with a sparkle of amusement in his eye. Seeing him stilled some of the wild anxiety in her chest. They still hardly knew each other, but he calmed her all the same.

"Yes." Her shoulders relaxed a little. "I'm doing well."

He gestured to the hanging sheet. "Hiding?"

She gave a slow smile. "Perhaps."

"Good. Sometimes we all need to."

"I've been thinking about last night. What did you hear when you went back to Necce?" She leaned forward, eager to hear what La Salvatorra had discovered. Mateo and Benat had been out in the covens until late. She'd heard their whispers as they returned but had been too sleepy to leave the comfort of her new bed.

"Nothing new." His brow wrinkled as he wiped a bead of sweat off his cheek. "More hopeful talk about Mateo, overall. No attacks or rebel business, however, which surprised me."

"Does it mean something?" Vittoria asked.

He frowned slightly. "Maybe. It could mean they aren't organized enough to take advantage of such an unexpected opportunity for chaos." He shrugged. "Or maybe they're surprised. Curious. Overly cautious. It's hard to tell." He glanced around her room, clearly bored with the topic. "You're comfortable in here? Zuri get you everything you need?"

"Yes, it's lovely. Thank you. I slept better than usual last night. The ocean so close is . . . lulling."

"Very." He grinned. "Like a lullaby."

She gestured around her. "It . . . it feels like too much, though."

"It does at first, but soon I hope you'll grow comfortable with it. There's something powerful about having your own space."

Vittoria fidgeted with the fold of her dress. She'd never had her own space. "My family. Are they all right?"

"Yes!" He chuckled. "Benat's men were quite taken with Eneko. They gave him a wooden sword, and he's been hacking at bushes. They're settled in a small house near the quarry. I checked on them myself yesterday. Later, at dinner, I'll take you to them."

Vittoria's first full smile found her. "Thank you!" she cried with relief. "I can't wait to see Eneko with real toys."

Mateo chuckled again. "He's quite fierce with that sword. The apothecary will be there soon to see your pere. Today, I hope. Your mere agreed to help me with some things at the quarry. They're happy."

Vittoria beamed. "Thank you, Mateo."

He nodded. "Zuri will come and go if you need anything, but you can help yourself as well. Food is in the kitchen, blankets in the hall, that sort of thing."

"Thank you."

Mateo studied her for a second, and she wondered what he saw. Her fear? Her relief? Her homesickness already? Maybe all of it?

He extended a hand. "Come with me? There is something we should look at together. I owe you a full explanation of what's to come with the

Law of Rights, and this may be the best place to start. Then we can talk about your place in my plan to help the Network find stability again."

Vittoria stood and accepted his hand. The warmth of his palm was reassurance against all the doubt. Her fears vanished in the certainty that they would venture into this unknown world together.

"What is it you want to show me?" she asked.

His expression turned grim. "The arena, which is where the Test of Courage will take place. It's the place of my victory, or my grave. Might as well go now, while I'm sweaty. We won't get any cooler out there."

Vittoria's head spun as the transportation spell ended.

Mateo held onto her arm as she attempted to gather her wits. For all its conveniences, magic was not a fun experience. The spinning sensation ebbed, which took the wobble out of her knees.

Mateo put a heavy hand on her shoulder. The weight grounded her. She opened her eyes to find him only a breath away.

"Better?" he asked quietly.

Not recognizing any of her surroundings, she simply nodded.

Heavy, dense air pressed upon her, wet and thick all the way to her lungs. A trickle of sweat ran down her spine. Greenery tickled the back of her neck like reaching fingers. She shivered and stepped away, only to feel the frond of a fern on her arm.

The Saltu Jungle.

Mateo clasped her hand in his and tugged her to stand in front of him. He pressed a finger to his mouth to indicate a need for silence, then gestured behind her with one finger.

Vittoria glanced overhead, then behind. Thick branches tangled in a dense jungle canopy. Curling vines, leaves as tall as her body, and cascading flowers created the appearance of a ceiling. So many shades of green unfolded before her that she couldn't even count them. Just beyond the foliage lay hints of a bright sky.

"What is that?" she mouthed as Benat and two of his men faded into the jungle. She pointed toward where a vague shape seemed to coalesce.

His lips brushed the shell of her ear as he whispered, "The landowners call it the *poena*. It's the arena where the first Test of Courage will take place. It means *the agony*."

She shivered. The *poena* wasn't the only danger here. Ghost panthers ruled the Saltu. They were dark as night and mean as Hodei. Witches in the farmlands and the city feared the jungle. While fleeing the farmlands years ago, Vittoria and her family had been forced to skirt the edges of the Saltu on the way to Necce. She recalled the strange noises and shifting shadows with a bone-deep shudder.

Mateo motioned her forward a few steps, then pulled away the foliage. She peered between thick, glossy leaves to see the world fall away beneath them. They stood at the edge of a massive crater the shape of an oval. Rich, black earth had been excavated away until it reached muddy sand fathoms below. The entirety of the hole could house Magnolia Castle ten times over. On the far side, the jungle spilled over the edge and into the middle of the arena. Plants sprang to life along the ground before her very eyes, unfurling a leaf at a time. The sheer height of the straight drop made her dizzy.

Around the edge of the *poena* were seats for spectators. Each row of seats was wider than the last, until the final row stopped just below the treeline. Vittoria stood with Mateo at the edge of that layer now, barely hidden in the foliage.

Workers were carving more seats into the *poena* with tools that looked like long, flat scrapers, flattening the earth and then discarding the extra into a bucket. Mud coated their calves and arms in the sweltering heat. A lower-level landowner followed them. The muddy benches hardened behind him, apparently with magic. He eyed the workers warily. Red stripes across the workers' backs dripped blood in crossed lines. A whip hung from the landowner's hand.

"By the Givers," she murmured.

Mateo pulled her back. She doubted they'd be seen, but she was relieved to look away anyway. Benat returned with a nod to Mateo.

"This is where the first Test of Courage will happen," Mateo said, just loudly enough to be heard over the sounds of the jungle. Benat stood near them, head cocked as he peered into the Saltu. She wondered if Mateo felt any fear. If not, she felt enough for both of them.

"In four days, Romeo and I will meet down there to prove our courage." His stoic expression didn't waver, but his voice softened a little. "The actual task will be unknown until we both arrive."

"Who decides the task?"

"Historically, the Head of Guardians. Since Pere has given that title to himself, then it goes to the second-in-command. That is an ambitious witch named Balta, who wants to be the Head of Guardians and would do a good job of it. Of course, Pere shares nothing. Certainly not power," he said sardonically. Then he gave her a little wink that loosened some of the tightness in her chest.

"So, the task could be anything?" she asked.

"Anything. But I'm willing to bet it has something to do with the jungle, considering." He motioned to the labyrinthine greenery below.

He was probably right. She doubted the jungle would spill into the *poena* otherwise.

"Are you prepared to kill your brother?" she asked.

"No. Not remotely." He sighed heavily. "Fortunately, we don't fight each other yet. I have time to . . . wrap my mind around it."

She shuddered. "Barbaric," she murmured. "The whole Law of Rights."

"Effective." He shrugged. "It has been invoked in the Castaneda family six times. Only once by a brother. Most were cousins. One was between an uncle and a nephew. It's supposedly an honorable way to claim the throne, too, although I would question any landowner who uses that word while working conscripted witches to death."

She scoffed. "Honor among landowners."

Mateo laughed without amusement. "Honor is their religion as surely as Givers are for workers. Pere's ancestors were nothing if not pompous. Many of them believed that dying without honor would ban them from returning to life. They believed death to be their entry to the next life. Without honor, they are denied entry and are simply gone forever. Honor, supposedly, is fighting for your life."

"Then workers all die with honor."

"I agree," he said quietly.

She frowned. While landowners believed in honor, workers believed in fate and Givers. But Mateo seemed to straddle the lines. "Do you believe in honor, Mateo?"

"Not as landowners see it."

Another of the men returned and reported something to Benat. They spoke quickly, their voices a blur she couldn't make out. Finally, Benat motioned the other guard toward the trees. He obeyed, positioning himself between the *poena* and Mateo.

"One more," Benat said to Mateo.

"One more what?" Vittoria whispered.

"Woman left to report back to us."

"Spies?" she asked.

"Spies."

Mateo parted the leaves again. Vittoria leaned forward and followed his gaze. Toward the top of the arena, the benches gave way to a flattened space beneath a canopy of woven fronds. Tables and lounge chairs filled the shaded area. Several female workers bustled around, carrying baskets filled with what appeared to be starched tablecloths.

"They're preparing for the event," muttered Mateo. "During the test, many landowners and their wives will eat there, maybe several times, while waiting to hear what happens to us. No doubt there will be spells in place to protect them so they can enjoy their entertainment. Hodei keeps a dedicated staff at the arena. Those women live here. They sleep outside, fix the meals for the arena staff, and then serve guests at the games."

"The games?"

"It's hard to see clearly with the jungle growing down there, but there's a fighting pit where landowners watch various barbaric events. Workers battling each other, animals fighting, you name it."

The wall with hanging neck and leg manacles required no further explanation. Nor did the obvious bloodstains on the walls, the floors, the rows closest to the bottom. The jungle continued to creep forward one budding plant at a time. Where it had overtaken the edge of the area on the far side, full-sized trees had already grown. Who gave magic to such a horrific thing?

The third guard returned, reported to Benat, and fell into place near

Vittoria. The second guard shifted to accommodate him. She felt marginally better for their presence. Mateo sent a questioning look to Benat.

"No foul play suspected," Benat said. "The women report no interference from Romeo or his men so far."

"You expect your brother to cheat?" Vittoria asked, voice lifted in surprise. Wasn't *honor* first and foremost?

"One always does," Mateo murmured. "Thank you, Benat."

"May we leave now?" Benat asked. "I don't like it here. I can't guarantee Lady is safe if she can't transport away immediately."

"Soon."

Benat and his men had started calling her *Lady* after the betrothal announcement last night. An official title she wasn't entirely comfortable with, but didn't want to take away from them. She tried to ignore it, but it made her grit her teeth. An ungainly reminder of a future she hadn't yet fully embraced.

Shouts rang up from below, and Vittoria shifted closer to Mateo. One of the workers, in a vain attempt to hurl himself down the steep stairs to die, stumbled over a tool. The landowner in charge tossed the whip, caught the witch around the mouth, and yanked. A shrill scream issued from the witch's throat as he writhed on the ground. Lash after lash bit into his skin. His face, filleted halfway open, cheek dangling uselessly on the stone floor, chugged blood onto the ground.

Vittoria blanched but didn't look away. Her stomach churned painfully. She thought she might vomit. *I'm sorry*, she thought to the man. *I'm sorry.* Mateo tensed next to her as the punishment continued until, finally, it stopped.

The worker twitched once, shuddered, then lay limp on the stone. Blood pooled around him in a river.

"Vittoria—"

"No."

Her voice was husky but firm. Benat glanced at her. But Vittoria kept her eyes trained on the bloody stump of a witch and the humiliating agony of such a death. The other workers didn't look. Didn't falter. They continued forming benches out of sand. The landowner returned to his previous position.

The bloody arena claimed another life, and the world moved on.

"Honor," she muttered.

Mateo took her hand. "I'm sorry," he whispered.

She nodded, and it was all she could do.

A rustle in the jungle caught her attention. Another of Benat's men appeared. "Trouble," he whispered just as the landowner below called out a halt to all the workers. Mateo peered through the foliage as a figure emerged from a tunnel onto the arena floor.

Romeo turned, seemed to look right at her, and lifted a beckoning hand.

9

MATEO

Mateo transported Vittoria to the arena floor, then braced himself in front of her as she stood like a board at his side. He wished Romeo hadn't seen them crouching in the jungle, but there was no changing history.

A voice in his head screamed like a madman. *Don't let her meet him!*

He shouldn't bring Vittoria down here. Not so close to Romeo. He didn't know his brother as well as he might have liked these days. Was it beyond Romeo to sacrifice honor and kill her now?

Not likely. He couldn't protect the landowners if he were dead.

Besides, Romeo wouldn't fully understand Mateo's plan yet. That might be the reason he'd come today. Mateo dismissed his concerns. Let Romeo think Vittoria was just a way to get workers' attention and nothing more. But setting his hope for Vittoria's safety on a tenuous thing like honor didn't help this feel any safer.

I wanted her to meet him, he reminded himself. It didn't soothe his deep, instinctual fear.

Benat and his men followed close behind. Benat shifted to put his body between Vittoria and the Guardians who trailed Romeo. One of his other men took up her opposite side. She didn't seem to notice.

Instead, she studied Romeo with a pale expression.

"Mateo," Benat drawled. "This isn't—"

"Patience, Benat," he murmured.

Mateo widened his stance as Romeo strode toward them, his clip steady.

More for Vittoria than Benat, Mateo explained, "Honor won't allow him to harm her here. Not unless she actively threatened his life. He would lose the Network to me and die in dishonor."

Benat snorted.

Vittoria's hands shook at her sides.

Mateo resisted the urge to comfort her as his brother closed in. Romeo's severe countenance gave him a formidable appearance, but he lacked Mateo's innate confidence. Romeo ignored Vittoria completely as he slowed to a stop a few paces away and regarded Mateo through slitted eyes.

"Mateo."

"Brother."

Romeo's hard expression didn't relax.

"To what do I owe this dark pleasure?" Mateo asked. "A visit from a busy man like you is no small gesture."

He kept his body in front of Vittoria to give her a moment to prepare herself, but she emerged from behind him on her own. To her credit, she didn't say a word. Just studied Romeo with an uncanny gaze.

"So, you are the girl," Romeo said as he cast a glance at her. A veiled insult. Vittoria was no girl. She wisely didn't take the bait, just regarded him carefully. The two of them stayed locked in a silent contest of wills for an interminable time.

She didn't curtsy, the way a landowner would have. She watched. Noted. Ascertained him as equally as he did her. Maybe out of sheer fear and lack of know-how. Romeo shifted one shoulder back after the silence extended beyond formal comfort.

"My name is Vittoria," she finally said. Although her voice trembled, it didn't detract from her power. "One day, you may call me Majesty."

Romeo lifted an eyebrow, glancing at Mateo in question. Mateo stared back. The urge to laugh nearly overcame him.

"You have come to ensure fairness, I assume?" Romeo said to Mateo as if Vittoria hadn't spoken.

"Always."

"Are you satisfied?"

"So far."

This meeting was no accident. Mateo had told Benat's guards not to be too careful as they gleaned information and surreptitiously offered generous food buckets to the witches. He wanted Romeo to know he had come. Wanted Romeo to meet Vittoria on his terms, away from Hodei and before the fight.

Likely, Romeo had wanted the same thing. To suss Vittoria out. To sense the edges of Mateo's plan, or figure out *why* Mateo would make such a move.

"Are you prepared for the Test of Courage, Mateo?" Romeo asked.

"Of course."

"With a *lavanda* maid and a handful of defected Guardians? Quite the support system you've built up all those years wandering the streets, dodging responsibility. I imagine you're eager to rule the Network with such workers behind you."

Mateo almost laughed again. *Wandering the streets. Dodging responsibility.* As if Mateo hadn't spent the last decade working as hard as Romeo to one day rule the Network. But Pere and Romeo had never acknowledged him. Part of their psychological warfare, no doubt.

Mateo smiled. "I'm very eager to change the Network for the better."

A twitch of a sneer ghosted Romeo's pale lips. "Of course," he murmured silkily. "It's easy to be arrogant when you have the luxury of ignorance, isn't it? I guarantee you a fair playing field. No traps."

"The entire thing is a trap."

Romeo conceded with a slight nod. "Regardless, I guarantee the honor of our tests and our match."

"And the honor of a landowner is a precious thing."

Romeo said nothing at first. He opened his mouth, hesitated, and finally stated, "Pere was too unwell to get out of bed today, or he might have come to meet her himself."

With that, Romeo shuffled back. Mateo wanted to feel a stab of concern for Pere but couldn't conjure it. Only a dull numbness lingered there.

Besides, that random comment had to mean something. Why did Romeo want him to know?

"Forgive me," Romeo continued coldly, "but I must be going. The East End rebels have burned down two landowner stores since your announcement last night. I'm to get the responsible parties on a pike."

Vittoria didn't even flinch. Mateo's admiration for her warmed.

Romeo walked away, his uniformed Guardians following. Only one remained behind to watch Mateo's party and Romeo's back. Mateo stood there until Romeo transported away and the final Guardian followed.

Vittoria stared at the spot they disappeared, deep in thought. Her trembling had subsided. Mateo wanted to reassure her but didn't know what to say. Truly, was there any reassurance?

Benat stepped forward. "Shall we go, Majesty? We may speak of this further at home."

"Yes."

Vittoria turned to face him, a completely unreadable expression on her face. That seemed far easier to deal with than fear, so Mateo didn't question it.

"Thank you," he said to her.

"For?"

"For your loyalty."

She frowned but gave no response.

Mateo ran a hand through his hair and sighed. "Let's go home," he said. "It's been a long day already."

10

VITTORIA

"After Romeo's little appearance, I've requested that Benat keep a few more men on duty tonight," Mateo said when they returned. He fought back a yawn. "Precautionary. I doubt Romeo plans to follow or act, but one never knows."

They were back at the house, a strange silence between them in the aftermath of the unexpected encounter. Vittoria stood in the middle of the room, uncertain of what to do next.

"Thank you," she managed. "I appreciate the caution."

He waved it off.

Her mind spun back to the events of the day. It was hardly noon, but she already felt tired. Meeting Romeo had been disorienting, but it was the arena that frightened her. The generations of spilled blood.

Death in the air.

It was a dark place where men went to die.

"I promised to explain more of our plan. Allow me to do so now?" he asked.

She nodded. Mateo straightened. Fatigue undercut his movements, which seemed heavy and slow.

"For now, my plan is to continue what we have been doing. You will remain out there distributing food buckets while we support the needs of

the workers as best we can. Benat, his men, and I will continue our work as
La Salvatorra."

"But why?" she asked, finally able to voice the question that had
haunted her for months. "Why do this at all?"

"For one, it helps workers feel safer with us and know we're on their
side. You're one of them, and they recognize that. Secondly, they need
another figure who is a landowner, but isn't La Salvatorra. I will never
reveal that I was La Salvatorra because it would threaten what little trust
the landowners have in my name. So someone else must arise. And the
workers love you already. Many of them have known you for months. Now
we'll take you to different parts of the Network where they don't know you
yet. Eventually, I want all of the Eastern Network to know of you. Then, I
want you and La Salvatorra to be seen together."

She blinked.

There was more strategy behind the plan than she'd expected. Part of
her had thought he gave the food buckets out of guilt or a sense of oblig-
ated reparation. Maybe just to build up loyalty to her so that when she was
announced as his betrothed, the workers subsequently trusted him more.
But no—he was downright tactical.

"That's . . . fairly simple," she finally said.

For half a breath, there was hesitation in his face. A sense of something
he wasn't saying. But a weary smile swept that away. "Simple plans often
work."

"I will just continue to do what I've been doing while you fight out the
Law of Rights?"

He nodded. "Essentially."

Relief followed her surprise. Knowing the nature of his plan made this
all seem less overwhelming. The ability to help workers made the separa-
tion from her family bearable. She felt surrounded by luxury in this new
world, and the guilt nagged at her. She did no work, yet she—and her
family—ate. They lived in a safe place, too. It didn't seem fair to have so
much.

Distributing to the workers, however, felt like it balanced her stroke of
good luck. The plan gave her firm footing. Action. Something to do. It

would occupy a few hours during the day, at least, and help her make a difference.

She drew in a breath and nodded, relief apparent in her voice. "Thank you, Mateo. I'm grateful that I can still help."

He smiled. "Always. If you ever need anything, just let me know. I'll be sleeping in the room down the hall if I'm not outside. Knock anytime. Also, if you're agreeable, I think it would be beneficial if you learned how to read. Zuri has volunteered to teach you in the mornings when she brings the food for the buckets. Magic, too, if you'll have it. Are you interested?"

She considered the parchments outside her room, stacked on a shelf in the wall. She loved the idea of seeing her name written out. As if understanding the letters made it her own, somehow. Mere had admonished her to take her magic-learning opportunities where she could. Although magic made her uncomfortable, it *could* make her safer also.

"Of course I'm interested," she said slowly. "But how is all of this possible? The food buckets. The tutor. The house?"

"Mere."

She blinked. "Your mere? But I thought . . ."

Mateo grinned wryly. "Yes, she is dead. Died when I was fourteen. But she was a great collector of expensive things. It's easy to spend the currency of a High Priest, isn't it?"

A flash of amusement in his voice hid something else.

Pain, perhaps?

"She constantly traded with the Southern Network. They took our goats, green vegetables, and seashells while she took their gems and silk. When she died, my friend and I hid her wealth away so it didn't fall back to Hodei."

He tilted his head to gaze on the room, then lifted both hands. "It pays for this. For all the food you've distributed. There are landowners in the farms who don't want Romeo to take the throne, so I've formed friendships and agreements with them. I sell Mere's stash and buy food from the willing farmers. Zuri prepares the food after it arrives, and I use magic to transport it to the bucket."

Vittoria laughed. "Very sneaky," she said with admiration. "I would never have guessed so much is involved."

His smile widened. "Sometimes, we must be sneaky. The supply won't last forever, of course. For now, it's sufficient."

For now echoed in the room. It didn't need to last forever, did it? He'd either die or become High Priest. The thought made her sick to her stomach again.

"Since we are speaking of business matters," he continued with a deep breath. "We are betrothed and will, given my success in the arena, eventually be handfasted. You are in total control of all aspects of that. You will never be forced into anything, which includes the intimate aspects of our relationship. I only ask that we hold off on the handfasting until the Law of Rights is settled."

His expression was inscrutable until she gave a small nod indicating she understood. Her knees spasmed at the thought. At least he'd answered her unasked question, and there was a sense of relief in knowing she wouldn't be a widow.

They felt like strangers all of a sudden. Cordial but distant. She hated it, but welcomed it at the same time. He gave her power, which so few workers gave to their wives.

"Thank you."

Mateo straightened. "I will do everything in my power to keep you safe, Vittoria."

"And if you die in four days?"

One of his hands rested on the doorknob. "Benat will get you out of here, and his men will help your family. There are many witches outside Necce who are loyal to me. They have already agreed to take in you and your family. Some places in the Central Network will take you in as a refugee if it becomes necessary."

Of course he'd thought of this already. But who thought of him? No one, it seemed. For being the High Priest's son and a man of considerable stature, he was arguably the most solitary figure she'd ever known. No one to truly support him. No one to stand by him, save Benat and his men.

It broke her heart, for Mateo was good. Confusing, but genuine. The words she spoke next took her by surprise.

"I will always be at your side, Mateo," she said. "I see the sacrifice you are making for your Network. You don't do it alone anymore."

He reached up, touched her face, and gave a small smile that spoke worlds. "Thank you, *masuna*. I can't tell you how much that means. Tonight, after some rest, I will take you to your family. You may see them as much as you wish. Until you can learn to transport yourself, you need only ask."

With a slight bow, he faded into the hallway. Vittoria watched the space where he disappeared, her heart hiccupping.

Sunlight tangled with Vittoria's dreams when she awoke four days later.

A gentle breeze rushed across her skin as she opened her eyes. The gauzy curtains drifted into the room, reaching for her, and the bed creaked as it rocked. She drew in a deep breath of salty air, stretched her arms above her head with a little squeak, and let her eyes flutter closed again.

Five days of this elegant lifestyle, and she still couldn't blink herself out of her stupor. Her half belief that this was all a dream.

If this weren't destined to be such a bloody day, she'd almost call it *lovely*.

Hints of fresh-baked *pitta* stirred her awake. Zuri must be here already. Vittoria threw her covers off and slipped into the balmy air to help Zuri finish the food preparations. Time for a trip into Necce, then.

Not to mention the desperate fact that she needed a distraction from the impending Test of Courage.

Midday, Mateo had said last night. He'd stared at the fire until she'd slipped away to go to bed. *We'll meet at the arena just before midday. The spectating landowners will already be there. You and Benat will follow separately. He'll keep you safe.*

Five hours, she thought with a quick glance at the sun in the sky. She slipped into the subtlest dress she could find, and a knock sounded at the door.

"Come in, Zuri," she called, eager to see her new friend. Life in the covens hadn't given her time to make friends. But now, Zuri's maternal warmth had been a safe spot in the midst of all the new things. Even though Vittoria saw her family every night before Eneko went to bed, she'd desperately needed Zuri's motherly touch here. Zuri had already started teaching Vittoria the basics of the alphabet and how to spell her name. They practiced simple magic every day in the sunshine.

Zuri opened the door and cocked a hip. "Well? You ready to go?"

"Just about."

Vittoria reached into a basket next to her door and extracted an elaborate candlestick that, she felt some certainty, was made of pure silver.

"Where did you get that?" Zuri asked.

"One of Benat's men brought it to me last night," she said as she flipped it over. "It was discarded from the castle because there's a slight imperfection at the bottom. Can you believe that? A silver candlestick cast away for one little mark."

"They are all kinds of sick in the head up there." Zuri folded her arms and pursed her lips. "Are you ready for the Test of Courage today?"

Vittoria wrapped the candlestick in a pillowcase and avoided Zuri's studious gaze. The tone of her voice suggested she wouldn't tolerate Vittoria avoiding the conversation.

"Not in the slightest," she admitted.

"He's going to be okay," Zuri said. "Mateo has always been a survivor. He will be one today also."

Vittoria nodded. "I trust him."

She felt a rush of fear. She and Mateo were friends now that they'd spent the last five days living in the same house. Distributing food buckets meant more now that she knew the person tailing her—and that all this work meant something. *We're so close!* she wanted to shout to all the workers. *Mateo will bring us peace! Just hold on a little longer.*

But all the *what-ifs* ran through her head so quickly they made her dizzy. Her hair rustled as she tied it away from her face in a braid that no landowner's wife would be caught dead in.

"Did he leave already?" Vittoria asked.

"This morning." Zuri nodded. "I think he went back to his old estate to find some peace. He has gone there before."

"Why there?"

"It's where he last saw his mere. No one else has inhabited it. They say ghosts live there." Zuri shrugged.

Vittoria's lips rounded into an *O*. She did the same thing when she missed Anton. Searched for ghosts of the past for comfort—only she turned to Eneko. Wrapped her arms around his warm little body and remembered Anton's bright personality and infectious laugh.

Mateo had none of that to snuggle up to.

Zuri bustled up behind her to pluck a string off her shoulder, then nodded. She tilted her head toward the door. "Well, let's get going. Benat is waiting for you, I'm sure. Don't worry about Mateo, *masuna*. He'll be just fine."

Vittoria followed Zuri out of the room with the fervent hope that she was right.

"Did you have any family, Benat?"

"No, Lady. Just me."

Benat stood with Vittoria in an alley not far from the *eliza* of the Giver La Principessa. It was her favorite spot. Crowds gathered here daily now, waiting for her to appear. The stench of urine and dirt filled her nostrils. Despite the rank smell, there was an odd sort of comfort in the familiarity of it. Witches bustled around, clutching bags or baskets, or poorly attempting to hide half-full pockets of food.

"How did you meet Mateo?"

"Luck."

She thought of asking what that meant, but didn't. If he wanted her to know, he'd tell her.

His rough features softened. Scars peppered his face and neck, some edging along his hairline, others deepening his scowl.

He thrust a white cloak at her. Intricately embroidered magnolia flowers covered the back of the cape in a wreath design. The creamy silk material would make her stand out from a coven away. The top of the cape, near her neck, boasted a gentle blush color, as if a magnolia petal were unfolding on her back.

"Here. Mateo wanted you to wear this."

"White?" she gasped. "You must be kidding. It will be filthy in a moment's time."

He shrugged and motioned her forward. She twirled the cloak on with a sigh, then stepped out of the alley and emerged into downtown Necce with a bucket in hand. The cape billowed at her back as she hurried down the street. Newsbook hawkers and flower girls called out over the din of clopping horseshoes. The air of the alley smelled thick with brine and fresh fish.

She approached a huddled figure on the dirt near a pile of discarded fish guts. The half-sleeping figure stirred when Vittoria pressed a *pitta* into his clawlike hand.

"May La Principessa bless you," she murmured, as she always did. Mateo's voice rang in the back of her mind.

La Principessa is the most powerful of all Givers, he'd told her several nights ago. *What is more powerful than hope? Whether you believe in her or not, invoke her name when you give them food. Remind them they have reason to hope. We make sure of that every day.*

The man, ragged beard crusted with filth, blinked rapidly.

She smiled, then moved down the alley toward a blacksmith's shop. There, a man stood behind an anvil, near a fire where a young boy shoveled coal. Heat thickened the air. The man regarded her cloak, then Benat. Children sprinted by outside, singing, "La Immanuella will avenge us."

"*Allo,*" the blacksmith said.

"Can you split silver?" she asked.

He nodded.

She extracted the elaborate candlestick. "I'd like this to be split into chunks. Maybe the size of the end of my thumb? As many as you can. I'll happily give you one or two for your time." Her gaze darted to a book behind the desk. "No notation of work necessary. You won't have to share it with your landowner."

When she pushed it toward him, he stepped back.

"No."

Her brow furrowed. "Why not?"

"It's a test."

"Oh, no. I can understand your fear, but it's not a test."

He shot a dubious glance at her cloak. She glared at Benat as if to prove her point, but he just shrugged again.

"You stole it," the blacksmith said. "They'll blame me."

"I didn't. It was given to me, and I don't need it. I want to distribute the silver to witches. You, your assistant, your family. You may all have one."

His suspicion turned to incredulity in seconds. "Then you're a fool." He put a hand to his forehead. "Touched with the mind fever. Why would you give away silver?"

She laughed, then shrugged. "I'm a *lavanda* maid."

His gaze tapered. "You're that witch, aren't you? The one who gives away food. The one who . . ." He eyed Benat again. Some of his apprehension faded.

She brightened. "Yes!"

He frowned, then made a sound in his throat while he glanced over the candlestick. She held his gaze, not daring to breathe. The boy behind the blacksmith paused, a shovel of coal held halfway to the fire. The blacksmith looked from Vittoria to the candlestick and back again.

"Pere," the boy whispered. "Please."

"Three pieces for you," she said. "Make them as large as you want."

With a reluctant sigh, the blacksmith held out a sooty hand and flicked his fingers once. "Quickly," he said. "Before my landowner comes."

Twenty minutes later, Vittoria slipped out of the smithy, forty fingernail-sized silver chunks clinking softly in her pocket. She'd given a *pitta* bread to the blacksmith and the boy, then stopped in front of an alley, near a man with a leg cut off at the knee.

"*Allo*," Vittoria said softly. "Here. A piece of silver. La Principessa watches over you, *maltea*."

The shriveled man looked at her through one eye, the other sealed shut and crusted over. The eyelashes merged into one thick line as he curled his fingers around the silver.

"Do you have somewhere to sleep?" she asked.

He gestured to the ground.

"Then I shall bring a blanket next time." She put a hand on top of his. "Perhaps two of them."

Whispers followed her as she advanced farther into Necce, distributing the silver pieces to children and adults. Witches crowded around them as she proceeded down the alley.

Under his breath, Benat said, "We must return, Lady. You are drawing a crowd again."

"It's not the first time, Benat."

"It is for a crowd of this size. You have drawn more attention than usual with your silver."

She cast a quick glance behind her. Her stomach caught. Indeed, quite a few witches followed them now. No more than twenty, but enough to draw the curious gazes of other workers. They seemed more curious than threatening.

For now.

"We're giving away silver," she murmured, then tossed a few pieces of silver to the witches. They scrambled after them. "Of course we'll draw a crowd. I'll be quick about the rest. Just twenty left."

Benat pressed his lips together and followed her quickening steps. For the next twenty minutes, Vittoria approached any beggar with an apparent and desperate need for help. The whispering crowd continued to grow. The bucket disappeared when she handed out the last piece of food. She spoke with each worker she passed, attempting to learn more about their story.

"Lady," Benat said. "Mateo will face his first test soon. We must go."

"Three pieces of silver left," she said. "There's a woman who begs on the next corner. She's a friend of mine. I'll give them to her. It's this way."

She grabbed his arm to move away from the crowded marketplace and nearly ran into two young men.

One of them startled. His gaze dropped to her cloak and the silver in her hand. He cried, "La Principessa! So it's true?"

The other gaped. "A Giver. A Giver is here in the flesh!"

"What?" she whispered.

Benat pulled her back and stood between them with a scowl. The first witch turned and called to someone behind him, "La Principessa! She is here! Find your mere. La Principessa will heal her."

Cries rang out from the stalls where workers bought and sold for their landowners. The flood of witches who had been following converged with a surge of curious onlookers from the market.

Benat shoved several more witches back but couldn't keep them at bay. "Lady—"

"Transport us, Benat."

Before he could touch her, two workers gripped her arm from behind. Their hands groped her clothing. Something tore.

Shouts filled her ears, disorienting her. She whirled around as a cool brush of air fluttered against the back of her arm where her sleeve had once been. With a gasp, she tried to duck away. A wall of witches filled the alley now, blocking all exits.

"I have the sleeve of La Principessa!" a voice shrieked. "It will heal all of us. Touch it and you shall see!"

Vittoria turned. "No," she called. "Please! I am not La Principessa. I—"

Her words were drowned in the chaos as Benat struggled to stem the tide. He reached for her, shouting her name, but his voice, too, was lost in the din. More witches gathered from the far reaches of the marketplace. Vittoria ducked under their grasping arms in a poor attempt to find her way out of the madness. They tugged her hair. Groped for her skirts, which tore. With a bellow and several violent shoves, Benat reached her side again. He held firmly onto her shoulder and pulled her close.

Still, the witches pressed toward them.

"I can't transport us like this," he called. "We need to get away. The transportation magic won't work if someone else is touching us."

The cacophony reached a crescendo as the two of them struggled against the mob. A break near a corner allowed Vittoria to stumble away. Benat gained the footing he needed, then hauled her into his side and ran. Vittoria struggled to keep up. The remaining pieces of silver scattered on the ground behind her. Cries rang out.

"Silver!"

"She cares for all of us!"

Witches mobbed each other for the silver pieces. Three of Mateo's men appeared to block the witches from following. A shrill scream arose from the other side of the marketplace. The workers dispersed.

"Guardians!" someone shouted. "Run!"

Benat skidded to a stop. The odd tingle of the transportation spell washed over her, but the hard clamp of a hand on her arm stopped it. Her heart barely had time to squeeze before she saw an emerald cape. A helmet

and a set of half-armor made of metal and leather decorated a broad-shouldered Guardian.

Her head tilted back to look into a pair of cold, dark eyes.

Benat was torn away from her. Then she heard the clank of swords on
stone. Screams of pain and flashes of fire in the background meant the
Guardians had come to the covens.

And they had her now.

"You're wanted by His Majesty, Hodei the High Priest," said a firm voice.
"Come with us."

"No!" Benat shouted as he lunged. "Lady!"

He struggled against four Guardians who silenced him with a spell.
Another incantation dropped him to the ground. Vittoria met his livid gaze
seconds before the Guardian forced her into the pressure of a transportation spell.

Everything went dark.

11

VITTORIA

Vittoria sat on a plush chair in a long hallway lined with sprigs of ivy. Gulls chanted in the background as she waited, heart pounding. Three Guardians surrounded her. Their broad bodies blocked her view of the area, but she knew where she was.

Magnolia Castle.

The castle had always loomed large and beautiful and pristinely white in the distance of her life. Extensive gardens dotted with magnolia trees surrounded the flowing structure. Its white stone sprawled across the beach.

A lovely building filled with landowner snakes. Now she sat in the middle of it, alone. Unprotected.

Oddly, she didn't fear for herself yet.

Did Benat and his men get away? Her stomach clenched at the memory of Benat's horror. What was happening with Mateo? Based on the location of the sun, they were probably just minutes away from the start of the first test.

What had she done?

The slam of a door reverberated down the white-walled hallway. She jumped as a scratchy voice declared, "Bring her in."

The Guardian from the marketplace motioned for her to stand. When he took her arm, it was with a gentle touch. He was oddly . . . kind. The intensity of his expression had faded. In the aftermath, he appeared younger than she'd expected. Only a few years older than her. Perhaps a bit thinner, even. He didn't make eye contact, but closely watched her.

Instead of shoving her the way she'd anticipated, he guided her through a double-door archway that appeared out of nowhere in the white wall. A spell, perhaps, to protect the entrance to the High Priest's office. Her stomach felt leaden as she followed him through the arch. She risked a glance up, but he still didn't meet her gaze.

What would Mateo say to her now? Her first chance to truly support him, and she was gone. He'd worry about her, and that would distract him. She hoped that Benat and his men were able to get free of the mob and that they'd lie to Mateo. That they wouldn't tell him the muck she'd gotten herself into, that they'd find her later without involving him. Surely, Hodei wouldn't just . . . *kill* her.

Would he?

Well, why *wouldn't* he? Fate had her now. Nothing to do but see where it took her.

"Vittoria, do come in."

A broken, bent man stood in the middle of a circular room. Windows dotted the far wall, lined with emerald glass and colorful seashells along the edges. Bookshelves filled the rest of the round walls. The warble of a songbird issued in the background, strangely at odds with the shadows in the man's stare. A musty smell lingered in the air, as if the windows hadn't been opened in years.

Vittoria stopped halfway to him. His oddly curved spine made him equal to her height. All the paintings depicted him as a hulking, strapping man. Like Mateo.

How far he had dwindled.

For years, rumors had circulated among workers that Hodei's evil had warped his spine. That he paid for his sins through physical torment. La Tourrere, the Giver of Peace, had abandoned him, they claimed.

Somehow, immobile before him, she believed it.

They regarded each other with unchecked curiosity. Vittoria fought off a little shudder. Hodei. Possibly the most frightening witch in all the world.

She stood alone with him now while her only hope battled for all their lives.

Givers, but she'd messed up.

"Have a seat," Hodei said.

A chair knocked into the back of her knees and forced her to sit. She gripped the arms before it toppled backward. It was a heavy thing, made of carved wood, and didn't fall as she'd expected it to. In fact, she didn't move at all. Magic bound her to the seat.

Hodei called across the room, "You may leave."

She glanced up and swallowed a scream. A worker shuffled out of the shadows. He wore the usual emerald-green garb of castle workers, but his eyes were sunken in, as if permanently bruised. Slashes of black twine crossed his lips, sewing them shut. The edges were a bright red and tinged with blood, as if fresh.

She fought the urge to vomit.

A personal worker, no doubt. Hodei smiled as the boy passed, but it was glacial and calculated. He'd had the worker appear just now on purpose. He *wanted* to scare her. Vittoria suppressed her panic. The door shut behind the boy, sealing them inside.

"There's nothing I hate more than traitors," Hodei mused in a light tone as he stared at the door. "Once a liar, always a liar. Now, on to business. Your betrothal to Mateo took me by surprise. Might I say it also impressed me. It's been a while since someone has been able to startle me. Congratulations, Vittoria. I did not anticipate you."

His hoarse voice harbored no amusement. The cold chair felt like slivers of ice against her skin. He leaned toward her, the knuckles that held his cane blanching white. Despite his diminutive size, she felt small sitting before him.

"You must be more comfortable in your new lifestyle," he said.

She didn't respond.

Hodei continued, "In fact, that's a very interesting cape you have on. Far beyond anything you've ever worn before, I would venture. Do you know the significance of it?" His eyes studied the ivory cloak more closely. He made a sound in his throat.

Vittoria swallowed. Unsure of what to say, she remained silent and tried not to look afraid.

Disappointment crossed his features. "No? Well, that's odd. Most workers love their La Principessa. Doesn't the magnolia symbolize your Giver?"

"She's not my Giver," Vittoria heard herself say.

Hodei blinked. "No?"

This time, she clamped her mouth shut. Hodei mumbled something. She caught only the word *interesting* in the garbled sound. He shifted in his seat with a grimace he tried to hide.

"You surprise me again," he managed. "You were hoping to watch Mateo in the Test of Courage today, I assume?"

She reluctantly nodded. He glanced at the window.

"Shame," he said with a *tsk*. "Your first opportunity to show loyalty to him and it's . . . gone. You are here, with the witch he hates more than anyone in the world, instead of at his side. How do you feel about that?"

Vittoria's breath sped up as she attempted to hold in her panic.

Oh, what a wily, aged bag of bones.

He continued, "It's odd, you know. Having two sons who both hate me but want the same thing. Two sons willing to battle to the death for the prize. Such a prize it is. Leadership. Power. A Network to control."

His wrinkled skin showed no change to support the drawl in his tone. Despite his gasping, wheezy breaths, his mental faculties seemed sharp as needles.

From the far side of the room, a birdcage slid across the floor and stopped in front of him. He reached a gnarled finger through the slats. The yellow songbird, a little thing no bigger than her palm, let out a strangled sound. It shied away when he touched it, then stopped, as if something held it there. Its feathers fluffed out as it gave a strangled warble. Hodei stroked the downy wing while the bird trembled.

"I didn't start this war between workers and landowners, you know. Nor am I the reason it has escalated to such tragic heights," he said.

Vittoria bit back a scoff too late. A peep burst out of her throat. Hodei ignored it.

"She did."

Her mind worked desperately to ascertain what he meant. She? Who was *she*? His nostrils flared, and his hand shook as he stroked the terrified bird.

"Esperanza."

Vittoria wracked her mind. That name should mean something to her. There, on the edge of consciousness, was a tingle of familiarity. It disappeared as quickly as it had come.

Who was Esperanza?

"My sons may hate me, but it's their mere who stands guilty. She consigned them to this fate. Without her betrayal, I would never have taken Romeo. Would never have pitted them against each other."

Of course. The deceased High Priestess, Esperanza.

A witch rarely spoken of in the worker world. And, she imagined, the landowner world as well. Bits of memory served her, hazy and incomplete, swirls of rumor and speculation. Tragedy on one end. Death on the other. Something about misaligned sympathies and banishment to the country.

There had been true anguish in Hodei's voice, but he'd already schooled his expression back to one of annoyance.

"Romeo has always been the weaker of the two boys in some ways," Hodei continued, as if discussing insignificant details of his day, "which is why I could mold him. But he has slowly taken over my role with more talent and ruthlessness than I expected. He fancies himself the High Priest already, while I am yet alive. Can you imagine?"

Bitterness edged his voice.

"And you resent that?" she asked.

Hodei smiled with paper-thin lips, and it sent a chill through her. "It is *my* power he plays with, Vittoria. Borrowed power. I am not dead yet, no matter how much you and my sons may wish it. But that's not what calls you here today."

"Then what does?"

"Mateo is the weaker of the two in all the ways that hurt the most," Hodei said as if she hadn't spoken. He tapped the side of his head, then his chest. "He is weaker here, and here. He forms attachments. Gives in to compassion. No ruler can afford compassion, Vittoria. It means that Mateo will never be able to kill his brother."

Despite her terror, she kept her expression even. He didn't look at her. Didn't gauge her reaction. He spoke in an even cadence and then seemed to think about what he'd just said.

Ice flooded her entire body as she sat there, wishing she'd listened to Benat. The songbird gave a pathetic *bleat* as Hodei ran the tip of his finger over its frozen face. Then, after a firm tap of Hodei's finger on the top of its head, the bird crashed to the bottom of the cage in a flurry of feathers.

Dead.

Hodei canted his head, regarding the bird. Then he cleared his throat and turned to Vittoria.

"I brought you here to meet you, Vittoria. You who are the key to undoing all my hard work. Likely the only witch who can skirt the two worlds I've carefully created for the good of our Network. You could unravel everything I have done, and even that may be acceptable. The world will change after my death. I cannot stop that. But borrowed power. Betrayal. Those things are *not* acceptable, and I shall not let them go unrevealed."

Her mind whirled when his gaze dropped to her cloak, then to her. A silent, rapt fascination had overtaken her.

Hodei smirked, looking like death before it pounced. "Mateo may think you're safe with him, but you should know you never are. Secrets are not safe from me, Vittoria. None of them. I always find out. I have allowed you to live for one reason and one reason alone: there is something I want you to seek."

"What?"

"The truth."

Her brow furrowed. "The truth about what?"

His chilly eyes met hers like daggers.

"Why, Vittoria?" he whispered. "Why did Esperanza stay?"

"Stay where?"

He lifted both hands, as if to encompass all of the world, and ignored her question. "Esperanza stayed, and *that* is why I sit here today. Why you are a worker with no rights whatsoever. Why your nephew starved in the streets and your pere lived a painful life as a broken man. It all comes down to that one single question: *Why did she stay?* You are the only witch who can answer that question. Because sometimes even the witches we trust the most will make fools of us."

"Me?"

Truth rang in his voice, but it seemed like a matter-of-fact statement, as if he were merely still puzzled how someone had managed to best him. There had to be more to the story, which was the most frightening part.

Hodei shifted in a move that seemed an attempt to conceal pain. "Your path is set now, and to stray would remove what little honor life has gifted you. Or is it fate that you workers believe in? Even fate has brought you here. You'll find the answer to my question with the rebels, because you are the only witch who can reveal this truth. Answer it and return to me, and I shall let you and your family live. Refuse me, and you and your family shall die."

A knife appeared, gleaming, at the base of Vittoria's throat. The edge of it prickled her skin. Her heart thumped, veins pulsing against the razor edge. She sucked in a sharp breath. For several interminable seconds, she thought about the weight of what both father and son asked of her. About this frightening world. Overturning a government. The ice in Hodei's eyes.

Hodei sank down. A chair appeared behind him. They were almost eye-to-eye now.

"You may be a worker, but you're no fool." The knife pressed deeper, slicing into the skin at her neck. Blood dribbled onto the blade. Her cottony mouth longed to swallow, but she feared it would be her death.

Vittoria fought for something to say, but her thoughts were too loud. Moved too fast. Instead, she held Hodei's gaze by sheer force of will. Her knees trembled like the silenced songbird.

"Your pere is sick, isn't he?" he asked. The knife cut deeper yet again. She squeaked. "Disease of the lungs, likely contracted on the farms. Not to mention a broken back and partial paralysis. A poor stroke of luck. Particularly when your mere just disappeared from her conscription to the landowner Moretti. An offense that could earn her the pike if she were ever found again. And your nephew, little Eneko—"

A spark of fear flared in her chest.

"I'll do it," she cried.

One second she was staring at his livid gaze, the next she felt a cool balm on her neck. The knife disappeared. She drew in a shuddering breath and grabbed at the wound, but no blood showed on her hand.

Magic had healed it?

Hodei pushed out of his chair and shuffled closer. The magic held her fast as he pressed an arthritic hand to her cheek. Yellowing, pointed nails stroked the sensitive skin by her eye. His clammy palm felt like cold death.

"You really shouldn't let your weaknesses show so easily, my dear girl. Go to the rebels," he whispered, his breath sour on her face. "Find Esperanza's story, and report back to me. This is your only chance to avoid a traitor's death and spare your family from pikes outside the castle."

"Why?" she managed to whisper. "Why do you need to know?"

"Because," he said, "I will not be deceived. I will not be played. Borrowed power is no power at all." His nostrils flared, and his entire body vibrated with a rage that seemed to permeate all the way through his soul. "I will not be made a fool, not even in death."

He straightened, and the madness seemed to have passed. Something like admiration replaced his wrath.

"Such a lovely face," he said. "All the landowner wives will hate you for it. Allow me to help with that?"

He tapped her cheek gently, then slashed his nails down the side of her face with a savage growl. Vittoria cried out as hot blood collected on her skin and dribbled toward her jawline.

He sneered. "There. Now they won't hate you so much. Such a perfect complexion deserves a little . . . texture. You'll thank me for helping you one day, Vittoria, for there's nothing more vicious than a threatened landowner. The final gong at the *poena* should be sounding right now. You wouldn't want to disappoint Mateo, would you? Hurry, hurry. Honor awaits."

Hodei disappeared.

The magic that held her to the chair tingled as it faded. Vittoria leaped away from the chair, threw open the closest window, and vomited onto the sand outside.

12

MATEO

In, Mateo thought. His lungs expanded with lush air. *Out.*

Even in his controlled breaths, he found little stability. Considering their reputation as a society that allowed their wives and children little exposure to violence, the crowd of landowners was an oddly even mix of female and male today. Witches milled in the seats in their elegant dresses and silk shirts, focused on the entrance to the tunnel at the bottom of the arena floor. Mateo stood in that stale tunnel that led to the jungle, out of sight thanks to a spell. For some reason, he couldn't face the landowners yet. Not without letting his loathing for them show. One day soon, he'd have to be their leader.

Today, he couldn't stand the sight of them.

Romeo strode up from behind him and stopped. Mateo let the magic go. Romeo didn't spare him a glance when he said, "Are you prepared?"

"How can either of us be?"

A gong rang in the distance, an oddly keening sound. Four more and this debacle would start. Silence fell on the arena.

Outside, a voice resounded over the crowd. From where he was standing, Mateo struggled to make out the words, but he knew the voice right away. Balta, who would be Head of Guardians if Hodei wasn't so tightfisted about his military power. Balta was the planner of this event, and he wouldn't hold back. Not with the military precision he'd used to carefully sculpt his career and his life. He'd prove out his next High Priest with skill and tenacity.

Whatever awaited them out there wouldn't be easy.

Mateo's fingers ground together, the knuckles popping. He drew closer to the mouth of the tunnel to hear better.

"The Test of Courage begins after the final bell," Balta declared. "Each contestant will seek out an elusive ghost panther and bring it back alive. Romeo's panther is marked with a blue cloth around its neck. Mateo's with yellow. They will each bring their assigned ghost panther back, unharmed, for inspection. Any magical interference will meet with execution. They have one full day to bring the panther back, or they forfeit the task and the throne."

Nausea bloomed in Mateo's gut at the second gong. He chuckled, drawing an annoyed glance from Romeo. By *any magical interference*, Balta meant any magic at all. They could use no spells. No invisibility. No incantations. They had to not only survive an encounter with the massive, bloodthirsty beast, but bring it back alive.

Without magic.

"Suicide," Romeo muttered.

Ghost panthers were notoriously quiet, agile, and ruthless. When hungry, they stalked with relentless and silent precision. Ghost panther meres were especially violent. If a ghost panther whelp had ever been seen by a witch, none had survived to tell the tale.

Did he imagine that Romeo looked pale? Mateo felt the loss of blood from his tingling fingers.

Balta continued, "This test is meant to prove the candidates' bravery in the face of danger. Their ability to form a plan, remain calm, and execute said plan in spite of difficulty, danger, or unexpected twists. For what plan ever unfolds the way it should? Even in politics?"

A cheer rose from the crowd. Mateo felt sick all the way to his toes.

"To guarantee compliance," Balta continued, using a spell to project his voice over the crowd, "we have placed a barrier around the edge of the arena that prevents the use of magic within. Any interference from the crowd will result in an immediate negation of the test and withdrawal of the assisted candidate."

The third gong tolled.

Mateo wondered if Vittoria was waiting outside yet. There was a specific spot set aside for her where Benat could keep her safe from the landowners.

"Honor awaits," Balta said.

The fourth gong answered.

Mateo's stomach felt watery. Not much frightened him, but the unknown had always had a wary hold on him. For what felt like an eternity, he stood there, trying to slow his heart rate, to no avail. The Test of Courage was bad enough as stated, but he knew there would be a twist. Something tossed at them at the last moment. His instincts were already prickling.

The final gong sounded.

"Honor to you, brother," Mateo murmured.

Romeo ignored him and strode into the arena.

Cheers filled the air as Romeo appeared at the mouth of the tunnel, in the small section of arena that remained free of the jungle. He spread his arms in acknowledgment of the crowd's support. Sunshine broke across his face as he spun, encompassing all with a fierce smile. The thunderous sound of his adoring public shook the ground. Mateo paused, allowing it to run for several more seconds.

Then he slipped into the arena, ignoring the onslaught of low jeers. Instead, his gaze flickered to the top left. A glass dome surrounded a small, square area where Vittoria could sit. It lay empty. His stomach twisted.

Why wasn't she here already?

For a moment, he felt panic. Was something wrong? Had she come to harm? He slowed his heart by sheer force of will. No, he couldn't do this. He trusted Benat to get her here safely.

Focus. Focus.

Romeo stood a few paces away. He held out a hand. "Honor to you, brother," he said.

No doubt the observation of the public had something to do with his sudden willingness to exchange honor. Mateo clasped Romeo's upper arm and nodded. They parted an instant later. Two machetes stood in the ground only a pace or two away. Romeo grabbed the one marked in blue, glanced back at his crowd with a wave, then headed into the jungle to the left.

Mateo paused to gather his bearings. He ripped the yellow-marked machete out of the earth and studied everything he could see. The sun warmed his back. Shadows had moved across the doorway of the tunnel as he'd waited inside, which put the direction he was facing as east. Why it mattered, he didn't know, but he oriented himself all the same. A quick glance confirmed that Vittoria still hadn't arrived. Or, if she had, she hadn't shown herself.

Landowners hissed at him as he turned to face the southern edge of the arena. Romeo had turned north. The jungle was sparser there, allowing a little more sunlight. Better visuals, for sure. Less chance that something could be hiding in the shadows, ready to spring.

Now, Mateo thought. *Go now.* He'd already waited too long. The landowners started to shout at him.

"Honorless," they chanted. "Honorless."

A ripple of movement caught his eye. Mateo looked up to see Vittoria rush to the glass wall and press her hands against it. Her lips moved. Benat stepped up behind her with a firm nod to Mateo. Mateo could barely see them from this far away, but he thought he caught his name on her lips.

Bolstered, he nodded once to her. She clung to the glass for a moment. There was no farewell in her gaze. Only heart. Courage. Bravery. Light. Everything he needed to prod him into the darkness.

Mateo shouldered the machete and moved south.

Mateo stumbled on a tree root for the thousandth time, caught himself with the tip of the machete, and glanced down. He rolled his eyes at the sight of the squished, slimy little bloodsucker that had tripped him. The length of his thumb and twice as wide, bloodsuckers congregated on tree roots after crawling out of the soil, as if they could suck blood from the sap. They made the ground slippery as soap, too. Mateo reached down, pulled another one off his ankle, and chucked it into the forest.

He paused to try to gain his bearings, skin sweaty and clothes already damp from the baking heat. The jungle was oddly calm, although some of the usual animal life remained. The gentle caw of a bright *daw* bird with its rainbow-colored feathers and ebony beak. The shuffle of something in the underbrush, then a little trill of song. Talking birds meant no predators nearby.

Better to keep moving.

He couldn't be quiet on the ground, and any movement spread his scent, so he gripped the machete in his teeth and scaled the closest tree. Vines abounded, but there weren't enough strong tree branches to make this easy. Ghost panthers, if he remembered right, preferred solid ground even though their claws allowed them to climb any tree. The ivy repulsed them, he'd once heard, but that seemed unlikely. Ivy draped ground, tree, and sky here, so they'd run from everything.

Carefully, and with precision, Mateo moved through the trees. He felt no rush. Didn't matter who found their ghost panther first—just that they found it. Besides, the panthers wouldn't be active now. Too warm.

Mateo stayed high as often as possible. He shuffled across the ground only when he needed to study the jungle from a new vantage or to cross a stretch of the arena that lacked supportive trees. The trees grew close as braids here, the vines clustering with thick abandon. It wasn't difficult to move up high.

By instinct, he plunged into the darkest part of the arena, but stayed close to a quiet stream because everything had to drink.

After testing a vine to make sure it would hold his weight, he swung across an unusually open spot of ground, caught another vine on the other side, and clung to a tree with his free hand. His shoulders burned like fire after hours of such physical exertion, but he pressed on.

Except now the jungle had fallen silent.

Mateo found a foothold and a better grip. Such stillness felt at odds with so much teeming life. Even the flies seemed to have fled. No sound met his ears. Not even the revel of the landowners, likely chanting for his death.

Nothing.

The slightest flicker of movement drew his gaze to the right. Verdant life abounded everywhere here. Emerald leaves set in a backdrop of black made it impossible to tell what was really watching him. Shadows were a natural result of such packed space, but what he saw now was *moving* blackness.

Mateo held his breath when the slinking, steady shadow passed behind several tall bushes. The blackness moved to the left, as if circling him, then paused. If he hadn't known any better, he would have guessed that embodied darkness was following him.

But he knew. A ghost panther had finally arrived.

And now he realized his folly.

Finding the animal wasn't the issue. Eventually, he was destined to meet it. The arena was big—but not *that* big. The problem was taking the panther alive to Balta without magic. He should have spent more time planning what he'd do when he found the beast. This might not even be the panther he should claim.

But now that he had a chance, how to win?

The shifting shadow stopped moving. A pair of blood-red eyes blinked as they assessed the area. The shine of a black nose reflected in the dim light of the jungle as the panther sniffed. The movement brought its head out of the foliage and into Mateo's line of sight. Though its coat was deep black, flashes of lighter, circular rosettas were just visible in the right light. Like an overlay of black on top of a regular panther.

Mateo slowly let out his breath, not daring to move. That's when he registered one very important detail.

There was no collar—yellow or blue—tied around its neck.

A moment of confusion preceded a gentle scratching sound, then a squawk. A flash of yellow at the ghost panther's feet drew Mateo's gaze down. His heart nearly stopped. A squabbly little whelp, likely no older than a month, laced itself between its mere's thick legs. Around its neck was wound a cloth of bright yellow. Seconds later, another whelp tumbled into sight with a scream the mere ignored. It wore the blue collar.

He felt the realization like a cold fist to the stomach. By honor, but he and Romeo had to take ghost panther *whelps*. Somehow, he had to get past *her* to get the whelp.

The mere tilted her head back, sniffing. She seemed to smell him but hadn't found him yet. She focused her attention on the ground, as he'd suspected. That would change in moments, he had no doubt.

Mateo clutched the tree tighter. A bloodsucker inched closer to him, one antenna on the tip of his finger. The sensation of a needle prick distracted Mateo only momentarily, but he didn't flick the bloodsucker free in case the movement or sound drew the mere's attention.

The mere swung her large head toward him.

A moment later, the family of ghost panthers disappeared. It didn't take long to comprehend why. Romeo stumbled into the small clearing, machete held out, at the very spot the mere had just vacated. The ground would still be warm from her paw print, but Romeo wouldn't pay attention to details like that.

Mateo dropped to the ground. Romeo jumped, whirled his machete toward his brother, then relaxed slightly.

"Just saw them," Mateo said, gesturing to where Romeo was standing with a nod. "They were right there. We're to take two whelps."

Romeo paled. "What?"

"Listen, without magic we'll never do this alone. The whelps are young, maybe a month old. Their mere is going to be fierce, and we don't stand a chance." Mateo glanced at the bloodsucker on the tip of his finger. "But I have an idea, and it could work if we do it together."

Romeo studied him.

Without having seen the sheer size of the ghost panther, would Romeo be able to appreciate the odds against them? Besides, Balta had said nothing about what would happen if he or Romeo interfered with the other's panther. A truly ruthless opponent would kill the mere and the other ghost panther whelp, then take their own. Working together could be a fast track for a betrayal.

But Mateo saw no other way. He waited.

"You could betray me and let the ghost panther kill me," Romeo said.

"Same, brother."

Romeo grunted.

"But I doubt you'd stake something as valuable as your honor on it," Mateo continued. "Together or not?"

Romeo's jaw tightened. Mateo could see the moving thoughts in his eyes. No doubt he was considering the likelihood of killing the mere himself.

"You have a plan?" he finally asked.

Mateo flicked the bloodsucker free and tapped his bloody finger against his palm. He tilted his head back to study the trees. "Yes. Something like that. It's not perfect," he said, "but it's something."

Finally, what felt like an eternity later, Romeo reluctantly nodded.

"Together."

An hour later, Mateo silently cursed his own stupidity and spat another mouthful of dirt back onto the jungle floor. Romeo was just visible on the highest branch of a tree near the whispering stream. Mateo stood in the running water, digging bloodsuckers out of the rich ground where his smell wouldn't linger. The bloodsuckers populated like leaves when he didn't need them, and now disappeared like magic once he did.

Six bloodsuckers hung off his arm, filling their disgusting bodies with his blood. One of them, engorged, nearly dropped back into the stream. He snatched it before it disappeared in the water, then cut its head off with the machete and placed it on a rock near the edge. A subtle break in the thick foliage likely indicated a spot that animals had come to drink before.

Then he stepped on it. Blood squelched beneath his shoe, shooting straight out in an arc that spread droplets at least four paces.

This place would look—and smell—like a murder scene.

Not far away, just down the stream, Romeo stared into the jungle canopy with his hands on his hips. Looking for a branch to hide on, and a path to get up the tree to it. They were still near the spot where Mateo had spotted the mere. Mateo assumed she'd prowled here before. Two suckling whelps would guarantee a return visit to the stream at some point, because nursing meres were thirsty. She wasn't likely to travel too far with the whelps, and the smell of blood would draw any of them faster than water.

Which was just when Mateo would pounce.

He foresaw two scenarios here. The first had the whelps running to the stream when they smelled the bloody bloodsuckers, and Mateo and Romeo could grab them and run for their lives ahead of the mere. In the second, the mere smelled the bloodsuckers and drew the whelps closer to her. Mateo would drop on the mere, Romeo would grab the whelps, and they'd hope Mateo figured out a way to subdue her.

Blood dribbled down Mateo's arm. He let it drip to the jungle floor. Another bloodsucker fell off. He grabbed it, repeated the beheading process, and pitched it into the dirt a few paces away. When the blood-suckers were all finished, a trail of blood led to the stream bank. His head spun a little as he stood up, but he shook it off.

Romeo whistled once to indicate he was ready. Mateo glanced up, able to see Romeo only because he knew where he'd be. The jungle hid him from sight. But would his smell fade? Would the mere come back this way? A thousand questions plagued him, but he shoved them away.

It had to be enough. They'd figure it out later if they had to.

Mateo reached for a vine dangling over the stream and pulled himself onto the closest branch. It was flimsy but held his weight as he went a bit higher. He climbed carefully, allowing blood to trickle down his arm and onto the ground. Once he reached the overhanging branch he'd already picked out, he crouched.

His stomach churned at the thought of what lay ahead, so he pushed it out of his mind. Didn't think about the ghost panther. About dropping from the trees. About how he'd subdue the mere without killing her, because why kill a mere with whelps? Nor did he think about a sudden, intense rush of thirst that tickled the back of his throat.

Twenty minutes passed.

Thirty.

Maybe an eternity.

His pulse slowed only slightly as he waited, not daring to breathe. Sweat trickled down his face and along his spine. His shirt was soaked through.

Darkness began to fall in earnest. The sun would be higher in the sky than it appeared now, because the jungle's dense canopy cast early shad-ows, but night would come soon. And panthers could see at night. Mateo might not even know he'd died until he woke up on the other side with fate, honor, or the Givers.

His heightened nerves kept his body tense and on edge. He wondered if Romeo felt the same dreadful anticipation.

Then he heard a yowl.

In the growing shadows, he could just make out the movement of a small figure and a flash of yellow. A flash of blue followed. The whelps tumbled with each other not far away. Then, one of them stopped. It pressed its nose to the ground, then seemed to catch the scent of his blood. The baby panther raced forward, tripped over its own feet, and tumbled into a dead bloodsucker.

The whelps mauled it, all snapping teeth and angry growls.

Mateo's heart raced. He should drop, grab the whelp, and dart away as fast as possible before the mere appeared. It was possible she'd let them venture ahead, so this could be his only chance. But not knowing where the mere was kept him on the branch a few moments longer.

He shifted ever so slightly. The whelps, distracted by the second dead bloodsucker, had no idea he was hovering a few paces away. He thought he heard the rustle of a branch. Romeo, likely.

Until he heard a low, throaty purr just behind him.

Mateo sucked in a sharp breath. Slowly, he looked back over his shoulder. The glow of crimson eyes hovered in the darkness just behind his branch. He swallowed hard, face-to-face with the mere, the slap of her rancid breath like a death knell.

"Romeo," he shouted. "Now!"

The mere lunged.

Mateo sprang off the branch, leaping away from the whelps, and grabbed whatever ivy he could wrap his hands around. He tumbled to the ground. The tangled ivy slowed his fall, so he didn't break a leg but did lose his breath. The mere slinked out of the tree behind him with a hiss, moving like vapor. She pounced, ears back, coming within a pace of his ankle with the gleaming talons of her right claw. Her scream set his hair on edge.

Mateo scrambled out of her reach as Romeo streaked behind them, grabbed both whelps, and disappeared into the trees.

The mere leaped again.

Mateo rolled as her claws slammed into the dirt where he'd just been lying. The ivy wrapped around his body, tangling around his throat, but he leaped to his feet anyway and landed in a crouch. The mere advanced with a swipe, but moved back. She twitched, nose jerking back and forth.

There *was* something in the smell of the ivy she didn't like. It hadn't been a legend.

"Your babies have been taken from you once already for those stupid collars, Mere," he whispered soothingly. "I get it. No wonder you hate us. But I swear no harm will come to them. Just afford me this one chance to save my Network."

At the sound of his voice, she shrank back for a second. He rustled the ivy and she recoiled, then screamed. He felt her third attack more than saw it, and although he ducked and avoided her teeth, her paw chuffed him on the side of the head. Mateo crashed to the ground, ears ringing.

His mind moved slowly. He saw her blood-red eyes. Smelled the metallic breath of death. Sensed her looming over him.

At the last second, he rolled onto his back, threw his left arm in the air, and felt something close on it instead of his head. Teeth sank into his forearm. The bones cracked, sending pain through his body like an earthquake. Mateo shouted, rolled with whatever momentum he could muster, and used all the power in his body to stand.

The unexpected movement threw the panther off-balance. They both stumbled, but she didn't release him. Her teeth shredded his arm and jerked on the broken bone. Mateo growled. He kicked at her to jar her concentration, but she sidestepped, crimson eyes focused on him.

Until the terrified scream of one of her whelps issued through the air.

Startled, she released her grip for half a second to look up. Mateo wrenched his arm out, ducked, and threw himself behind her. Half-blind with pain, he launched himself onto her back, gripped her body with his legs, and hooked his right arm around her neck.

The panther thrashed and screamed, but Mateo clung to her. He felt the edge of her jaw against his hand. The strain of his right arm as he tightened his grip.

Tightened.

Tightened.

Every jerk of her thrashing body sent agony through his broken arm. He tried to brace it along his body, but that hurt worse. Twice he almost passed out. Twice the night seemed to have overcome him, but he brought himself back before his grip loosened. Three times he overcame the urge to use magic to deepen his hold.

Wheezy and weakened, the panther eventually slowed, struggling under his weight. Mateo pulled tighter with a yell, his face pressed into her rough fur. She canted to the right. Her neck jerked. Her tail whipped around. They slammed into a tree.

And he held on.

With the sheer power that comes only from certain death, his good arm held until the panther's front legs collapsed. Her ear twitched, and her face went slack.

He loosened his grip slightly with a bolt of panic. No, he didn't want her to die and leave those beautiful whelps abandoned. His arm unwound. He pressed an ear to her chest. The faint thump of a heartbeat responded.

Passed out, not yet dead.

But soon awake.

Mateo struggled to his feet with a shout of agony. Heat streaked through his arm with pulsing pain. The world swam. By sheer willpower, he kept himself from passing out. He leaned against a tree, yelled himself awake again, and forced his feet to move.

Blood gushed over his arm. It felt sticky on his fingers. Hot on his already-hot skin.

"Romeo," he yelled, half-blind from the pain. "*Romeo!*"

His mind spun. Had Romeo abandoned him? Taken the whelps, doomed him to certain death? The mere would awaken any moment now. Was there more honor in victory if Mateo died for Romeo?

Surely . . .

Mateo fell to his knees. Breathing hard, he gritted his teeth and forced himself to stand.

"*Romeo!*"

Out of the night came a simple voice.

"Here."

Mateo stopped and blinked several times before the picture clarified. Romeo stood in a rough animal trail, two squalling whelps dangling by the scruffs of their necks. Red slashes dotted his arms and face. His shirt was clawed to ribbons, but the whelps seemed calm now. They growled, occasionally batting with a paw, but were mostly docile. The unreadable expression on Romeo's face caught Mateo's attention, even through the pain.

Romeo held out the yellow-collared whelp.

"So," Mateo panted. He grimaced as another spiral of pain wound all the way to his shoulder. "You didn't betray me."

"I wouldn't say that," Romeo drawled, his face darkening. "Let's just say ... I owe you something."

With that, Romeo spun on his heels and disappeared into the jungle.

"Honor awaits," Mateo muttered to his whelp.

13

VITTORIA

By the Givers, Vittoria thought she couldn't get any more frightened than she'd been with Hodei, but this awful arena beat everything else for fear.

"Tell me what happened with Hodei," Benat said for the fifth time. "Your face? How did you escape? What did he say?"

"Later, Benat."

"Lady—"

"Please." She pressed her fingers to her wounded, stinging cheek. The blood had dried, thankfully, but it still hurt. "Your men found me outside the castle as soon as I climbed free and brought me here safely. Everything ended well. That's enough for now. Let me focus on Mateo, and then I'll confess everything."

Her knees still felt weak and wobbly hours later, like jellyfish dead on the sand at low tide. Her face flushed, and her heart raced. She felt weak as she tried not to cling to the glass, tried to affect a brave face. Focusing all her attention on Mateo helped.

"Five hours," she hissed. "It's been five hours, Benat. Five hours of no sound. No word. No sign. How much longer?"

"Lady, please sit. Have some food or—"

A shout broke the silence from the depths of the arena. That wasn't just any shout. That was agony. Guttural, deathly agony. And there was no doubt who it belonged to.

Vittoria sucked in a sharp breath and pressed herself against the glass, as if that would allow her to see him.

Even the bustling landowners with all their food and laughter and flirtation fell into utter, stony quiet.

"Benat?" she asked, her breath fogging the glass.

He stood behind her to peer over her shoulder. All eyes seemed trained on the open space near the tunnel where both Romeo and Mateo would appear . . . if they survived. Ice shot through her body when, minutes later, another desperate shout rose from the jungle.

"Romeo!"

Vittoria reached out to clutch Benat's hand.

"He's alive, Lady. That's something."

Her heart bruised itself against her ribs as she waited an interminable amount of time. Just when the landowners started stirring and speaking among themselves again, movement came from the edges of the jungle. The witch named Balta advanced out of the tunnel, and Vittoria's heart leaped into her throat.

Romeo appeared out of the Saltu, holding a panther whelp.

A whelp? What in the Givers . . .

He was a bit bloodied and his shirt shredded, it appeared, but largely fine. Vittoria swallowed hard as Balta carefully accepted the yowling whelp and handed it to another witch behind him.

How had Romeo emerged alive?

Would Mateo?

Then Balta clapped Romeo on the shoulder with a wide smile. Romeo kept his back to the jungle and nodded, bending over as if exhausted. Seconds later, a team of witches surrounded him. Apothecaries, likely.

Landowner cheers drowned out the blood rushing past her ears.

Almost as an afterthought, Mateo appeared. A whelp dangled carefully from one hand. Vittoria let out a little cry of relief, then alarm.

"There's blood everywhere," she whispered. "His arm. Something has happened to his arm."

Even Balta paused at Mateo's appearance, then shook his head and accepted the whelp. The raucous landowners quieted, no doubt thirsty for the gory story. Balta spoke with Mateo. Mateo nodded once, then shifted his weight as if to ensure he'd remain standing. His shoulders were heavy. She couldn't see his face from this angle.

Balta turned to the crowd. "The Test of Courage," he called, voice ringing on a magical spell, "is completed on both accounts to my satisfaction. Both will advance to the second test."

The pervasive sense of disbelief shattered moments later. Cheers erupted again. Mateo dropped to his knees, forehead pressed to the ground, as Balta advanced on him. Romeo disappeared into the tunnel with his team of witches, but without a glance over his shoulder.

"Come, Lady," Benat murmured with relief in his voice. "Balta will bring Mateo back home. Let us prepare to take care of him."

Inky darkness comforted Vittoria as she sat next to Mateo, watching his chest rise and fall. A shiver slipped through her every now and then when Hodei's wrinkled face appeared in her mind's eye.

It all comes down to that one single question: Why did she stay?

Her mind spun fast as a whirlpool and twice as violently. Why was she the only witch who could find the answer? Why did it matter?

Her bleary eyes burned like a vat of seawater had been poured into them. It must be almost dawn. She rubbed her face, nearly lulled to sleep by the gentle roar of the ocean.

Hodei was just a bitter old man, likely. She didn't know Esperanza's whole story, but it must be cloaked in deceit, or something worse. Had Esperanza fooled him, somehow? If so, why hadn't he found the information he craved sooner?

What was his game? Were these just deathbed questions? Or was there something more he wanted Vittoria to discover? He'd spoken bitterly of Romeo, of borrowed power.

An opportunity to get rid of her, possibly, while casting the blame elsewhere. If she went to the rebels and started asking around, they'd probably kill her. She'd almost be safer with landowners—at least they believed in honor. The rebels had falsely twisted fate to their own purposes, and that was just as terrifying.

Still, the High Priest's threat loomed large in her mind. Hodei had so easily taken her from Benat. Had known so much about her family. Even with Mateo protecting them, might a powerful man like Hodei get the best of them?

Was he really *allowing* her to live?

The biggest question loomed in her mind like a bubble, crowding out all the other thoughts that vied for her attention.

Would she tell Mateo?

The arguments for and against moved like the tide, ebbing and flowing. Yes, she should tell him everything. The threat to her family. The strange request. She could trust Mateo, and he didn't control her.

But would he stop her?

No, came the rebuttal, she couldn't tell Mateo. Her family was at stake. And, perhaps, she felt a flicker of curiosity. What was Hodei's motivation? What if there was more that a little searching would reveal?

Was there something *bigger* at work here?

Mateo stirred. She straightened, breath held, and untangled herself from thoughts of Hodei. A female witch—an apothecary—awaited them at the house when they'd returned. Mateo arrived shortly thereafter, transported by Balta, who left immediately.

The apothecary had used magic to straighten Mateo's bones and clean the puncture wounds that had been so deep they were nearly black. Then she dumped a viscous green potion over the top. It sizzled and smoked with a painfully disgusting smell.

"A rare potion called remoulade," she'd murmured while Vittoria hovered anxiously nearby. "Most expensive potion on the market. His bones will heal fast with how much I used. In time for the Test of Magic, at any rate. Fool. Lots of blood loss. Puncture wounds indicate bloodsuckers. He'll need to drink a lot of water. Hold off on any strong ipsum for the time being."

Vittoria had been relieved when she left. Mateo, thankfully, had remained unconscious the entire time. She'd held his hand while she waited for him to wake up, gratefully aware of every breath. A white bandage covered his left arm all the way to the bicep, with no blood peeking through. Perhaps the potion had served him well already.

His eyelashes fluttered open. With a sharp intake of breath, he sat up in a panic. "The whelp!"

Vittoria rested a calming hand on his naked shoulder. "Mateo, you're home. The whelp is already reunited with its mere. It's over."

It's over. Until she whispered those words, she wasn't sure she'd fully comprehended it herself.

His eyes were cloudy still, no doubt with pain. He winced and lay back, his torso slowly relaxing against the pillows. One moment at a time, the clouds parted in his eyes until he looked at her with utter fatigue and disbelief. She sat with him on her right. No candles lit the dark, hiding the marks on her left cheek.

Unable to help herself, she reached out and brushed a lock of hair off his forehead. He closed his eyes and leaned into her palm.

She cupped his face. "You did it, Mateo."

"*We* did it," he murmured. "Romeo didn't betray me. He could have. He so easily could have . . . he said something odd . . ."

The whole story hadn't surfaced yet, though Benat said various speculations had been circulated in the newsbooks. She didn't care what the gossip said. It was over.

"You're tired," she whispered. "Go back to sleep. I'll be here if you need anything."

He chuckled, then nuzzled his face into her palm. His breath was warm and wispy against her wrist.

"I don't want to sleep," he said softly. "I want to stay here with you."

She leaned forward and used the tip of her finger to trace a line down the side of his face, then his jaw. She did it again and again until his expression softened. He looked like Eneko, almost, with his thick eyelashes closed and his body slack with rest.

"Not fair," he murmured drowsily.

She quietly laughed. "My nephew has taught me the subtle art of soothing finicky males."

His eyes opened again, clear as a midnight sky. "Stay with me?" he whispered. "Please?"

Vittoria gave him a soft smile. "Of course. Go to sleep, Mateo. I won't leave your side."

His eyes closed, and he dropped into sleep.

14

MATEO

Vittoria stared at her lunch with unusual intensity the next morning when Mateo sat in the chair next to her with a barely suppressed groan.

"Something on your mind?" he asked dryly.

She wore a simple ivory gown without ruffles, as usual. It was fitted to her elbows, scooped around her collarbones, and drew attention to her lovely neck. He wanted to run his thumb across the seam of her lips.

Instead, he waited.

Vittoria swallowed, but she wouldn't meet his gaze. She rubbed her left arm with her right hand, brow knitted together. Then, seeming to feel the weight of his stare, she turned to look right at him. All hope of a relaxing meal vanished when three catlike scratches across her cheek caught his gaze.

"What happened?" he whispered, his voice stark.

With a soft inhale, she reached up and touched them with her fingertips. She looked back at the table. "It was nothing."

Gently, he took her chin in his hand and turned her face to see the marks better. Though they were still swollen and crimson, they looked too shallow to be from an animal. They stretched from the top of her cheekbone nearly to her mouth. A dark feeling settled in his belly.

"Pere," he said.

Her gaze met his for a brief moment, then she pulled away from his touch. Lazy curls fell to the bottom of her shoulder blades, and the gentle slope of her nose was silhouetted against the sunshine outside.

Vague memories flickered through his mind from last night. Her face hovering over his. Locks of hair tickling his cheek. A warm murmur. A soft touch. She'd cared for him all night. It was the first time in over a decade that he hadn't felt quite so alone.

With that sense of belonging came a surge of protective rage that he carefully schooled into concern. "What happened?"

"My fault," Benat said as he entered the room. He stood near the doorway, arms folded over his chest. His scowl would have set water on fire. "There was a mob in Necce. The Guardians came, grabbed her, and transported her away before we could get out."

Mateo frowned.

"It was my fault." Vittoria held her chin a little higher. "Benat kept me safe. Without him, I might have been killed by the mob."

With a jerky nod, Mateo motioned for Benat to sit. "Tell me everything."

Vittoria obliged with careful calm. "A crowd mobbed me in Necce, and while Benat was trying to get me out, a Guardian grabbed my arm. They took me to Hodei." She looked at her hands in her lap and sucked in a sharp breath. "He forced me into a chair with magic and then . . . spoke with me."

Mateo's shoulders tightened. He put a fist over his mouth and waited.

She trained a wary gaze on him, then continued, "At first, he just said he was impressed because we took him by surprise. He spoke about you and Romeo." Her brow furrowed. "He mentioned something about my cape and La Principessa."

Benat's gaze flickered to him, but he ignored it. Vittoria shook her head as if to clear her thoughts.

"He said he brought me there because he wanted to meet me, but I think he just wanted to scare me. He spoke about my family. He knew what had happened to my pere, that Mere had worked for Moretti and that her disappearance meant she could be piked if she were ever found. He knew Eneko's name."

She bit her bottom lip, the skin turning white beneath her teeth. Mateo's jaw tightened at the fear in her gaze.

"He said I wasn't safe. That he was allowing me to live."

"Why?"

The word came out of Mateo with a raspy breath. The force it required to restrain his rage cost him precious energy, but he held it together.

She hesitated, her mouth half-open. Then she lifted her shoulders in a delicate shrug. "I don't know. He spoke about your mere." This time, she met his gaze. "He said she had betrayed him or . . . something."

Mateo sucked in a sharp breath through his nose. "How did you get away?"

She blinked. "He let me go, eventually. I ran to the window. When I stumbled onto the beach, in the garden, Joska appeared. He brought me to Benat."

Mateo's nails ached from digging into his palm. He made a mental note to personally thank Joska later. He must have gone right to the garden near Hodei's office. A smart man.

With a shudder, she said, "It . . . it wasn't as bad as it could have been, but I am afraid for my family. Mateo, if something happens to them—"

"It won't, Lady," Benat said. "I've already sent a man to stay there all day."

The firmness of Benat's tone seemed to steady her. Her shoulders relaxed a little.

"Thank you, Benat."

Mateo leaned forward, put a hand on hers, and said, "I'm sorry, Vittoria. Hodei was trying to get into your head. It's what he does. He plays mind games with witches. He wanted to make you afraid of him so you'd give up. Run away. He'd do anything to keep me from the throne. You are safe with me, I guarantee it. All of us would give our lives for you."

A troubled expression crossed her face but quickly disappeared. He wondered what it meant. Then he reached up, caressing the skin beneath the slash marks. Guilt warred with rage. He'd spent so long protecting her, only to fail her at this precious stage.

"I'm sorry he was able to hurt you. I blame myself."

She put her hand over his. "No, Mateo. I—"

"I'm afraid what Hodei did was vengeful," he said before she could absolve him. "He was trying to mar your face. Landowner women regard their complexion as their greatest asset. Perfection is paramount. They transport all the way to the Western Network to get to a certain clay that helps the skin. That's so far that witches have died in the transport. Or they spend currency on potions that make their skin appear perfect. It was a catty attempt to foil your future success."

She managed a small smile. "Fortunately," she said, "I don't care all that much about landowner beauty ideals."

Mateo smiled softly. Fate must have given her to him, indeed, for he couldn't imagine how lucky he'd been to find her.

"I'm sorry," he murmured. "We will never fail in protecting you again, Vittoria."

Her expression tightened, and she nodded.

Benat stewed with an ugly glower. Mateo's mind, still foggy with residual pain, worked slowly through her explanation. Something didn't quite add up, but he wasn't in the right frame of mind to figure it out. At least his anger had taken his mind off the pain. He thought of Pere with another twist of fury that could power him through anything.

"The Test of Magic is in two weeks," Mateo said, and Vittoria seemed relieved at the change in topic. "Balta sent out a letter this morning."

"Will you be healed?" Benat asked.

Mateo shrugged. "Doesn't matter. It still starts in two weeks."

"What is the next test?" Vittoria asked, poking at a bit of soft goat cheese with a fork. She seemed less wary now that she'd told her secret, but still didn't quite meet his gaze.

"Not sure of the details," Mateo replied. "But it won't be as physical and will involve magic. Complicated, ancient magic, I suspect, if Balta's involved. Probably with some sort of military slant. The only thing I know is that it will somehow involve magical skills that I'll need as a High Priest."

Vittoria nodded.

Mateo turned back to Benat. "While we wait, we need to try again to contact the rebels. Try the ones in Necce Coven, this time. Mayfair's ignored us too long. Then send two men to try to speak to the rebels in the orchards again. I don't want to proceed into the battle against Romeo without a plan in place for the rebels, or else anarchy will break out once I take the throne. It's what the rebels want."

"They want anarchy?" Vittoria asked, looking startled.

"Yes, so that they can put their own High Priest on the throne," Mateo replied. "They are always looking for an opportunity to do so. As soon as I take power, the rebels will try to kill me and Romeo to destroy the Castaneda line in a public way."

"But why not do that now?"

"It wouldn't be as dramatic," Benat said with a scowl. "The rebels want to show their power and take the throne violently from the Castanedas. Not only that, but they want revenge for all that workers have been put through all these years. And they may not be able to strike unless both Romeo and Mateo are distracted. They are both powerful magic users with witches who protect them."

"If they incite chaos and a civil war . . ." Mateo allowed the silence to fill in the rest.

No doubt Vittoria could easily piece it together in her mind.

"But who would they put in place?" she asked.

"That's the biggest question," Benat said. "We've tried for years to figure it out, but no one knows the leader of the rebels. Or *if* there is a centralized leader. Rumors say there are several. Others say there is one and he is highly protected. Either the rebel groups aren't working together, or they sow chaos among their own to protect whomever is behind it all."

"Once Romeo or I win," Mateo continued, "we must be ready for the rebels' response. For ten years, I carefully and slowly set up a relationship with the rebels. They talked to me. Never too much. Never too close. But I had witches there who would listen to me. The last year?" He shook his head. "They've shut us out."

Stunned, she just stared at him.

The surprise in her face upset him. He wished he could take it from her. Make this somehow easier. She'd been snatched from an unsafe but unchanging world and shoved into one that was as steady as an earthquake. Of course, there was nothing he could do about their current circumstances. Not immediately, anyway. He needed time. Yet time was the one thing they didn't have.

He shouldn't care about her this much so soon. No son of Hodei should carry this much emotion in his heart. Compassion. Empathy. Such characteristics were lost on Pere. Even on Mere, to some extent. She'd viewed the world through the lens of *what can I lose next and how will I stop it?* Emotion was expendable. Mere had been a true child of the streets.

Which left him in that strange in-between yet again.

Vittoria cleared her throat, which brought him out of his spiraling thoughts. His arm ached beneath the bandage. He wanted to wrap himself in a dark world and fall asleep for days, but there was business to attend to.

"Would you mind if I went into Necce again today?" she asked.

Benat's eyes widened, but before either of them could protest, she held up a hand.

"I know it may not be safe after the mob, but I want to go somewhere specific. Benat may scout it out ahead of me, meet my sister-in-law to confirm it's all right for me to go, and then transport me there, if that's safer."

"Sannara?" Mateo ventured a guess.

Vittoria nodded. "When I saw my family last night, they told me they haven't seen Sannara since they moved out there. I promised them I'd find her after the Test of Courage. Eneko misses his mere."

"And you," he added quietly.

She hesitated. "I'm concerned. Sannara has always been in and out. She rarely stays, and Eneko is used to that. I . . . I am more of his mere than she is, but still . . . we're worried about her."

"Of course." Mateo gestured to Benat. "Benat and his men will keep you safe. Let's do your usual food buckets out at the eastern farms today. They won't have such a response there, and they haven't seen you yet. It's a longer transportation, but worth the work."

Vittoria smiled with some relief. She must have been afraid he'd try to keep her back. Then she excused herself.

Once she was out of earshot, Benat leaned forward. "Did something happen with Hodei, you think?" he asked. "She's . . . different now. Quieter." His countenance darkened. "Of course, he slashed her with his nails and revealed his dark soul, so maybe she's just frightened."

Mateo frowned. There was definitely something different today, and he didn't think Vittoria was frightened. She seemed distracted. Concerned. Of course, that could be about Sannara, but the instinct that had kept him alive thus far denied that.

"Yes," he said. "Something else is happening. Likely, Hodei is trying to manipulate her. Keep your eyes open, and keep me informed. I must speak with Balta in the meantime."

15

VITTORIA

A bark of laughter sounded from the other side of the Wench, but Vittoria ignored it. Benat shifted behind her, more in the shadows than out. She didn't need to see his face to feel his tension.

The Wench was a worker pub and little more than discarded boards nailed together in an alley between buildings. Rainwater leaked through a hastily constructed roof made of straw and mud that smelled moldy and crumbled in the middle. Gaping holes revealed wide swaths of grumpy sky overhead, and puddles collected on the muddy floor. The slate clouds left the square space shrouded in darkness, lit without candles. What worker had wax to burn? A raindrop splashed on the back of Vittoria's neck and trickled down her spine.

The Wench was a seedy place, not really a true pub. No entertainment graced these cobweb-ridden walls, and the only drink it offered was weakened ipsum. The dregs of workers came here, most of them surrendering the last morsel of their food bucket in exchange for the watery brew.

Ipsum was the only grace the landowners allowed the workers. Here, it was so watered down that there was little chance of getting truly drunk from it. For some, however, it took the edge off of a hard life. Workers in the breweries received cast-off ipsum instead of food buckets for pay. They exchanged that ipsum here for food from other workers desperate enough to buy it.

But that was all a cover. In truth, the Wench was little more than a trading ground, run by a thin, shrewd worker named Michal. He used to work for the breweries. Now, he quietly ran an underground black market and avoided Guardians at all costs.

Vittoria stood in the back corner in a plain cloak. Witches lined up out the doorway, food tucked into their pockets. Michal stood behind a wooden desk, alternating between beckoning workers forward and silencing those who were too loud on the other side of the room. No need to draw the Guardians in.

If Michal was lucky, the Guardians would only demand a barrel of ipsum to pay for not taking witches to prison. If he wasn't lucky? Well, the Wench had been burned down before.

Vittoria's eyes darted over the crowd again, but she shrank back when she didn't see Sannara.

"What," Benat muttered, "are we doing here?"

"Sannara comes here more than anywhere," she said. "She'll be here."

Twenty minutes later, a lithe figure stepped through the doorway. She wore a chocolate brown cape over a head of thick hair that barely brushed the tops of her shoulders. Vittoria stepped forward. Then she stopped, utterly astonished by what she was seeing.

The Givers, but Sannara looked . . . *healthy.*

Vittoria took two steps before Sannara's sharp eyes jerked to hers and comprehended her for a full moment. Then she smiled widely. Her face wasn't so gaunt. Her cheeks had filled out, and her eyes were bright. Sannara lifted her gaze to Benat, smirked at him, then looked back at Vittoria.

"Come," she mouthed.

Michal glanced up, saw Sannara, and discreetly waved her on. She motioned for them to follow. Wordlessly, they did.

What had happened to her sallow, sickly, on-the-edge-of-death sister-in-law?

Sannara navigated the growing crowd with surprising ease. The men seemed to part in front of her. Her dress was clearly a worker style with no extra layers and elbow-length sleeves, but looked like old velvet. Quiet elegance in a place like this.

She led them through a darkened doorway and into an open space. Along the walls of the alley were small rooms built with boards scrapped together, likely scrounged from fallen buildings. Five boards served as doors, two of them closed. Moans came from one. A chuckle from another.

Sannara turned into an open room. This one had full walls with no holes, as if someone wanted it secure. Vittoria stepped inside to find a thin straw mattress on the floor and nothing else.

With a wave, Sannara beckoned them in. Benat gazed around the windowless space, and Vittoria could practically hear his thoughts. One wall matched the aged wood of the building next to them. The rest were thin pieces of scrap wood salvaged together. The whole place would collapse in a good wind. But the other rooms hadn't been so well put together—they'd had holes, missing boards, a half a door.

He shook his head. "I'll stay out here."

Sannara shrugged, then shut the door. The moment it closed, she yanked Vittoria into her arms. Light spilled through slats in the wooden ceiling, giving just enough illumination to see Sannara's relieved expression.

"Thank the Givers," Vittoria whispered thickly, "you're all right."

Vittoria held Sannara for so long that Sannara had to eventually pull away. Tears filled Vittoria's eyes. They stared at each other for several long moments. Vittoria couldn't help but think of Anton, who had loved Sannara so deeply.

"Eneko misses you," Vittoria blurted out. "He's doing so well. He's eating three meals a day. He has toys. They live by the quarry where they're well hidden, and there are trees and fresh air. He runs all day!"

Tears sparkled in Sannara's eyes. She laughed. "I'm so glad to hear it!" she cried. "He deserves all that and more. And you? Are you safe? When the betrothal was announced, I was terrified for you. I tried to find you through my . . . contacts, but Mateo keeps you hidden away so well."

"Fine." Vittoria squeezed Sannara's hands. "He's a good man, and he's taking care of me and the family. I'm safe for now, as you can see. Mere and Pere are worried sick for you. Why haven't you come home? They said

Benat's men offered to take you there but you refused them. Is everything all right?"

Sannara smiled, but it was tinged with sadness. She reached up and touched Vittoria's face. "I'm glad you're safe," she said. "But you play a dangerous game. This is the world of the High Priest, Vittoria. They are . . ." She shuddered. "They are ruthless, even to the very end. They're willing to do anything to get what they want."

"I know. I'll be fine. Sannara, why won't you go live with Eneko? You'll be safe. Fed. You can finally be with your son! Although maybe you don't need it." Vittoria stepped back. "You look so healthy."

A flash of something appeared in Sannara's eyes, then faded. In the aftermath, she seemed more tired than ever.

"Yes, I am . . . well cared for."

"How is it possible?"

Sannara laughed without mirth. "A very complicated web, I assure you. Not one I would relate to you yet."

"Tell me about it. I can take it."

"I can't, Vittoria." Her voice was strained. "There are . . . there are attachments here in Necce that I cannot leave."

"Greater than your son?"

"It's not fair to Eneko. I realize that." Sannara turned away. "He haunts me every night. I am no mere to him, Vittoria, and I never have been. Please, ask me no more. Now, tell me why you have come. Do you need something? I don't have long before I must start work."

Sannara's voice remained low, as if she were still afraid she'd be overheard. She gestured to the bed behind her before Vittoria could answer.

Vittoria's heart plummeted. Sannara did many jobs to fend off starvation. Did she also sleep with men in exchange for food, as Pere had suspected? Is that how she looked so well? Did she find a wealthy landowner? It wasn't unheard of. Sannara's natural grace and delicate features made her attractive regardless of her low birth. Few landowners would tolerate the touch of a worker, but some . . .

Hot tears stung the backs of Vittoria's eyes. If Anton had never died. If the plague hadn't swept his life away . . .

She blinked those tears back. What-ifs were wasted time.

"It doesn't have to be this way anymore, Sannara," Vittoria pleaded. "I agreed to be betrothed to Mateo so you don't have to live like this anymore. Anton—"

"Don't say his name to me!"

The harsh response sent a shock through Vittoria. Astonished, she simply stared.

Sannara's proud expression slowly crumpled. She shook her head and swallowed back tears. "I'm sorry."

Her hair swung around her face in long strands, giving off the cloying scent of roses. "I'm sorry, Vittoria. I just . . . I cannot. I cannot think of Anton, or Eneko, or the grief overwhelms me. The missing. The ache. He was . . . I loved him more than I've ever loved anything. But he is gone, and I've had to pick up the pieces of my life. I can't say more than that. Trust me. What I do, I do for Eneko's benefit. For . . . for everyone's benefit. It was the only way I could provide for him after Anton's death, and now . . ."

She closed her eyes with a sigh.

Unable to stop herself, Vittoria pulled Sannara back into her arms. Her heart broke all over again. For Anton. For Eneko. For Sannara. A peep of a sob escaped Sannara, and she pulled away again. Her eyes glittered, but she didn't let the tears go.

"What do you need, Vittoria?" she whispered. "Why have you come?"

"I simply wanted to check on you. To see you. Mere and Pere are worried, and so was I. We love you. Eneko misses you."

A ghost of a smile appeared on her lovely lips. "I'm sure he does, but we both know who his true mere is. Thank you, sister." Sannara kissed her hands. "Thank you for your care and love. I'm well. I'm thriving in my little niche in the world. I'm doing what must be done. As always, the best way to help me is to love Eneko. *You* are his mere. Not me. One day, I will make it up to him. Now, if I need you, how can I get hold of you?"

The words wouldn't come at first. The resignation in Sannara's voice cut deep. Vittoria wanted better for her. Had *created* better for her. Why wouldn't she take it?

"I'm in a shack on the beach, out west of Necce," she finally said. "Come out there. Benat's men will see you before you see us, and will bring you in. I'll tell them you might come. If you ever need anything. Food. Shelter.

Escape." Vittoria fought not to stare at the bed. "A new life. I'm here for you, Sannara."

Sannara leaned forward, kissed Vittoria on the cheek, and squeezed her hands. "Thank you, *masuna*. I will do that."

Benat knocked on the door. "Lady?"

"I must go." Vittoria gave her sister-in-law one last kiss, then stepped away. "Take care, Sannara."

Vittoria backed out of the ramshackle room, her heart in her throat as she walked away.

That afternoon, Vittoria stared at the churning, angry ocean as raindrops tapped against the window. Her mind drifted to Eneko. He had an inherent restlessness on rainy days. Most worker children were products of the outdoors. They lived in the nooks and crannies of the streets because even that smelled better than the dank holes they slept in. But when it rained, going outside wasn't worth the muddy battle.

Nor the cold.

With a shiver, she pulled a wrap more closely around her. A warm fire crackled in the hearth. Zuri bustled in the background, humming under her breath as she sorted through a few scrolls. Their daily reading lesson would begin soon. After that, magic.

Zuri had taught her a few easy incantations. Turning water into wine, then back again. Moving a scroll to the bed from the counter. Today, she'd practice being invisible. She taught all of it to Mere, Pere, and Eneko on her nightly visits. Eneko was so fast, his mind so quick.

When Vittoria asked when she'd learn to transport, Zuri waved her off.

"Milk first," Zuri had said with a prim purse of her lips. "Meat later. Get this right, and then I'll teach you to be invisible, then to transport. Transportation is dangerous until you really know what you're doing."

Vittoria's thoughts drifted to Sannara, then to Hodei. A chill slipped through her.

The mystery of Esperanza still troubled her, but not more than Mateo's cold, closed-lip reaction when she'd mentioned his mere's name. Nor his righteous indignation when he swore they would never fail in their protection of her again.

No, he'd never let her find the rebels. Did she blame him? No. The rebels were almost as frightening as Hodei. Their desperation was palpable. Which made the situation that Mateo and Benat had discussed that morning all the bleaker.

But could he really stop her?

He didn't have the power to command her to *not* go, because he wasn't her husband yet. But surely Benat would tighten security. They wouldn't let her leave at all, maybe. She didn't want to lose her opportunity to distribute the food buckets, nor did she want to endanger her family if Hodei truly knew where they were.

Her only hope lay in Mateo giving her an explanation of his mere that would fill in some holes. Maybe she wouldn't have to visit the rebels if Mateo could suss out what Hodei wanted.

But that didn't seem right, either.

She had the urge to ask Zuri about Esperanza, but held back. Such a question should go to Mateo first. She owed him that courtesy. But how to ask without explaining what Hodei wanted her to do?

Her determination doubled. She'd figure this out. She couldn't put a finger on *why*, but she had a feeling it was all interconnected.

Somehow.

"Come, Tori." Zuri waved for her. A box of wet sand and a stick waited at her feet. Vittoria would draw the letters in sand first, then switch to quill and parchment later, once she felt more confident in it so the parchment and ink weren't wasted. "We're ready to start practice."

Vittoria brushed her thoughts aside. First, she'd ask Mateo about his mere. If that didn't go well?

She'd have to find the rebels herself.

16

MATEO

Mateo smiled warmly as his oldest friend and closest confidant, Balta, greeted him with a grip on his right shoulder.

The plump, wizened man grinned as he looked Mateo up and down. "Must have bathed in remoulade to look this recovered," Balta said. "You were a mess, and you're insane."

Mateo just shrugged.

Balta snorted, then nodded to the other side of his office. "Have a seat."

He lived in the thick of the landowner peninsula, in a three-story townhouse that opened to an elegant garden in the back. A wrought-iron fence surrounded it, and a whitewashed exterior made the whole place shine. The home was sparsely decorated with military memorabilia and a couch here and there, as if comfort were an afterthought.

Balta made himself comfortable on a chair behind a thick, mahogany desk.

"You already know that I can't speak a word about . . ." Balta cleared his throat. An incantation prevented him from speaking about the Law of Rights or its tests, to prevent cheating.

Mateo waved that off as he sat in a chair across from his old mentor. "You know I wouldn't ask. Besides, we've kept our friendship from Pere and Romeo this long. Wouldn't do to make them suspicious now."

A crisp fire crackled in a hearth not far from Balta's cluttered desk. For a man of such military discipline and precision, he couldn't seem to keep the space clear. Two quills wrote on parchments near the fire, where the ink would dry faster. One of parchments folded itself into a letter and zipped under the doorway.

As a young High Priest, Hodei had kept control over the navy instead of instituting a Head of Guardians. At the time, it had been an unprecedented and bold move that went unchallenged because of imminent threats from the wild witches in the mountainous North. Hodei's eye for strategy defeated those fools who attacked the East, and earned the grace of the nobility at a time when he'd just ascended to power. No one challenged him when he kept the position afterward.

In the minds of the Council, they didn't need to fix what wasn't broken.

But all of that was about to break.

Balta's keen military mind and magical prowess—not to mention noble birth—kept him in Hodei's good graces. For now, Balta was the second-highest-ranking commander and managed the captains. As Hodei's health declined, Romeo had given Balta most of the responsibilities of a Head of Guardians, but not the official title. No reason to incur Hodei's feeble wrath while he was alive. If there was anything Hodei hated, it was giving up control.

The rest of the room drowned in military paraphernalia. Swords. Coats of mail. Historical Guardian armor. Maps, cudgels, even navy weapons that Mateo only vaguely comprehended even though he'd served nearly two years on a navy ship after Mere died.

Mateo recalled the briny days with a pang of homesickness. Such a regimented world had been exactly what he'd needed those years after her death. But he'd left it behind gladly for his real path, fortunate that Balta's influence allowed him to withdraw without question.

Balta poured a glass of mulled wine and sent it to Mateo with a spell. Warm spices filled his mouth as he took a sip. As a military man, Balta always kept his wine weaker than most. No reason to get drunk and lose his ability to reason.

"Nothing like mulled wine on a cold day," Balta said, lifting his glass. Rain plunked on the windows outside. Three of Benat's men hid at various places on the property to keep an eye out, just in case. Mateo thought briefly to Vittoria and her meeting with Sannara.

Balta pulled his attention back.

"All that I'm going to say," Balta said, "is that I'm relieved to see you alive, and I apologize for nothing that has come or will. You know that I'll prove out my next High Priest." Balta paused here, and a twinkle appeared in his eyes. "But I'd hate to see you die after all the work I've put into you over the years."

Mateo laughed.

"Still," Balta muttered, "even Romeo would be better than the rebels. You know there's a rumor that Xavier is still alive and that they want to appoint him as High Priest in a takeover?"

"One would hope not," Mateo said.

The name *Xavier* sent a shudder through him. Xavier was Mere's older brother and an unconfirmed martyr to the rebel cause. Rumors resurrected him every few years. Mateo had never met him and never wanted to.

Balta shot him a look that suggested Mateo had lost his mind if he didn't believe it, and they fell into companionable silence. The warm wine soothed Mateo's stiff muscles as he regarded his greatest ally. Balta had saved Mateo's life all those years ago. When Mere died at the country estate where she and Mateo lived, Hodei had sent a few witches to kill him. Balta showed up unexpectedly, told their paid workers to leave, and yanked Mateo away just before the would-be killers showed up.

It had been the first assassination attempt.

That night, Mateo and Balta had snuck back into the house and hidden away all of Mere's treasures. Once that was done, Balta shoved Mateo onto a ship in the southernmost regions where not even Hodei would look for him. For two years, Balta kept track of him through letters and occasional visits. Mateo served the navy, then returned to Necce and stayed with Balta on and off. Balta guided his education. Taught him magic. Trained him how to work as a diplomat and a landowner.

Meanwhile, at Balta's urging, Mateo roamed the Eastern Network and learned the ways of the workers. Made his face and his name known. Saw every inch of the Eastern Network.

"How can you lead," Balta had grumbled at the time, "if you don't know your Network? Romeo has already seen all of this. Met all of them. You must as well—or no one will know your name, and you won't have any support when you assert your right."

Eventually, at seventeen, Mateo broke out on his own. But Balta always stood behind him. A guiding star.

Now, a bristling salt-and-pepper mustache covered Balta's upper lip. Age had made his bones a little weaker, though his attitude hadn't waned. He leaned back in his chair and studied Mateo, the way he always had.

"How are you?" Mateo asked.

"My mistress left me, so I'm heartbroken again, but already taking applications for a new one. So, things are fine here."

His eyes twinkled as Mateo huffed a laugh. Balta bragged about a healthy respect for carnal delights but had never actually been *seen* with a mistress. If gossip was to be believed, he was more inclined toward men.

Balta sobered. "It's been a few months since we've talked. What's on your mind?"

Mateo leaned forward, shoulders expanding as he pulled in a deep breath. "I can't get an audience with the rebels, and I'm concerned. Benat has sent our usual messengers through several channels, all to no avail. They've clamped down and, so it appears, won't let anyone speak with them. Six months ago, I could at least meet with their leaders, even if there wasn't much progress in our relationship. The country was open, the city was wary. Now, both are sealed."

"Have you been down to the catacombs yet?"

"No, never. They wouldn't let me. Didn't want me to see any entrances."

Balta frowned. "I see."

"Feels like I wasted a lot of time."

"Rumors abound, of course . . ." Balta trailed off, getting lost in thought. He shook his head and came back to himself. One graying, bushy eyebrow rose. "Think it means something that they're hunkered in?"

"Yes." Mateo leaned on his elbow. "I think they're preparing."

"For what?"

"Attack? Takeover? They probably know how sick Hodei is. But I don't know. This started long before the Law of Rights was invoked, but surely it's correlated."

Balta shrugged. "They may have known your pere was sick for a while."

"Maybe," Mateo replied. "Likely, they can't afford the risk that someone will leak their plans, so they're tightening up. Why not attack during a transition of leadership? It'll certainly engender the chaos they need. They've never been shy about their plan to destroy Hodei's legacy."

"It's what you've always feared," Balta said.

"Yes."

Balta gestured to the window. "And your betrothed?" he asked, as if Vittoria stood outside. "How is that going?"

Mateo stood and started to pace, wincing when he jarred his left arm. "Almost perfectly. She took the broken candlestick and went to the city to split the silver, as I'd hoped. She's proven herself."

"Could still be seeking safety and food."

"Undoubtedly she is," Mateo murmured. "But that's never been a problem. It's whether she'll remain the witch we need as High Priestess. I think she's purehearted. I think she's perfect. My qualms are gone now that I've lived with her."

"She could be a spy for the rebels, you know."

Balta said it gently, but Mateo glowered anyway. "She's assuredly not a spy. I trust her. She . . . has no guile."

"Your pere thought the same."

Mateo sent him a quelling look. The last thing he wanted to do was bring Mere into this conversation.

"Speaking of Pere, I'm suspicious that Hodei has a claw in Vittoria." He related her story of Hodei's capture of her. "Something is . . . missing there. Pere wouldn't call her into his office just to scare her."

Balta blinked, and warning rang in his tone. "Far more complicated than you expected. Are you sure this is your best plan? La Salvatorra was an accident. No one thought that they'd make a Giver out of you. Now, if you reveal yourself as Mateo *and* La Salvatorra? Why wouldn't the workers follow you?"

He shook his head. "It's not enough. The workers could feel duped. Betrayed. Lied to. Plus, it would infuriate the landowners. Would they trust me after that? Never. No, Mateo and La Salvatorra must be different people. This is the *only* plan. The workers need a Giver to follow, and it can't be me.

Besides, Romeo won't see her coming until it's too late." Then he tacked on, "Hodei will, I would guess."

"You think the two of them won't talk?"

Mateo shook his head. "Things don't seem right between them. Pere has little vitality or power these days, from what I saw and what I read in the newsbooks. It's not explicitly stated, but it's there between the lines. Pere doesn't like Romeo any more than he likes me these days."

Balta agreed with a shrug. "You always thought for yourself, but were too emotionally based for Hodei to trust. Romeo works off the facts, takes emotion out of his decisions. Plus, he's smarter than Hodei."

Mateo snorted.

"My informants say that rumors of La Principessa in the flesh have started," Balta said. He twirled his glass. "But only in a few places in Necce. Mayfair Coven, mostly."

"Good." Mateo rolled his neck to loosen the stiffness. "At least it's starting."

"You need it to spread further. You're not moving quickly enough. You must get her out there more often. You can't just have workers in Necce recognize her. It must also happen in the country."

"Tonight," he promised. "We've already expanded to the orchards and the farmlands."

"Benat's men will protect her ... except they won't *entirely*, correct?"

Balta's drawl set Mateo's hair on edge. The insinuation that they shouldn't suppress a mob annoyed him, even if it was somewhat correct. Mobs spurred gossip. They needed the rumors more than ever—so the bigger the mobs, the better.

But not at Vittoria's expense.

Mateo frowned. "She's not bait, Balta. She will not be sacrificed to this plan."

"I didn't say kill her. I said be aware of the circumstances, and make sure word spreads."

Mateo let out a heavy breath. "I know."

"You're fond of her."

"Yes. We're friends."

Balta grimaced. "Well, that was stupid of you."

"I know."

The admission cost him a moment of discomfort. Even in front of Balta, who had seen him at his worst and still come through for him, he didn't like the show of weakness. He *did* care for Vittoria, and it felt like a lie to call her a friend. She felt like so much more.

Balta waved a dismissive hand. "You'll win, Mateo. You're one of those witches. Success flows to you. It follows you. Success wants *you*. The question is: What will you lose to gain it? That's all we ever need ask. Unfortunately, you're fond of the thing you might have to lose."

Mateo's lips pressed together in a grim line. "You want me to sacrifice her to draw the loyalty of the landowners? Is that what you mean?"

He shrugged. "It's an option you need to consider. Mateo, their magic could suppress even the greatest of fights if they *really* came together. Sure, landowners bicker like little children, but to save their wealth? They'd unite. They'd use their magic. And they'd win."

Mateo scowled.

"I think you're underestimating their ability to defend themselves," Balta continued. "You're underestimating them, period. Some of them will play dirty to keep their wealth. If you win and a civil war starts and the landowners pull ahead, you may have to sacrifice your Giver to win them back. If you don't, the landowners will kill you and then all hope is gone. Once you're High Priest, you can slowly make changes for the workers."

Rage streaked through Mateo, but he schooled it. Emotions made terrible decisions, and he did need to remain open to all possibilities. Even the ones he didn't like. Balta watched him carefully. He'd earned Mateo's respect and loyalty because he was willing to say what others wouldn't.

Worse, he had a point.

"I will not kill Vittoria, Balta," Mateo said firmly, "or allow her to be killed. But I'm aware of alternate . . . possibilities if things go badly wrong."

Silence reigned for several long moments before Balta leaned forward. "Being a leader isn't easy, my boy. In this kind of climate, leadership will be ruthless to you, so you must be ruthless back. I'm simply preparing you, as I always have."

Mateo nodded, then stood. "I must be going. I need to sleep and then figure out a way to prepare for the second test. Not to mention a way to get

Vittoria in front of the landowners. She must make her impression there as well." He rubbed a hand over his weary face. "There's not enough time in forty years to accomplish all I need."

Two envelopes appeared, one in front of each of them, as Mateo turned to leave. Mateo's name was scrawled across the front of a heavy parchment that looked similar to the letter that had come to Balta. What were the odds they'd both get the same message at the same time?

Unless . . .

Mateo's stomach felt hollow all of a sudden.

Balta's opened on its own as Mateo snatched his from the air. After skimming the words, Balta looked at Mateo with a wry grin.

"Looks like your Lady may get her chance." Balta tossed the parchment in the fire with a spell. "There's to be a ball, thrown by your brother, to celebrate the Law of Rights the night before the second test. It's like Romeo anticipated you."

Or wanted to trap him.

A postscript caught his eye at the bottom of his invitation.

You will be admitted to Magnolia Castle for this special celebration.

—R

"Well," he muttered and crushed the invitation in his hand. "At least they're letting me back in the castle for one night."

Balta laughed.

Mateo grunted, but his gut rolled within him. This had strategy written all over it.

Shrewd, brother. Rope Vittoria into a dinner with etiquette and expectations before she even knew her way around the castle. While she had fresh scars on her face. Not even Zuri could educate her on everything she'd need to know to avoid being a laughingstock. But he couldn't say no. Nor could he show up without her. No, they had to be there.

Vittoria would do it. She had a way of making things happen.

Balta's eyes held a dark mirth, even concern. "I suppose I shall see you there with your betrothed? Best of luck, Mateo. Hopefully she can swim in deep waters."

"Go, be with your family tonight, Zuri," Mateo said with a dismissive wave. "Things will get busy the next couple of days while we prepare Vittoria for the ball."

Zuri glanced around, a hand on her hip. Her gaze dropped to his arm. "And how are you healing?"

He held it up. Only a small scab remained, thanks to the magic of the remoulade potion. He'd applied his last bottle an hour before, and it still stung. "Almost there. Still hurts, but it's sealed over."

"No infection." Relief laced her voice as she poked at it. "You're one lucky landowner."

He grinned. "You're my good-luck charm."

She snorted. Then she tilted her head to the other room where Vittoria awaited. "She's doing good with magic," she said. "Letters, too. You picked a smart one. She has a fast mind. If she were a landowner, she would have done very well in life."

"She'll do very well in life as a High Priestess. You'll see to that, won't you?"

She rolled her eyes and pointed at him. "Don't flatter me, but yes. I'll be back in the morning. You be good while I'm gone."

He gave her a soft nudge on the shoulder, and she disappeared.

The rest of the house lay quiet. Benat and his men were on their own breaks while Mateo was home with Vittoria. Mateo grabbed a fresh bottle of wine, pulled out the cork, and poured a glass.

Flickering candles illuminated a simple but robust dinner. Soft white cheese flecked with dried currants. Warm bread shaped into squares with massive air pockets that tasted like heaven. And the rare but tasty find of chicken simmered in broth and wine.

A shuffle came from the hallway. Vittoria appeared, a shawl around her shoulders. Her startled expression gave him a moment of amusement.

"Dinner, Lady."

"Oh." She wrapped her shawl more firmly around her shoulders. "It looks"—she stopped for a long inhale—"and smells delicious."

He motioned to a chair. "Have a seat."

With a rosy color in her cheeks, she obliged. The tall candles stood between them, casting warm shadows on the table. Outside, the rain had abated after darkness had fallen, but the wind still whipped past the house with long, mournful wails.

Vittoria studied the food for a minute, looked at him, and smiled. "Thank you. This is perfect."

"Not too overwhelming?"

"Not at all."

Landowner custom dictated elegant, elaborate meals on the sixth and last day of the week. The *ultima*, or final day, was usually celebrated even by the workers. Not with food, of course, but with their weekly trip to the *eliza* of the Giver La Principessa. She gave them hope for a better week. A better world. It was one of the many reasons she was considered the greatest of all Givers.

They ate quietly after Mateo gestured for Vittoria to dish hers up first. She took small portions, which he ignored. He'd goad her into eating more later, when he brought out his hidden stash of Western Network chocolate.

"Benat's men brought something here today," she said as she took a sip of wine. "They said it was discarded from the castle."

"Oh?"

"A box of silver utensils." She gestured across the room with a nod. "They're all broken or bent or crooked. Discarded."

Mateo snorted. "They're nothing if not perfectionists there."

"May I . . . may I have them?"

"Of course."

"I want to go back to Necce with them. There's a blacksmith there, not far from the *eliza* of the Giver La Principessa. He'll split them so I can give it away again."

Mateo nodded easily. "I know the one."

She paused, as if feeling him out. Then she pressed further. "I want him to cut the utensils up so I can distribute them among the workers like last time."

"I assumed so."

"You're fine with this?"

"I have no ties to the silver myself."

A ghost of a smile crossed her face. "I understand that. But last time it wasn't entirely safe with the . . . the mob, and then Hodei . . . I thought you might have an opinion on it. Might try to exercise some control over where I go or what I do."

She'd tensed slightly, but he tried to act as if he hadn't noticed. "I think you should do it, but let's do it together. I'll go as La Salvatorra with you. It's a good opportunity to start revealing us together. I know the blacksmith—he's a good man. He'll split the silver outside his usual hours. Your mere has been helping us make more blankets to distribute, and just sent some earlier today. We can take those too."

Vittoria opened her mouth to speak, then closed it again. She went out every day at some point, but never at night, and never with La Salvatorra. Balta's nudge to move the plan on faster had nipped at Mateo's heels all day. This would be the perfect opportunity.

Eventually, she smiled. "You think you're ready for the plan to progress to that stage? You're not just trying to prevent me from going out without you?"

He frowned. "No," he drawled. "It's not a matter of control, but of safety. You know better than anyone how unsafe the streets are. Without you, the workers have little hope of a better situation."

She softened, and what tension had been in her ebbed slightly, though it didn't disappear.

"Thank you. I would . . . I would like to appear with La Salvatorra."

He smiled warmly at her. "It's my pleasure."

"You're not so attached to things like silver or blankets or time?" she asked. "Not like landowners, anyway?"

He shrugged as he grabbed another square of bread. "Not really. Possessions come and go."

She seemed to think that over, then reached over her plate to dip her bread in the saucer of chicken and broth. Then she paused, alarmed.

"Is that wrong?" she whispered. "Is it bad manners to put my bread into the sauce dish?"

He laughed. "Help yourself. When you're here, you're home."

Her shoulders immediately relaxed. "Thank you."

Mateo turned the conversation to Eneko and watched in fascination as Vittoria lit up like a star. He laughed, delighted with every recounting of what Eneko had been doing that afternoon, until the wine had loosened the perpetual knot of tension in his chest. The Test of Magic may as well have been a million years away.

When the humor subsided and most of the dishes were empty, Mateo sat back. He admired her in the candlelight. She was simple elegance. Unbound grace. Although she'd spent a life disregarded as a *lavanda* maid, he saw all the dignity of a Giver in her.

"You are lovely, Vittoria. Did you know that?"

She managed a stumbling smile, her cheeks bright. The wine had brought more words out of her than he'd ever heard. Although out of her element here, she was clearly warming up.

"Thank you."

He leaned forward. "Earlier today, I received an invitation to an event hosted by Romeo. A ball. I wanted to ask if you'd attend with me."

Her eyes grew big as the saucer of broth. The easy air shifted as she set down her wine glass.

"A ball?" she asked.

"Thrown by my brother to celebrate the Law of Rights."

"To celebrate it?" She frowned. "What is there to celebrate about killing your brother in the name of a throne?"

Mateo shrugged. "Trust a landowner to celebrate something so stupid. Regardless, I think Romeo has deeper intentions here. He's trying to suss you out."

"What does that mean?"

"It could be a lot of things, or nothing. Perhaps Romeo is simply trying to get a lot of his supporters in a room with me because he wants them to shun me and he thinks I'll care. Or maybe he wants you to be frightened of the landowners." Mateo shrugged. "It's hard to know exactly. The only thing I'm certain of is that this ball has some kind of angle."

A thousand thoughts seemed to appear in her slack expression all at once. She sat back, as if staggered by them, and fell quiet. Mateo let the silence ride until she asked uneasily, "Would it be safe?"

"You wouldn't leave my side," he said quickly. A rush of protectiveness startled him, but he embraced it. She would soon be his wife. Of course he'd feel this way for her.

"I mean . . . it's not so bad here at the house." She gazed around. "I don't mind it here because I'm so far away from all of them. From . . . their world. But this would force me into it. There's no hiding the fact that I know nothing about their customs. I dipped my bread in the sauce bowl!" she cried. "Surely that wouldn't have been allowed?"

He would have laughed—because she was absolutely correct—but he kept a steady expression.

"An unfortunately necessary step," he said. "It's easy to imagine that all landowners are monsters, but it's not true. With this change in leadership comes a change for them as well. Many of them, particularly the women, are as swept up and chained to their lives as you. We cannot forget that the landowners represent a part of the Network as well. Without knowing and acknowledging them, we *do* risk civil war in the transition. This is an opportunity to at least understand them better. I'm not asking you to like them. I'm . . . I'm asking you to see them as witches who will also need to make major adjustments and changes in their lives. It's the same courtesy we will ask of them and of workers. Do you see that?"

Vittoria's shoulders lifted and fell with faster breaths now. She pressed her lips together and attempted to speak several times, but fell back into silence. It was a hard mental transition for her to comprehend, no doubt. The landowners were at fault for the state of the Network in many ways, but not all of them participated in the abuses. Shifting out of that mindset had been difficult for Mateo when Balta had first spoken with him about it.

Mateo had lived with his worker mere all his life. Heard the plight of the worker, the agony of their lives from her lips. These truths about landowners hadn't come easily, but eventually he understood that he couldn't hate them *and* enact positive change for the Network. Diplomacy had to have eyes for all. Now Vittoria had to come to terms with that under the pressure of time, while he'd had years.

Finally, she nodded warily. "I see your point. And, of course, I'm willing to do my part to keep my family safe and better the Network. But what if I make a fool of myself? What if they laugh at me or I make a mistake or—"

"We have nearly two weeks until the ball," he said. "Zuri has already come up with a plan to teach you everything you'll need to know. I'll be holed up in the office refreshing myself on all the magic I can possibly comprehend to prepare for the next test, anyway. Not to mention going out as La Salvatorra at night, if you'd like to come with me. Two weeks is plenty of time."

"Yes, of course."

He reached across the table and put his hand over hers. She turned her hand over, pressing their palms together in a move so instinctive he doubted she realized that she'd done it. For a long moment, he could only stare at her.

"This is likely a terrifying idea," he whispered, "but you're not alone. I'm with you every step. If you really want to change the world, we can't leave you in here forever."

"I'll go." She gave a determined nod and a little smile. "I'll do it happily and make an effort to understand them better."

He squeezed her fingers gently, as if he could impart strength through touch. She was a marvel.

"You delight me, Vittoria, and your courage gives me courage. The next week or so will be busy while you prepare for the ball, we continue to distribute our buckets, and I brush up on my magic. The days will pass quickly, I'm sure."

He pressed a quick kiss to her hand and saw goosebumps rise on her skin. Then he stood up and gathered the plates. Vittoria joined him, the dishware clinking.

"May I ask you something?" she asked. Her shoulders had tensed, and she avoided his gaze.

"Anything."

"What happened to your mere?"

He froze, a pile of plates and utensils stacked in his hands.

"Mere?" he asked, keeping his voice carefully controlled. By honor, that was the very last question he would have expected from her, and the very last thing he wanted to talk about.

"Yes. You never speak of her. In fact, no one speaks of her. Even though she's dead, it does seem odd. Why is she never spoken of? Not even among landowners or newsbooks or history or . . ."

"Because she's gone."

"But surely—"

"And that is where she shall stay. Trust me, Vittoria. It's best that she remain in the grave, for there was nothing joyous she brought here."

He didn't mean to sound so firm, or hardened, or like Hodei, but the words flew out of him just like that. Before he could call them back, he stacked the dishes in the sink around the corner, issued a spell to take care of the rest, and stepped outside without another word.

Eventually, he heard her shuffle off to her room, and he closed his eyes in relief.

Later, he promised himself. *I'll explain that whole mess later.* For now, he had to focus on the Test of Magic and on keeping them all alive.

"You're perfection."

In wry amusement, Vittoria glanced at Mateo out of the corner of her eye. "Thank you. You're quite handsome yourself."

Mateo wore a pair of black slacks, elegantly pressed into lines, and soft leather shoes. A starched black shirt with emerald buttons lay beneath a well-fitted gray vest. With all that, and his hair worn to his shoulders and a freshly shaven face, he was handsomeness personified.

They slipped through the wide, elegant halls of Magnolia Castle, headed toward the ballroom. Vittoria fidgeted with the end of her sleeve and tried not to be overwhelmed by such unfettered wealth. Zuri had spent the last three hours tugging Vittoria's hair into a complicated mess on top of her head. Four magnolia flowers graced each side of an elegant tower of curls, filling the air around her with their heady perfume. Vittoria had nearly insisted against such lengths just for hair, but Zuri had begged for her trust.

"It will not be so complicated or elegant as most," Zuri had muttered, pins held between her teeth as she stacked the curls. "You will stand out on your own merits. The other ladies will have hair added to their styles that's not even their own. For some women, their hair takes days and they sleep on wooden boards to preserve it. Idiotic, isn't it?"

Already, she had a pounding headache.

Zuri had costumed her in a thick dress with a main layer of velvet that kept her warm from the chill of the cool night. Beneath the crimson velvet and lace outerlayer of her skirt, five thin layers of fabric wafted around her legs with every step. Though almost monstrously large in comparison to her single-layer dress as a *lavanda* maid, it wasn't as large as the dresses she'd seen most landowner women wear just in the streets. There were no hoops in the long, fitted sleeves, either.

Still, she felt like a thorn among roses.

"Tonight, the goal is to feel out your general reception," Mateo said, tugging her from her thoughts with his rich voice. "See how they respond. How you feel. What are they saying? I'm as unappreciated by some landowners as you are. Perhaps, in some ways, more so. But not all landowners are hostile to me. At least, not outwardly. I'll seek them out and talk to them. Let their thoughts be heard if it's safe. For both of us, this shall be a revealing evening."

The last two weeks had been surprising and frustrating and lovely. Mateo's intelligence and compassion had charmed her at every step. No mobs had threatened her in the darkness. The workers they helped were loving and filled with gratitude, particularly on their visits to orchards and farms. The smell of damp earth gave her a physical thrill. She missed her early life in the fields, even if the work had been backbreaking.

But she'd been wildly frustrated at each turn. There wasn't a moment when Benat's men didn't have eyes on her or the house. When she could sneak out for just an hour. Even if she had, how would she find the rebels? She had no plan except for one sliver of hope at the ball.

So she'd clutched that, paid attention, and waited.

While she'd learned how to sit without her back touching the chair, Mateo had been locked in a room. Flashes of light and odd sounds had appeared from the rim of the door as he scoured old grimoires and attempted different spells. Zuri had laughed while Vittoria practiced landowner meal etiquette and accidentally spilled her soup. And Vittoria still spent time with her family every evening. Mateo would give her a kiss on the cheek and they'd quietly part, her heart longing for more time with him.

And every day, rain or shine, Mateo fought Benat for hours with wooden sticks, swords, cudgels. Any weapon imaginable, Mateo had some prowess with it. She loved to stand at the window and watch him spar, like a dance.

At night, she stayed awake. Thinking of Hodei. Esperanza. Every time they ventured into Necce, she watched for rebels. Signs of entrances into the catacombs beneath the earth. She saw nothing, but it was clear she was on her own. How could she find a way to the rebels without Benat knowing?

"Do you have any friends besides Benat, Zuri, or Balta?" she asked as they sashayed down the halls. His gaze kept darting around, as if he vaguely remembered the castle.

"A few," he murmured.

"As in three?"

His mouth twitched. "Maybe four, the butler included."

Vittoria grinned as they turned a corner. For the first time, she imagined that perhaps they had a shot at changing the Network. Together. Surely, such an optimistic hope would carry her through this evening.

Even if it wasn't true.

To bolster her courage, she pictured Eneko. Pere. Mere.

Mere was bright with joy at all the work Mateo sent her way, and Pere improved daily. One of Benat's men had constructed a chair with wheels that allowed him time outside. She'd spent all evening with them yesterday. The joy in Eneko's face and the feeling of his strong little body in her arms was all the reminder she needed.

For them, she could do anything.

A pair of double doors spread open before them as they approached the ballroom. Tangles of dresses and music spilled into the hallway. This was elegance unleashed. The landowners in their prime. She drew in a calming breath, eager to get this over with.

"If you need anything, simply tug on my jacket or my sleeve," Mateo murmured. "I'll make an excuse to get us out of whatever conversation we're in. Anything at all."

"Thank you."

"I anticipate you'll stir up a lot of curiosity. Are you prepared?"

Her face crinkled as she recalled the hours of lessons Zuri had managed to pack in. While brushing her hair. Curling it. Serving her food. Vittoria had eaten seven different practice meals—she wouldn't need to eat for a week. The sheer amount of food gave her guilt. She'd saved whatever she could and given it to children in the orchards.

Aside from Mateo, she had no allies here. No friends, no family, no one who knew her. Which made this all the more terrifying.

"As prepared as I can be," she said. "I hope I don't embarrass you."

He laughed, clutching her hand a little tighter. "You could never do that."

With that, he swept her past two Guardians and into the ballroom. Most of the landowners had already arrived. They were packed around the open dance floor, while an orchestra warmed up on the other side of the room. Mateo had told her they were arriving one minute before it would have been considered rude, to give them the advantage of a crowd. More bodies made it easier to disappear.

The dinner laid out was extraordinarily lavish. Oysters in shells with a rich ceviche topping. Lettuce cups filled with flaked crab in butter sauce. Steamed clams. Braised shark steaks soaked in milk. Piles of caviar set among wafer-thin crackers.

It was greater than anything Vittoria had ever seen before. Several witches sat at a long table, already eating and talking. It seemed less an organized affair, more a free-for-all. They could mingle, dance, or eat whenever they wanted.

"Romeo has swamped the room with glamour," Mateo said. He tightened his hold on her arm as they passed two landowner wives, necks laden with gems the size of Vittoria's palm. Their hooped sleeves bounced by their waists. "Flood you with glory, then shame you for not keeping up. Welcome to the world of the landowners."

Still, the dazzling spread of food, the sparkling glasses, the quiet mingle of murmuring voices struck her deeply. There was enough food here to feed her entire coven. Enough fabric to clothe all the children in Necce.

"Will they waste all this food if it doesn't get eaten?" she asked.

"Leftovers go to the staff for dinner."

She felt slightly better but doubted much would remain.

For the next hour, Mateo toured through the ballroom with Vittoria on his arm. Her head turned as she canvassed the area. No friendly faces revealed themselves. Most witches ignored her completely. A few would speak to Mateo now and then, but blithely passed her by. He spoke to her under his breath, telling her names, ages, facts. She couldn't keep up with it all and didn't try. It breezed past her, leaving her with the acute awareness that she didn't belong.

And she wasn't sure she wanted to.

Instead, she studied the women's dresses and played a game as to which potion she'd use to clean them. Silk, mostly, with yards of fabric that restricted their movements on the dance floor. Many wore flowers in their hair, but none wore magnolias. Vittoria eyed the driftwood fire in a great hearth that intermittently sent up colorful sparks. Strings of shells adorned the walls. Music, mostly flutes with some low, thrumming drums, played in the background.

When the decorations bored her, she turned back to the landowners and thought of what Mateo had said. *Try to see them as witches.* Vittoria ignored their dresses and tried to see the pain behind their eyes. The witches behind the glamour.

What did *they* worry about?

Did such wealth feel slippery? Did they worry about feeding their children also?

Most of them pretended to laugh with others. The conversations all felt stilted. Strange. As if no one really cared. Could she ever agree with these witches? Ever understand their views? She sensed a hunger for . . . something. Or maybe desperation. Once she peeled away the haughtiness, she saw the same unhappiness she'd found in the covens.

It was just different here, and all the pomp seemed to cover up their own bleak reality.

"Mateo!"

A voice called out to them, drawing her attention. Balta stood near the left wall in an obnoxious emerald-green outfit, a goblet in his hand. He raised it, then beckoned them closer.

Mateo turned them that way, whispering, "You're doing magnificently,

Vittoria. Balta is our greatest ally here. Be prepared, however. He says what he thinks."

She squeezed his arm in response.

Balta nodded as they approached, but kept his gaze on Vittoria. "A pleasure to meet the bravest witch in the Eastern Network," he said in a booming voice. A few heads turned their way, but only for a moment.

"I'm honored," she murmured with a smile.

"You should be. You've done the unthinkable and haven't been murdered yet. That's something in a room like this."

Mateo reached for a wine goblet on a waiter's tray. His hand rested on her back and nudged her a bit closer to his side. Landowners continued to ignore them. Vittoria was relieved to stop walking.

"How are you doing in your new life?" Balta asked her. His tone spoke of genuine interest. "*Really* doing? Anyone can put on a pretty face and stiff-smile through an evening, but I'm curious what you think of bridging the two worlds."

Vittoria hesitated. How honest should she be?

"It's . . . interesting."

He laughed loudly, drawing a few more stares, as if witches were eager to hear but didn't want to be *too* obvious. "Very few witches can truly understand what this is like for you, I bet," he said, then brightened. "Oh, perhaps La Salvatorra? I bet you that Mateo could pin that landowner down. He moves between the classes as fluidly as water."

A sparkle of challenge met her in his eyes. She nearly smiled back.

"He's also a bit mercenary," she drawled instead. "I'd be afraid to know a man like that, I think."

Balta's expression didn't change. "And who said you wouldn't have to be to survive such a gap?"

There was entirely too much gravity in his tone now.

"Then again," he reasoned, "you are still very much protected by the workers, are you not? You could at least go out among them without fear. No landowner wife can do that. Perhaps you are the freest witch in the Network?"

"While some of my class believe I've sold out? It's not entirely safe."

He shrugged. "As witches do. Can't control their thoughts. Regardless, you're in a position of some power. If Mateo, by some miracle, does win the throne, then you'll be handfasted to the High Priest. You'll be safe among the landowners—though likely not welcomed—because they have to respect you. They'll be monstrously unkind, but words don't kill."

They can sure come close, she thought.

Balta was the first witch to put into words what had been swirling around her head all this time. To articulate the strange position the betrothal had thrust her into. She belonged to no one. None truly or readily accepted her, but neither did they shun her in violent ways. Would she always live in those in-betweens? It seemed lonely.

The words *position of power* rang through her head.

Balta let out a long breath. "Doesn't matter anyway, Vittoria. You and your workers can keep praying to your Givers. Let them believe in La Principessa or La Salvatorra, if they must have something to believe in."

"It's more than that," she said, startling herself with a sense of defensiveness. "The Givers are hope."

He rolled his eyes. "La Salvatorra. La Christianna. Whatever you want to call them, they're all the same thing. Tales created by desperate minds. Do you see the madness in it? The witches have *created* the idea of La Principessa, and now they believe in her as a blessing from a sea goddess no one believes in anymore."

Vittoria clenched her fists. What frightened her most was just how close to her own thinking he'd come. So why did it bother her that he held the same opinions she did? Why should she care what a landowner thought?

Mateo gripped her hand so tightly her bones ached. She squeezed back, and he eased off.

"Not unlike honor," she replied, "which has no corporeal form, nor capacity for intervention, but is allowed to decide the course of your lives?"

Balta laughed. "You're brave, *maltea.* I honor that wholeheartedly."

Another voice broke into the conversation. Both Vittoria and Mateo turned at the same time. A young man approached with what could almost be called a warm smile. Vittoria was eager to see someone else in order to get away from Balta's intensity.

Perhaps shunned silence was better than discussing such matters with landowners.

She may not believe in the Givers any more than they did, but she didn't ridicule her witches for their beliefs.

The approaching witch was likely no older than twenty-one and had the beginnings of a sooty beard on his face. Vittoria studied him, startled by his open curiosity as he regarded Mateo. The young man and Mateo grasped arms.

"I'm Iker," the young man said. "My pere just died and left me with a prodigious inheritance and much property. I'm . . . curious about your ideas if you win the throne. My uncle says he's listened to you and liked some of your progressive ideas for the economy. Would you be willing to discuss them?"

Vittoria released Mateo's arm and shuffled back a step. As exciting as this sounded, she'd rather do a bit more exploring away from the landowners. Their general stony silence over her was clear enough. Besides, what harm could she possibly come to in a world where she was all but invisible? Benat and Joska were mingling in the crowd, anyway.

Mateo grinned at Iker. "I'd be more than happy to. Please—"

He turned to check with Vittoria. She gave him a quick smile and a wave, already several paces away. Let him work his leader magic. She wanted to find the *real* heroes of the castle, and she didn't need him to do that. Concern flitted across his face, but she gave him another confident glance and a small nod.

Slowly, he nodded in return.

"I'll give her one thing," Balta's muttered words faded as she slipped into the crowd. "She certainly has courage, doesn't she?"

Vittoria eased into the throng of witches.

Don't walk alone, Zuri had said. *A landowner wife should never leave the ballroom without their husband. It's a recipe for scandal and disapproval.*

She couldn't fathom why. Vittoria had roamed darkened streets in the middle of the night as a *lavanda* maid, armed with only a metal pipe.

Slowly, she circled the edge of the ballroom and tried to find another passing waiter, but they seemed to have disappeared. Even alone, she practically didn't exist. Among the glittering gems and dresses, she sought out a familiar uniform. Green and gold. The workers. Not an easy task, considering most workers were trained to be unobtrusive. Her best bet would be to wait near the food.

Even there, the dishes seemed to refill by magic, somehow.

Finally, she found a worker. A butler, she imagined. He wore an emerald uniform with gold edging and a white shirt underneath. He had to be middle-aged, which was almost ancient for a worker. Then again, castle workers lived in a bubble. They were mostly born and raised here. Never allowed to leave the grounds. Constantly assessed and tested to be sure the nobles in the castle would be safe from them. They lived in quarters behind the castle, not in leaky hovels in the street. While they might not eat a lot, they did eat more.

This butler had thinning hair, a trimmed goatee, and hazel eyes. He roamed just along the edge of the ballroom and seemed to be looking for something. Whenever his eyes swung her way, he gazed beyond her, as he would any other landowner. She winced. Would they all see her as another landowner now? That felt unacceptable, but inevitable. Of course, the landowners would always see her as a worker.

Balta's assessment had been spot-on.

With her shoulders straight, she approached the butler with a warm smile. "*Allo.* I'm Vittoria."

A brief second of confusion registered on his face, then gave way to understanding. His gaze darted to the magnolias in her hair and back to her face. His mouth rounded into an O.

"Might I ask your name?" she asked.

"Ah . . . Zaldar."

"An honor to meet you, Zaldar." She curtsied to him, the same curtsy Zuri had taught her to use when meeting a landowner. Behind her, someone gasped.

Alarm filled Zaldar's gaze. "Is there some way I may serve you, La Pr— Lady?" he asked with a little bow.

"Oh, no. Nothing I couldn't do for myself, thank you. Actually, I just wanted to meet you. How long have you worked here?"

He blinked. "Meet me?"

"I've never known a worker from the castle. I've been a *lavanda* maid for the last several years. Before then, I came from the farms. You?"

Zaldar struggled to respond at first, so she gave him the space to wrestle his shock.

"Ah . . . I've been here my whole life," he finally managed. "My mere was a maid when she had me, and they conscripted me at the age of three. My wife was also conscripted here as a child, and so were our daughters."

"I was born on the farms," she said with a little smile. "I often went from field to field through the spring, summer, and fall. We moved all the time through the land, so I can't imagine staying in one place like this."

Vittoria felt, more than saw, his sudden tension. "Is it safe for you to speak with me?" she asked quietly. "If you shouldn't be seen with me, I would understand. I'll leave immediately, in fact. I'm just . . . I'm looking to find a friend here." She gestured to the crowd behind them. "They all hate me, or fear me, and maybe I don't blame them."

His shoulders relaxed a little. He studied her more closely. Finally, after what felt like an eternity, he said, "It's . . . safe."

But his eyes flickered back to a balcony not far away, swamped with landowners and their frippery. Most of them were young men, flirting with girls younger than Vittoria. The girls leaned on the banister near the edge of the half dome and batted their eyelashes.

"Do you enjoy it here?" Vittoria asked.

"As much as anyone would, I imagine."

"All this . . . stuff?" Her nose wrinkled. "I can't make sense of it. Can you imagine owning so many things? What would you do with all of it?"

Amusement crossed his gaze. "Indeed, after the farms, I can imagine not. I've heard that workers sleep outside, on the ground."

"We did."

"Did you like it?" he cried.

She grinned. "Very much. At least, in the summer. When it was too cold in the winter, there were crude shelters that kept us this side of death. Are your accommodations better here?"

"Yes."

"You mentioned daughters?"

The ice in his expression seemed to melt. He beckoned her to follow and moved along the edge of the room, away from the balcony. For the most part, they stayed out of the way of the landowners. No one seemed to notice her there. While Zaldar spoke warmly of his daughter and two grandsons, Vittoria reveled in finding a new friend.

"My only daughter who survived childhood is Melda. She was conscripted to the castle at three, and she still works here today. Her two boys are in the stable now, conscripted at three also. It's a good life, comparably. Except for those unfortunate enough to be personal servants to . . . certain witches, they don't beat us here."

Vittoria sighed. A rarity these days, when the rebels engendered fear and landowners responded to attacks by tightening their control.

"I'm glad to hear it," she said warmly. "Do you mind if I ask you a question? If you have been here so long, Zaldar, do you remember the High Priestess Esperanza?"

The question was a wild shot, but it seemed to hit the mark. His expression clouded. Vittoria forced herself to hold his gaze while he stammered for a reply.

"E-Esperanza?"

"Yes."

"Why do you ask?"

"Curiosity." She turned to see Mateo through breaks in the crowd. The music sang in the background, coaxing couples onto the dance floor. "He says so little about his mere. In fact, no one mentions her much. Given that I will be the next High Priestess, I wanted to learn from the previous ones."

Her response had given Zaldar a chance to recover his composure.

"The days of Esperanza were interesting, of course," he said slowly. "She was a beautiful woman. Elegant. A natural in such crowds. Had a talent for reading a room and knowing who to talk to."

Vittoria managed a light laugh. "Unlike me, you mean."

He cast her a wry, sidelong glance. "Not what I meant, of course. But you . . . you were not born to this. Then again, neither was Esperanza. But there was something in the way she carried herself . . ."

"Wait, what do you mean?"

"Esperanza was a worker." Zaldar's eyes wrinkled as he frowned. "She pretended to be a landowner but was actually a rebel when she handfasted Hodei. Even he was fooled."

Something cold flowed through Vittoria's blood. Esperanza was a spy? Her mind could hardly fathom it.

"Oh," she whispered.

"Fearless, really." He sounded distant until he turned back to her. "Like you."

Vittoria bit back a startled laugh. "Did you meet her?" she asked instead.

"Not officially. She played the part well and mostly ignored us. But I did work around her and assisted several times in her personal quarters with the boys and with other little things."

"Was she kind to you?"

Zaldar appeared lost in his own thoughts, as if recalling a memory. Eventually, he nodded. "Yes, she was kind. There was a sense of hesitation between her and the workers. The truth of her story didn't come out until much, much later, of course. After we all found out, her life here made more sense. She was always cautious. Too cautious to be a regular landowner, and she asked little of the workers who served her. But not little enough to draw suspicion."

"But why did she do such a thing? Why was she not piked for it?" Vittoria couldn't hide her astonishment.

Was *this* why Mateo didn't want to speak of his mere?

Zaldar shrugged. "She was a rebel through and through. I assume that's all the motive she needed. As for piking, I'm not sure. Hodei, for lack of a better word, loved her. At least he seemed to. I remember when they met. He was sotted, certainly. Most landowners were too dazzled by her presence to be otherwise. And it was more than just beauty," he added. "But . . . grace. The way she carried herself. She believed she was a High Priestess. With her keen mind, one would have almost thought *she* could have ruled."

He laughed at that, and no surprise there. History had recorded no female leaders in the Eastern Network. Other Networks, such as the

Central Network, had no such restrictions. But it wasn't done here, and certainly not during the Castaneda Dynasty.

Vittoria's mind spun with questions. So many of them rushed her at once that she was struck momentarily quiet. Zaldar, meanwhile, glanced at the balcony again. He nudged them back a few steps.

"Do you think they actually loved each other?" she finally asked, recalling bent, shriveled Hodei with a shiver. Could the man who sent assassins to kill his own son ever love anyone?

"Oh, yes." Zaldar nodded, though he appeared troubled. "Back when such a man was capable of any selfless emotion, yes. Some say that finding out the truth of Esperanza is what made Hodei the monster he is today."

"What happened after he found out the truth?"

"I don't know how he found out," Zaldar said. "Just that things changed. One day everything was normal. The next? Hodei sent her and their sons to the country. After that, we never saw her again. Rumors around the castle were that she found refuge in the country and preferred it there. She lived there until she died. A quiet exile," he added gently, "but far better than a pike."

A distant gong announced the twelfth hour. There was still so much history left in the gaps of what Zaldar had said that she only had more questions. Did Hodei want to know why Esperanza stayed with *him*? Or why she stayed in the country? Or why she stayed . . . somewhere else?

Was she desperate to leave? Because she sounded rather at home in the palace.

Zaldar, occupied with staring at the balcony outside, missed her soft intake of breath. A familiar, aged man stood across the room, his bent back giving him away. His head canted up to stare straight at her. Hodei. The chill in his eyes sent a shiver right down her spine. Vittoria's stomach clenched. Her body flushed with cold.

His parchment-thin lips moved. Seconds later, she heard a whisper, as if he stood at her ear. Sent by an incantation, no doubt. By sheer force of will, she didn't turn to look at the spot next to her. Instead, she held his glacial gaze.

"You," Hodei whispered in the dark tones of his gravelly voice, "seek information in the wrong place, La Principessa. There is much for you to discover. Your nephew's life is at stake. Or have you already forgotten?"

An image of Eneko slipped through her mind, then. The sunlight dancing in his hair as he ran through the trees near the quarry, a giggle on his lips.

"Don't be a fool."

His whisper faded away. A landowner wife sashayed by, breaking their eye contact. When the woman passed, her exorbitant skirts trailing paces behind her, Hodei was gone.

Vittoria felt as if all the warmth had left her body.

La Principessa?

Zaldar sucked in a sharp breath. "The time has come," he murmured, then put a hand on her wrist. Only a worker who deeply trusted her would dare touch her, even if she only masqueraded as a landowner.

"Mateo need not look far to find his friends here," he said. The sudden intensity of his voice startled her. "Castle workers are considered apart from the others, but we aren't. We think of ourselves as one of you. Keep that in mind if the worst happens, for all will need saving. Go to the far edge of the room immediately. Take your betrothed with you and wait there. I'll come find you and help you get—"

A distant screech cut through the air, like a flute had gone off-key. A stunned silence followed for half a breath just as a scuffle broke out on the balcony.

"Go, Vittoria!" Zaldar cried. "Run."

Shouts came from the edge of the room. Zaldar thrust her behind him as a swarm of witches stormed the ballroom from outside. They wore dark-gray robes, black breeches, and deep hoods.

The rebels had come.

18

Mateo tried not to let his eyes cross.

Iker was a polite young man, but dull as a rusty blade and ambitious as mud. While Mateo politely answered questions and attempted to find something they had in common, his mind ran to Vittoria.

Was she safe?

Did she feel lonely?

Had anyone been rude to her?

Benat tried to blend into the crowd not far away, looking somehow out of place despite his elegant attire. Joska would be somewhere on the grounds by now. Mateo managed to catch Benat's eye in silent question. Benat tilted his head to the right. Vittoria was speaking to a butler near a bookshelf on the other side of the room. Relieved to have eyes on her, he turned half his mind back to Iker.

Until the air in the room shifted.

The effect was subtle. Flutes played. Couples danced. Food filled the room with delicious aromas. But he felt the odd change like a cold breath on the back of his neck.

Benat looked at him immediately. Mateo nodded to the balcony—the only true weakness in a place like this, open like an invitation—and clapped a hand on Iker's shoulder.

"Sorry, *jauna*. Must find my betrothed."

A scream interrupted the night.

An awful squawk filled the air as a flutist missed their note. Then another woman screamed from somewhere outside. Mateo was halfway across the ballroom when the first rebel made it in. Benat swung around his right flank, headed toward Vittoria. Panicked witches bolted to the other edge of the ballroom, away from the balcony.

By the time he waded through the disarray, Vittoria had moved.

"Vittoria!" he called.

He towered over most witches, but all he could see was chaos. Rebels poured into the ballroom, ringing the sides. They held no weapons, producing terror by their presence alone. Likely, snaking around the edges was an attempt to force all the landowners into the interior of the room.

Overhead, chandeliers threw bright prisms of light on the checkered tile floor, reflecting off the expensive gems. Landowners screamed. Men shoved women behind them. A few girls hid behind chairs and sobbed.

Mateo grabbed a chair and stepped on it while witches streamed past. In the melee, he caught a glimpse of a magnolia flower. Seconds later, he stood next to Vittoria. She clutched a heavy candlestick like her metal pipe and kept her back to the wall. Her eyes watched the rebels as they stationed themselves in front of exits before anyone could escape.

"You're well?" he asked, breathless.

"Fine," she said without fear. "The rebels, I presume?"

He nodded and pulled her close. The butler stepped forward. Zaldar. Mateo recognized him from his time here as a young boy.

"Majesty," he said to Mateo, one hand on his heart. "Allow me to escort you and Lady out of here, to safety."

Mateo studied him. The title of *Majesty* and *Lady* from a butler in the castle? He wasn't sure what it meant, but it was unexpected.

"Thank you," he said cautiously, "but I will stay. Do you know which rebels are infiltrating?"

Zaldar hesitated.

"Who is it?" Mateo said more sharply.

"The rebels from Necce Coven, Majesty. At least that's what rumors say."

The man knew which coven these rebels were from, had kept Vittoria along the far edge of the room, and also addressed him as *Majesty*? It made no sense. Zaldar's affiliations were mixed. But Mateo set that aside to think about later. The rebels were steps away.

When three rebels advanced toward him, a nearby landowner grabbed Zaldar, put a knife to his neck, and shouted, "Stay back!"

The three rebels immediately stopped. Vittoria sucked in a sharp breath of surprise. The landowner's gaze darted from Mateo to the rebels.

"Well?" he shouted at Mateo. "Aren't you going to stop them?"

Mateo stared hard at him. "Only if they attempt to harm someone. At this moment, *jauna*, only you have done that."

"This . . . isn't acceptable!" the landowner cried.

"I agree," he said calmly. "Let us hear out their reasoning."

One of the rebels snarled while another, the smallest, seemed to focus on Vittoria. The screams of the landowner women had localized to the middle of the ballroom now, where they'd been herded like sheep.

Vittoria stepped forward. "Drop your knife," she demanded to the landowner holding Zaldar. "Or we will allow the rebel witches to overtake you."

"You're with them!" the landowner cried.

"Not yet," she muttered.

Mateo used a spell to freeze the knife in the landowner's hand. It crackled with the sudden chill, and the man screamed as it burned his palm with a frigid kiss. The knife toppled to the ground. The landowner shoved Zaldar away.

"Lady," Zaldar said with a hand held out to Vittoria, "please! Allow me to take you to safety."

The landowner darted off. All around the ballroom, landowners had gone on the attack, fighting back. Incantations, curses, shields. Lights of different colors and sizes came from thrown blighters—glowing balls of magical power with various effects. A tangle of retreating rebels nearly knocked Zaldar over in their haste to get to the food on the other side of the room. Mateo grabbed Zaldar's shoulder and held him upright.

"Get back," he said to Vittoria. The last thing he needed was her getting injured. She ignored him, gaze trained on the battle in the center of the room. He watched, stunned by the back-and-forth between landowners and rebels. For the most part, the rebels didn't seem fazed by the magic, though they weren't using any obvious magic themselves.

Did they also have magic?

Why were they here?

Magic had been outlawed for workers for almost twenty years. The younger generation supposedly had no skill, but the older generation did. It would have been easy enough for them to teach it underground, in the catacombs where Hodei dared not send his magic-seeking Guardians. One good fight down there, and the whole leaky catacombs could collapse, taking the city of Necce with it.

But what were the rebels doing here, anyway?

Now that all the landowners had been pushed to the center of the room, some rebels were raiding the food tables. Others plucked crystals off the chandeliers. The rest engaged with the fighting landowner men. Largely, they . . . did almost nothing but steal.

Except for a rebel on the far side of the room, who slipped through a secret door. Another spoke to a butler, hidden in curtains. Did Mateo see shadows climbing the walls outside, through the window?

Odd.

Five rebels headed toward him, drawing his attention back. He, Zaldar, and Vittoria were the only non-rebels on the edge of the room. Even Romeo stood in the ring of landowners, shouting orders.

The incoming rebels' faces were hidden in the deep hoods of their dark cloaks. Their ratty boots thudded as they marched with stern determination. Vittoria sidestepped Mateo, putting herself directly in their path. Before he could reach out to pull her back, all five witches stopped.

Mateo moved behind her, a warning on his face. But the five witches seemed, again, to be staring at Vittoria. Zaldar stood at her side, trembling. The knife had nicked his skin, and blood smeared his wrinkled neck.

"What do you want?" Vittoria asked.

Two of them fell to their knees in front of her.

"La Principessa," one of them murmured. "Why are you here?"

"Did you know?" asked another, guilt in their voice.

His stomach twisted. La Principessa? By the Givers, not here. This was not the time or the place for her to have this revelation. Mateo shifted to stand in front of her, but Vittoria put out a hand to stop him.

"Wait."

"La Principessa?" whispered a rebel who stepped forward. Female, by her quiet voice and slender shoulders. She seemed more confused than shocked. "Is it really ... are you ... ?"

Vittoria's face turned white.

"San—"

The witch cut her off. "Are you really La Principessa?"

Vittoria reached a hand to the magnolia flower in her hair. If the rush of understanding that filled her expression meant anything, Mateo's entire hand had just been revealed to her. To her credit, she didn't look at him. Didn't scream. Instead, she just stood there in pale shock. Another rebel advanced, nearly shoving the first to her knees.

"Lies," he snarled. "You're no more La Principessa than I am La Tour-rere. On your knees, landowner wife."

"Not while I live," Mateo muttered silkily, stepping in front of her. "Would you like to challenge me?"

The rebel stumbled back a step, stuttering.

An unusual quiet had fallen on the room, and Mateo felt the weight of many stares. He could not be seen as in league with the rebels, but nor would he give the rebels a reason to hate him more if it could be avoided. An impossible task. Half the rebels now ringed the throng, fighting off curses, hexes, and other magic from the landowners. The rebels didn't reciprocate with blatant magic, but Mateo saw the ripples of shields every now and then.

Interesting.

The rest of the rebels stared at Vittoria instead of fighting. Even the landowners had slowed their blighters and were looking at her now. Whatever the Necce rebels' plan, it had just begun to crumble thanks to Vittoria's distracting presence.

Seeming to understand this, Vittoria brushed past Mateo and strode into the fighting crowd before he could stop her. Her lips moved over and over again. "Stop. Stop now!"

But the cacophony prevented her from being heard. Mateo followed her, casting a spell to amplify her voice.

"Stop!"

Her shouted command echoed through the ballroom. For a breath, the chaos calmed. Nearby rebels dropped to their knees in a circle around her. The landowners hesitated, magic sparking in the air, no doubt wondering what had just happened. Mateo moved as close to her as he dared without blocking her. Vittoria slowly turned, comprehending the whispers of *La Principessa* from the rebels on their knees at her feet.

Her expression paled further.

Across the room, Romeo stared at Mateo with dark, glittering eyes. Mateo met his stare without a flicker. Did Romeo see it now? Did Romeo comprehend what Vittoria just barely understood herself? He must, because rage pulsed in his throat.

Mateo fought off a smile, but not too hard. His lips curled up slightly as he looked at his brother.

Oh, yes, this was a plan that not even Romeo could have anticipated, and *that* was why Romeo looked ready to kill. Romeo's nostrils flared as he shoved his way through the crowd.

"That's enough!" Romeo shouted as he stepped forward. "Seize every single one of them! They will all taste death tonight."

The rebels disappeared at once.

Their sudden absence sent a gasp through the room. Only two stragglers remained, held by a burly landowner and unable to transport. They landed a pair of well-aimed punches, and the landowner fell unconscious as the two rebels vanished. Mateo darted forward to grab Vittoria. His hand closed on her arm just as he finished muttering the transportation spell.

Darkness fell as Romeo advanced, a knife gripped in his white knuckles. But Mateo was already whisking Vittoria far away.

19

Vittoria stared at the shifting shadows of the ocean for a long time. The flicker of movement as Benat's men patrolled the house reassured her. Mateo and Benat were in the dining room, their voices a low rumble.

The safety of Mateo's house gave her a physical sensation of relief. It allowed her mind to unwind and process what had happened in the ballroom tonight. She leaned against a pillow in her curtained-off area and stared out at the sea, her mind rolling back.

Back, back, back.

Vittoria thought of the smelly Necce streets that she knew so well. The workers she'd visited there with Mateo the last several nights. With Benat. The magnolias in her hair. On her cape. On her dress during the betrothal. She remembered the mob and what they'd cried. *La Principessa!* Mateo's lack of concern over her going back into Necce. The silver that Benat's men just happened to find and happened to give to her.

She remembered everything.

Especially the quiet female rebel at the ball, who had asked, "La Principessa? Is it really . . . are you . . . ?"

In that moment, Vittoria had comprehended three things: the workers thought she was a Giver come to life. Mateo wanted them to think that. And she knew that rebel's voice.

Vittoria thought about the rebels next. The power of their palpable desperation. The way they'd stormed the room but didn't attack. Thankfully, no one had died tonight. This was more of a scare than an attack. She'd seen no faces in that raid. Had the Necce rebels hoped to test themselves against the landowners? Were they there to harm anyone? They clearly had some magic, but was it enough?

Their attack had been haphazard, at best. Poorly organized. It could never have worked, and they left so early.

So, why attack?

Pikes would stand as punishment for this. There had to be a reason.

Her mind skipped around, unable to focus. Some of the rebels seemed to really believe that she was La Principessa. Or had that just been their hope?

Were belief and hope different things?

Had Mateo been using her?

He hadn't told her everything, and that stung. Now her faith in him felt shaken. What else didn't she know?

"Your world here has never been safe, *masuna*," Mateo had whispered as he left her in her room to think. "But now it is deadly. Romeo will kill you the moment he has a chance, so please don't leave before I can explain more."

Vittoria rubbed her fingernail over her bottom lip. Mateo had clearly been afraid she'd cave. Abandon this mad plan that made her a Giver, of all things. But wasn't it too late now? She effectively had *nowhere* to go. And Romeo would want to kill her. The screams of the landowners rang in her ears. When she blinked, she saw the way Mateo had snatched her at the very last moment. She'd seen Romeo for only a breath. The knife in his hand as he headed straight for her.

Oh, yes. He'd wanted to kill her, honor be damned.

A soft knock on her door interrupted her thoughts. She straightened, then called, "Come in."

Mateo's heavy steps advanced into the room, along with the flicker of a single candle. He set down the light with a little clatter. Then the sheets parted as he peered inside her hideout.

"May I come in?"

She gestured to the wall next to her. She was clad in her usual white dress. The flowers and pins had been removed from her head, leaving her hair on her shoulders. He'd changed into a fresh white shirt and a pair of brown pants. He sat down heavily and sighed. For several moments, neither of them spoke. She was grateful for the silence, because she wasn't sure what to say. She wasn't sure what she was feeling. Every time she thought of the ballroom, prickles attacked her heart. Was this feeling betrayal?

Fear?

Relief?

Finally, he broke the silence. "I thought it would be more genuine and more successful if I didn't tell you the ultimate goal of all our work."

She laughed, but it held no amusement. "You thought I wouldn't agree to impersonate a Giver? To pretend to be something that I'm not? Well, you were correct."

"You were a giving person long before I met you. I saw it in you, which is part of the reason I was drawn to you in the beginning."

She sucked in a sharp breath but refused to look at him. "I am Vittoria Nerea Antoinetta Guita, daughter of Nerea Antoinetta Isabella Sal and Ander San Guita of the Mayfair Coven. A *lavanda* maid. There is nothing powerful about me."

"And yet you have already given your witches hope, food, warmth. Your very presence tonight stopped an attack on the landowners that could have resulted in bloodshed on both sides."

She frowned. "You don't know that's why they stopped."

"I know half the witches in the room were kneeling to you, and if even fifteen of them had knelt, that would have been enough to cripple any plan."

A thousand rebuttals surfaced on her tongue all at once, then dissolved at the same time. She closed her eyes and leaned her head back against the wall. The rhythmic crash of the ocean soothed her.

This is *not* what she'd wanted. To be a Giver? That pressure? The idea of having to give hope in a world like this . . .

"I'm angry that you didn't tell me." Her fists clenched. She edged away from him, almost without realizing it. He let her go but eyed the new space between them. "I feel . . . left out."

"I know." He swallowed. "And I'm sorry, Vittoria. It wasn't fair."

"I don't even believe in the Givers!" she cried. "How can I pretend to be one?"

"Perhaps that's the reason why you can."

Her thoughts felt crowded—she didn't want to figure it out. To pretend to be something she wasn't. That felt wrong. But, then, hadn't she already agreed to that? She was Mateo's betrothed.

A fake landowner.

The overwhelm led her to plant her forehead on her knees and take a deep breath. All her emotions were tangled up together.

"I never wanted to do anything to break your trust," he continued. "But everything else was already so overwhelming for you. And, in the beginning, I didn't know if this wild plan would work. Those months when we didn't speak? I was just . . . trying to prove it would work. Then it started to, and we had to move quickly."

Mateo stared at his hands, where his fingers were tangled together, and continued, "I meant it when I told you that I can't do this without you." He ran a hand through his hair. "The East is split three different ways. The landowners, the workers, and the rebels. The only place where there is crossover is between the rebels and the workers. Workers flock to the rebels because they're frustrated or scared. Without the workers, the rebels wouldn't exist. If we can stop the workers from fighting as rebels, we have a chance at quelling a civil war when I take the throne."

"And the landowners? How will you cripple them?"

Her voice sounded sharper than she intended, but she didn't regret saying it. Did Mateo's roots keep him prejudiced in favor of the landowners? Was that part of what he meant when he said he needed her to bridge the gap between the classes? To represent the workers?

"The landowners are protected by the Guardians," he said, "but the Guardians are *also* workers, for the most part. My hope is that it works the same way. If we can stop the Guardians from protecting the landowners because they believe in La Principessa, the landowners might have to negotiate."

"Might?"

"Magic." He shrugged. "They have it. They could be powerful enough to defeat the workers by sheer magic, but it's hard to know for sure. Regardless, there's only one way to get *all* workers, most of the Guardians, and some of the rebels to follow something."

"The Givers," she murmured.

"Exactly. It's the only common thread among them. In a conflict such as this, they need something bigger to follow. They're too afraid to choose sides on their own, and why shouldn't they be? It's death either way. Side with the rebels and fight with no guaranteed success against Guardians and powerful magic. Side with the landowners, become a Guardian, and they may have to kill their own families in defense of witches they can't stand. The workers needed . . . a sign. A symbol. The *most* powerful symbol."

"La Principessa," she whispered, and her voice sounded stark. Hollow. So colored with disbelief it didn't sound like her.

"Yes." He leaned forward, passionate now. "It's the only thing that Romeo and my pere would never have seen coming. They could fight me and maybe win, but how do they fight a Giver? How can they stop what we've started? The rumors of La Principessa are already crawling among the workers. After tonight? It will be a wildfire. And when hope sparks a flame?"

"It turns to fire."

She looked at him, then. Despite her disgruntled frustration, she admired the way the shadows highlighted his jaw, his cheeks. He was pure, bottled power when he looked at her like that. As if he really believed this madness could work. That he could embody an idea as potent as a Giver through *her,* a *lavanda* maid. Being a High Priestess seemed like a stroll compared to this.

"Your pere and Romeo can still get rid of me," she whispered. "The name La Principessa doesn't protect me. In fact, tonight just made everything more dangerous. More difficult."

More impossible, she thought morosely as she recalled Hodei's brief appearance at the ball.

"Yes. It's why we must be so careful. Romeo responded rashly tonight. After some time, I think he'll work through it. Realize that you're of more value to him alive than dead. If he kills you, the civil war is unstoppable because the workers *will* rise for their Giver. But if he shatters their belief in you? Then hope is gone. His only chance to win against La Principessa is to prove you're just a witch. That's why we must be careful."

The audacious plan came together one piece at time. She sank into it. It sent her mind down different paths, attempting to suss out just how wrong this had to be. How could it actually work? It was insane. Desperate. Wild.

And yet . . . so precise.

In fact, it seemed so clear she was startled she hadn't seen it before. Perhaps she didn't want to.

She wanted to remain furious that he hadn't been open with her. She wanted to smack him until her palms sang. But she clenched her fists as the ire died away. In truth, he'd been correct. She would have thought him totally unhinged. She never would have ventured out to give away food or silver. The witches never would have seen her among them, and this almost-bloody night could have sparked the civil war they all feared so much.

"I understand," she whispered reluctantly.

Mateo studied her uneasily. "Do you hate me? Because I would understand if you do. And while I can reassure you there are no more surprises that I'm aware of myself, I wouldn't blame you for not trusting me."

Her lips twitched. "I thought I did hate you for a while, but . . . no. I could never hate you, Mateo. I see why you did it. And you were right—I never would have gone along had I known. But I do wish . . . anyway. No more secrets?"

"I swear it." The earnestness in his voice convinced her. "Do you see that this is the only way?"

"Yes."

He reached out, fingers on her chin, to gently persuade her to look at him. Nothing but concern shone from his dark eyes in the fading candlelight.

"Will you be La Principessa, Vittoria?" he murmured. "Now that you know, do you see how important you are? How worthy you are? Whether you see it or not, you have always been La Principessa. You have always given hope. To your witches and to me."

Her heart quivered at his words.

"I will be what my family and my witches need," she whispered. "I vow it to you."

"Thank you."

There was so much that lingered in the words. Vittoria leaned into him until he pulled her close. She closed her eyes. His warm breath felt like a caress on her cheek. He wrapped an arm around her shoulders and held her against his side. She luxuriated in the heat that radiated from him, a sharp contrast to the cool wall at her back. His comfort tonight, of all nights, sang through her blood. She needed it so desperately. Needed to feel as if there were a safe escape somewhere.

A shocking thought struck her, and she drew back.

"The Test of Magic is tomorrow!" Her brow knitted together. "I had put it out of my mind. Are you . . . can you . . ."

He put a hand on her face. "I'll be fine. I'm ready."

Her panic faded in response to his calm. "Can we really do this, Mateo?" she whispered, searching his eyes. "This plan feels so impossible. So overwhelming. There are so many things that can go wrong."

"Yes. We can do this, but only together," he murmured.

She nodded and put her hand over his. Tomorrow, he'd face another harrowing test. Tomorrow would be another defining moment in this obnoxiously complicated plan he'd cooked up.

Tomorrow could be another victory that moved them closer to freedom. To stability for her family and Eneko. To clothes on their backs and education in their minds and hope in their hearts to stay.

And it was comfort enough.

20

MATEO

A warm breeze fluttered through Mateo's hair the next day, as if the old sun god wanted to comfort him.

The Test of Magic, he seemed to say, *is yours to conquer.*

Then a contrary wind blasted him. It roared across the ocean and sent frothing whitecaps over the ridge of each wave. They crested and slammed into the sand to whisper near his bare feet. His heart felt just like one of those waves: hammered by the sheer anticipation of what came next. The scar on his arm hurt, as if the ghost panther had attacked again. He rubbed it and forced his thoughts away.

Balta stood a few paces away on a barren stretch of beach far beyond Magnolia Castle. Romeo was next to Mateo, white shirt flapping in the wind. He wore a pair of linen pants that made him almost appear normal. Like a sailor on a day off. The wind ruffled his short-cropped hair. Vittoria had tied Mateo's hair back, out of his face, with a piece of leather.

"Mateo." Balta nodded to him, then turned to Romeo, hands clasped behind his back. "Romeo. Welcome to the Test of Magic. Unlike the Test of Courage, this will be private. There are no spectators allowed, and no one has been informed of where we are."

The silence on the beach felt oddly surreal. Not having a sea of eyes staring at him this time certainly helped, but his palms still felt clammy.

Undaunted, Balta continued, "As soon as I am finished here, I will transport each of you to separate boats in an unknown location. Due to the dangerous and violent nature of this task, you'll be alone and far from our shores. As this is a test of your magical skill, of course you must use magic."

Romeo shifted. Mateo forced himself to stay still. To *not* think about what this meant. The stakes if he lost. Was his power strong enough? Did he know enough? The water should have comforted him, but today it felt more like foe than friend.

"Once you're on your boat, you will encounter a sea wyrm. Your job is to remove the threat from Eastern Network shores. You will be required to prove your work after the task by leaving this token." Balta sent each of them a necklace with a spell.

Mateo caught it—a gnarled piece of seaweed on a cord of black leather. Magic hummed from it.

Balta continued, "I will then go to your token and assess whether you've sufficiently neutralized the threat. If the wyrm is within a day's swim of our borders, you will fail. Be aware that returning without completing the task will count as failing."

Balta glanced to Mateo, then Romeo with an almost-bored expression. Neither of them had said a word.

"A High Priest is only as good as his magical ability, as you already know," Balta said. "Today, you are to prove your talent. You have until the sun descends below the horizon to finish. May the magic of the gods serve you well today."

Mateo's gut churned as he comprehended the challenge.

Sea wyrms were nothing more than big, fat, blind snakes that lived in the ocean. Some historians linked them back to dragons and believed that the sea goddess Prana messed up when first forming sea dragons—and that wyrms were the mistake. Though there was nothing dragonian about them.

They were hairless, toothless, gray, and wrinkled, but that didn't mean they weren't dangerous. They were absolutely gigantic and had drowned plenty of sailors by rising into the air and plopping their bodies onto ships, reducing them to nothing more than splintered wood.

Plus, if the legends were true, they were seeking, ruthless creatures that lived for something they couldn't have: magic. Lore stated that the sea goddess, offended by their ugly bodies, cursed them to crave magic all their days. They would die for it if they could find it in large enough amounts. When a wyrm found a source of magic, it would use one of its two pointy ends to prod the magical object, then consume whatever item, or witch, it found.

But was that part really true? No one knew, because sea wyrms were as visible as Givers. Inland witches scoffed at all the stories, as if they didn't believe wyrms were real. Sailors who claimed a sighting were often ignored or disregarded or made fun of.

But the sea wyrm wasn't the strangest part of this task.

Balta's phrasing rang through his ears like a dull knock on hollow wood. *May the magic of the gods serve you well.*

The magic of the gods? Such a thing didn't exist. The gods, when they lived in Alkarra at all, gave no magic to their mortals. They hoarded it, jealous of the ease and power it bestowed. Balta wanted them to use a nonexistent magic system to defeat one of the largest creatures in the ocean?

No, it had to be a trick, just like the ghost panther whelps. Mateo searched his memory for any scrap of recollection of what *the magic of the gods* could refer to.

Gods, as opposed to goddesses, were impatient. They were jealous protectors of their mortals and their magic and cursed witches because witches were too like their goddess sisters. They were selfish creatures, banished by the goddesses to the other side of the world, far from Alkarra, over a thousand years ago.

Mateo shook his head. Sea wyrm. The magic of the *gods*. By the Givers, but the Law of Rights would kill them all. Romeo struggled to hide his perplexed expression as he stared at the sand.

Balta gestured Romeo forward. "Romeo," he said. "You shall go first. Mateo, do not move from that spot."

"Go with honor, brother," Mateo said.

Romeo ignored him as Balta gripped his arm, and they both disappeared. Mateo's thoughts spun to the wyrms he'd heard so much of on the navy ship.

"Restless," his navy captain had once told him with a little shudder.

"They're strange, restless creatures. Some say they crave magic and will do anything for it. That's why they attack boats. They can sense the magic. They want it. Saw part of one once. Felt fortunate to escape with a boat and my life, if I'm honest. They just seem . . . restless."

A blood-red sun lingered not far from the horizon. Mateo hazarded a guess that they had about an hour, maybe less. As it stood, he'd much rather take his chances with the ghost panther whelps again.

Balta returned, his face blank. "Any questions?"

Mateo shook his head.

"Then honor awaits."

Balta grabbed his hand, and Mateo felt the tug of a transportation spell all the way to his navel.

Mateo landed on a boat in the middle of an angry ocean.

The moment his feet touched the wood, Balta left. Mateo saw only a blur before he was adrift, alone on the water.

An agitated sea churned below him, white with waves. Utter silence and glittering blue brilliance glimmered in an unending circle. The wind had stopped here. He must be some distance away from shore. Based on the position of the setting sun over the watery grave, the boat faced north, which meant the Network would be to his left somewhere. Within a day's swim for a wyrm, he presumed, which also didn't tell him much because he didn't know how fast they could swim.

By sheer force of will, he forced his pounding heart to calm while he clutched the sides of the pitching boat. The wooden boards practically hummed beneath him. Magic hung heavy in the air. Of course. What else would guarantee an agitated sea wyrm the moment he arrived?

Some navy ships in the deep oceans used magic only in times of emergency to avoid attracting wyrms.

Scarcely ten seconds after he landed, the sea calmed.

"Oh no," he muttered.

A fleshy, monstrous body broke the water to his right. Mateo straightened, half in terror, half in awe. A sea wyrm rose from the endless ocean beyond him, the heaving body climbing higher and higher in the air until it exceeded the height of the Saltu Jungle arena. The thickness of its massive body would have fit at least a full landowner house. Deep wrinkles lined its shiny, leatherlike skin.

Struck by the sight, Mateo simply stared as it rose, rose, rose, only twenty paces from his little skiff.

Then he scrambled for an oar.

As quickly as the wyrm ascended, it began to fall. The snakelike body plummeted back toward the ocean like a toppling tree and slapped the water. From the depths of its belly came a distinct groaning, as if the ocean herself wanted to complain and vented her pain through the wyrm.

Too late, Mateo pushed his oar in the water and tried to get away. The wyrm slapped the surface of the ocean with its other end, let out another keen, and disappeared below the waves. Water sloshed over the sides of the boat.

In the distance, the sun crept closer to the horizon.

Now, Mateo could hear a strange singsong. The wyrm slithered with lightning speed beneath him, skimming just under the surface, appearing with a flash of light in the water.

Mateo struggled to keep his focus as the waves crashed into his boat, then began to calm. He couldn't just fight—he had to think. Had to go on the offense, or the wyrm would drown him and then eat him.

Salt water poured down his neck and saturated his hair. He shook it off and braced his legs again. His goal? Get the wyrm away from the Network. He glanced out at the endless sea. At least he knew what direction to go. If he accidentally brought the wyrm closer to the Network, he'd lose the throne.

Sea wyrms wanted magic, simply put.

But then what?

Mateo conjured a ball of light and used magic to throw it far away from him, to the east. The magical ball bobbed in the water just as the wyrm reappeared. The wyrm slithered toward the ball, body canting to the left and the right like a snake. It consumed the light with its massive jaws.

Then it groaned.

Mateo paused as silence fell over the sea. Surely, it couldn't be that easy.

That had been a stupidly simple spell. A desperate attempt to draw the wyrm's attention away from him ...

He swore under his breath as the wyrm spit the magical ball back out, then thrashed back and forth.

"All right," he muttered. "You don't like that."

That broke the assumption that wyrms wanted to eat any magical item, anyway. At least, not items conjured from that kind of magic.

The wyrm disappeared, then surged out of the water next to him, so close he could have reached out to touch its strange skin. Water sprayed off its mottled body as it rose back into the air. The boat heaved and pitched Mateo off the side. The wyrm slapped the ocean again.

Cold water encompassed Mateo all at once. He struggled back to the surface. Waves drove him back under. He fought in and out of the agitated currents for several eternities before using a spell to vault himself to the surface.

Once he broke into the air, he gasped and sputtered. The boat had broken apart in the violent waves, leaving pieces of wood floating around him.

The wyrm was more agitated than ever. While Mateo struggled to swim to a piece of the boat, the wyrm swam in circles around him, creating a circular current that pulled Mateo in.

While riding the current, he forced himself to focus.

Did the wyrm want something more than just a magical ball of light? Mateo shouted out a few more spells, throwing anything that might satisfy it. Cracks of light popped just over the water.

The wyrm ignored them.

He conjured a school of glittering red fish that swarmed it.

The wyrm thrashed them with a tail until they were stunned, then died and disappeared in the depths. Frantic, Mateo cast any spell he could think of. Spells that brought light, seaweed, turtles, anything. He tried several different types of magic, to no avail. Modern magic with simple spells. Cabrerran. Almorran. Declan.

The magic seemed to call the wyrm, then fade. The wyrm was restless. Agitated.

Searching.

Always searching.

But for what? Witches assumed it was magic, but he'd disproven that. It wanted something else.

The wyrm seemed to understand that the magic came from Mateo, so it didn't try to harm him. Perhaps it understood him as the source. Perhaps it was sheer luck. It just kept swimming, keening, lost. Its mouth, which tapered to a gradual point like an earthworm, probed around the water. Poking. Prodding. Popping out into the world, then back again into the water with growing frustration.

Mateo risked a quick glance at the sun.

Halfway down the horizon.

"All right," Mateo shouted. "You and me, wyrm. What's the magic of the gods, eh? Do you know?"

The wyrm paused, head poised half out of the water like a forgotten mountain in the middle of the ocean. Mateo blinked.

Had it *heard* him?

"Hey!" he shouted, bobbing in the water. "Hey! Over here."

The head rose, whirling around as if it were searching for him. Then the wyrm headed his direction. Mateo's heart thumped as he transported farther away to buy himself a moment to think. Too much of this didn't add up. If the wyrms really sought magic the way witches assumed, why was it getting more agitated?

The more magic he conjured, the more frustrated the wyrm became.

No, it wasn't magic the wyrm wanted, it was something else. The wyrm tussled with the water as if it were . . . hungry.

But for what?

Magic of the gods, Balta had said. *Magic of the gods.*

The gods were nothing but a fuzzy blur in the realms of history. Historians who still believed in that paradigm claimed that the gods had magic they never shared, but that it was . . . archaic. Simple. So simple it insulted the goddesses.

But how could that help here?

Or maybe it was a trick. Balta hadn't said to use it. He'd said, *May the magic of the gods serve you well today.*

Water churned around the wyrm as it opened its mouth, drawing the ocean into its dull lips. The keening sound strengthened into a roar that nearly rent the air. Mateo realized with a start that the wyrm meant to eat him.

He transported to another spot as the wyrm closed in on him. The wyrm spun, no doubt honing in on the magic, and headed for him just as quickly again.

Mateo transported away, farther out. Time was of the essence. If he just kept transporting, it would follow, but not far enough away. He had to have enough magic to draw the wyrm away from the Eastern Network *and* return to shore. There wasn't time. Sea wyrms clearly moved extraordinarily fast in the water. He'd have to swim halfway around the world to prove that he'd led it far enough away.

Which meant he had to *neutralize the threat* as Balta put it. All he'd done so far was prove the wyrm could swim.

No, he was missing something . . .

The wyrm closed in on him, forcing Mateo to transport even farther away. As if the wyrm had finally found an outlet for its frustration, it charged through the water at an impressive speed.

While Mateo racked his brain, he kept transporting farther into the middle of the ocean and then to the north where the waters grew cooler. Although he wasn't certain where Balta had sent him, he had *some* idea based on his navy years. Wyrms were reputed to prefer warm, coastal waters, which is why they wreaked havoc on marine life.

Was he near that cluster of sand-only islands he'd seen on so many naval maps?

He fingered the gnarled seaweed as the wyrm charged faster at him. The idea that formed in his half panic wasn't a solution, but it was something.

A flash of lightning streaked across the sky in the distance. The wyrm startled with a giant twitch and turned toward it. Another moan issued from the depths of its belly. Mateo glanced beyond the wyrm to a charcoal-dark skyline. Another flash of lightning from the high tempest.

Another keening bellow.

"You're hungry?" Mateo murmured. Water splashed his face as he swam in place, keeping his head barely above water. "You're sort of half dragon, and you live in a world of water. So, what is the one thing you can't have that you desperately seek? It's not magic. You have plenty of food. You hate witches. But if you're part dragon, or almost a dragon . . ."

On a bold hunch, Mateo kept an eye on the lightning and cast a fire spell.

He sent it far away from him, forcing the wyrm to turn the opposite direction. The wyrm swung around. And slowed.

And stopped just below the flame, as if transfixed. For the first time since Mateo's arrival, all lay quiet.

Within seconds, the bottom half of the wyrm popped out of the water. Both ends appeared at the same time, the tops of its obnoxiously large heads bobbing up and down. Then the wyrm rose slowly, water surging around it, to caress the bottom of the fire.

The fire was extinguished.

The wyrm roared.

Mateo cast another fire spell, this one brighter. The wyrm paused again, silent.

A quarter of the sun remained above the horizon now. He had seven minutes, tops. While the wyrm stared at the fire in fascination, Mateo swam in a circle. Nothing but water. Water everywhere. To follow through on his hunch, he needed an abandoned island where the sea wyrm could beach itself, and he could give it *real* fire.

The magic of the gods.

Mateo's heart nearly stuttered. Wait. *That's* what Balta meant. When the gods were banished by the goddesses a thousand years ago, legends said they'd created their own land away from Alkarra, on the other side of the world. Gelas, god of ice. Solus, god of sun. Ventis, god of wind. Tontes, god of thunder. Ignis, god of fire. They took seawater from Prana, their most beloved sister, who opposed their banishment, and formed their land.

He had to form his *own* burning island, just like the gods.

Simple magic. *Archaic* magic. Turn water to earth.

Frantic, Mateo cast the same spell of fire thirty times just to keep the wyrm busy. Then he summoned all the power he could draw from his body and chose a simple Cabrerran spell. He'd found it in an old gardening grimoire as a teenager. The grimoire dated back centuries. It had helped several workers at the farms out of a pinch when crops were low and landowners threatened punishment for it. It was sluggish magic at first, but picked up speed quickly.

The magic drew from the elements around him to form earth. A flicker of fire could become earth. Water could become earth. Rocks could become earth. Then it multiplied itself. He chose water.

He wouldn't be able to anchor the makeshift island all the way to the ocean floor, but he could, hopefully, make it float with an incantation taken from Duran magic, which he'd studied last week.

The two magics had never interacted before. As far as he knew, all the magic in the Eastern Network originated from Prana, not one of her sisters. Magic could sometimes clash when it crossed goddesses. And when magic clashed . . .

Well, there would be no wyrm *or* Mateo to recover.

He grasped water in a cupped hand and started the Cabrerran spell. The water particles trembled, then crashed together into a loamy fistful of dirt. Under his breath, he cast the incantation again and again and again until the words formed a rhythmic chant. The loamy earth thickened until it filled both palms. He held his hands close to the water. Magic flowed out of him and into the dirt, turning to earth at his fingertips. It spread further out, tripling in size within moments.

The sun sank lower.

In the distance, the wyrm snuggled up to the fires, caressing each until they were extinguished. Then it let out a guttural roar and found the next one. Mateo kept only a small part of his mind focused on the wyrm, the rest on pulling magic from every portion of his body.

Every fleck of dirt that touched the water multiplied until it spread past his arm, his shoulders. It thickened and began to sink. Mateo weaved the Duran incantation into his chant to force the dirt to float. It stayed together now, but the growth slowed.

Frantic, he switched to mental recitation because he could think the magic faster than his lips could move. The thoughts streamed through him, and he focused only on the alternating spells. The dirt expanded until he clung to it instead of swimming. The wyrm approached the final, taunting flame, extinguished it, and shook the air with a livid bellow. It thrashed, looking for the next in an empty sky. Beyond it, the sun turned to a glowing fingernail of burnt orange.

Magic poured out of Mateo in sheer desperation now. Mud floated around his hands, stained his white shirt. He had to stop the incantations to cast a flame near him to draw the wyrm closer. The fire flickered overhead, massive in size thanks to the intense magic flowing out of him. The dirt began to sink again. With a shout, Mateo called it back up with Duran magic.

The island, longer than he was tall now, expanded more rapidly with each passing second. He poured out the magic, and the magic grew. It tugged at his brain. His muscles. Even his bones felt as if they were drained. The magic sped up, multiplying quickly.

Finally, Mateo climbed on top of the earth pile and stood there, chanting. The island bobbed in the waves, but remained above the water, as broad as his own house. He continued, but fell to his knees. The magic seemed to possess him now. Flew out of him. Drained him. Pitied him in its ultimate power. As if he'd become the magic, and the magic took over.

He gave it more, and the magic took it. The dirt grew into an island he could pace across, an almost-perfect circle. Fingers of dirt crawled from the center, expanding outward. The wyrm pursued the hot flame overhead, seeming to speak with deep curiosity as it pushed closer.

Exhausted, Mateo stepped closer to the edge of his new island. With each passing second, the island doubled in breadth. Its sheer size meant it touched more water, transforming it into dirt. It also required more power. Nearly all his life force.

Mateo stopped the loop of incantations. He cast a different spell to keep the island floating for a few minutes. His legs gave out as he lurched into the water the moment the sea wyrm arrived on the strange shore.

Paddling to the surface required more energy than he had to give, but he dug deeper. Forced himself up. The wyrm lay on top of the island now, prodding the fire with its mouth. More of the wyrm slithered onto the dirt. Mateo kept the island growing with silent magic as the wyrm coiled its body on the earthen rug in the middle of the sea.

The sun dropped, nothing more than a slice of heat the width of a sliver.

Mateo set the island on fire.

Flames exploded in a rolling ball that mushroomed into the air. He ducked under the water while the wall of heat passed, then he popped back up. His vision swam. He felt groggy from fatigue, from the absence of magic within him. As if using it all would separate him from life. Somehow, he kept his legs and arms moving, but his mind felt like mush.

Orange light consumed the island in between his long blinks. Seawater lapped at his face. The fire spell he'd used was simple and ancient. It could burn for an hour. By that time, the wyrm would be dead—he hoped—and the chunk of magical earth gone.

The wyrm made a high-pitched sound and slid its massive body onto the island in coils. It curled up to the fire and writhed happily within the flames. Mateo blinked. Was the wyrm shrinking in the fire? Was it a trick of the dying light, or was the wyrm actually growing smaller in the flames?

Its body began to char, but it snuggled deeper, deeper, deeper.

As the very last hint of sun sank just below the edge of the world, Mateo released his token onto the edge of the island and summoned the very last of his magic. He might not have enough to make it. Might die halfway through the transport.

He had never been so . . . tired.

The transportation spell tugged him away. Mateo barely felt the pressure. The rib-cracking sensation of displacing the world to move so quickly through it. Seconds later, the wet slap of sand against his face greeted him just before he glimpsed Balta's startled expression.

Mateo collapsed onto the sand.

21

VITTORIA

An hour and a half after he left, Mateo returned.

Two of Benat's men arrived with Mateo shuffling between them, his head bowed. His wet shirt trembled in the wind. She curbed the urge to run to him and throw herself into his arms. No, she didn't have that right yet. They were . . . friends.

She replayed the intimate moment from last night. The heavy touch of his hand on her face. The strange dichotomy of being so angry, then letting it go as she comprehended the bigger picture.

Was that friendship?

Was the drive to see him every day, to talk with him every night, something that happened to friends?

The only friend she'd ever truly had was Zuri, unless she counted Sannara—which seemed different. Vittoria and Zuri laughed together. Giggled over her strangely shaped letters or her simple incantations that went awry. Like the day she turned sand into an azalea but had wanted *azult*, a delicious bread made from grains that grew like melons in the farms.

Vittoria set those thoughts aside as Mateo approached. Friendship or not, she'd feared for him, and he'd clearly survived. She forced her shoulders to relax and her fists to loosen. Mateo stopped several paces away, just outside the beach house. Five of Benat's men ringed the perimeter and kept wary eyes on the horizon, the beach, and beyond.

Vittoria devoured Mateo with her eyes. His hair was waterlogged and covered with sand. He looked pale and exhausted, but he was alive and on his own feet. Mateo met her gaze as Benat's men returned to their positions, leaving the two of them alone.

"Are you all right?" she whispered.

"Fine. I promise. Just weary."

He held out his hands, which she accepted in hers with relief. His calluses against her fingertips proved all the reassurance she needed. His wet shirt felt cold, translucent even in the torchlight.

"You passed?"

He twined their fingers together, and her heart sang at the affectionate look in his eyes.

"I passed."

"And Romeo?"

A shadow fell over his gaze. "He passed as well, but I don't know how. I was too tired to ask. He finished just after me with only seconds to spare."

Darkness had fallen over the beach like a quiet blanket, revealing a few stars ahead of the impending storm. She felt disoriented with both relief and despair. A successful Test of Magic behind them meant they'd advanced. There was still hope.

It also meant he had to kill his brother.

Vittoria squeezed his hands. "I'm sorry, Mateo."

He studied her, then pulled her body against his and held her. He smelled like salt water and seaweed. The shirt was cold against her arms and wetted her dress, but she didn't care. His weight sagged against her for a moment, and she accepted it. If she let him, she had no doubt he'd fall asleep on his feet.

"Come inside," she murmured. "You can tell me everything in the morning, after you rest."

Relief and uncertainty permeated the foggy air the next morning.

While the ocean rolled outside under a white sky, Vittoria sat at the table next to Zuri, drinking sweetened hot coffee. Zuri skimmed through a newsbook that Benat had brought, murmuring under her breath every now and then.

"They're saying you're in league with the rebels." Zuri's finger tapped the front page. Then she flipped several pages. "But back here, they say that you saved three landowner wives from certain death when a bat attacked and then turned into a rebel at the ball. Why are bats always considered bad animals?" she muttered with a shake of her head. When she lifted her gaze to Vittoria's, amusement brightened her face. "You had a busy night at the ball, simultaneously destroying the Network yet saving the landowners. Are you tired from all that?"

A hint of a smile rose to Vittoria's lips. "Very tired."

Zuri patted her arm. "Have a drink. We're going to start transformation today. You never know when disguising yourself could save your life. I was most impressed with your everyday household incantations. Please, use your magic to clean the dishes whenever you like. If only my children learned to do that, my life would have been easier. Not that we had dishes to do . . ."

Vittoria did laugh this time as Zuri grabbed an empty plate. "Do you miss having young children at home?" she asked. "I miss Eneko, and he's not *truly* mine."

Zuri inhaled, then grinned. "All three of them were monsters when they were little, but I loved it. What I was able to see of it, anyway, when I wasn't working. Now they make grandbabies for me and they live with me, so I'm very happy. Especially since Mateo found me."

Vittoria frowned. All the time they'd spent together in lessons, and Vittoria still didn't know that much about Zuri's life.

"How did he find you?"

Zuri stood with her hip propped against the table, brow wrinkled. "My husband died six months ago. So I was alone in my closet of a house in Necce Coven. One night after his death, a rebel riot started at a nearby landowner tavern, and the flames spread. La Salvatorra came in, woke me, and pulled me out before my house collapsed. In the process, a board fell on my head and knocked me out. He and Benat nursed me back to health here." She lifted her arms. "And I stayed until I was better. Then he offered to pay me to help him with the food baskets and now to help you."

Vittoria felt a sense of affection for Mateo rise within her. He collected witches who needed help, then set them back on their feet to take care of themselves and help others. If there was any better definition of a Giver, she couldn't think of it. That was the Network she wanted for Eneko, and that was the Network Mateo fought for.

"You do the food preparation at home now?" Vittoria asked Zuri.

Zuri smiled warmly. "Mateo helped me find a place where my children and grandchildren and I could live together. I prepare the food and blankets there. I didn't want to be parted from my children, so we still live together."

With that, she spun and headed for the kitchen, plates in hand. It left Vittoria in the silence of the house, save for the swish of water and rattle of dishware. She eyed the open newsbook, able to pick out a few words. *Landowners* and *Vittoria* and *High Priest*. Zuri had been teaching her the most pertinent words first, even if they were longer.

Vittoria leaned back against the wall, adjusting herself on the floor cushion. The low table was right at her arm height as she reached for the coffee and sipped it. Thick, from the sugary pastry used to sweeten it, but zesty all the same. Her mind wandered back to a brief explanation of the Test of Magic Mateo had given her and Benat before retiring to bed.

Sea wyrms. Gods. Magic.

Every day, she felt more overwhelmed by this world that she knew so little of. Until she'd escaped Mayfair Coven, she hadn't realized that workers lived in bubbles. Starving bubbles. Desperate bubbles. Bubbles that kept them ignorant of the world around them.

On purpose, no doubt. They knew so little, how could they ever survive were the system to break?

The sheer amount of magic Mateo must have used to win awed her. No doubt his work as La Salvatorra helped enable such a feat. He'd spoken of the different magic systems he'd studied for years as he searched out incantations that would aid his work as La Salvatorra. Unknown magic that the Guardians weren't trained to anticipate or sense.

You feel magic, mostly, he had said through a yawn. *Sense it. When you're familiar enough, it's a part of you.*

She opened her fingers and studied them, as if her magic resided there. So far, magic felt like nothing more than words and study. Like laundry. Taking something from one state to another. Magic was more like cold, unexplained science than mystery. She felt no emotion about it yet.

Then again, she and magic were reluctant acquaintances.

With a shake of her head, she turned her thoughts. There wasn't time to focus on any of that. The Test of Courage and Test of Magic lay behind them. Now, she had to think about moving forward in the two weeks before Mateo would face his brother.

In other words, it was time to find Esperanza.

Hodei's whispered words at the ball were a stark reminder. But he'd revealed something else, hadn't he? *There is much for you to discover.* And, fortunately, the chaos at the ball had revealed that she knew a rebel after all.

"*Allo.*"

Mateo's sleepy morning voice came from just behind her. Vittoria straightened as he sat in the chair next to her.

"*Allo,*" she replied. "You look . . ."

"Like death?"

Before he fell asleep, he'd bathed the salt water out of his hair, which had dried in silky locks this morning. She barely kept her fingers from winding through the strands. Wrinkles still lined his weary eyes, but he wasn't so pale today. He fought off a yawn.

"I was going to say *better.*" She smiled at him. "But, yes. You still look as if you have some recovering to do."

He winked as Zuri bustled back into the room, a pile of things in her arms—a wooden spool of sewing string. An apple. A carved duck. A string of seashells. And a half-dead flower with leaves so thin they were as translucent as onion skin.

"Of course." Zuri sent him a sharp glare as she set each item down on the table across from Vittoria. "You *would* wake up just as I was going to start a transformation lesson with La Principessa! Now I have to go make your breakfast and interrupt my flow. You're trouble, Majesty."

He grinned at her. "I will happily get my own breakfast, Zuri. Somehow, I survived on my own for years."

"And it's a wonder to us all. No, I won't stand by and let you burn the house down. Thank you, but I'll grab it before we start."

The twinkle in her eye as she slapped his shoulder and brushed past them gave Vittoria a little smirk. Bluster aside, Zuri thrilled at any opportunity to take care of someone else.

Mateo settled back against the chair and rubbed a hand over his face. Vittoria stared at the items on the tabletop, wondering what Zuri would have her transform them into. Her thoughts were scrambled now that Mateo was in the room. Not knowing which direction to nudge them, she let them go. Thinking around him wasn't easy. He sucked up all her attention with his kind eyes.

Mateo blinked out of his own tunnel, then turned to her.

"Balta sent me a letter this morning." His voice was low and quiet, like the gentle roll of the ocean. "The battle with Romeo will be in two weeks."

Two weeks and the world will be decided, she thought. Mateo would be alive or dead.

Before she could feel her fear or ask how *he* felt about having to kill his brother, he continued, "Tonight, I would like to bring La Principessa and La Salvatorra together in downtown Necce, officially. We have appeared together, but not with you declaring yourself as La Principessa. Tonight I want to announce it. Are you ready to truly be her?"

Her entire body rebelled. She wanted to scream, *No!*

But how could she refuse when he'd almost died fighting for the Network last night? He seemed so fearless. So unafraid of what he was throwing himself into. He deserved loyalty, at least. Still, she trembled at the thought. She wasn't a Giver and didn't want to lie. But, in some ways, she *was* a Giver. Some perceived her that way, at least.

Could she take that hope away?

"Yes," she finally said.

He smiled at her hesitant response. She felt the warmth in his gaze all the way to her bones, as if he sensed her trouble and wanted to reassure her. Seconds later, his expression darkened. "I'm concerned for the workers in Necce Coven. Benat's men reported to me just now that Romeo sent

Guardians into the city last night to seek revenge for the ballroom incident."

She clenched her fist around her dress. "Is he piking them?"

"He's trying to, yes."

Vittoria straightened, her coffee forgotten in a sudden burst of dread. "But how could he know who they were? They all wore robes. There's tens of thousands of workers in the whole Network. Someone may have lied about it being the Necce Coven."

Mateo shrugged but appeared troubled. "He likely doesn't know, so he'll punish whoever he can find. He's already been on a rampage. My contacts say that ten witches were piked early this morning."

"Then let's go."

She started to stand, but he pulled her back down.

"Not yet, *masuna*."

The endearment calmed her, but she wasn't assuaged. "I cannot just sit here," she murmured. "What if—"

"It's why I want La Salvatorra and La Principessa to be seen together. The workers need hope more than ever. We'll be out all night, if you can manage it. There is nothing we can do this moment except get ourselves killed in daylight," Mateo said. His tone suggested he was saying it more for himself than for her. "The rebels acted, and innocents will bear the consequences. That's why the rebels are so dangerous."

"But this is wrong!"

"I agree." He put a hand on her flushed cheek. "Tonight, we will try to make it right, but we must be wise. While we wait, let's gather supplies to distribute. Benat and you and me will make a plan. It's likely that Romeo will act more dramatically at night. Do you agree?"

Her thoughts settled into an unusual calm. Thanks to his steady voice and reassuring gaze, it was clear to her. He was right. Acting rashly—no matter how much she wanted to—wouldn't serve anyone. With Eneko and her family safe, she had the luxury of waiting without as much fear.

Finally, she nodded.

"Then I ask only that you listen to me whatever I say tonight." He let his hand fall from her face, and she wanted to call it back. "It may require some courage to stand as La Principessa. But we will keep you safe."

"I will."

He smiled and brushed a warm finger down her cheek. "You'll do beautifully, *masuna*."

She longed for him to cup her chin and dissolve her into a kiss. To feel the heat and strength of his body pressed against hers in a physical reassurance that went beyond words. There was so much unknown between them, even if they were betrothed. Did she want to invest so much emotion into a man who might die in two weeks?

Instead of drawing his lips to hers, she settled for soaking up his touch.

"We leave at twilight," he murmured.

22

MATEO

The coppery smell of blood filled the air.

Mateo stood atop the *eliza* of the Giver La Principessa, a spell concealing him from sight. Instead of his usual rotating transformative magic, he settled on one persona for now. The lack of magical pull was a relief. Despite a day of rest and strategizing with Benat and Vittoria, he still felt drained. But this couldn't wait, and his energy had been replenished enough.

The sun sank in the distant sky, replaced by shadows from the other side of the world. Necce lay mostly quiet, except for muffled shouts to the northwest. Then a scream, and then another.

Vittoria stood next to him in her creamy cape, a magnolia rustling behind her left ear. "Romeo is attacking?" she asked.

"Yes. The East End Coven now. They moved through Necce Coven last night. Our spies tell us that Romeo received information that East End witches participated in the attack, but I think he's just using that as an excuse. He'll punish each coven, if you ask me. Let's go somewhere closer. I know a spot we can observe from."

Benat and his men had stashed several crates of supplies that La Principessa could give to the workers once Romeo's raids ceased. And not just food. Clean rags. Soap. Potions.

As he'd expected, Romeo had allowed the day to proceed with little action, but that truce had ended just before twilight. Workers in the East End Coven foolish enough to be in the main alleys were crying out in fear.

Such purges had happened before. Guardians were doubtless marching through the alleys, setting new pikes and seeking any witches still on the road. They'd pounce from the shadows to take rebels away to the *vinsela*, a special prison in the middle of the Saltu. If any rebel or worker could escape from its magic, they died in the jungle. If they didn't escape, they'd rot in a cell until they died of neglect or in a mass execution. The worst offenders, like landowners who sided with workers, ended up in Carcere, a special prison on an island down the coast.

Mateo reached over, grabbed Vittoria's wrist, and gave it a little squeeze. With a quick spell, he transported them to another *eliza*, in the East End Coven. La Christianna. This was much smaller. Two stories. Dilapidated stone. It had once been a small shop. When the second-story floor fell through, landowners abandoned it and the workers moved in. It was a quiet place amid the stench of the East End Coven, where the air always smelled like refuse and rot.

Mateo stood on top of the *eliza*, still concealed, with only Vittoria's warmth at his side. Benat followed. Mateo kept a firm hand on Vittoria's arm while he maintained his invisibility spell. She cast her own invisibility spell and held it well enough, though her feet and hair sometimes slipped past the magic.

Not being able to see one's own body was disorienting. Not seeing it while standing at great heights would likely dizzy her, but she remained quiet at his side. Still, he kept a hand on her, just in case.

Bursts of light came from the Road of La Immanuella. The magical fire would be from the Guardians, likely meant to disorient a group of witches or illuminate an alley so they could take them to prison or pike them.

"I must get closer," Mateo said. "Stay out of sight on the rooftops, but follow me. You'll know when you need to act."

"We will," Benat said from somewhere behind him.

"Be safe," Vittoria replied.

Mateo took two steps back, ran, and leaped onto the stone roof of another building, then dropped to a staircase tucked into an alley just off the Road of La Immanuella. As he'd expected, chaos unfurled in the streets.

Guardians swept down the road in groups of five. Workers had already scrambled to whatever holes they could find. He thought he heard a whimper below the stairs. One glance down confirmed that three children were huddling together. The oldest had his arms around two young girls. He stared at Mateo in undisguised fear when Mateo dropped the invisibility spell. Mateo shook his head once, conjured the glowing blue sign of La Salvatorra above his palm, and winked.

The little boy's face contorted with relief.

Mateo extinguished the sign and murmured, "Stay here until you've counted to one hundred, then take the back alleys until you find your home again. I will put a spell over all three of you that will keep you invisible for fifteen minutes. Can you return by then?"

The boy nodded. Mateo cast a spell on the children to hide them and moved to the edge of the alley. He grimaced. Each incantation tugged at his already-tapped resources. And it made him nervous to go out under one face instead of many.

Pikes stood at alternating distances along the road. They'd be filled with heads soon enough, at this rate. A shout drew Mateo's attention. He turned to find a circle of ten Guardians. Two of the regular five-man patrol groups had come together for something. Only a few steps more brought their voices into range. He kept to the edges of the street, casting spells to hide what witches he found trembling in the shadows.

"Kill him!"

A captain yelled the order. The most a conscripted witch could expect out of military service was to be a foot Guardian. The landowners sent all their sons for a stint in the military—the good ones reached the rank of captain, or higher. This captain appeared to be somewhat young. Maybe twenty-one, when few reached that rank before age twenty-seven. Had Hodei grown desperate? Why push such young men into leadership?

In the middle of the circle of Guardians was a young Guardian with armor too big for his gangly body. His helmet almost covered his eyes. He couldn't be more than thirteen.

In front of him knelt an even younger worker boy. Eleven, at most. He had scraggly hair that fell to his shoulders and dirt caked under his trembling fingernails. Blood stained his clothes in brown and crimson. Conscripted to the butchers here, no doubt. He'd probably been out on a delivery and returned too late. A sob peeped out of him as he tried to curl into a ball and hide.

"Kill him!" the captain yelled again.

"B-but sir!" the young Guardian squeaked. "I-it's my brother. He's done nothing wrong. He w-w-wasn't at the ballroom."

A hard silence fell on the circle of Guardians. Mateo didn't bother with a concealing spell as he slowly worked his way around the edge of the circle. He glimpsed the captain in between bodies. For a split second, indecision appeared on the captain's features. He'd already issued a command —he had to force the Guardian to see it through or be known as weak. But the other Guardians in the circle were young workers forced into the service. They lived in these streets. Knew these witches. Prayed to the same Givers. Could all of them overwhelm him? Possibly, if they pounced fast enough.

Mateo glanced above the road to the shadowy sky. A shape moved on a nearby rooftop and nodded once.

A vein popped in the captain's forehead as he finally screamed again, "Kill him or die yourself!"

The Guardian stared at his brother in horror. "I-I c-can't," he said to the captain. Tears made his voice wobbly. His knees quaked as he dropped his sword. It clattered against the ground with damning finality. "I-I can't kill him."

The captain grabbed the Guardian by the neck and shoved him down until the boy's forehead slammed into the cobblestones. His sword hissed as he drew it from his scabbard. Dazed, the boy blinked.

"Remove your armor," the captain muttered.

Another Guardian stepped forward to stop the captain, but was held back by a friend. The terrified young Guardian fumbled as he pulled off his half-leather, half-metal armor to expose his back. Old scars, silver in the dim torchlight, gleamed off his ribs.

The younger brother gaped, eyes wide with tears and horror. "No!" he screamed, a desperate, throaty sound.

The captain kicked him.

Mateo glanced up to see a definite stir of shadows atop the closest building. A flash of white in the night. He issued a spell as the captain put the tip of his sword against the young Guardian's rib cage.

"For your insubordination," the captain said.

A shocking blue light exploded overhead. The captain winced and held up an arm to shield his eyes. The sword tip dropped to the dirt as one of the Guardians cried out. The sign of La Salvatorra floated over the circle.

"La Salvatorra!" voices exclaimed.

A command rang from the rooftop. "Leave that boy alone!"

Vittoria stepped into sight in a circle of torchlight that Benat must have cast, magnolia flower illuminated behind her left ear. As always, she wore a simple dress with no adornments. The bluish glow from the sign of La Salvatorra cast her in an even brighter light. Her elegant ivory cape, so like a magnolia itself, rustled behind her in a gentle breeze. Her expression was firm.

Five of the ten Guardians dropped to their knees with startled cries. From a nearby window came the muffled sob of, "La Principessa!"

"If you value your life," Vittoria said to the captain, "you will leave those boys alone."

The captain gritted his teeth. "Pray to your Givers," he shouted to the Guardians on their knees. "I don't take orders from a woman. Now all of you will die!"

"Not necessarily," Mateo quipped as he advanced. He kept his eyes on the captain as he withdrew a sword. "Unless you would like to fight La Salvatorra?"

Murmurs rippled through the circle. Several emotions flickered through the captain's expression under the glow of La Salvatorra's mark.

"No?" Mateo tsked. "Well, that's a shame. Those pikes are waiting for a head, aren't they?"

Mateo issued a spell. Ropes snaked around the captain's hands. Another spell forced him to his knees.

"Traitor!" the captain finally sputtered. "You will see justice for this!"

Mateo smiled. "Correct," he called. "That is what I am, is it not? And that is La Principessa, Giver of Hope. I suggest you remember that we work together in defense of workers. And you have been found guilty this night."

The captain attempted to overpower Mateo's magic and free himself from the ropes around his wrists, but Mateo silenced him with a knock to the side of his head. He fell unconscious to the cobblestones.

From down the road, another patrol of Guardians marched toward them. No doubt they'd seen the sign of La Salvatorra. Mateo had only a few moments before they would go invisible and spring into an attack.

"I want no harm to come to this captain," Vittoria said. "He will be handled according to justice's demands. If the Network is to unite, we must stop the senseless killing and trust the Givers."

Astonished murmurs rippled through the crowd. Mateo mentally tipped a hat to her cleverness.

"The Givers have come," another Guardian exclaimed. "Our prayers are coming true."

Benat's men would transport the captain to the *vinsela* tonight and stash him in a cell. The Guardians there would find him in the morning or the next day, whenever the feeding schedule allowed it. Wallowing in a prison cell in the Saltu might give him some humility. The two young boys would be offered a chance to join Benat's men.

"Salvation has come!" A witch leaned out of a nearby window. "La Principessa and La Salvatorra are with us!"

Mateo bowed, gallantly sliding into his role as the somewhat-extravagant Giver. The larger-than-life personality sometimes confused or distracted the Guardians, allowing Benat and his men to more easily do their hidden work. It also firmly separated La Salvatorra from Mateo.

The footfalls of the oncoming Guardians sounded on the stone now. More witches spoke from the houses, the alleys. They spilled onto nearby rooftops as they emerged from hiding and dropped to a knee while facing Vittoria.

The Guardian reinforcements moved more quickly now, but they were a smaller group than when they'd started. Behind them, Mateo thought he saw Guardians kneeling on the road.

No time to wait.

Mateo grabbed the two boys by their arms. They hardly had time to gasp in surprise before he summoned all the magic he could pull out of his body and transported them away.

He could only take them to the rooftop behind Vittoria where they wouldn't be seen. Once there, he collapsed under the strain. He'd never transported two before—hadn't been positive it was possible—but was gratified that all his years of magical work were paying off. Benat appeared next to them. He rested a hand over the mouth of the youngest and motioned for them to be quiet.

Wide-eyed, they both nodded.

In front of them, Vittoria stood silhouetted against the mark of La Salvatorra.

"Peace is all that I ask," she said to those on the street. "It's all we want. Of my workers, I demand respect for our desire for peace. Bring no harm to the Guardians. Guardians, leave now with your lives. If we cannot respect each other and come to understand that we are all witches, no peace will be possible."

Mateo motioned Benat back to Vittoria with a jerk of his head. Benat disappeared under a concealing spell. He'd work any required magic in Mateo's place now. Just a regular night for La Salvatorra: Mateo distracted Guardians by being La Salvatorra, and Benat and his men used stealth and magic to save whomever they could.

A moment of silence fell over the scene in the wake of Vittoria's words.

Mateo struggled to his feet, exhausted already, and moved closer to the edge of the building. The newly arrived captain struggled to know what to do when the other captain disappeared without warning, transported away by one of Benat's concealed men.

"You have ten seconds to leave with your lives, Guardians!" Vittoria cried. "Or you'll see La Salvatorra's justice on your own heads."

Benat's men lurked unseen in the shadows. The Guardians, too distracted to feel for magic in use, wouldn't see an attack coming if they tried to press this.

Finally, the captain barked, "Guardians, return to your posts. Now!"

"Leave those Guardians who have shown obedience to me," Vittoria demanded. Her voice didn't waver, not for a moment. The Guardians who had taken a knee remained in their spots in silence. Some of them trembled and stared at the road.

Reluctantly, the rest filed away.

Benat murmured a command to three of his men, who nodded and disappeared. One of them reappeared in the middle of the remaining Guardians and began to speak to them.

Mateo stepped forward. Workers still watched from windows, alleys, storefronts, and hidden nooks.

"I am La Salvatorra!" he called. "For the last ten years, I have worked among you. Now, La Principessa and I are here to bring you hope and justice. You are not alone."

Muted cries followed. The sound of more screams, the stench of smoke, and the crackle of magic came from the entrances to the East End Coven. Mateo glanced that way, then pointed to Joska in the circle. "This is Joska. If you follow him, you'll be safe. You need not return to Hodei's service."

With that, the burning blue light faded. Once it was gone, Mateo collapsed wearily. In the darkness, Vittoria retreated out of sight of the street. Benat appeared next to him as Vittoria put a hand on Mateo's shoulder.

"Can you do this again?" she asked with worry in her gaze. "There are attacks in other parts of Necce. I can hear them out of the Samsa Coven now."

He looked at Benat, who nodded once.

"Add the two boys to the group of Guardians who will be defecting," Mateo said quietly. The two boys clutched each other with a mixture of relief and terror. "They'll be fine. So will I. I have the energy we need."

Mateo allowed Vittoria to pull him to his feet and ignored her skeptical expression. Her concern eased his mind, and he didn't know why. She put a hand on his face, tears in her eyes.

"Thank you," she murmured, "for saving them."

"It was La Principessa." He brushed a lock of hair out of her face. "You'll make a wonderful High Priestess, Vittoria. Come, let's see what more we can do. We need to let as many workers know of our work together as possible. Word has probably reached Romeo and Hodei already."

Worry crossed her face.

He put a hand on her cheek. "You will be safe from Hodei, I promise."

Something flashed in her eyes. She nodded. "I trust you."

Vittoria followed Mateo down a staircase on the side of the building. They'd use as little magic as possible in their quest to help workers, just to save him the energy. Benat and one of his men disappeared with the two boys.

Mateo pulled Vittoria toward the Samsa Coven, already alight with fire and screams.

23

VITTORIA

The next morning, Vittoria yawned as she ladled another helping of soup into a bowl, then passed it to the awaiting young man. He mumbled a thank-you, head bent low to avoid her gaze, then stumbled away. She ignored the awkward sense of awe that all these young men had toward her after she'd helped snatch them up from the streets last night. Then again, she was supposed to be a *Giver*, although she didn't think that title would ever feel natural.

Or perhaps they'd just never expected La Principessa to ladle soup.

Thirty refugees had joined them last night as they'd roamed Necce, distributing food, blankets, and healing supplies as they could. All thirty refugees were now packed into Mateo's house, filling every available space. Once they'd eaten enough to sate their seemingly endless bellies, Benat and his men would transport them to the quarry far outside Necce, near her family.

A restless energy made the house feel cramped, particularly with all the new witches. The desperate former Guardians found spots to sit, then stared at the floor as if stunned by all that had happened.

Had she looked like that when she first arrived? Were they able to comprehend how their lives had changed, or did they even try? The jolt of entering a brand-new world could be disorienting at best. Terrifying at worst.

How easily she remembered.

She gave them all a kind smile as she refilled cups of water. Zuri brushed by, two baskets of fresh *pitta* bread in her hands. All of these Guardians ate faster than Vittoria and Zuri could supply food. One of Zuri's daughters, a quiet young woman with a fast smile but little to say, had arrived to help in the kitchen. She disappeared every now and then to return to the farms for more food. Three burlap bags of grain lined the kitchen floor now, along with a few baskets of apples.

Mateo had retired to his room to rest. He'd collapsed on the bed and fallen asleep seconds later. At one of the tables, Benat and his men talked in the background. Vittoria loosely tracked their conversation, relieved to be back safely, but fatigued herself. Romeo's attempts at revenge last night had been harrowing. The Guardians had finally retreated for good after midnight, but she and the men had been out until dawn assisting workers who needed help healing, locating lost relatives, or just getting home.

"Ideal situation," Joska said, interrupting her thoughts. He was a strong witch, maybe eighteen, with a thirst to prove himself. When excited, he had eager eyes the color of chocolate. He leaned forward. "We keep doing this, Benat! Every night. It will pull the Guardians out of their force, losing Hodei his men. Then he'll be less likely to attack. It can only work to our advantage."

"Or he'll attack more," Benat muttered.

"The rebels will think we're in league with them, and they'll only grow bolder," said another. "We need to make our position clear to them, at least."

A frown marred Joska's expression, and his energy deflated. "The *vinsela* was empty last night."

Benat's brow wrinkled. "What?"

Joska nodded solemnly. "Empty. We hid the captain so he'd be out of hearing for the night, but they may not find him for a few days if it remains that empty."

Benat's fingers twitched as he shook his head. "Another mass execution."

No one said a word until Benat spoke to everyone in the room. "For as long as Romeo commits violence against workers and Mateo has the strength, we will continue this work." His gaze flickered to Vittoria. "La Principessa will always give her witches hope."

They'd stopped referring to her as *Lady* and solely called her *La Principessa* now. She thought of the dearth of rebels on the streets last night. How furious it made her that workers had paid for the rebels' crimes. Thoughts of the rebels led her back to Esperanza. Every hour that passed without information on the deceased High Priestess left her throat a bit tighter.

Did Hodei feel the same way?

Was he already planning how he'd harm her or her family?

Should she just confess it all to Mateo now and gamble on whether he'd stop her from going to the rebels herself? Maybe they could take her family somewhere else, at least?

A pot of soup bubbled in a cauldron over the fire. She stirred it with a wooden spoon, lost in thought. Zuri bustled by with a basket filled with apples and an exclamation about hungry men. The apples weren't crisp anymore, but the men devoured them anyway.

Finally, the food rush slowed.

Benat's men wearily transported the refugees away one at a time. Eventually, the newcomers were all gone, and Benat disappeared to rest. Three of his men stayed behind on duty. The rest left to sleep. Zuri's daughter transported away with a soft smile and a nod to Vittoria.

Only Zuri and Vittoria remained.

"Well." Zuri collapsed onto a chair. "I'm exhausted. You must be beyond so after being up all night *and* helping here. Thank you, though. That would have been a mess without your hands to feed those hungry mouths!"

She was far beyond exhausted. Still, her mind wouldn't settle. It felt like a school of fish, darting here and there.

Zuri waved at her. "Sleep," she said. "I'll clean up. Not that there's anything *to* clean. They even ate the crumbs. The poor souls."

"First, can I ask you a question?"

"Of course."

"It's sort of an odd one, and I would prefer you didn't mention it to Mateo."

Zuri's interest deepened. She set down the dishes she'd gathered and faced Vittoria fully. It gave Vittoria a moment to wonder whether she should have asked. The two of them had grown close, but would Zuri confide in Mateo anyway? Zuri gestured for her to continue with a nod.

"Do you know anything of Mateo's mere, Esperanza?" Vittoria asked.

Zuri's eyebrows knitted together. For a moment, she seemed puzzled, as if rooting through her mind. Then she shook her head. "No. I remember when she was High Priestess, of course, but he's never really spoken of her."

"Does Benat?"

She shrugged. "Maybe. If he does, he's never talked about her, either. Why do you ask?"

Vittoria forced a smile. "Curiosity, I suppose. Everyone is so secretive about her. Mateo. The newsbooks. Romeo. The average witch on the street doesn't know much, I'd wager." She put a hand on her chest. "She's . . . like a ghost."

"That's what death brings upon us." But Zuri eyed her more carefully.

"The reality that I may soon be High Priestess hangs over me," Vittoria said quietly. She picked at a loose string on her dress. "It . . . it makes me think of the others who have gone before me. Their stories. They were . . . they were likely so much more prepared than I feel. I'm not born to this the way they were."

Not that Esperanza was, either, she thought wryly. But Esperanza had a few years of preparation, at least.

Zuri pulled her chair back out and sat down. Her hand was warm when she put it on top of Vittoria's. "You can do this, *masuna.* You are made for great things."

Vittoria swallowed. A thousand thoughts rushed to the surface. Though she'd confessed her anxieties to distract Zuri, every word had been true. Now she swam in deeper waters than she wanted to admit. For weeks, she'd been ignoring the reality that one day—if things went right—she'd have to lead all these witches. Witches who tried to worship her or wouldn't even meet her eye. Now that she'd said it out loud, she couldn't take it back and it had become all too real in her own head. It was as if the ground had fallen out from underneath her and she was left grasping for purchase.

But what if I can't do this *great thing?* she thought. *What if Mateo takes us all the way through the Law of Rights, and somehow I mess this up?*

There was still so much she didn't know. What would they do with her as La Principessa *after* Mateo won? What if they prevented a civil war? Then what? Would the workers believe that a Giver could live among them? Would they feel betrayed that she really was just a *lavanda* maid?

Zuri pressed a palm to her warm cheek as if she sensed her inner tempest. "You are enough, *masuna.* Things tend to happen exactly the way they need to. And in the moment, we rise to the occasion. We become the person we need to be. So will you. You always have been."

"Yes, you're right." Vittoria managed a smile. She gave Zuri a quick hug just to break the intensity of the air, and quietly soaked in the warmth of her maternal touch. It grounded her, giving her just enough strength to push the questions back down where they could simmer out of sight again. "Thank you, Zuri. Sometimes I just need to find my courage again."

Zuri's curious stare followed her as she slipped into the hallway that led to her room. The air felt cooler here, a welcome kiss on her flushed face.

Once in her room, she moved to the doors and peered out at the ocean, her arms folded across her middle. Fatigue slowed her thoughts. Still, she thought of Mateo sleeping. Benat resting. Most of his men would transport somewhere else to rest for the day. A skeleton crew of three would be sufficient to patrol the grounds here.

But could she sneak away from them in her exhausted state? Find the rebels herself? Ask them the right questions and hope they didn't kill her? Or worse, keep her as a bargaining chip?

No. She didn't have the energy for that.

Not tonight, anyway.

Suddenly, she felt imprisoned here. She didn't want to tell Mateo that she needed to seek out the rebels for some purpose set by his pere, but Mateo wouldn't speak of his mere. And Hodei had made it clear at the ball that he wanted her to talk *to the rebels.*

Was it just a way to get her killed?

Maybe.

But maybe there was more.

Benat's men would follow her anywhere to keep her safe, so the question was how to elude them without drawing suspicion. She forced herself out of the spiral of thoughts and let her mind float. It fluttered to her family. To Eneko. Then finally, with a gasp, she settled on a plan.

Why hadn't she thought of this before?

She exhaled, relieved. This could work. Without knowing exactly what information she sought, she'd go to the rebels and ask her questions. Then she'd satisfy this plaguing curiosity, fulfill Hodei's requirement, *and,* possibly, find information that might help them win.

She didn't even have to go into the catacombs. She simply needed to talk to a rebel, one who could be discreet. That left one witch who could help her.

Tomorrow, she would find that witch.

24

MATEO

The lulling thrum of rain greeted Mateo.

Outside, a storm churned the ocean to frothy waves. Rain sluiced down clear windowpanes and gathered in puddles. He shook his groggy head, drawn from a sleep so deep he remembered nothing but closing his eyes.

"By honor," he muttered as he rubbed his stubbled cheeks. He rolled over with a wince. His arm still twinged near the ghost panther bite every now and then, and he'd slept on it awkwardly.

Shaking that off, he looked to the window. It must be late afternoon, almost evening. Was Vittoria still sleeping? Were the Guardians safe at the quarry? A rap on the door interrupted his murky thoughts.

"Majesty?" Benat called.

"Come in." Mateo slid off his hanging bed as the door swung open.

Benat filled the doorway. "Joska has been watching the Guardians at the castle for the last hour or so," he said. "There's no reports of them preparing to go back into Necce tonight. My scouts in the covens say things have been quiet. No sign of another rampage. For now, I think Romeo is satisfied."

Mateo frowned. Were two nights of pillaging the covens enough to satisfy the landowners who demanded vengeance even though none of them had died? His still-sleepy mind took a moment to catch up.

"Think it's because La Principessa showed up?" Mateo asked.

Benat shrugged. "It's hard to tell, but I imagine our presence factored into it at least a little. We have six captains in their own prison. They'll find them eventually, but for now they may have assumed we've killed them or taken them captive. Might not want to risk any others with the end of the Law of Rights so close."

"Thank you, Benat."

Benat eyed him. "Might I suggest we wait tonight, Majesty? Go out closer to midnight?"

Mateo rubbed a hand over his face. He could probably sleep for another six hours. "A wise plan, Benat."

Benat nodded once and stepped back to retreat into the hall, then paused. "La Principessa has been quiet in her room today. She's there, and safe, but . . ."

He trailed off, allowing the implication to hang in the air. Last night had thrust La Principessa into the world in a big way. No doubt she had some feelings about that. He'd had years to adjust to the idea of workers regarding him as a Giver. Vittoria had only just begun, and last night had revealed Romeo's brutality to a new extent.

That she hadn't fled was a miracle.

"Thank you, Benat."

Benat disappeared as Mateo changed into fresh clothes, tied his hair back, and ventured into the hallway. A shuffling sound came from Vittoria's room before he knocked.

Seconds later, she called, "Come in, Mateo."

He grinned as he opened the door. "You knew it was me?"

She sat on the edge of a floor pillow with a half smile on her face. Her shining hair lay around her shoulders. She set aside a comb fashioned out of a chiseled seashell and motioned for him to come in.

"You have a special knock," she said. She yawned prettily, so demure in every movement. Her head tilted to the side as she regarded him. "How are you?"

"Fine."

"You rested well?"

"Like a rock."

Her lips quirked to one side of her face. She canted her head. "How are you *really* doing? I mean, about the upcoming battle with Romeo."

His stomach clenched at the reminder.

Ten days until he'd face his brother in a hand-to-hand battle to the death. A newsbook on Vittoria's bed revealed an article about Romeo's training schedule. Trust a landowner to glory in tactics even when the goal was killing a family member.

The final battle was simple enough. The two opponents would fight to the death in an oval of fire, using their hands only. No magic. No weapons. Nothing but fists to the finish. Mateo had the advantage of size, but Romeo was slight. Fast. All told, they'd be evenly matched, and that's what worried him the most.

He'd kept the thoughts at bay on purpose. To set aside the ugly truth: that he'd have to kill his brother to set the Network right.

He regarded the gloom outside.

"Mateo?"

He startled, realizing he'd been lost in thought for too long.

"I'm sorry." He shook his head. "I . . . I haven't allowed myself to think too much about it. It doesn't feel good, I can tell you that."

She regarded him with concern and compassion. He wanted to pull her into his arms and find reassurance from the power of her touch, but he held back. They stayed so carefully distant. She seemed to draw close, then pull away.

He allowed her that because of all he asked of her. But oh, how he wished they could have met away from all this. On the streets, where love could have blossomed between them without the weight of a Network and the question of *will I die?* hanging between them.

Vittoria beckoned him closer with a wave of her hand. He sat next to her, then leaned against the wall. As if she sensed his mood, she wedged herself into his side. He put his arm around her shoulders, grateful for the soothing touch.

"I can't imagine having to kill Anton," she murmured. "So the weight of what you bear must be enormous. If there is something I can do to help . . ."

He squeezed her against him for just a moment. "Thank you, Vittoria. I feel . . . this is something no one can help me with. Honor demands it."

She leaned her head against his shoulder. He breathed in the fragrance of her hair. Lavender, both subtle and sweet.

"If we aren't going out tonight," she said, "I would like to see my family."

She stiffened slightly in his arms, but he couldn't imagine why. She saw them every day.

"Of course."

"I plan to stay the night, but should be back mid-morning. Will it be safe for me to continue to distribute food during the day like we used to? I assume not, but . . ."

"No." He toyed with a strand of her hair, rubbing it gently between his thumb and forefinger. "It isn't safe anymore. But we can still go together at night. After you return, perhaps? We need to go back to the orchards, and some of the farms in the south of the Network."

She relaxed. "I agree."

Mateo thought of Romeo again. Then Pere. Those thoughts led to Mere, a memory of her face. A vise clenched in his chest. Could he kill his brother? He pondered the question so long that he hadn't realized Vittoria had fallen into a light sleep on his shoulder.

He remained awake, feeling every breath against his skin, her heart a steady drum next to his. The rain thrumming on the roof lulled his thoughts into a single point of clarity. There *was* something else he could do—had to do—before he could really face his brother in the final battle.

Something he had put off for far too long.

That evening, Mateo transported Vittoria to her family in time to eat dinner with them. Eneko sat on his lap and tugged his hair while they laughed together. Vittoria's expression lit up every time Eneko snuggled her —which was often—or brought her all his new toys to play with.

Then Mateo had transported away from the happy scene and right into the landowner coven. An elegant mansion that could comfortably house thirty witches stood near the beach, glittering chandeliers with beeswax candles visible through pristine windowpanes.

Mateo landed a few steps away from the open glass door on the top-floor balcony. His gaze trailed over an abandoned table littered with used dishes, chocolate crumbs, and half-empty glasses of wine. Then he crossed to the banister, leaned against it, and stared at the ocean.

Eventually, a voice came from the darkness of the room inside.

"Ten days until honor decides which of us is the greater man, brother," Romeo said as he shuffled out of the room to stand next to Mateo. They gazed out at the view without looking at each other, but Mateo could feel Romeo's tension.

Mateo regarded his younger brother out of the corner of his eye. An older version of the little boy he'd been so close to. So fond of. The horror of the day Hodei had stolen Romeo away played back through his mind. The screams. The pain. He and Romeo were inseparable once. Back when Mere smiled because Romeo was there. Because Romeo was her deepest joy.

And Mateo was her deepest reminder of a husband she loathed. A reminder she didn't really have room for.

Now, Romeo might as well have been an unknown face in a sea of landowners. Hodei's influence did that to witches. Time with him separated witches from their emotions, taught them to strategize for their own personal benefit first, then created fanatics to the cause of the landowners. Mateo couldn't even blame Romeo for what had happened between them. Maybe it was his fault. He didn't stop Hodei. Didn't offer himself up. Didn't try hard enough to break Romeo free.

He should have fought harder.

Regret filled him, and not for the first time. Romeo had once been kind. Caring. They'd played together, and Mateo missed that boy. Missed the opportunity to see who *that* Romeo would have been.

What horrors did Romeo experience living with Hodei? Eventually, anyone would have become a monster. Mateo shoved those thoughts away to glance over the world behind Romeo's sprawling mansion. Leafy fronds. Trails through a garden maintained by magic because the loose, sandy soil yielded little life. The crashing sea.

"You have nothing to say, brother?" Romeo asked, breaking Mateo's thoughts. "No glib response that honor would only choose you?"

"Honor," Mateo said, barely able to wrap his lips around the noxious word. For their ancestors, *honor* may have actually meant something. "Perhaps."

A sheet was knotted around Romeo's waist. He wore nothing else, and bruises dotted his arms, no doubt from training. Romeo had bulked up the past year. His shoulders were strong, if not meaty. He had a wiry kind of power.

Mateo eyed him. Perhaps Romeo wanted this more than he'd thought.

"Catch you at a bad time?" Mateo asked wryly.

Romeo snorted. Mateo felt Romeo's scrutiny in the dim light. Time had a strange way of changing people.

"How is your betrothed?" Romeo asked.

Romeo's nonchalance was sickening, and his game of acting indifferent had Hodei written all over it. Was it a game, though? Or had Hodei's influence shattered all vestiges of empathy? Mateo had always hoped that Romeo's indifference to other witches was smoke and mirrors, but was it?

How different he wished this life could be.

"Does Pere know you have a peace agreement already arranged—unsigned, of course—with the Central Network?" Mateo asked.

It was a stab in the dark, of course. He hardly knew Romeo, but it's what Mateo would have done in his position. Romeo loved the landowners, and he'd want a smooth transition of power. Hodei had spent years trying to gain back land he claimed the Central Network had taken from them. Since Hodei's health had failed, Romeo had pulled the Guardians away from the border to focus on defending Necce and other cities from rebel riots.

Without a proper agreement in place, however, there was no doubt the Central Network would begin harassing the East as soon as Hodei died. The landowners wouldn't like it, which meant Romeo wouldn't, either.

Romeo paused for a breath, an indication of his surprise. Maybe a chance to decide how to respond to such a wild question.

"I assume he does," Romeo said. "Pere doesn't speak with me anymore. Hasn't since the fall."

Not surprising, but interesting.

"He'd never approve." Mateo tutted. His voice mimicked Hodei's. "*Peace is a weak idea. If you want something, you fight for it, and you live prepared to fight for it until your dying day.*"

Romeo didn't even flinch, but Mateo thought he detected something in Romeo's tight expression.

"Pere has his own ideas," Romeo finally muttered.

"Many of them." Mateo nodded. "He probably doesn't like your plan to disband the Council and install a younger generation of advisors, either."

Romeo cast him a sidelong glance. That had been another wild assumption on Mateo's part, but the annoyance in Romeo's face all but confirmed it. He'd be a fool *not* to get rid of the current Council. Young blood was far more malleable. It was half of Mateo's plan, at least. There were specific councilors he'd get rid of, and others he'd keep if they were willing.

But Romeo would want to drive his already-deep stakes further into his beloved landowners. Quietly retiring older councilors, and offering those jobs to the next generation. Likely, Romeo had already made promises to many of the old goats to install their sons and ensure a stable succession of power in the family.

"You have room to talk about Pere's disapproval?" Romeo asked.

Mateo laughed. "Not at all."

"Why are you here?"

A hint of something lingered in Romeo's voice. Mateo couldn't fathom why, but he thought he heard a little boy under the words. There were a thousand reasons he'd come, but they all came down to one point.

"Mere wept over you for years," he said.

Romeo stiffened.

"That day." Mateo shook his head. "That . . . that terrible day Pere took you away . . . she was inconsolable. One of the workers had to set a blessing on her to get her to calm down. She fell asleep but woke weeping in the middle of the night."

Romeo's jaw ticked.

"Pere almost knocked me senseless when he hit me," Mateo continued. "Staying conscious was a struggle at first. But I did come after you, Romeo. My vision was almost black, but I stumbled outside to run to the castle because I didn't have the presence of mind, or the power, to transport that far. And I tried. I ran for half an hour and screamed your name until my voice was hoarse." Mateo touched his head, recalling it all. "I passed out twice. Someone must have come after me, because after the second time, I woke up at home. Mere was crying in the other room. Her sobs . . . they rang through the house for weeks."

A gentle brush of wind stirred his hair. It pulled Mateo out of the memories. He turned to Romeo, not surprised to see a glassy expression and cold eyes. It's the way Romeo had looked before the Test of Courage, before he'd gone a bit noble and given Mateo the whelp.

Before his cryptic comment that he owed Mateo something.

"I don't want to kill you, brother," Mateo said. "I wanted you to know that."

Romeo contemplated that for a long time. Mateo couldn't take the burdened silence, so he finished what he'd come to say.

"Mere always preferred you. Always. You were the sweeter son. Softer. The one who cared for her more than I did. She saw too much of Hodei in me, I think. Why do you think he took you? Who do you think he wanted to punish? Mere. It was all about getting back at Mere."

Romeo's nostrils flared.

"This wasn't about us," Mateo said, "but we have to pay for it."

"It doesn't matter," Romeo replied. "The past is over. You're a fool if you stay in it, Mateo. A distracted fool. You can't win. You could never even anticipate what—"

Romeo stopped, as if forced.

"We can come to an agreement," Mateo said. "Something else. Anything but this. We don't have to kill each other to find whatever we're chasing. There has to be a way to dissolve the Law of Rights. I can offer you a position of power. A say in decisions. Something. Anything *but* this. Romeo, we're brothers. I haven't forgotten that."

Romeo stiffened, chin tipped back to meet Mateo's challenge.

Mateo forced his shoulders to relax. His voice to soften. "We will always be brothers."

A shuffle inside caught Mateo's ear. He issued a quick spell, amplifying the sound to hear a gentle sigh, then a gasp of surprise. Feminine, for sure.

Not paid, nor a worker in the house, for Romeo wouldn't ever allow a paid girl to fall asleep, and no worker would dare be caught in a landowner bed . . .

How interesting his brother had suddenly become.

Romeo's left shoulder twitched, as if he wanted to go. "Your Vittoria surprised me at the ball," he said. The tension had left his shoulders, but he still looked uncomfortable.

Mateo affected casual surprise at the change in conversation. An intentional switch, likely. Romeo wouldn't want to talk about dissolving the Law of Rights or reconciling as brothers . . . but he might not want Mateo to pay attention to the woman inside, either.

"Vittoria surprises me constantly," Mateo murmured, allowing his affection to bleed into the words.

It threw Romeo off, because Romeo studied him for a good five seconds before he continued, "Hodei will do anything to stop you. He's not dead yet, Mateo. His mind still works like a clock, and he refuses to accept that once he dies, he won't be able to control what we do. To him, that's losing."

"And only fools lose," Mateo said.

Romeo paused to take a breath. "It means he'll do anything. *Anything.* And there's . . ."

He trailed off again. This time he swallowed, as if his throat hurt. Rage flickered across his face, then vanished.

"Why are you telling me this?" Mateo asked.

Romeo ignored that question. "You've wasted your time coming tonight, Mateo," he said instead. "Whatever affection you hold for me is your business, not mine. This isn't personal. This is who I am, and I will see this plan through to the end. I've given my life to it. I will have honor . . . even if that requires your blood on my hands. I am ready and willing. Are you?"

A question Mateo had never truly entertained before flittered through his mind.

Would Romeo actually kill him?

Frost rolled off Romeo in waves. Like the ice god, Gelas, of whom ancient history whispered darkly.

Yes, Romeo would kill him. And he wouldn't hesitate. Mateo had revealed too much affection here. Too many cards. Romeo might have suspected Mateo's struggles, but now he knew them. He'd use them against Mateo in a few short days, during the fight. Somehow.

Mateo's palms turned clammy, unable to place the little brother he'd always known with this angry, bitter man. It saddened him so deeply that the pain cut all the way to his bones.

Was he truly meant for this?

Could he actually take his little brother's life?

"Your La Principessa is being spoken of in the city," Romeo said lightly.

"La Principessa is always spoken of."

"The workers will be devastated when they learn she is a mere witch, like the rest of them. Have you thought of that?"

A razor-sharp edge entered his tone. There it was—the threat against Vittoria he'd been anticipating. As he'd expected, Romeo didn't want to kill Vittoria. He wanted to kill *La Principessa*.

"Perhaps that won't be necessary," Mateo replied.

Romeo laughed, but it was mirthless. "That's always been you, Mateo. Carefree. One step behind a plan that you make as you go. You pop in and out of life with no steadiness at all. And yet you want to be High Priest?"

Mateo's jaw clenched.

Romeo's placid expression dropped into a scowl. Passion burned like flames in his voice. "How can you still hold onto this plan of yours? How can you even hold onto affection for me? Your plan is even wilder than I expected. La Salvatorra? La Principessa? You've been tromping around the city for two years helping workers?"

Mateo kept his surprise hidden by sheer force of will. If Romeo knew about his work as La Salvatorra, did the others landowners? He pulled himself back out of his shock.

"Ten." Mateo met his gaze with half a smile. "I've been doing it for ten years, but they just gave me the name the last two. Did you just find out?"

Romeo's nostrils flared. "You can never win the long game, Mateo. If you're really hoping to restore some sort of honor, you won't through your leadership. You will not save the workers by fighting for them. By *leading* them. To what? Death? Destruction?"

"To better," Mateo said. "I will lead all of the witches to better."

Romeo ignored him, disgust in his voice. "Workers cannot stand against magic and Guardians and progress. They will desert you before you can save them. Surely you must see that. So, why? Why make this worse for them? Insubordination will not be tolerated by the next leader."

Romeo hit a hot, painful mark inside him. It vibrated, shaking him.

Why am I doing this?

There had always been doubts and would always be doubts in a world such as this. But Mateo felt oddly exposed. Vulnerable. Open. A thousand new doubts whispered from the depths of his mind, finally uncaged.

He was doing this because he must. Because their family had brought this dark legacy to the East, and he would undo it to strive for something better.

That had to be enough.

He met Romeo's exasperated glare. For several long moments, they stared at each other. Then Mateo put a hand on Romeo's shoulder.

"I love you, brother. Even if you do kill me, I'll still love you and won't blame you. Let that be the end of it."

A vast, fathomless chasm lived between the two of them. One he had no idea how to manage. One he had no courage to cross. There had long been too much water under that bridge. Now the bridge was swamped. Gone. For all intents and purposes, his brother was dead. With a final thrum of agony, Mateo mentally separated the brother he loved from the usurper trying to claim the throne. In his little brother's place was the implacable Romeo.

A different man Mateo had to kill.

Mateo stepped back. Romeo's glare deepened as Mateo hesitated, then transported away without another word.

25

VITTORIA

E neko lay on the wooden floor, legs straight in the air, eyes glued on
his grandmere. Vittoria's mere stood above him, arms spread out to
encompass the massive sea dragon from her story.

"And then," Mere said, "the sea dragon hissed. Out of the ocean it
leaped to bite La Principessa in half." She stopped. Her back straightened
as she shook a finger back and forth. Her voice dropped to a dramatic whisper. "But the sea dragon could not."

"La Principessa stopped it with a single hand!" Eneko cried.

"That's exactly right. She banished that enemy back to the ocean, and it
has never been seen in all of Alkarra ever again."

"Just like she'll save us." He tilted his head to the side. "Only the dragon
isn't real. But she'll still save us. Maybe from Hodei?"

Mere leaned over to kiss his forehead. "*Wa*, my boy. *Wa*."

Vittoria watched the warm scene from where she sat curled up next to
Pere on his bed, her fingers braided through his. Their comfortable cottage
far outside Necce boasted a sturdy ceiling and wooden floors. The haze of
smoke from the city was only a smudge in the distance. Lush trees covered
rolling hills that led to the old quarry, a massive scar against the highest
hill. Dust filled the air and covered their belongings, but Mere didn't mind
at all.

Life here was full. Happy. Rich with fresh air and sunshine. Eneko had put on weight. He almost had dimples in his elbows, and he ran barefoot through the thick, rich dirt. Scrolls were scattered across the tabletop, and toys filled a woven basket in the corner. Benat's men rotated through to check on them in shifts every day. They had been teaching Mere and Pere simple magic. Even Eneko could do easy spells, like moving a cup across the room or making toys out of dust.

She felt a moment of longing—a desire to stay forever and experience it with them. To see Eneko wake up in this haven every day. To set aside the fear of civil war. Of Mateo's death. Of becoming a High Priestess. But an easy life would be empty without Mateo. Zuri. Benat. The purpose distributing the food baskets gave her. As if she'd found a second family and loved them both.

The quarry was an abandoned place, falsely believed by the landowners to be dangerous. Fortunately, it proved an effective training ground and hiding place for the refugees La Salvatorra and La Principessa now took on their nightly rounds to the farms and to Necce. Every now and then, dust rose from the cliffs as stones fell.

The sun sank lower, signaling the end of a lovely day. Eneko's eyes grew heavy. He grabbed his favorite wooden sea dragon, hugged Vittoria so tightly his hands dug into her ribs, and slipped into a small room that was his very own, with a broad glass window at the top. She marveled at the reality. Eneko sleeping in his own room. A luxury she'd never imagined.

"You must go?" Pere asked, breaking into her thoughts.

Vittoria squeezed his hand, gathered his water cup, and stood with a nod. Thanks to an apothecary, Pere's coughing fits had dramatically lessened. Pain no longer dulled his features. He'd never walk again, but he moved around the roomy house and outside in a chair with wheels on it.

"You are quiet," Pere said.

At the gentle concern in his voice, Vittoria turned to face him. His wrinkled face was lined with worry. Knobby, thin legs stretched out in front of him beneath the blanket, twisted at odd angles from disuse.

"Thinking, Pere."

"Of?"

She sighed. "Eneko's future and how much brighter it can be now. How I hope this doesn't end. How I . . ."

"Thoughts of the future lead to no productivity in the present."

She smiled. "I allow myself this one dalliance."

He grinned in return. "I can sense your thoughts are heavy," he continued, more seriously. "Are things that bad in the city?"

She'd given them no updates except to tell them that Sannara was well and hoped to visit again soon. La Principessa rarely came up as a topic, and she didn't encourage it much. They lived in a blessed bubble here. Mere cooked for Benat's men, and Eneko worked as an errand boy in the quarry training grounds. She didn't want real life to intrude on their dream. There was no telling how long this bliss would last.

"As bleak as it has ever been." She clutched his hand and forced a smile. "I think I'm just always sad to leave."

He enveloped her hands in his. His skin was soft, not calloused and brittle anymore, the way it had been on the farms.

"To have you here brings me great joy," Pere said. "You are always appreciated and welcomed, *masuna*. But your life awaits in Necce. There is much for you to do. I can respect that."

Her gaze drifted to the horizon. The sun was gone now, taking the last light with it. Mateo expected her to stay the night, but that had never been her real plan. She had a three-hour walk back into Necce. Four to get to her destination. If all went well, she'd be home by the time Mateo started breakfast in the morning.

Suddenly, she *wished* she'd learned transformative magic already, even if it frightened her.

"I must." She nodded. "But I will return."

Pere had been one of the lucky old ones—the last generation of witches who learned to read and write before Hodei implemented his education and magic ban. On the farms, they used to sit outside and watch other workers return to their makeshift homes. *Storymaking time,* Pere would say, and invent wild, hilarious tales about the witches as they passed.

A smile ghosted Vittoria's lips at the memory of the farms. The dirt under her fingernails. The thick scent of hay and manure. Being back in the country made her miss it. It felt like another lifetime. She tried to capture the memory and keep it close, because there wasn't a guarantee she'd ever see them again. The final battle was still weeks away, but one never knew. What would the reception of her amongst the rebels be? It was impossible to guess.

Saying goodbye was so hard. Already, their years in Necce seemed a lifetime ago. As if a different witch—a more frightened one—had lived it instead of her.

Unable to bear it a moment longer, she pressed a kiss to each of his cheeks and straightened again. Mere approached, a warm shawl tucked around her shoulders against the chilly evening. Winter would sweep in soon. This time, they would be fine.

For now.

Mere embraced Vittoria when she finished slipping her cloak on. Mere was a woman of the streets. A survivor. She hadn't made it this long with depths of affection. But now, safe in the country, she seemed to have an abundance of it. Vittoria mourned her lost opportunity to know this side of Mere better.

"Please," Mere murmured, tears in her eyes. "Let me plead to La Principessa, the greatest of all Givers, for you?"

Vittoria nodded, emotion thick in her throat. Mere put one hand on the carved figure of La Principessa on the wall and held Vittoria's hand with her other.

The carving looked a little bit too much like Vittoria for comfort.

"To La Principessa," Mere said. "May our bread be filling, our hearts be giving, and the moments of joy greater than the sorrow. Bless our daughter on her path." Mere lifted her head to signal the end of the plea. "Thank you for coming home, Vittoria. Now, go. Save the world with your power, whatever the power is that La Principessa grants you."

The Wench lay swathed in shadows.

Vittoria's heart beat double time in her chest, occluding her ears with the sound of rushing blood. Although weary from the long walk, off the edge of the road where she wouldn't be seen, the fear of what lay ahead kept her from feeling her fatigue. Scratches from bushes and trees marred her arms. A sting of pain warmed her cheek where a cutting branch had crossed the healed scars from Hodei's nails.

However tonight ended, her Necce family—Benat, Mateo, Zuri, and all the witches who worked so hard to keep her safe—would be upset about the risk she was taking. The lie of omission that brought her here. Maybe they would feel betrayed that she'd taken matters into her own hands and gone into the rebel world. Maybe she'd be kidnapped and disappear.

Maybe she'd get the information and everything would be fine.

Regardless, she'd have to repair the damaged trust. And she would. Eventually, maybe they would understand.

Despite that, her resolve was ironclad. She'd do anything to keep her family safe. Mateo had already refused to speak about Esperanza, and no one else knew much of the elusive High Priestess. Not Zaldar, or Zuri. Perhaps Benat, but she didn't dare risk asking him.

Besides, she felt deep in her bones that something wasn't right with Hodei's strange errand.

Something brewed in the subterranean depths of Necce. And now she was La Principessa. If she was going to save her witches and spark hope for a better future, she had to chase down every opportunity to prevent the brewing civil war.

The Wench proved unusually busy. Perhaps due to the new curfew implemented after the ball attack. All witches were supposed to be in their houses by dark, which meant that the younger, wilder workers naturally violated the rule as a means of quiet rebellion. The curfew made navigating Necce in the moonlight a terrifying prospect. Still, she'd made it. Her nerves felt frayed already, but she was here.

Vittoria gently pushed her way around idle men as they guffawed or brooded. She wore a black cloak with the hood pulled over her head. Unlikely, at any rate, that someone here would recognize her, but she wouldn't take any chances.

Finally, she managed to catch Michal's eye and lifted her hood ever so slightly. He saw her and waved her back. She navigated through the sweaty crush of bodies and half-empty food pails to the familiar hallway. This time, a burly male witch stood there to prevent access. One nod from Michal, however, and he admitted her.

What did it mean that Michal trusted her back here?

"Sannara?" she asked the witch.

He nodded to the same room as before, then gave her his back.

Vittoria stepped closer to Sannara's room, trying to ignore the noises coming from behind the closed doors.

Hurry, hurry, her thudding heart seemed to say. She had no idea what the time could be, but it likely encroached on midnight. Safely working her way here had taken longer than she'd expected. What if Sannara wasn't here?

The scuttle of rats in the walls made her shiver as she lifted a hand and knocked softly. A moment's pause came just before the door opened.

Sannara peered out with a frown that deepened when Vittoria pulled her hood back. She reached out, snatched her arm, and yanked her inside. "What are you doing here?" she hissed.

Vittoria shoved her hood off. "How long have you been with the rebels?"

The ballroom attack flashed back through Vittoria's mind with new urgency. There was no doubting the thin figure in the gray robe. Or Sannara's astonished voice. *La Principessa? Is it really . . . are you . . .*

Vittoria had known the moment she heard the voice who hid in that hood. Only shock had kept her from tearing Sannara out of the castle and shaking her. Then Sannara had left with the other rebels.

Now, the guilt in Sannara's eyes spoke worlds. She released Vittoria and folded her arms across her chest, appearing more troubled than angry.

"Years now," she murmured, gaze downturned. "I don't know how many. It was before I met you." She shrugged, arms spread helplessly. "What choice did I have at the time? I was young when my parents died from the winter fevers. Not old enough to do the work of a *lavanda* maid, and no one would conscript an orphan. It was sell my body or work for the rebels."

Vittoria gestured to the straw mattress on the floor. "But don't you—"

"No." Sannara shook her head. "No, I haven't sold my body that way. I'm a messenger. This is all just a cover for the rebels." She waved a hand, and Vittoria wondered whether she meant the room or the Wench. "Rebels bring me messages from the catacombs. I organize workers on the street who report in every night, and we run messages between rebel groups. Most rebels can't read or write, though some can. I'm in charge of making sure that rebel groups still communicate."

Vittoria frowned. It explained the errands in the middle of the night. The food. The secrecy. The long disappearances. How many days would it take to go to the furthest covens? Weeks, for some parts of the Network.

Sannara likely hadn't told anyone because Pere would have been so against it. *Violent,* he always said. *They stir up anarchy, but that solves nothing. They're too wild. Too impetuous. A better life does not come from that path.*

Her responsibilities also implied that the rebels weren't as fractured as Mateo thought.

"Can't you leave it now?" Vittoria asked. "Now I can guarantee food and a safe place, at least for a while. I—"

Sannara emphatically shook her head. "Among the rebels," she said, "there is no leaving. My life is decided, Vittoria. I chose this path so I could eat and be sheltered, and now it's set. It's a roulette game I've played since before Ant—before I met you. It's nothing you can save me from. I accept it for what it is."

"Did Anton know?" she asked to buy time. To figure out a way to convince Sannara that Eneko needed her. *They* needed her.

Sannara laughed, but it was more bitter than amused. "Yes. It's where we met."

Vittoria's eyes widened.

Sannara grimaced and sighed again. "Anton joined the rebels as soon as your family arrived from the farms. Rebel contacts were how he managed to get your mere work in the Moretti house and all of you a place to sleep. At least initially. He never told you because he feared your pere's displeasure."

Another rat scuttled across the far wall. Somewhere in the distance, someone muffled a scream. A woman cried out, then fell silent after a *crack*. Vittoria comprehended almost none of it.

"Anton in the rebels," she murmured weakly. Things had been bleak when they first sought refuge in Necce after Pere's accident. They'd been near to starvation. Anton, an ideal older brother, had always tried to protect her.

Sannara's voice sharpened. "Your parents must never know."

"Of course not."

"The attack at the castle," Sannara began, then halted. "When I saw you? I was . . . shocked. Rumors of La Principessa had been swirling, but I hadn't known it was you."

"Why were you there?"

Sannara snorted. "I shouldn't have been, but . . . someone special wanted me to go." She wouldn't quite meet Vittoria's gaze. "I think he wanted to show me what he thinks he can give me after . . ."

The implication was clear enough. *After the uprising.* A dark feeling crawled through Vittoria's chest.

"Who is this man?" she whispered.

"Doesn't matter," Sannara said. "He's very possessive and determined to have me. He . . . loves me, in his way. There's no denying him."

"Are you safe with him?"

"Yes. It's fine. Vittoria, why are you here? It's not safe for you to be anywhere." Sannara gazed around, alarm in her eyes. "Where is that man who came with you before? Are you here alone?"

"Yes, I'm alone. I came to ask a favor."

"What?"

Vittoria pulled in a breath, but the words wouldn't come. How could she explain this crazy errand? She was admonishing Sannara to leave the rebels even as she *sought* them. Finally, she managed to say, "I need to speak to someone in the rebels. After the ball, when I realized you were one of them, I thought to come to you."

"What?" she snapped. "Not on Mateo's behalf, I hope. That—"

"No!" Vittoria shook her head. "No, Mateo doesn't know I'm here. That's why I'm alone."

Sannara's gaze narrowed. "Then who do you need to speak to?"

"Anyone who might remember Esperanza. I need information about her."

A full three seconds passed before Sannara seemed to grasp the words.

Something like astonishment clouded her features. "Why would you say that name?"

"I need to know more about her."

"About the dead High Priestess?"

"Yes."

"And you're asking the *rebels*?" Sannara's voice was too carefully controlled now. Blank, almost toneless. An equally empty expression had slipped over her face.

"Yes."

"Why?"

Vittoria hesitated. What was this change that had come over Sannara? It meant something, surely. Fear lingered in her gaze. Uncertainty. Her eyes darted to the door, then back to Vittoria.

"Hodei sent me," Vittoria said. "He's threatened to kill Eneko if I don't find out some . . . information about Esperanza."

Sannara sucked in a sharp breath. The sound of footsteps came from outside. She yanked Vittoria away from the door and motioned for her to be quiet. Then they heard the clipped voices of two men.

Sannara paled. "You must go!" she whispered frantically. "He's early."

"Who is early?"

"By the Givers, if he finds you here . . ."

But there was nowhere to go. Nowhere Vittoria could hide. Helpless, Vittoria mouthed, "Who?"

The footsteps stopped outside Sannara's door. Sannara's terrified eyes widened. She gripped Vittoria's hands in her own, her fingers a cold vise.

"I'm sorry." The words fell off Sannara's lips as the door creaked open.

A familiar face entered the room, then stopped. Dread filled Vittoria like a rising tide as she took in his strong shoulders. Serious expression. Hazel eyes and black hair. He blinked, mouth half-open in an exclamation.

"Romeo," she whispered.

Shocked, he looked from Vittoria to Sannara and back again. Questions filled his silent gaze, then seemed to vanish as he stepped into the room. Something cold came over him and hardened in his eyes like a glacier.

"La Principessa," he muttered. "How delightful to see you again."

The door closed behind him.

26

Mateo stared out at the churning ocean as night descended. His jaw felt tight, and his teeth ached. He realized he'd been grinding them together as his mind wandered to the battle ahead.

Less than two weeks.

He shook that thought off.

With Vittoria visiting her family for the night, the house had been quiet. Even if she didn't speak much when she was here, her presence had a way of filling the space so it didn't feel so cavernous. His mind wandered down darker paths whenever she was gone. His lips twitched, however, when he thought of Eneko. Give the kid a few years, and his natural drive and curiosity would keep Vittoria's hands full.

No, *their* hands full.

Chuckling to himself, Mateo turned. A message appeared in front of him. Balta's handwriting. He reached for it just as heavy boots issued from the front door and Benat called out.

"Mateo? Are you ready for your training session?"

But Mateo only vaguely heard him over the sudden roar of his heart in his ears. Heat rushed to his face while everything else inside him turned cold. In moments, he felt like a glacier had carved a chunk out of him and left him frozen and half-empty in its wake.

· · ·

Mateo,

I suggest you come to the castle. Hodei is on his deathbed.

—Balta

Mateo vaguely registered Benat's form in the doorway as he read the message twice, then a third time. The words finally sank in. His hand dropped to his side.

"Mateo?"

He glanced up.

Benat eyed him with concern. "Are you all right?"

Wordlessly, Mateo passed the note over.

Benat skimmed it, then let out a long breath. "You must go."

Must I?

The thought startled Mateo. He didn't *have* to go anywhere. Hodei didn't deserve any sort of absolution—nor would he seek it.

Still, the thought of Pere dying without something said sat like a lead ball in his stomach. He'd had no chance to part with Mere, and that had haunted him for years. He held no love for Hodei, but he didn't want to wonder later.

Mateo nodded. "I will go. Now."

He hesitated only a moment more to gather his thoughts. To rein in his emotions. The strange sense of calm and chaos surprised him. More than losing his only parent—and one who had attempted to kill him several times—Hodei's death would mean an acceleration of the final battle of the Law of Rights. The battle with Romeo would happen immediately. Within a day.

Perhaps this was the beginning of the end.

With a shake of his head, Mateo pushed those thoughts aside. He'd think through the implications later.

For now, he would visit Pere.

Mateo stood in the doorway of a shadowy room.

Hodei's rooms occupied the entire top floor of the west wing of the castle. Most of them were reportedly empty. Maids cleaned their skeleton interiors once a month to wipe away the dust and cobwebs, but no one ever visited them. Not even Hodei, according to rumors.

Not since Mere died.

How like Hodei to take up space he never used, all while children died of hunger and cold in his Network.

Mateo ignored the empty places and the ghosts of memories as he walked past. He had lived here once. Grown up here. Taken his first steps in this castle. He barely remembered those days. Mostly just flashes of white marble. Glittering chandeliers. Flutes and drums from the ballroom and a stoic pere who spoke little.

No one stopped him as he advanced. Perhaps Balta had prepared them. The Guardians glanced at him but made no move to prevent his entry to Hodei's private quarters.

Mateo pushed the door open, allowing torchlight from the hallway to spill inside. Deep, raspy breaths filled the room, the only sound except for the occasional shuffle of a worker in the distance. The air smelled stuffy, with a lingering hint of eucalyptus. A salve for his chest, perhaps. Mateo stood there for too long, expecting Hodei to snap at him to shut the door. He wanted to move forward, but his legs wouldn't take him there.

No one else lingered in the room. It lay, still as death and just as dark, in Hodei's final moments. He wondered if Balta had even come up, or just passed along the news. Mateo's thoughts skipped around, unable to settle on, or accept, the shriveled old man on the mattress.

Where was Romeo?

Why hadn't Romeo written to him?

A wistful, foolish thought. Romeo didn't care about Mateo, and he certainly didn't care about Hodei. Would it have been better if Hodei had just slipped away in the night, with no one at his side? No one to ease his passing into the oblivion that surely awaited him?

Not even honor would accept Hodei.

Landowners believed the next step after death was the interim. The place in between where witches go to be judged by their honor in life. Honor—a vague cloud. A sense. Not even a being, just an intuition that would grant them their just due. To be weighed worthy of moving to their next life, and if so, whether that life would be better or worse. But even if honor were the judge, surely it would not grant Hodei another life. No, Hodei had left nothing good behind.

So, this life would be his last. The final breath.

The *ultima mort.*

Last death.

Mateo advanced into the room with cautious steps, but left the door to the hallway open. A sprawling bed, large enough for all of Vittoria's family to lie side by side and still have space, swamped the middle of the room.

It would have been a warm, inviting place if Hodei had any sense of warmth himself. Instead, the wooden panels, marble floor, and flickering candles took on a grim appearance. As if death had already arrived, but was waiting for something. No fresh air drifted off the sea. Heavy damask curtains shut out the world. Not even a painting cheered up the walls.

And on the massive bed lay that bent body.

Mateo stopped, not far from where Hodei curled in on himself, half-alive. His breaths were intermittent. Labored. As if he scrounged for air from inside his chest.

A rush of pity took Mateo by surprise. The great Hodei had been toppled by his own body. Now, one of his sons would ascend his throne, and he wouldn't know which. He could be erased from the timeline of history, or remembered as the tyrant who lost his power at the end of his days.

Whatever he meant to achieve by his reign of terror would never be realized, because Hodei had never been satisfied. No power was enough. No sacrifice was enough. No amount of currency could buy whatever it was he sought.

And now, he would end instead.

"You," came the raspy voice, "are the last witch I expected to see in my final moments."

On instinct, Mateo almost retreated, but he tucked his hands into his pockets and forced himself to stay. Hodei's eyes remained closed. He panted in between the words, and struggled to regain breath.

"I thought she'd come." Hodei gasped. "Taunt me from death."

"Mere?"

Hodei coughed, a weak, gurgling sound. His eyes remained closed as he sought another breath.

"Balta told me you were dying." Mateo shifted his weight. "I came after I received his message."

"I am," Hodei snarled.

Mateo said nothing.

One of Hodei's eyes fluttered open, then closed again. He lay on his side, face pressed into a pillow where spittle dribbled every now and then. A blanket covered half of his body. The skin of his arms had turned pale, and his fingertips were tinged blue in his clawed hands.

"You always thought I was your enemy," Hodei said. He managed one word at a time, each wrenched from a breathless, air-starved body. "It wasn't me."

Mateo's brow wrinkled. "Pere, you have enslaved half of our Network. You've killed thousands in the name of prosperity."

"I said *your* enemy."

The emphasis sent a chill through Mateo. Of course Pere had been his enemy. He'd sent assassins. He'd taken Romeo, abandoned Mere. Ignored him.

Hodei coughed again, but it was a petulant wheeze at best, followed by several minutes of agonized panting. Mateo sought for words, but found none. He'd dreamed of this moment for years. The blistering words he'd say to Hodei in exchange for the years of fear. The agony of rejection. The loneliness and uncertainty.

Now, he had nothing to say.

A dreadful sort of numbness had replaced the emotions of the last ten years. He leaned into the emotional reprieve, certain this would hurt in excruciating ways later when he had time to think about what he should have said.

Hodei forced both his eyes open. "The assassins?" he growled. "Not mine."

Mateo crouched down, barely able to hear the words. Surely, he'd heard wrong. At any rate, Hodei must be half-delusional at this point, so hungry for breath.

"They were Guardians, Pere. All three attempts."

Hodei shook his head, a pathetic back-and-forth that could have been a twitch. "Not mine. Don't be a fool."

"Then who?"

"Her."

"Who?"

Hodei tried to swallow, but it sent him into another pitiful coughing bout. His eyes closed. The heavy, frantic breaths calmed into ten seconds of total stasis. For a second, Mateo thought he had passed, but then Hodei gasped in another ragged breath. His eyes rolled back in his head. He wasn't dead, but likely wasn't conscious, either.

Mateo stumbled back.

A deathbed hallucination, certainly.

Even so, his mind chewed on the thought. If Hodei hadn't sent the assassins, then who had? Mateo sank into a nearby chair, his mind awash with hazy memories. The first attempt had been the day after Mere's death, right when he'd awoken from his fever. Balta had shaken him out of his half-delirious stupor and forced him to leave, mere minutes before the assassins arrived. The second had been years later, just after he'd returned from his time in the navy, while he was walking through Necce. And the third was after La Salvatorra had made a name for himself. All of the would-be murderers had worn Guardian uniforms. They'd been better trained than the average Guardian, of course.

His mind stuttered to a stop.

Or *were* they Guardians? Why would an assassin wear the uniform? It would be very conspicuous of them.

Mateo felt sick to his stomach as he turned to look back at Pere. What if

Hodei was telling the truth? What if this wasn't some delusion of his dying mind? If not him, then who?

Her?

Agonized breaths shuddered out of Pere now. His hand, curled until the fingers pressed into each other, rested on the pillow next to him. His dry, pale lips gaped open, and a long, cold breath escaped him.

Mateo stared at his bent body, his own breath held, and waited for Hodei to gasp again.

The muscles around Hodei's shoulders slackened. His face drooped. No breaths came. The High Priest was dead. The final battle of the Law of Rights would have to take place as soon as possible—before the world found out.

And before the civil war began.

"Whoever tried to kill me," Mateo whispered, "you certainly didn't stop them."

With that, he tucked all the strange emotions farther into his mind, shut them there, and transported back home.

27

VITTORIA

A dull pounding pulsed through Vittoria's head.

She moaned and attempted, unsuccessfully, to open her eyes. The air felt heavy with a smell she couldn't quite peg. Age? Decay? Earth? Pebbles ground into her arms and her back, wet and slippery.

With all her might, she forced her eyes open.

Several seconds passed before she comprehended that her eyes were, in fact, open. She saw only darkness at first, until a limp torch became visible in the distance. A tinkle of moving water came from far away, and a wave of the malodorous smell followed. The ache in her head intensified.

She closed her eyes again and sought her memories. Where was she? How did she get here?

The recollection returned sluggishly at first. Mere. Pere. Eneko. The Wench. Sannara. Romeo. Then pain in her head and total darkness.

All at once, she remembered everything. Romeo had advanced on her, and that had been it. He'd easily toppled her.

"Givers," she muttered.

"They don't come here. At least, you may be the first one."

The voice reverberated as if she lay in a cave. Romeo. Vittoria's eyes flew open again. She canted her head to the left in the direction of his voice, only to find darkness. Her hands were bound in front of her by wiry rope that dug into the skin. Her eyes had adjusted to the darkness a bit more, enough to make out crude buttresses overhead. The arched supports were spaced out here and there, some crumbling after years of water erosion. Dark lines in the walls dribbled water. Any surface the light touched appeared to be slippery.

Vittoria fought to keep her panic under control. The catacombs. This had to be the catacombs.

Now the rebels had her.

But if the rebels had her, why was Romeo here?

Approaching footsteps rang in her ears. She blinked as a broad figure stepped closer.

"I expected you to be a bit less . . . frail," Romeo said. "You act like you're made of such strength when you're with my brother."

Vittoria fought back a moan. Romeo chuckled, straightened, and moved away.

While his focus was elsewhere, she peered around. Rough, uneven bookshelves had been chiseled into the stone walls. Scrolls and books and more scrolls lined every available space. She was in some sort of cavern, if these were the catacombs at all. But why wouldn't they be? Her head ached too much to think through it. A rickety desk sat in front of the closest bookshelf. Romeo stood behind it now, staring at her.

"You're a fool, you know," he said.

"Why?" Vittoria croaked. She struggled to sit, then gave up. Her head throbbed too much. Her ankles were tied as tightly as her wrists. The grain of the rope rubbed against her skin and felt wet. Blood, likely. There would be no wiggling free.

He lifted two of his hands, as if to encompass the bleak space. "Because you sought a dead witch at the behest of Hodei, who is the cruelest witch of this century."

"Sannara told you?"

There was a smile in his voice when he said, "I know more than you think, Vittoria."

"Are you Xavier?" she asked, recalling the brief conversation she'd had with Mateo about the elusive, possibly not even real, rebel leader.

"No."

"Then why are you in the catacombs with the rebels?"

"It's a stroke of luck that I caught you tonight, of all nights." A tinge of amusement filled the words, but his nonchalance seemed forced, at best.

Why wouldn't he answer her question?

Vittoria grimaced against another wave of pain. She let out a long breath to relax the muscles in her shoulder, which also hurt. Had he hit her on the side of the head? The neck? How did she get here? Someone transported or carried her? The questions flooded her with every passing moment. She forced herself to set them aside and focus on what he'd said.

"Tonight?" she asked. "Why tonight?"

"Now that I have you, everything changes." He sounded stone-cold. The lack of inflection sent a chill through her. "Because you are in my power, Mateo will not be able to win the final battle against me. How easy to distract him. To anger him. Not that his bleeding heart would have let him win, anyway. Tonight, the throne is won, and it is won for us. Would you like something to drink?"

Vittoria's throat ached with thirst after the long trek into Necce, but she shook her head, then regretted it when pain bounced around her skull. What time was it? Time probably didn't exist down here in the belly of the earth. Had hours passed?

He'd said, *It is won for us*. Who did he work with?

What was Mateo doing right now?

"Tonight," she murmured. Her mind sped up slowly, absorbing the words too long after they were said. Panic tightened her chest, made it difficult to breathe. Now she understood. Now she saw what he must mean.

"Hodei?" she asked. "Is he dying?"

"Dead. Or will be soon."

"Mateo?"

"Will shortly receive a message from me," Romeo said. He folded his hands behind his back and strolled toward her. "In that message, I will inform him that the final battle will commence immediately. As the initiator of the Law of Rights, I get to choose the place of the final battle, although Balta declares the time."

Vittoria swallowed, feeling cold. If nothing else, she had to keep him talking. Get more information. Buy time until she figured . . . something out. Because she had to find Mateo. Tell him that Romeo was something. A traitor? Working for the rebels?

She didn't even know herself.

"Sannara?" she asked. "Is she all right?"

Romeo paused, studying her with a dark expression. It cleared almost as quickly as it came. "She's no concern of yours now. She is mine."

"She's my sister. Her son is—"

"She is *mine!*"

His shout rippled through the empty corridors of the catacombs. *Mine. Mine. Mine.* Vittoria swallowed again, although her mouth and throat were bone-dry. Romeo's flaring nostrils calmed.

"Fine." Vittoria winced. "She's yours. I won't ask about her again."

The pulsing in her temples subsided slightly.

Romeo straightened his coat. "See that you don't," he muttered.

Vittoria attempted to see more in the cavern, but the darkness was static now. Pervasive. There was nothing else she'd be able to see without more light. She had a feeling there wasn't enough light for a reason. Romeo didn't *want* her to see. The vague shapes of dead candlesticks were barely discernible in the dark.

A distant squeak sounded behind her, as if a tunnel led to—or past— this cavern. Rumors whispered that the catacombs were hiding places first created by the Old Ones who lived in Necce long before witches ruled Alkarra alone. During the time of the mortals, before the great divide, when gods *and* goddesses reigned, the Old Ones had used magic to sculpt the catacombs and protect the mortals who hid from the wrath of the goddesses. The sea goddess, Prana, supposedly created the magic for these catacombs to protect the mortals and anger her sisters. Some of the cata-combs stretched beyond Necce's borders and under the ocean.

Was she beneath the ocean right now? A chilling thought. Such ancient foundations couldn't be safe. How they stood now, she couldn't imagine. The magic would be ancient, and likely faded.

Would all of Necce crumble when the catacombs fell?

Canals must connect the caverns, if the constant sound of water meant anything. Which meant she could escape this cavern, but to where? To stumble around in the depths of the earth, risking the rest of her life in the dark channels? She could wander forever. Maybe drown, get lost, or go mad.

No, she couldn't escape and wander on her own. She had to be brought out.

"Since you know why I'm here," Vittoria said when the silence stretched too long, "will you tell me about Esperanza?" She swallowed hard and tried to sound bitter. "If you're going to kill me anyway, what does it matter?"

He laughed, a surprisingly lyrical sound. "Why would you seek a dead woman's mysteries? It's not very landowner-like of you. We're all terrified of ghosts, aren't we? I confess, I thought your motivation was made up. Then again, Hodei did love wasting other witches' time."

"Hodei wanted me to come to the rebels and find the answer to a question." She monitored his placid face. He returned the same studious attention.

"What question?"

Deciding to throw caution to the wind—for Romeo surely wouldn't allow her to live, and if Hodei was dead, then Mateo would be busy fighting for his life soon—she said, "He wanted to know why she stayed, even when she wanted to leave."

Romeo blinked.

"What were his exact words?" he finally asked.

The reverberating pain had ebbed to a dull, persistent throbbing, but it still made thinking difficult. Vittoria closed her eyes, even if the room was already so dark. It was easier to think back to that day without his eyes boring into her soul. She licked her dry lips.

"He said, 'Why did Esperanza stay?'"

Romeo's face split into a wide grin.

"You're a fool, Vittoria," he said quietly. "A good-hearted fool. You see what he did now, don't you? A wild chase. An attempt to keep you busy and get you out of my way. If the rebels had you, then Mateo didn't, and that was all Hodei wanted. He wanted me on the throne, not Mateo."

"Does he know you're a member of the rebels?" she asked.

He laughed. "Pere believes himself far cleverer than he really is. Do you think I'd still be alive if he even suspected? I've been hiding this secret for over a decade, Vittoria. Don't insult me."

Vittoria's heart did a double *whomp*. She comprehended in that moment what she'd always known could be true: that all of this was nothing. She may have brought herself to her own end without Hodei stepping in. Genius, really. Hodei could, with very little effort, get rid of her and all the hope she brought to her witches. Romeo would ascend the throne unimpeded.

Except for one thing: Hodei knew Romeo's secret.

She recalled that day in Hodei's office, her heart pounding with sudden understanding. The dry wheeze of Hodei's voice scuttled back through her mind. The strain in his bitter, wrinkled face.

Because sometimes even the witches we trust the most will make fools of us, he had said.

That hadn't been about Esperanza.

Somehow, Hodei had known Romeo was in league with the rebels, so he sent Vittoria down here to ask about Esperanza. Eventually that would have led her to Romeo.

Then she would have seen the truth: that Romeo had been betraying Hodei all this time. Playing both sides. Then she'd tell Mateo, who could use that information against his brother. Perhaps Hodei even knew about Sannara. Wouldn't that explain his other comment?

You are the only witch who can reveal this truth.

Only Vittoria could answer the question because she knew Romeo's lover *and* had Mateo's trust. Mateo would believe Vittoria when she told him about Romeo, but wouldn't have trusted the same information from Hodei. If he'd simply executed Romeo, Mateo would have taken the throne, and Hodei didn't want that either.

Her heart raced with the implications. If Romeo were in league with the rebels, what did it mean? What would the landowners say? Did it truly give Mateo an advantage? The thoughts made her breathless. It was almost unbelievable—except she *had* to believe it because Romeo was in the catacombs with her right now.

Everything felt scattered. She couldn't pull all her thoughts together into a cohesive puzzle in her aching mind, so she trusted her instinct and the vague plan that was slowly cobbling itself together.

"You're not the leader of the rebels," she said to the sudden stillness. "At least, not yet. Xavier is still alive, isn't he? Your uncle. And now you're working with him."

Romeo stilled.

"That's your great plan to unite worker and landowner, isn't it? Xavier will draw the loyalty of the workers in Necce, and you will bring the landowners. Maybe your agreement is that you rule as High Priest?"

He didn't react, but even that told her she must be on the right track.

"If that's true, then Xavier needs me, doesn't he? The workers *might* follow Xavier, but that's too great a risk to take when facing the landowners' magic. Workers will surely follow La Principessa, however. That's why you didn't kill me back at the Wench. It's why you brought me here."

Romeo shifted his weight. "You're no use to us dead. Not yet, anyway."

"I'm no use to you silent, either," she countered. "You want to destroy belief in La Principessa, but you're a fool if you do."

"A fool? Hope is a great force. You, of all witches, should know that. We take away their Giver of Hope and—"

"And you have insurrection. Rage. The desperate power of hopelessness. If you want a great insurrection on your hands, kill La Principessa. Or the idea of her. Even if you keep me alive but try to destroy the Giver I have become, you'll be killed in the bloodshed that follows."

His silence gave her a flimsy hope that she could get out of here. A tiny spark that meant she at least had his ear, so she might be able to talk herself out of this. She suspected he wouldn't ask any questions, so she kept going.

"You need La Principessa to *support* Xavier. To throw her weight behind him. I suspect that while you are fighting Mateo, Xavier is supposed to rise to rally the workers. Because we both know that the workers are the real deciders here. The rebels are small in number compared to the Guardians. Without workers flocking to your side, you'll fail immeasurably. And you know that, don't you?"

Vittoria laughed, but it was mirthless. Romeo's treachery occurred to her in a whole new light. The landowners. He professed such admiration and love for landowners but all along had been stabbing them in the back. He'd been planning to use the rebels to defeat them for . . . how long now?

A decade, had he said? How deep could this blackness extend into his being?

He surely had no soul left. A true son of Hodei.

She swallowed and pressed on, warming to it. The pieces fell together in her mind. "Except the workers might not listen to Xavier, and that's a risk you cannot take. So you need La Principessa to call to them." Her voice hardened now. "But they won't follow if I don't say a word. So you don't need La Principessa dead. You need her vocal."

Romeo advanced so quickly she almost didn't see him coming. One moment he stood behind his desk, the next he'd landed in front of her with a snarl contorting his handsome features. He stood over Vittoria, a hand to her throat. When he grasped her neck, fingers bruising her windpipe, she felt the darkness around him.

Her heart thudded against her chest as she tried to gasp for air.

"And yet," he whispered, his grip tightening, "you *will* speak."

"Why should I?" she mouthed.

Romeo sneered, and it curled like a cruel hiss around his lips.

"Bring him!" he shouted.

A sharp cry issued from outside the cavern, but the sound was familiar. Fear coursed through her, so strong it gripped her like death. Him? No. It couldn't be. Romeo loosened his hold with a growl. The blood drained from Vittoria's face as she coughed, sucking in a lungful of air.

"You wouldn't," she whispered.

"Tori!" Eneko's little voice cracked as he called her name from somewhere she couldn't see. Vittoria whipped her head toward the entrance of the cavern. Just beyond was a flickering torch. Then came a scuffle of sound and the shadow of a little body on the far wall.

"Eneko!" she called.

"Tori!" He sobbed. "Where are you? It's dark. I'm scared."

Vittoria cried out when Romeo picked her up off the floor by her neck. He gripped her so tightly she couldn't breathe. Her head pulsed with a fresh wave of agony, and white stars exploded in front of her eyes.

"Because if you don't," Romeo whispered, his lips brushing the shell of her ear, "he will die. You think Hodei was terrifying? Just wait until you face my wrath. I am more terrifying than my pere, because nothing that he cared about could ever be good. I am what they made me to be, Vittoria, and now they will pay for their choices."

Vittoria gasped as he shoved her to the ground. She landed on a rock on her back, wincing, and curled onto her side. Eneko had faded away, his keening cry disappearing into the darkness. Tears clouded her eyes as Romeo stalked off, barking orders to witches she couldn't see. Then she heard manacles scraping across the ground.

"Eneko!" she screamed. "Eneko!"

A distant voice called, "Tori!"

"I will find you! I will come after you!"

"Lock her up until I give you the command," Romeo said to two wraith-like witches. "Let no one else in here while I'm gone."

Romeo left the cavern amid a rustle of fabric.

"Sannara will never have anything to do with you after this!" she shouted. "Never!"

But he ignored her, and as her words echoed into the vast chambers of the catacombs, even Vittoria wondered if they were true. Sannara had never put Eneko first, and Romeo's hold on her was clearly absolute.

Another sob ripped through her.

The torch went out.

28

MATEO

Mateo paced back and forth across Vittoria's bedroom, his thoughts fragmented.

How long had passed since he'd left Hodei's deathbed? A few hours, maybe? Ten minutes? Time felt like a blur. He'd told no one that Hodei had died, but they'd find out soon. Someone would check on the ailing High Priest. An apothecary, most likely. Or maybe Balta.

The news would ripple through the castle and the landowner coven, but not likely beyond. No, the landowners wouldn't want anyone to know until the final battle of the Law of Rights was over. Which meant he'd hear from Romeo or Balta in the morning, most likely.

Mateo shoved a hand through his hair. At least Vittoria was safe at the quarry. He could go warn her of Hodei's death, but then she'd insist on coming back to support him in the battle. But he didn't know yet when it would happen, so why break her peace? He'd find her when he knew more.

If the question of succession had been decided when Hodei was alive, there might have been less uncertainty. As it stood, whoever gained the throne would have to implement their plan at once.

Which meant rebels and landowners alike would be scrambling to prepare the moment news of Hodei's death broke.

No, Vittoria should stay at the quarry for now, with Eneko. Joska was assigned to check on her, and he'd just left. Then, if the worst happened here, Benat and Joska could take Vittoria and her family away immediately. Joska was as good as Benat, if not a bit youn—

"Mateo!" Benat barked. "It's Vittoria."

Mateo's head popped up. He stopped pacing, arrested by the panic in Benat's tone. Joska followed Benat into the room, pale.

"What?"

"She's gone."

"Gone where?"

Benat's nostrils flared as he motioned to Joska, who stepped forward and spoke.

"We're not sure, Majesty. Two men are looking for her now. Nerea said she left a few hours ago, around sunset. They thought one of us transported her back here."

"No one did?"

"No."

Benat confirmed it with a shake of his head. "I've spoken with all my men. They've been assigned to other places tonight. The ones patrolling the quarry said they saw no sign of her and thought she was still inside."

"There are tracks through some bushes and on a path that leads to the road that match her foot size. No other prints to suggest someone else took her." Joska gave Mateo a helpless shrug. "If she went that way, she would have been hidden from the guards. The tracks initially head toward Necce, but they disappear into the underbrush almost as soon as they enter the road. We've combed the road—still are combing the road, just in case—but so far have found nothing."

Mateo scowled. "Why would she walk away from her family on the road back to Necce without telling us? It doesn't make—"

His mind flitted back to the morning after the Test of Courage. When Vittoria's cheeks were bright red with catlike scratch marks, and her expression stoic. He'd wondered then if something had been wrong.

"Hodei," he whispered. Was it possible? Had Hodei sent her to do something while he was on his deathbed?

Benat stared at him, then seemed to remember that day himself. He nodded wearily. "Hodei."

"She didn't want us to know," Mateo murmured. "That's why she said she wanted to stay overnight. Now she's walking back into Necce alone because she's doing something for Hodei tonight."

"A trap," Benat snarled. "It must be. La Principessa would not betray us."

"Hodei?" Joska asked softly. "But . . ."

"Joska, go to Vittoria's family and double their guard. I want you with them. I want someone with Eneko. No, Vittoria hasn't betrayed us," he added, more to himself than them. "I believe she's acting to protect her family. Hodei has threatened her, somehow."

"What would he want from her?" Benat asked.

Mateo suppressed the urge to put a fist through the wall. He should have gotten to the bottom of it. Should have talked to her, or built up her trust, or figured this out sooner. Instead of throwing something, he began to pace again. He set aside all thoughts of Hodei, the Law of Rights, and Romeo. Vittoria was the priority.

"What could Hodei want from her?" Mateo murmured. "It doesn't make sense."

"It may not be Hodei," Benat said. His countenance darkened as he opened his mouth, then closed it again.

"What?" Mateo snapped.

"She . . ." Benat closed his eyes. "Is it possible she's a rebel?"

Mateo stopped pacing to glare at him. "If you are suggesting—"

Benat held up two hands. "We have to explore all possibilities, Mateo."

"She's *not* my mere."

Joska averted his gaze. Benat said nothing.

Mateo raked a hand through his hair. "What would Hodei ask her to do that she would try to hide from me?" These threads had to meet some-where—and they had to meet back with Hodei. Or, he thought with a visible shudder, Romeo. "Why would Hodei want Vittoria? He's dying. Dead."

"Because she threatens his legacy?" Joska asked.

Mateo shook his head. "No. *I* threaten his legacy. If Hodei wanted some-thing from Vittoria, it would be to punish me."

"A trap set by Romeo?" Benat offered.

Mateo chewed on his bottom lip. "I don't know. I don't know what he's asked of her, but it must be something she doesn't want me to know about."

"Because you'd stop her."

Mateo met Benat's hard gaze. "Exactly. And there's one big thing in Necce that I wouldn't allow her to get involved in."

Benat swallowed. "The rebels."

Mateo stopped. His stomach clenched as he whispered, "The rebels."

"She's gone to the rebels?" Joska asked.

"We must assume so," Mateo said, "but it doesn't mean anything yet. There are a dozen reasons she may have been led there."

Benat looked away again.

Mateo tilted his head to one side. His neck cracked. "All right. That's where we'll start. We'll assume she's gone to the rebels for . . . some reason. We need to infiltrate the catacombs. Benat, we'll each lead a team. Sanja can lead the third. Pull some of the men from the quarry. Grab the ones who have been there the longest. We'll—"

"No, Majesty," Joska said quietly.

Mateo's head snapped up, and he snarled, "Did you just refuse me?"

Joska held up two hands and stood his ground before Benat could advance on him. "I know it's insubordination to refuse a command, and by the law of the Guardians you could have me killed, but on this point, let me speak. Please?"

Mateo hesitated. The last thing he needed right now was mutiny, but even he could admit that he wasn't at his most logical. Thoughts of Vittoria in the hands of the rebels . . .

He shook that off and gave Joska a hard nod.

"You just said that Hodei has died, which means the Law of Rights will be fought to the end at any moment now. You have to be available if Balta declares the start of the match."

"The message will find me in the catacombs," he snapped. "I'll transport."

Benat's brow rose. "Are you sure?"

"Majesty," Joska hurried to say, "the catacombs are known for having dead spots where magic doesn't work. I've been there. I've felt them. The magic there is powerful. Ancient. Unstable. Sometimes it changes the way other magic systems work. A message sent to you may not arrive."

Mateo frowned. He'd never actually been in the catacombs, but he wasn't about to surrender Vittoria, to leave her to be a puppet for the wild rebels.

"Then I'll return every fifteen minutes and see if a message has come," he said.

Benat put a hand on his shoulder. The firm weight grounded Mateo, even though he wanted to shake it off.

"Majesty," Benat murmured. His nostrils flared as he sent Joska a warning look. "He's right. The catacombs are too unknown. You cannot be the witch who goes in there."

Mateo turned, gaze tapered in a challenging stare. "You'll stop me?"

"With my life, if I must."

"The catacombs are bigger than Necce, Majesty," Joska added. "The Old Ones who built them were more powerful than any of us. Their magic, though weak, is still active down there. It's the only reason the catacombs haven't been flooded by the sea. You'll get lost. Some of the canals are still functioning traps set by the Old Ones. And we don't know for sure that she's there. It is, perhaps, a trap for *you*."

"You think Hodei set this up as a trap for me to walk into so Romeo wins the Law of Rights?"

Joska shrugged, but Mateo read through his silence.

"You think Vittoria has deceived me?"

"We didn't say that," Benat said.

"But you can't deny it?"

Joska kept his gaze on the ground, but Benat didn't even flinch.

"I will remain open to all possibilities until the truth is known," Joska murmured, "because that is how I keep you safe and serve you best."

Mateo growled, barely reining in his rage. Would Esperanza never cease to haunt him? Could her legacy never die? He was on the edge already and the fight with Romeo hadn't even been declared yet.

Why did he feel so wild? So infuriated?

Was there a kernel of doubt within him? Even a hint of question about his betrothed? Vittoria certainly could betray him. Esperanza had done so to Hodei, hadn't she?

Unable to even consider it, he whipped back to Joska. "Then what do you propose I do?" he snapped. "You must have some sort of brilliant idea if you're willing to believe so ill of your future High Priestess?"

Joska hesitated, eyes darting from Mateo to Benat. "I propose that you allow us to find her in the catacombs."

When the rage flared within Mateo like a fire, Benat stepped between the two of them.

"You can't do anything about it now, Majesty, except go to that fight when the call comes for you," Benat said. "My men will save her if she's down there. If she's not, we'll find her."

A thousand scenarios ran through Mateo's mind. Romeo could have her. The rebels. Hodei's Guardians. A group of desperate landowners hoping to sabotage him. Who knew. The endless possibilities made him sick.

"I can't accept that, Benat."

Benat put a hand on Mateo's shoulder. "You must," he said quietly. "Joska is right. This could all be a trap. An elaborate way for Romeo to pull you away and win by default. Vittoria would agree that you must save the Network first, and then her."

Benat didn't choke on the words, at least, which left Mateo wondering where he really stood.

Mateo glanced between them. "I don't like this, but obviously I have no choice. And yes," he added, "I trust both of you to do the impossible without me. Benat, bring her back at any cost."

29

VITTORIA

Vittoria shivered with cold.

Her dress lay damp across her shoulders and back, and her teeth chattered like old bones. Every now and then, a rustle came from beyond the cell, but the darkness was pervasive. At least they hadn't kept her shackles on in here.

When she felt along the wall behind her, wet rock met her fingertips. A door of thick iron bars blocked her exit from the small cell, which was five paces wide at its broadest. How much time had passed since Romeo had her locked in this dent in the rock, she had no idea. It felt like hours.

Every now and then, Romeo's murmurs broke the silence. She strained to hear, unable to make out even the faintest consonants. Two witches had dragged her here and slammed the door after her.

Other voices rotated through Romeo's little lair, mostly female. Zuri had taught her a spell to amplify sounds, but she had no idea if Romeo would be able to detect the magic. Undoubtedly. But would he be paying attention to it? Would magic even work down here?

Was Romeo preparing to fight Mateo and sending messages about his conspiracy with Xavier?

The witches speaking with Romeo could be rebel messengers like Sannara. They might be bringing information about what was happening aboveground. But despite the temptation, she'd wait, just in case. The right moment would present itself.

Not many more minutes passed before a voice called to Romeo from deeper in the caverns. His footsteps retreated. Vittoria knew that voice.

Sannara.

Vittoria cast the simple sound-amplifying spell and winced as the grating crunch of shoes on rock rippled through her ears. *Every* sound was amplified, but at least their words were clear.

"Go to the country house," Romeo murmured. "Don't make me order you to do it. It's not safe here. Not now."

"You want me to abandon you when you need me most?"

A rustle of something. Clothing. Hair, perhaps?

"You serve me best by remaining safe," Romeo said. There was genuine warmth in his words. The coldhearted man who had kidnapped Eneko couldn't be the same witch. "All of this will mean nothing if we're not together at the end of it. After all we have been through . . ."

"She is my sister. My son needs her, Romeo. And you know I will do anything for him that I can."

Sannara said it quietly. It sounded more like a statement of fact than a plea. Vittoria's heart pinched.

Romeo's tone hardened. "It doesn't change the plan."

"Romeo, please."

Vittoria's heart slammed in her chest. Did Sannara know he had Eneko? Did she know what kind of monster she loved?

"Sannara," Romeo said like a caress. "Trust me, please? We will be together, finally. When this all comes together, she will—"

Silence. A muffled sound, like a kiss.

"He has Eneko!" Vittoria screamed. "Sanny! He has Eneko. He's holding him hostage so that I'll do what he wants. Save him! By the Givers, Sannara. Do the right thing for your son. Forget me. Save him!"

"Eneko?" Sannara whispered.

The light beyond the cell brightened. Vittoria barely had time to stop the spell before Romeo appeared in the narrow entryway to her small cavity. He slammed a torch into a holder on the wall and stalked toward her, fury on his face. Vittoria lifted her chin and forced herself not to step back as he approached. With a growl, he grabbed the metal bars in white-knuckled fists. They rattled against the stone.

"You know nothing," he snarled. "Nothing!"

"I know what kind of man you are," she hissed, "and it's not the man that Sannara deserves. You steal children. You betray everyone."

"I will save this Network! It is my duty."

Vittoria stared at him, startled by the unhinged fire in his eyes. Angering Romeo wouldn't help Eneko. In fact, it might make things worse for him. Instead, she had to delay Romeo and buy Sannara time to save Eneko.

But would she?

Vittoria hated herself for the question. Might Sannara have already known? No, she couldn't have known. Her voice had betrayed her shock.

Vittoria steeled her resolve. She couldn't give up hope that Sannara would finally choose her son. Would finally do the right thing. She had to at least give her a chance.

She swallowed. "I'm sorry, Romeo. I didn't mean to anger you."

He glared at her in stoic silence. But her placating humility seemed to do the trick. He stepped back. She followed until the bars stopped her.

"Xavier?" she asked. "Is it him you're frightened of? Is that who you're trying to please?"

"Who said I was frightened?"

"Your eyes."

She said it softly, and she expected him to reach through the bars and strike her. Instead, his jaw tightened. Then he leaned closer, face almost pressed into the iron. The utter fury of his twisted expression sent a spike of fear all the way into her gut.

"You asked about my mere," he murmured hoarsely. His eyes tapered. "Do you really want to know our dark, dark legacy?"

At his words, her heart slammed against her chest. Was this some sort of trap? He looked like he wanted to strangle her.

She nodded.

He laughed, but it was cold.

"That means Mateo told you nothing about her?" Romeo's brow rose. "With good reason. He didn't want to frighten you away."

"No, he didn't tell me."

Romeo scoffed. For a second, he seemed to war with himself, an internal struggle visible in his twitching cheeks. Finally, he drew in a deep breath.

"Mere was raised as a worker and known for her beauty. She had an older brother, Xavier, who was protective of her."

Vittoria mentally shivered. So there *was* a Xavier, and he was their uncle after all. If Romeo noticed her surprise, he ignored it.

"Their parents died in a plague when she was seven and he was ten. Mere was conscripted to a landowner house, while Xavier worked for a blacksmith. They managed to scrape out a life on the street, created a family of misfits. Over time, their family grew to a neighborhood. They pooled resources and took care of each other. Word spread. More joined."

"And so the rebels were born?" she asked when he paused.

Firelight flickered in his eyes. "So they were born," he muttered bitterly. "Xavier was an ambitious young man who hated Sodor, my grandpere, the High Priest. Sodor had imposed heavy taxes and tightened his control on the Network. By that time, Xavier was eighteen. Mere was fifteen. She would have done anything for her brother."

Vittoria's stomach clenched as she remembered Zaldar's revelation before the ballroom attack. *She pretended to be a landowner,* he had said, *but was actually a rebel. Even Hodei was fooled.*

Water pooled at her bare feet. Her dress trembled from her shivers while she waited for him to continue. Romeo stared at the glimmering rock wall behind Vittoria, seemingly transfixed by the cadence of the story.

"A sympathetic landowner named Raphyel took her in. He taught her reading. Transformation. Transportation. Simple spells. Magic wasn't yet banned, but few workers knew much of it. Raphyel supplied Mere with dresses and jewelry. Just after she turned seventeen, she entered into society as his niece."

There were chilling similarities—though stark differences—between her and Esperanza. The similarities made her ill. Did Romeo see it? Is that why he stared at her with such disdain?

"But wouldn't she have been recognized?" she asked.

He shrugged. "She could have been, but wasn't."

"To what end?"

"To gain Pere's attention, of course," he murmured silkily, but there was ice behind his tone.

Although she'd expected that truth, it still startled her. Romeo leaned away from the wall but didn't relax his intent stare. Like he wanted to peg Vittoria down and make her suffer for something.

"Mere caught Hodei's eye at a ball, and they fell in love. That gave Xavier access to Sodor. At the betrothal dinner, Xavier posed as one of Mere's servants and slit Sodor's throat when Sodor left to empty his bladder. A Guardian noticed and advanced. He claimed to have cut Xavier's head half off with a sword, but no one found the body. Nor a blood trail. It's as if he just . . . vanished. Hodei became High Priest at twenty-nine. He was eleven years older than Mere."

"Did Xavier actually die?"

"Mere and Pere were handfasted just before Hodei officially took the throne." He ignored her entirely. The hard edges in his voice sharpened, and she wondered if it was because of his pere or his mere. "Mere grieved her brother and continued on with the lie, even though she wanted to go back to the rebels. She didn't want to wait around for Hodei to find her out. She knew he'd destroy her in the most painful way possible."

Vittoria suppressed the urge to gasp. Was *that* what Hodei wanted? To know why Esperanza had stayed with him when she wanted to go?

Romeo continued, "She claimed that her feelings for Hodei were real, of course. But Mere always knew how to lie. She said she cared for him. Loved him. All the while knowing that Hodei would eventually find out and kill her. The rebels pressured her to stay and spy while their numbers grew. Then she fell pregnant with Mateo and stayed out of fear. Things could have grown worse for the rebels, but she prevented a lot of deaths. Then she had me a few years later."

Thoughts formed in Vittoria's mind like slow-swelling clouds. How desperate Esperanza must have felt, torn between her scrabbled-together family and ruthless husband. What daily terror did she endure, knowing Hodei's wrath could be directed toward her at any moment? Vittoria recalled the servant with the sewn lips. The heads on the pikes in the street.

Was it love or fear that drove Esperanza to stay?

And is *that* what Hodei had really wanted to know?

"Then Mateo's tenth birthday happened," Romeo murmured, oblivious to her thoughts. His expression had turned hard as stone. "I was seven. We were living in the country because it was safer there and, unbeknownst to me at the time, much easier for the rebels to communicate safely with Mere. The riots had started in earnest. That day, Hodei showed up. I remember them arguing. He screamed almost senselessly. I'll never forget his rage. Mere cried. Then he slapped her. He grabbed a knife on his belt and lunged to kill her, but Mateo threw himself between them and fought for her. Hodei won and nearly killed Mateo in the process." Romeo shook his head. "He took me, and here we are."

An icy feeling settled deep in the pit of her stomach, frozen colder by the depths of the shadows in his eyes. *Here we are.* What had happened to Romeo in the years between then and now? Was the fury that rolled off him in waves a result of his time with Hodei? His grief for Esperanza?

Who had loved him?

Who had been Romeo's ally? No one, she imagined. Dark legacies, indeed.

"You weren't there when your mere died," she whispered. "That must have been awful. Mateo said she was fonder of you than him."

"You have your answer now, Vittoria. Mere was a bitter, determined woman who chose the workers over her family. She died alone in the country, the way she deserved. That's all there is to it. Why did she stay?" he scoffed. "Because she loved the rebels more than she loved anyone. Hodei was never able to accept that she turned him into a fool."

Vittoria remained silent, her emotions tumultuous after hearing such a bleak history. Her heart ached for Mateo. For Romeo. For Esperanza.

"Why did you tell me all this?" she asked.

Romeo hesitated in the doorway. He half-turned and said, "Because you won't survive the night. As much as I hate Mateo . . . I . . ."

Before he could say another word, he walked away. The torch remained, flickering on the wall. She stared at the fire longingly but couldn't feel its heat from here. Romeo's departure gave her space to think, and her chest tightened.

For an interminable amount of time, Vittoria paced her cell. She rubbed her arms for warmth, desperately cold. It distracted her, made it difficult to think. Esperanza's story ran through her mind again and again. From Mateo's perspective, and then Romeo's, and then Hodei's, and then Zaldar's. *The days of Esperanza were interesting, of course,* Zaldar had said. *She was a beautiful woman. Elegant. A natural in such crowds.*

Esperanza must have been multifaceted, like a diamond, to harbor such secrets for years. Strong. Maybe even bitter, as Romeo had said. How else would she have gained the strength to survive a world that wanted to destroy her? Had it been difficult to stand by—and love or pretend to love —the man who caused such despair for her witches? To be a puppet for her brother and in fear of her husband?

What a horrifying existence.

Vittoria's mind spun back to the day she met Hodei. There had been real pain, however brief, in his rheumy eyes. Deep bitterness. Did Hodei just want closure? No, he'd wanted more than that. Hodei would have wanted revenge against both Esperanza and Romeo.

Maybe even Xavier.

Was she destined to the same fate as Esperanza?

A female voice whispered outside the cell. Moments later, Romeo stepped back into the narrow doorway. A piece of parchment was on fire above his hand.

"Wish me luck," he said, eyes bright in the light of the flame. He smiled coldly at her. "The time is set when I shall kill Mateo. I'm sorry it had to happen this way for you, Vittoria. Once Mateo is dead, you won't matter at all."

30

MATEO

T he final battle of the Law of Rights commences in twenty minutes at the eliza of the Giver La Principessa.

— Balta

Mateo stared at the hastily scrawled message.

Why so soon? He'd expected this news to come early the next morning.

Balta must know something he didn't. Or feel some sense of urgency for the safety of the Network. For the first time, he wished Balta wasn't the moderator. Before, he appreciated the assurance of fairness, but now he wanted a friend. If Balta hadn't been the moderator, Mateo could have turned to him for help. Wisdom. Sage advice. As it was, Balta could interact with neither Mateo nor Romeo.

Still, Mateo couldn't help but wonder.

Why would Romeo choose the eliza? There was a flat, open space on the gabled rooftop that would allow for a good match, but it was in the heart of Necce and far from the palace. Not to mention stories high. What better way to send a beacon to the rebels that Hodei had died?

There were standard rules, of course. An oval of fire would be conjured. Both fighters would be kept inside until one of them died—unless conditions made it impossible to continue. A match a century before had been called off halfway through due to a tidal wave.

But why that *eliza*?

A dark feeling told him that the *eliza* of the Giver La Principessa hadn't been chosen on a whim, and that made him more nervous than the thought of killing Romeo. The question of *why* rippled through his head in waves. Benat entered the room with heavy footfalls, so Mateo sent him the letter on a whispered spell.

Benat read it, then swore under his breath.

"Any news from Joska?" Mateo asked.

"Not yet. They left an hour ago and should be in the catacombs soon. If all goes well," he tacked on. "The entrance that Joska was aware of may be closed now."

Joska had brought the news of Vittoria's disappearance hours ago. Since then, Mateo had been pacing the house, waiting for the letter. Waiting on fate. Or honor. Or a Giver. Some force outside himself to push this along already. Now that the letter had come and fate had pushed his path directly into his lap, he wanted to shove it back and tell it to hold on for a bit.

He *wanted* to find Vittoria.

"Are you ready, Mateo?" Benat asked.

Mateo scoffed. He felt knocked off-balance. Vittoria gone. Hodei dead. Romeo at large and preparing to kill him. How could anyone be ready to kill their brother for a throne? To watch the world dissolve into civil war?

Vittoria might be the rebels' hostage by now, and surely, they'd use her against him. La Principessa could be humiliated, harmed, or destroyed. Maybe Romeo had Vittoria and wanted to distract him in the middle of the fight.

Maybe none of that was even true, and the worst had come to pass.

Mateo shook his head to clear his thoughts. He had to decide what mattered most, because this was the very moment he'd spent his life preparing for. He had to choose his witches. Choose peace over anything else. This was the moment that Mateo the High Priest must take his first breath.

Vittoria or not. La Principessa or not.

Plans or not.

With a deep inhale, he nodded. Setting thoughts of Vittoria aside caused him physical pain. He still wanted to hit something, but reined in the rage. He had to save his anger for the oval.

He had an overly motivated, arrogantly ambitious upstart of a brother to kill and a Network to save.

"Yes, Benat." He nodded. "I'm ready."

Benat clapped him on the shoulder. "Then I am behind you, Majesty. You were born for this. Now, let's see it done."

31

Vittoria paced her cell for warmth and out of a wild need to release her energy, despite her fatigue. Eneko clouded her thoughts, distracting her every time she tried to deduce Romeo's true game. Why was Romeo with the rebels? Who was really in control here? It all gave way to the memory of Eneko's frightened voice.

Was he safe?

Was he cold?

Had they hurt him?

Had Sannara found him? Would she look?

"Oh, Eneko." Tears filled her eyes, hot and stinging. She blinked them away. She had to focus on getting out of here so she could find Eneko. Then Mateo. Then . . . something. There were too many ways for this night to unfold.

Romeo had taken the torch this time, plunging her back into the unforgiving darkness. There were several witches around—or ones who quietly moved position often—because she seemed to hear sounds from everywhere. Movement beyond the cell. The occasional grunt of what she assumed was a guard. A trickle of a waterfall down the wall behind her.

An earthy, salty smell filled her nostrils. She tried to drink the water as it trickled down the stone, but it was too brackish. It was like sucking on a piece of salty metal. Ocean water, for sure, tainted with other things. How far under the ocean were they, anyway? Would this place collapse if the magic didn't hold?

She shuddered, unnerved by the thought.

A noise from the hallway caught her attention.

"Who's there?" called a wary voice. She jolted when the unmistakable shuffle of feet came next. Whispers. Torches flared to life, illuminating her cavern again. She winced against the unexpected light.

Guards filled the doorway now, standing shoulder to shoulder. Three of them. More than she'd expected, because they hadn't spoken. They stood according to height—the tallest on the left, the shortest on the right. All of them were thin, with ragged clothes. One clutched a hoe as a weapon.

"Stand back!" shouted a firm female voice.

Vittoria's heart fluttered. Sannara!

"If you don't stand back, you will die."

The shortest guard twitched. The three of them had their heads turned to the left, peering down what appeared to be a narrow hallway. Sannara's voice came from that direction, but Vittoria couldn't understand what she was saying.

"Not worth our lives," the short one muttered. "If it's Mateo come for her, he'll kill us in a second."

"What're these witches gonna do to us if we don't?" said the middle guard, gesturing toward Sannara. "They're rebels like us, aren't they? They can't have any better weapons than you and me. I say we take them on. Romeo said nothing was to happen to her."

The one on the left scoffed. He touched a short sword in a scabbard on his belt, but the trembling in his hand suggested he might not know what to do with it. Based on the way the other two seemed to await his command, she guessed he was the unspoken leader.

"It's Sannara coming," said the tallest with a little gulp.

"I'll not fight Sannara," muttered the middle guard. "Like a cat, that one. If you hurt her, you'll face Romeo's wrath too. He'd kill you like a crazy witch. You'd probably never die, just lay around in agony."

"Then what do we do? Protect Vittoria or hurt Sannara? We're dead either way!"

"Give Vittoria to Sannara and we can leave!" The shortest tilted his head back to glance overhead, then winced when a drop of water plopped into his eye. "This place is going to collapse any second now, and we all deserve to watch the final battle. It's the sign, right? So why are we stuck down here when everybody else gets to fight the landowners up there? We're rebels too!" His words ended on a squeak.

"I'm warning you!" Sannara called. "I'll blow this place up and you'll drown."

"She will," cried the middle guard with a note of hysteria. "She has access to the powder."

"Quiet!" the tallest snapped, but a strain of uncertainty colored his voice. He turned to the middle one, his tone quiet. "Could she blow it up?"

He shrugged uneasily. "She'd have to have stolen some of it, but you know Romeo has given her access to almost everything. No one would deny Sannara except . . ."

"She'd blow it." The tallest nodded. "Maybe we should give her the girl and go. Romeo won't find us in the battle, then we'll disappear back to the farms."

"If he even survives," muttered the shortest.

All three of them hesitated now, and a swell of silence fell over the cavern.

Blow it up? Vittoria thought. *What does she—*

An explosion reverberated through the cavern with a blinding flash of light. Rock and dust swelled into the room, and she couldn't duck away fast enough. Shards of rock slammed into her cheeks, scratching her face. A percussion of air shoved her against the wall, where she grunted from the unexpected pain. Her ears rang.

When the chaos settled, she peered through her hands.

The three guards lay on the ground, faces coated in dust. One of them screamed, hands over his ears. Blood trickled through his fingers. For ten terrifying seconds, she heard nothing at all. Then her ears began to pick up sound slowly, like listening through water.

A flicker of light, then a lithe body slipped into view from a hole blown in the wall. The gauzy folds of a dress were just visible in the moving shadows. Sannara.

She held a torch out in front of her, eyes darting all over the room until they landed on Vittoria. Her shoulders slumped with relief. She stepped over the guards—only one was conscious, and he wouldn't stop screaming. A fine powder lightened her dark, lustrous hair and covered her overcoat and dress.

"You're all right?" she whispered.

Vittoria grabbed the bars and nodded. "Fine."

Two witches trailed Sannara like wraiths. Their mouths had been sewn shut so many times that scars remained on the top and bottom of both lips, though they weren't sewn now. Hodei's servants—or used to be, anyway. No doubt Hodei had used the thickest twine possible just to make a lesson out of the agony.

Had the rebels recruited them, somehow? Their faces were thin and so pale she could see veins tacking through their skin. Maybe they'd escaped his evil by living in the catacombs.

"We must be quick," Sannara said. "How's your head?"

Pounding more than ever, but that didn't matter in light of breaking free. "I'll be fine."

"He's going to blow open the door." Sannara tilted her head toward one of the figures who had followed her. "A few clever rebels found ingredients that make an explosive powder. They plan to use it in the uprising tonight. We'll just use a little here, enough to break the iron doors, but step back and protect your head. Cover yourself, and prepare to go quickly." She eyed the wet rock overhead. "Romeo kept his office far out of the usual catacomb traffic. We're under the ocean now, so this could get ugly fast."

The man advanced. He wore a too-big shirt stained with sweat and dirt. He couldn't be much older than sixteen. He held a wooden box in his trembling hand. A piece of flint was carefully tucked in the other. He carried both with extreme care, every movement deliberate.

"Careful," Sannara warned.

Vittoria opened her mouth to say *thank you,* but a movement from the doorway caught her gaze. The middle guard had woken up. He stood, grabbed the hoe from his still-unconscious friend, and snarled.

"You attacked us!" he cried. "You're supposed to be on our side!"

Sannara whirled on him. She nodded to Vittoria. "She's the Giver La

Principessa here to save us. You want to imprison her? You want to suffer as a worker for the rest of your life?"

He paled and mouthed *La Principessa* as he stared at her. Rumors of her betrothal had surely reached all the farms by now, but her position as a Giver clearly hadn't. Vittoria tried to force a serene expression, entirely at a loss. It was easy to be La Principessa when she was giving hope in the form of food, warmth, and medicine. But to be the symbol of hope that prevented a war?

Her throat nearly closed off at the thought, and this was just one man. She couldn't do this. Not while Eneko was locked away. Not while Romeo was at large.

This *couldn't* come down to a *lavanda* maid.

The farm worker hesitated, clearly torn as to whether he believed it or not. No doubt Romeo had chosen these three because they'd come right from the farms. Though obviously not talented, they had brawn that would serve them in a fight. This witch had a body large enough that he could use his size like a boulder. All he had to do was crash into them to stop them. But he didn't.

And that hesitation bought Sannara time to withdraw a sword and point it at his neck. He stopped, throat bobbing as he swallowed and stared at his reflection in the sword.

"If you value your life," Sannara muttered, "you will leave right now."

"O-of c-c-course." He held up both hands. "I-I didn't know. I swear. La Principessa, forgive me." He hesitated, then quickly added to Sannara, "Romeo will kill you for this. You know that? He was firm. Explicit. She was to be kept here no matter what."

Sannara snarled. "Don't tell me my business, you fool. Now, go. Take your friends with you. And if you know what's good for you, you'll head back to the farms and avoid Romeo."

Frantic, he nodded. He shook his friends, and they groggily sat up.

Vittoria's heart slammed against her rib cage. The pale witch with the box had been crouched down all this time, carefully pinching some of the powder and weaving it in a line around the bars. Pieces of it fell to the stone and scattered, and he gingerly swept them back together.

Vittoria pressed her face to the bars as a gush of water spurted from the ceiling near the new hole in the rock. Sannara eyed the water warily.

"Eneko?" Vittoria whispered.

Sannara's expression grew haunted. "I will soon. I realized I had to break you free first, then I can get Eneko while Romeo fights Mateo. Thank you, Vittoria. I . . . I didn't know."

"Where is he?"

"Safe."

"I must—"

"He's safe!" she snapped, a wild look in her eyes. "He has to be. I-I can't fathom a world where he would . . . I'll find him no matter what it costs me. Even my life. I owe my son that much . . ."

She trailed off, eyes watery.

"Ready," the witch murmured as he replaced the lid on the wooden box. He stepped back, flint in hand again. Little shavings littered the floor in a small pile. Sannara pulled off her cloak and shoved it through the bars to Vittoria.

"Stand back," she said. "Put this over you. Protect your head, and keep your toes as far away from the ground as possible, if you can."

Heart pounding, Vittoria climbed up on a little ledge of rock and held herself against the wet wall so tightly that the stones pressed into her stomach. The witch murmured something—a spell—and sparks flared with light. Vittoria screwed her eyes shut.

"Ready," he called.

Fire hissed, and feet shuffled back. Seven seconds later, a percussive *boom* exploded around her yet again—this time unbearably loud. She thought her teeth would be shaken out of her head. An acrid scent filled the air. Debris and dust filled her lungs. She coughed, the powder grinding between her teeth and stabbing her tongue.

The iron bars slammed into the wall next to her. One struck her shoulder with a *thud*. She cried out, but the sound was lost. Only a ringing noise swelled around her now. Vittoria's head pounded until she felt a hand on her back.

"Come!" Sannara shouted, seemingly from far away. Water poured into the cavern. Rocks crumbled under its power. In seconds, she'd be trapped in the flood.

"It's all going to fall now!" Sannara yelled. Vittoria understood her more from the movement of her lips than from hearing the words. "We must go!"

Vittoria shook Sannara's cloak off. Dust and rock fell to the water pooling on the floor. Sannara motioned for her to hurry, mud coating her face as she grabbed Vittoria's arm and wrenched her away. The crushed rock ground into Vittoria's feet as she sloshed through the water. The three guards had disappeared, leaving a wide-open exit.

Sannara pulled Vittoria out of the spray and pointed to the two men she'd brought with her. They eyed the salt water warily, stepping back. The waterfall widened every second.

"Follow these two out!" Sannara yelled over the crash of the water. "They'll take you back to the surface. Mateo and Romeo are about to fight at the *eliza* of La Principessa. Let Mateo see you. Let the workers see you. He needs you, Vittoria. If you aren't there, the rebels will take over. What they have planned, no one will recover from. Only you can stop it!"

"What about you?" Vittoria squinted against the seawater. "Where are you going?"

"To my son!"

She shoved Vittoria toward the doorway. Vittoria only saw Sannara's wet hair clinging to her face before she darted away, following the wraiths of the catacombs.

32

MATEO

Firelight flickered over Romeo's stony face as he stared at Mateo from across the roof and bounced on the balls of his feet. Mateo hardly recognized this livid, wild man.

Mateo, Romeo, and Balta stood atop the *eliza*, near a waist-high wall around the perimeter. Crumbled stone littered the rooftop, painting Mateo's toes with dust. Romeo wore thin leather shoes, but Mateo kept his feet bare. Easier to gauge the position of the fire that way.

A black oval smoldered on the ground, but all three of them stood outside it. Balta's expression was carefully neutral. He looked to neither Mateo nor Romeo, and Mateo was glad. He could only focus on Romeo.

Romeo the usurper. Romeo the destroyer.

Despite the gathering crowd below, the world felt oddly empty up here. Calm. From below came the clamor of a growing crowd. Workers, but no clear rebels. No dark-gray cloaks with hoods. Rumors of Hodei's death swirled in the uncertainty, he was sure. Why else would they hold the battle early? But with no firm information, it was all speculation. Until they knew for sure, he doubted the rebels would act.

No, the moment to fear was when he or Romeo died. Then the rebels would advance and sow chaos. Mateo didn't hear the individual whispers from below. He heard nothing but his heartbeat and steady breath.

Because he was finally ready.

Tonight, he had to kill a man who had chosen to be someone else. As repulsive as it was, it had to be done—because Romeo would do more than kill him. Romeo would take his rage and destroy everyone Mateo cared about. The incensed expression on Romeo's face left no doubt of that.

Mateo didn't fight for his own life—he fought for Vittoria. Benat. Zuri. For all of the Network.

Balta gestured to the ring. "Contenders," he called. "Advance to the oval."

When they stepped up to the edge, the flames simmered to life, rising just inches from the rooftop. Barring a disaster that threatened both of their lives and prevented a reasonable conclusion to the fight, he'd be in that oval for his last breath—or Romeo's.

Vittoria intruded on his thoughts, but he had to push her aside. They'd find her as soon as he could. Benat and Joska were still searching for her. That would have to be enough.

Three of Benat's men waited in the crowd. The rest were looking for Vittoria or keeping an eye on Necce.

Below, the throng grew with every passing second. Landowners weren't visible anywhere—they would be hiding. It was late night—or early morning? Did it matter? Rumors of Hodei's death would have kept Necce up all night.

"Brothers," Balta called, loudly enough for all to hear. He hesitated only a moment. "The rules are explicit. A fight to the death. No weapons, no magic, no outside help. If you leave the oval before I authorize it, you forfeit. This is the battle for the throne. Are there any questions?"

Neither brother spoke.

With a heavy swallow, Balta nodded. "Then honor awaits."

They stepped into the oval, and the smoldering fire sprang upward into a shimmering orange wall twice as tall as Mateo. Balta was just visible through the thin flames.

Dirt ground beneath Mateo's heel as he stepped forward. The heat urged him further into the ring, which was twenty paces wide. Enough space to grapple, but they were still likely to get burned. Historically, most contenders used the fire to their advantage. Pushing their opponent into the flames, attempting to throw them out of the oval. A dirty way to win, but it had been effective.

Romeo hadn't looked away from Mateo since he'd arrived. His oddly intent gaze seemed hungry. Intense. Perhaps maniacal. The sounds of the crowd died away entirely in the oval, replaced by the snap and crackle of fire. The smell of an impending storm, swirling with the stench from the wharf, disappeared too.

For a moment, Romeo stood there, regarding Mateo. Mateo returned the scrutiny. "Honor to you, brother," he finally said.

Romeo glared. He shifted to the right. Mateo braced his weight evenly on crouched legs. All his lessons with Benat settled into his muscles. He knew this work well enough that instinct would take over once they got started.

"Come at me, brother," Mateo said with a jerk of his fingers and a cold smile.

Romeo's nose twitched.

They circled for another breath before Romeo advanced. Although he was fast, Mateo anticipated the move and dodged. It had been an exploratory advance, not meant to hurt him. Just to gauge his reach. Romeo danced back, then feinted again. Mateo slipped to the side. Romeo was moving too quickly and had to skid to a stop before he hit the edge of the oval.

"You," Romeo ground out, "were not meant for this, Mateo."

"As eldest son, you mean?"

"They chose me."

"They?"

Romeo yelled, then barreled at him again. Mateo dodged, but Romeo anticipated him and they collided. They toppled to the stones together. Mateo cradled his head with one arm, and his wrist took the blow instead of his head. The moment his spine hit the ground, he rolled. Romeo attempted to gain control by straddling him, but Mateo moved too fast. In seconds, they broke apart.

Blood oozed from Romeo's right nostril.

"You don't know what you're up against, Mateo. This is not what you think." Romeo cracked his neck. "There are things at play you have never dreamed."

"Oh? Like what?"

Romeo crouched. The fire danced eerily over the top of him like a dark omen. Both of them already glistened with sweat. The heat from the oval pressed on Mateo with sweltering fury. Sweat trickled down his back. If Romeo kept moving so quickly, it would make it almost impossible to peg him down. Eventually, he'd tire, but so would Mateo.

Mateo faked an advance, and Romeo feinted left.

"It's nothing you want to be involved in," Romeo muttered. "Concede the throne to me. I know our enemies far better than you ever will."

"I disagree."

Romeo screamed as he charged again. They met in the middle like clashing sea dragons. Romeo reached for Mateo's throat, but Mateo's arms were longer. He dodged the hold, wrapped his arms around Romeo's leg, and slammed him to the ground. Romeo grunted, the force of the impact taking his breath away. He tried to hook his legs around Mateo's hips, but his paralyzed lungs weakened the attempt. Mateo stepped out of his way as Romeo regathered his breath.

"You won't win, Romeo!"

"I have already won." Romeo grinned. Blood dribbled onto his upper lip and stained his teeth pink. "Your La Principessa is in *my* control."

All of Mateo's training kept him on the offensive. For half a second, he almost reacted. Almost gave into the temptation to be afraid for her. Instead, he drove his head into Romeo's midsection and dropped him to the roof. Romeo lifted a bent leg to Mateo's chest. Unable to reach his neck, Mateo punched. The blow grazed Romeo's cheek. Mateo threw another, but Romeo batted it away, grabbed his arm, and twisted.

Mateo grunted and slipped free of his grip. Romeo shoved back, separating them until they both stood apart again.

Romeo straightened, fury etched on every feature. But he was playing at this. He wasn't serious about killing Mateo yet, or he wouldn't be talking so much. Was he stalling? Nervous?

Why didn't he just go for it already?

Romeo danced back, spitting. "Mateo, forget this! You cannot win."

Mateo ran at him and dropped a shoulder. Romeo moved like a cat. He slipped out of the way, forcing Mateo to fall to his back to avoid the flames. Romeo took advantage and pounced, but Mateo rolled out from under him.

They toppled, one over the other, to the other side of the ring. Mateo's knuckles ached when he landed a fist on Romeo's jaw. Undeterred, Romeo scored a punch near Mateo's left eye. The skin bubbled with pain that Mateo barely felt. He used his legs to push Romeo off. The fire caught Romeo's shirt, and he jerked back, yanking it off.

Mateo leaped back to his feet. Romeo stared at him from across the oval, wary now.

"You're fast," Mateo panted, "but I'm stronger. Romeo, stop this madness and come to an agreement with me. I'm prepared to kill you today, but I don't want to."

With a guttural shout, Romeo advanced again.

Mateo waited. The three seconds it took Romeo to cross the oval seemed to slow to a lifetime. At the last second, Mateo dropped to one knee and hooked an arm around Romeo's neck. Romeo's body snapped back, turning with the sweeping movement. Mateo moved with it as he pulled Romeo close, put his chest to Romeo's back, and dropped his weight on him. Romeo hit his knees.

"Submit, brother," Mateo grunted. His other arm snaked around to reinforce the first. Romeo kicked, but Mateo's long legs wrapped around his waist. He rolled onto his back, tightening his body around Romeo like the ghost panther mere.

A crushing elbow in Mateo's ribs almost forced him to loosen his grip for just a breath, but he held on. Ferocity kept his arms locked despite Romeo's squirming.

"Why?" Mateo yelled. Tears prickled the back of his eyes. "Why didn't you trust me? Why didn't you give me a chance?"

The moments passed like hours, and a distant part of Mateo thought this must be another nightmare. This couldn't be the real thing, because back in the depths of his mind, in the furthest reaches of his soul, he hadn't really believed he'd be able to do it.

Romeo's entire body tensed like a whip beneath him. He tried to thrash, but Mateo held too tightly.

"Why?" Mateo shouted, even though he knew his brother wouldn't answer. "Why, Romeo? I always loved you!"

Romeo's pounding hand weakened. Mateo choked off a sob as he tightened his grip. For a moment, he faltered. The memory of Romeo's wide, terrified eyes when Pere snatched him away haunted him.

Romeo's movements slowed.

Mateo choked on his own grief. A few more seconds. Just a few more—

The fire vanished. Balta stepped through the smoking ring, one hand held out, and commanded, "Stop!"

Mateo released Romeo.

Romeo rolled to the side, eyes half-open in a violent coughing fit. Balta pointed to the east, toward the harbor, with terror on his face.

Fire dazzled the sea as boats burned bright in the harbor. Bodies could be seen in the light, jumping free of the ships and into the ocean. Mateo blinked several times. Cool air settled on his hot skin. Flames, dizzyingly high, lit up the sky behind Magnolia Castle. A loud, percussive sound issued from the top of the castle just before pieces of rock flew everywhere, collapsing the top of the bell tower. The tall structure crumbled in a pillar of dust.

"By the Givers," Mateo muttered.

Romeo groaned as he tried to get his body under him.

"The rebels!" Balta cried. "They're setting fire to everything in the landowner coven. Some of them are headed to Necce now. Look!"

A mob of witches with torches was headed this way. Behind them, the east wing of Magnolia Castle had just started to burn. Thick, choking smoke billowed into the sky. Mateo stared at it, breathless. Torches couldn't have caused that explosion. The rebels must have something else. Something dangerously flammable to have created such destruction in mere moments.

Romeo gasped, head pressed into the ground. "It's only going to get worse, Mateo," he muttered, hoarse. "All of Necce will burn. All of it."

Draped down the front of Magnolia Castle was a sprawling banner—an ivory swan on an emerald background. That wasn't the sign of the rebels. Nor was it anything he recognized.

A booming sound came from the landowner coven, followed by a flash of light.

Something . . . explosive.

Romeo's head dropped back to the ground as he wheezed for breath. "Finish this," he ground out. "Kill me now, take your Network and your life. You don't know what awaits you, Mateo. If you can't kill me now, you won't survive what's coming."

Mateo pushed to his feet with a grimace. "I cannot win while both of our lives are in peril. The oval has already vanished. We stop the rebels together, then we return and let fate decide."

Romeo glared at him. A captain transported to the top of the *eliza,* near Balta. Soot stained his face and clothes. He doubled over, panting as if he'd run there.

"Forgive me." He bowed to Romeo and Balta. "But rebels have overtaken the castle. They're torching the boats on the beach, threatening to kill all the landowners. The landowners are barricading themselves in the castle and fighting back, but the rebels have a powder. It's exploding rooms. Setting things on fire. Not even our magic can stop it. What do I do, sir?" he asked Balta.

Balta looked to Mateo.

"Stop this rebellion, Mateo," Balta muttered. "Right now. I will subdue every rebel that threatens any life."

A second captain appeared, terror in his eyes. "Rebels in the orchards, sir. And the farmlands. They're all rising against the landowners. The landowners are transporting into the peninsula now, running for their lives. Everything is on fire."

"Kill me now, Mateo!" Romeo screamed. "Or you will never win this throne. Prove yourself worthy!"

Without the roar of the flames in his ears, the sounds from below grew louder. Witches screaming. Women running. Every road in Necce was a mad scramble of fleeing bodies. Mateo ignored Romeo. Ignored the unfolding chaos. His thoughts focused on Vittoria. Forget the Law of Rights. La Principessa needed to come *now*. Mateo looked at Balta and pointed to the oval, now a line of ash.

"Can I leave it?" he asked.

"The oval is gone," Balta said. "The fight has been jeopardized by outside circumstances. We will resume after the rebellion is quelled."

Mateo cast one last glance at Romeo. "We are not done, brother."

He transported away.

He had his High Priestess to find.

33

VITTORIA

Vittoria's body felt as if it had taken a beating.

Her head pounded, still angry about the wallop from Romeo that had started this whole mess, and now exacerbated by the explosion that had granted her freedom. She forced her eyes open, aided by the chilly air of the caverns.

She struggled to stay conscious as the two witches led her through the catacombs. They waded through canals and endless streams of water that flowed past her ankles, icy cold and salty. Her skirt clung to her skin, tying up her legs. Each of the males held one of her arms and quietly stumbled along without a word.

Darkness was their ally and their foe. Twice, they took wrong turns and doubled back, sometimes groping in the dark. The two witches constantly glanced behind them and kept a careful eye on the water levels at their ankles. Whenever the panicked cries of other witches rang down the corridors, they stopped, pressed her into a wall to protect her, and waited.

"Flooding!" the fleeing witches screamed. "Get out of here!"

Once the witches passed, the three of them would start again.

Despite their thin, malnourished bodies, they navigated the catacombs with impressive skill. Clearly, they knew this world. How long had they lived here? How did they escape Hodei? A thousand questions plagued Vittoria, but she quieted all of them.

She had to find Mateo.

The cycle of running and hiding happened so many times Vittoria wasn't sure whether she was in a nightmare or a waking dream. She was so thoroughly disoriented and confused that when one of them put her hands on a flat piece of metal that stuck out from the cave wall, she had to shake herself. They grabbed her arm and tugged her up with a throaty grunt. She reached higher in the darkness to find another metal bar.

Rungs of a ladder.

Between the two of them, she climbed, slipping every so often on the mossy metal. Fifteen rungs. Twenty. Thirty. When the lead witch grunted, she stopped climbing on rung forty-two.

A knock came next. Then the scuffle of voices and feet, and finally, a crack of light overhead.

She stumbled onto a street, emerging onto a cobblestone road not far from the beach. When she whirled around, her escorts had disappeared. Only the giant sculpture of a sea dragon—an entrance to Necce on the opposite side of the city, as far from Magnolia Castle as she could be— stared back at her.

Did that statue hide an entrance to the catacombs? More of the strange magic that kept the catacombs from collapsing, perhaps? Where exactly had she been in the depths of the earth? Somewhere under the ocean, clearly.

The ground trembled as she stepped forward. She paused and looked behind her. There was no earthquake, but the trees lining the road shivered all the same. No doubt their foundation was collapsing. Water was filling the catacombs now, destroying the old foundations.

Vittoria ran.

The cold stones at her feet had an oddly grounding, awakening effect as she raced away, heart in her throat. She slipped into Necce, which hadn't collapsed yet, so she slowed. Maybe it wouldn't all fall.

A scream issued behind her. Vittoria whirled around. Flames danced high in the air. Rebels in their gray cloaks scuttled around, some with torches, others herding frightened children away from fires. Smoke billowed over Necce and the ocean, filling the air with the smell of char. Panic infused the city, thick as the smoke.

Vittoria stood there for several seconds, taking it all in, putting the pieces together.

Romeo actually led the rebels in some fashion—or worked for them.

Mateo was now fighting for his life.

The uprising had begun.

Trees toppled as the ground underneath them gave way, collapsing. It seemed as if the very earth was angry and fighting back. Alkarra, taking its revenge for such rampant brutality. Everything was about to fall apart.

Which meant it was time for a Giver to step up and save her witches. And somehow, *she* had to be that Giver. The thought made her knees weak. Did Mateo know she'd been taken? Was he worried or frantically searching for her?

Vittoria put a hand to her head, brushing the grit and dust from the explosions in the catacombs. She looked—and smelled—worse than anyone else she'd seen. No one would believe her to be a witch imbued with lifesaving magic.

How could she possibly pull this off?

Yet, her witches still needed a Giver. To be that Giver, she had to cross the city, find Mateo—if he was still alive—and somehow stop a disastrous rebellion.

First, find Mateo.

"La Principessa," she murmured, clenching the folds of her filthy dress in her hands. "Bless me this night."

She plunged into the smoky streets.

Wet skirts clinging to her legs, Vittoria raced through Necce.

Workers looted landowner stores, breaking windows with rocks and rushing in and out with goods in hand. Silk from the dressmakers. Candles. Potion bottles. The stolen items poured into the streets and disappeared. Currency, mostly gold coins, was thrown into the road and scavenged by any worker rushing by. Several food shops had been ransacked, discarded baskets empty on the ground beneath crushed food.

No one stopped Vittoria, nor recognized her. No one wore the gray robes of the rebels, though the rebels wouldn't be here, would they? They would be at the battle—near the castle or in the landowner coven beyond.

So, where would Mateo be?

The *eliza*, still? The battle for the throne had clearly sparked the uprising. Hadn't the farm workers said it was the sign? Maybe all this was meant to distract Mateo and give Romeo the advantage? She growled in frustration—there was so much she didn't know. She should never have gone by herself to the Wench!

The harder she ran, the more her head ached. Her hearing returned as she headed down alleys, twisting through crushes of looting witches. Rage and frustration and vengeance burned bright in their eyes. This was Mateo's nightmare come to life. As if all the powers of evil had converged on their world at once.

She rushed past the chaos, lungs burning. Her eyes were trained on the sky as a burning oval on top of the *eliza* came into view. Her heart nearly stopped. So this was the brutal battle that landowners claimed as honorable. Two figures moved within the flames, but the curtain of fire distorted their movements. Benat would be up there, surely. *Someone* would be there.

Then the oval disappeared.

Vittoria skidded to a stop with a cry. What did that mean? Was Romeo dead?

Mateo?

Workers streamed toward the castle. Were they workers? Some of them wore the pocketed robes of the witches in the orchards. Some carried tools from the farms. Pitchforks. Rakes. They were dull objects, but still formidable enough in a hand-to-hand fight. Nothing against magic, of course.

Her throat nearly closed off at the thought of those workers going up against the landowners with *rakes*, of all things. The civil war truly was unfolding before her very eyes. Mateo had always believed rebels had some influence in the farms, but the number of witches marching from the countryside had turned formidable.

But were they rebels or workers?

And did it matter anymore?

Vittoria slipped into a side alley that flowed back to the *eliza* of the Giver La Principessa. She dodged mud puddles, someone crying out for help, and a pool of broken glass. Panting, she stopped at the circular street that surrounded the *eliza*. Everything lay empty. Had no one been watching the fight? Or had they already fled?

Strewn parchment scuttled past, borne by a breeze. Cast-off food. Some clothing. The ravages of a massive crowd remained. Then she gasped. A few unmoving bodies littered the ground. Landowners, all of them.

Vittoria released a shaky breath. "Mateo?" she called. "Mateo? Benat? Joska?"

No one responded to the plaintive cry.

Frantic, she darted to a bigger alley and followed the crowd that chugged toward Magnolia Castle. The press of buildings looming overhead opened up to the barren stretch of beach that separated Necce and the castle. A firm dividing line between classes.

Vittoria sucked in a sharp breath.

Two lines had formed on the beach. On the far side, near the castle, stood a line of furious male landowners. The air shimmered in front of them with some sort of shielding spell. A few had soot marks on their faces. All appeared livid, their mouths open in rage-filled shouts she couldn't hear.

Balta stood on a large rock in the midst of the landowners, presumably barking commands to Guardians. The landowners held the rebels at bay with their invisible shield while the Guardians prepared to attack. The air crackled with the tension of magic.

The landowners wouldn't give up their peninsula, or their castle, without a fight to the death. And with powerful magic on their side, it seemed more and more unlikely to be *their* deaths.

Fifty paces away stood the rebels, interspersed with workers, in a line of their own. They conjured no visible magic, but didn't appear afraid of the landowners. Small balls of energy, some red, some magenta, others golden yellow, zipped out from the landowner line and across the space. Before they could hit the workers, the balls faded and dropped to the sand, inert.

So they must be using *some* magic.

Behind the line, several rebels carried small wooden barrels forward. Vittoria's stomach clenched. Barrels of that terrible powder that Sannara had used to set Vittoria free? What would they do with that? Utter destruction, if the pulsing rage of this crowd meant anything. An entire barrel could wipe out the whole castle, she'd bet.

Vittoria scanned both crowds. Where was Mateo? Benat? Any of them? What if they were out looking for her instead of here? A chant rose from the crowd of workers. A terrible song that turned her blood to slush.

"Death to honor. Death to honor."

The line of workers swelled to astonishing numbers. She even saw a few dusty faces that certainly had come from a quarry somewhere. Had the Guardians Mateo saved returned? Benat's men? She'd never be able to figure it out from where she stood. Like Balta, she needed to *see*.

Over the raucous crowd, she heard the roll of Balta's voice, amplified by magic.

"Guardians!" he roared. "Prepare yourselves."

Vittoria turned back around and headed for the closest building. Shoving her way through the press of bodies took time. Most witches ignored her. Some scowled. Others pushed back. Vittoria elbowed her way through until she came to a small shop on the furthest outskirt of the city. A rain barrel, half-full, stood at the corner. With a grunt, she heaved it over, sloshing water onto the cobblestones. She stood it back up so the open side was down, then climbed on top.

The view of the whole battlefield was far grimmer. Guardians stretched all the way to the castle, which smoked now instead of flaming. Beyond the castle, the burning landowner houses illuminated the sky like hot coals. Landowner women gathered on the beach in a long chain, using spells to send buckets of water on their houses, to no avail.

"Romeo," she muttered. "Where are you?"

Wouldn't Romeo be here, leading them? Or would Xavier? What was their plan?

But there was no discernible leader here. Just a group of witches staring at the opposing line. Some of them fidgeted, eyeing the magical wall warily. Some laughed, trying to catch the balls of magic and pretend they weren't terrified. But the front line of rebels, the most formidable and clearly the strongest, simply stared at the landowners. Their lack of emotion unnerved her.

"Who," she murmured, "is leading you?"

Balta turned, squaring himself to the rebels, his countenance grim. He projected his voice with an incantation that broke through the clamor.

"Rebels," he called.

A hush fell over both lines.

"I will give you one chance to stand down. Should you choose to fight us, you will be held guilty of inciting violence and will all meet with death. Every last one of you will be killed for insubordination. This is your only chance to get out of this with your life intact."

Vittoria heard her own breaths in the silence that followed. If he killed this whole crowd, who would hold up Necce? Who would work? Clean the houses? Prepare the food? He couldn't be serious.

But the expression on his face *was* serious.

Balta waited a full ten seconds that felt like a sordid eternity. His lips twitched as he held up both hands.

"Will you withdraw?"

"No!" shouted a voice. "We will not withdraw."

Rebels glanced around as if they, too, were surprised that someone had spoken on their behalf. Balta paused another few breaths. Then he nodded, as if resigned. "Guardians!" he shouted. "Advance!"

Vittoria held her breath. The rebels at the front braced themselves. Not far from where Vittoria stood, the landowners parted to make way for a contingent of ten Guardians. The magical shield shimmered dully, then floated forward to allow the Guardians space to stand in front of the landowners, but still be protected.

Nine more contingents moved through the landowner crowd—one hundred Guardians in all—and joined the new front. The Guardians were safe behind the shield, and the landowners were safe behind the Guardians.

Vittoria's heart broke. The end of this battle was already clear. Although the rebels and workers far outnumbered the Guardians, there was no fighting magic with hoes and rakes.

Then again, the landowners were powerful, but the rebels were desperate. And that desperation shouldn't be underestimated. No witch could hold up a spell forever—especially not something so energy-consuming as that shield. If rebels could break it, who would die first?

The young Guardians with trembling knees and pale expressions, most likely.

Rebels would have to kill Guardians to get to the landowners, and most Guardians were workers. Too young for such a life. Forced into serving their High Priest. Vittoria thought of the two brothers they'd rescued in Necce, and her stomach flipped. She wanted to vomit in the sand but couldn't summon the strength to move.

La Principessa, she thought, *is supposed to stop all of this.*

But how?

For a long breath, nothing happened. She needed Mateo and his infernal plans. His ideas. His . . . confidence. But how could a mere *lavanda* maid stop this? This battle had been decades in the making. The brewing tension had thickened to the point where it felt hard to breathe under the strain.

As if the crowd knew they could soon lose their lives.

"Ready!" Balta called.

Only the crashing waves broke the silence. The Guardians clenched their fists. Some of them shifted their footing in the sand. Small twitches rippled across the line.

The rebels didn't move, but tension filled the air. It would take only a few seconds for each side to race into the middle and attack—if the Guardians left the safety of the shield at all. Would they stand behind the magic and let the rebels fall at their feet? That seemed most likely.

Vittoria's heart banged against her ribs as Balta lifted an arm.

"Attack!"

The Guardians lifted their weapons, shouted something unintelligible, then turned around . . . and attacked the landowners.

Stunned landowners fell beneath unexpected blows. Blood sprayed in the air. The shield wobbled. Parts of it broke entirely, fading in the first hints of morning light. With guttural shouts, the rebels advanced forward to back the Guardians, throwing themselves into the fracas.

All down the line, the magic fell apart.

The violence rippled back in a sweeping tide of bloodshed. Some landowners attempted new spells, but the attack came too swiftly. Others drew swords but didn't seem to know how to use them. A few were expert swordsmen, but they were quickly overwhelmed by the rebels who poured onto the beach.

Rebels carrying tall torches broke away from the surge of angry witches and shoved through the crowd. They moved back toward Necce. Bright-blue flames sprang to life as they strode past Vittoria. Workers running to join the bloodbath dodged out of their way. Vittoria leaped off the barrel as a witch headed right for the shop behind her.

"Stop!" She planted herself in front of him. "You can't burn down everything! This will punish the workers, not the landowners!"

He snarled and heaved her aside. Vittoria stumbled into another witch, who pushed her away with a menacing laugh. She righted herself just as the rebel set fire to the dry roof. In seconds, the blaze crawled greedily up the brittle reeds. What few workers didn't surge into the battle stood back, watching with open mouths.

"Stop!" Vittoria screamed. "Stop!"

The crowd streamed around her, oblivious. Like the fires, fury built within her. They would destroy everything. Everything.

And how could they be stopped? Mateo had been right. The rebels led a force that was unimaginable in number, and growing. With the Guardians turning against the landowners, there would be new annihilation—and when would the bloodshed end?

This is what it felt like when there was no hope.

No hope for her family. For Eneko. For the future of an entire Network. Tonight, they swapped one regime for another. This was anarchy and bloodlust and years of pent-up rage. It wasn't a path that would yield a better world.

This was annihilation.

They would battle each other until landowners and rebels and workers were nothing more than piles of bones. Their history would be written on sand. No one would remember them. They'd fade into the bleak annals of time.

And La Principessa wouldn't stand for it. She couldn't. Because there was Eneko and Mere and Pere and Mateo and Zuri and Benat and always—always—room for hope. Righteous indignation filled her, swelling like a storm.

"I am La Principessa," she whispered furiously, fists clenched. "I am the Giver of Hope. I *am* La Principessa, and you will fear me!"

Vittoria pushed through the crowd, headed toward the battle where blood and death and destruction reigned. Screams. Crunching bones. Crashing swords. The smell of copper and smoke.

Nearby, a group of landowners had barricaded themselves back-to-back in a circle, magical shields barely holding off the wrath-filled rebels. Without the line of landowners in their way, rebels sprinted through the sand, toward the castle and all the landowner houses that lay beyond. Soon, the bloodbath would extend to women and children. Down the beach, landowner women shoved children onto rowboats and pushed them out to the ocean.

Hadn't the plan always come to this moment? This is what they had all been working to stop. This is what she was always meant to do. She didn't know *what* she'd do, or how she'd do it, but power propelled her forward all the same. The power of the Givers burned through her now, and she couldn't stop it.

This was how she saved her family.

"I am," she said, setting her shoulders, "La Principessa. You," she shouted to the oblivious crowd, "will one day call me *Majesty*."

Vittoria turned and strode into the war.

34

MATEO

"The catacombs are crumbling, Majesty. No one knows how it started." Joska dropped to his knees, panting. Water soaked the ground at his feet as it dripped off his clothes. "The sea nearly swept us away before we made it out. The land is collapsing on the far side of Necce, near Samsa Coven. Buildings falling." He shook his head. "I . . . it's all collapsing."

Mateo blinked, unable to comprehend the news. The catacombs? Terror snaked through his chest. By honor, if Vittoria were—

"Vittoria?"

"No sign anywhere. No one that we saw knew anything, and we saw almost no one. They were all coming here to attack."

Sorun, a man in his mid-thirties who had been assigned to Nerea and Ander, stepped forward with a grim expression.

"She's not at her parents' house, Majesty." He hesitated, then bit out, "Eneko is gone too."

"What?"

Sorun's face twisted in a flash of pain. "I didn't know, Majesty. I swear I didn't know he was gone until just now. Nerea and Ander didn't know he was gone, either. They thought he was sleeping. I had a feeling and . . . they checked on him. He wasn't there, but his window was open. They've sensed no disturbance at all. They're . . . they're terrified."

A roar filled Mateo. He kept it restrained, but he quaked with the force of it. Romeo. This had Romeo written on it. Romeo had been right—he should have killed him when he had the chance. Mateo's throat went dry.

"Sannara?" he asked hoarsely.

"No sign of her," Sorun said. "I sent men searching at the Wench, but it's deserted. She's not there."

"Send men to Romeo's home and his office at the castle. Scour every place possible looking for Eneko. We must find him. No luck on Vittoria in Necce?" he asked Benat.

"No, Majesty."

Mateo peered out on the devastation. They were just outside the city limits, on the far edge of the beach, watching the two sides clash. He'd winced when the Guardians turned on the landowners, but hadn't that been inevitable? Romeo had refused to see it.

And why?

Mateo had always known it would happen. Now that it was unfurling before his eyes, he hated himself for not preventing it. But who could have?

"She'll be here!" Mateo said. He thumped a fist over his heart. "I can feel it. We just have to find her. La Principessa will not abandon her witches. Our place is with her. Now, we find her to stop this war."

He headed for the madness. Benat trailed him as he wound through the crowd of workers on the battle's edge. There were so many they'd already started to overwhelm the landowners.

Then he saw a flash of something out of the corner of his eye. The hair rose on the back of his neck. He stopped.

And there was Vittoria.

Barefoot, filthy as a pig in mire, but with a ferocity he admired, she strode toward the battle. Dust caked her hair, and her dress was stained four different shades of brown. Blood marred her cheek.

But she was alive.

Clearly, she had no plan. Hadn't seen him.

But she was here.

Relief. Frustration. Love. Annoyance. He felt it all at the same time, a complicated tangle of emotions made worse by how beaten she looked. Mateo scowled. She expected to just walk into the chaos and survive?

Well, she would survive. He would see to that.

"Vittoria!" he called.

She spun to look at him, her hair hanging in clumps around her shoulders. He sucked in a sharp breath, stunned by the intensity of her expression—and the wounds on her face. A moment passed before he could recover his control. Whoever hurt her would get their due.

Once they stopped this madness.

Something settled on her. Calm. Peace. Resolve, perhaps. "Help me!" she cried.

"I will stop this!"

Disbelief that he'd found her at all weakened Mateo's knees. He took in the fury in her eyes. The uncontrolled rage in the hard angles of her jaw. And he knew that everything he'd wanted her to be had come to pass.

She *was* La Principessa.

So he nodded. Her face relaxed, then she whipped around to stride into the melee.

"Benat," he called. "Tell your men to get to Necce. Put out the fires. You and Joska will provide backup for me and Vittoria. Keep your eye on her, and stay with me. Be ready in case I can't maintain the magic."

"Yes, Majesty!" Benat broke through a crowd of workers and scrambled to keep up with Mateo, barking out directions to his men.

Mateo's heart beat in his throat as he advanced, following Vittoria's footsteps until he nearly caught up with her quick strides. He muttered a shield incantation he'd learned from a tribe in the South a decade ago. It would dissolve any flying objects before they hit her. Even now, spraying sand disappeared in puffs as the magic formed an invisible barrier around her. A flying shoe fell in shreds to the ground before it could slam into her shoulder.

He wanted to cast a floating incantation—ancient magic, Declan, perhaps. But he had to have Vittoria in his full sights when he started it, or it would lift someone else. She disappeared behind a rebel attempting to strangle a landowner. The landowner cast a curse, and the worker doubled over to vomit. Free, the landowner scrambled back.

Mateo dodged them, plunging farther into the chaos with his attention focused on Vittoria. Joska darted to his side and parried the swing of a wooden stick. Benat cast a shield spell over Mateo's back seconds before an errant curse would have hit him.

Mateo moved without thinking until Vittoria came back into sight. He chanted the elevation spell. She took a step, but her feet never hit the sand. He stopped to put all his attention on the initiation. Declan was a complicated magic, and spells like this unfolded in stages. Initiation. Maintenance. Conclusion. The layers gave it strength, but required concentration and time.

Benat and Joska flanked him on either side as magic lifted Vittoria off the ground. She startled at first, tensing. Then she realized what was happening and composed herself. Despite the blood pooling beneath her feet from dead or dying witches, she didn't seem afraid.

That blazing indignation had replaced terror and uncertainty. And Givers, was she a sight to behold.

Her lips moved, but he heard nothing. Mateo cast another spell as the Declan magic shifted into the maintenance stage. This new spell was easy magic. A sound amplifier that was static and didn't require constant repetition or energy. Even Vittoria could do this one. Simple, but effective. He could keep her elevated and her voice amplified for at least ten minutes.

"In the name of La Principessa," she cried with fury. "I command you to stop."

Shivers raced down his spine. The noise died away immediately around them, but men were still in a blood fury further out. They fought with weapons, fists, swords, pieces of wood, swinging anything they could reach without mercy.

Mateo cast about for a different spell. A louder one. Something that would get their attention. He turned to Benat.

"Light her up," he called.

Seconds later, lights exploded over her head, falling to the ground in the shape of magnolia flowers. At the loud popping noise, Vittoria glanced at Mateo, startled. He met her gaze and nodded. Her look of fear vanished. Seeming to gather her courage, she opened her mouth. Mateo finished a second incantation to amplify sounds. This one required a bit more time to say and only lasted ten seconds, but it would reverberate all the way to the orchards.

"In the name of the Giver of Peace," she shouted, "I command you to *stop!*"

The words rippled through Necce, expanding over the clash of weapons. Her voice echoed back as it reached beyond the orchards. Past the marshes. Over the Saltu. Through the farms. Vittoria's command carried louder than the screams and agonies of war. Witches ducked, hands over their ears.

Then workers dropped to their knees all over the beach. Landowners stopped to stare, mouths agape.

A strange silence followed.

Mateo lifted her higher. The incantation raced through his mind. If he said it once a minute, she'd maintain her position in the air.

He said it again. And he waited for La Principessa to save her witches.

More witches fell to their knees. Mateo cast another spell that slipped down her dress like a wind, cleansing the dirt and blood. Then he cast another—this one from a dressmaker's grimoire Mere had kept stashed away—that made the material glow. Workers all the way to the farmlands would be able to see her white dress, like a beacon.

He pushed her higher. She floated, brilliant gown waving in the breeze that blew in from the ocean. Even the landowner wives on the sea watched her. The chaos had calmed. No more screams interrupted the gray dawn.

"You desire peace," Vittoria cried, this time with less anger, "and yet you murder? This is not peace. This is anarchy."

With another spell from Mateo, a magnolia flower bloomed on her chest, another behind her ear. She acted as if she didn't notice them, but a murmur rippled through the crowd. Magnolia petals fell from the air behind her, fluttering in a light breeze.

Vittoria hovered fifty paces overhead now. Her hair trailed in ribbons off her shoulders. She was otherworldly in her indignation. If fire could burn in someone's eyes, Vittoria's were an inferno.

"We are at a crossroads," Vittoria said. Her voice echoed as it wound through the buildings in Necce, still borne on the power of magic. "We can destroy each other. We can destroy what we, and generations before us, have already built. Or we can start again on new ground with equal footing."

An earthquake rumbled Necce. Screams interrupted the low tremble of the earth at their feet. One of Benat's men transported next to him, wide-eyed.

"The city," he murmured. "It's collapsing. Slowly, but it's happening."

Mateo recast the dressmaker's incantation. Vittoria's dress brightened doubly, the white so blinding it almost hurt to look at. But he couldn't look away. The fierce expression on her face held him captive. He could stare at her forever.

His soon-to-be High Priestess.

"To bring equality to a failing system, we need a leader who will fight for all of us," she continued. "Not for the workers. Not for the landowners. But for both. We need a leader who can break down the weak parts of our society and make them strong. We need a leader who can unite us as broken brothers and sisters. If the Eastern Network is to survive, we must find our strength within. A weak leader has passed. It's time for our true leader to emerge. I call upon Mateo and Romeo to complete the Law of Rights. Let honor and fate allow the proper course to come to pass." She gazed down on Mateo. Her affection appeared in a soft smile meant only for him. "So that the true High Priest may take his throne."

Mateo nearly dropped the incantation as he recited it in his mind. She gazed down at him, but there was no question, no apology in her eyes. Nothing but firm resolve. He had to play his true part now, just as she had played hers. This battle had been stopped, but the war had just begun.

His time had truly arrived.

Mateo nodded once to her.

"Then may the oval be cast." She spread her hands. "And the Network be saved."

The sand burned beneath the flames.

Mateo stood in the oval again, eyes on a jittery Romeo. Blood smeared Romeo's face. Heat built up around them, adding to the already-thick air. Every now and then, the sand trembled at their feet. If Necce was truly collapsing behind them as the catacombs slowly filled with seawater, they had an hour to finish this fight and get these witches somewhere safe.

Outside the oval waited hundreds of witches, more joining the crowd every minute. A tenuous peace had been called, but it felt like a single spark could reignite the violence. Landowners watched from one side, workers from the other. Mateo could feel the weight of their stares. Their expectations.

He'd never felt more ready.

Blood streaked Romeo's shirt in lines of crimson and pink. It had torn at the top seam, revealing his shoulder. Romeo shifted uneasily in the sand. His gaze darted outside the circle. Vittoria stood there, her dress still lightly glowing, flanked by Benat and his men.

Workers stared at her in fear and awe. Whispers of, "La Principessa," circled through the crowd.

Vittoria ignored them.

She just watched Mateo and Romeo circle each other, as if she could guarantee the outcome by sheer force of will.

"Contenders," Balta called again. His voice broke, and he fought to hide a grimace. His left arm was still leaking blood onto a hastily tied bandage. A streak of his hair had been burned off by a blighter gone wild, and one of his front teeth was missing. But he would see this through, even if he was swaying on his feet.

"Advance."

Mateo braced himself, ready for a quick attack from Romeo. Romeo's nostrils flared, but he didn't move.

"I still don't want to kill you, brother," Mateo said quietly, "but I will, and you know it."

Romeo's hand trembled as he reached up and touched his swollen lip. Blood came away on his finger. He looked back through the flames, southward, to the char on the landowner peninsula. The bodies of the dead filled the beach behind them. Despite the low hum of the crowd and the snapping embers of the fire, Mateo thought he could still hear the wail of widows.

"She wasn't supposed to attack the landowners," Romeo whispered.

"The landowners were to be surrounded and forced to surrender, but not harmed."

Mateo straightened. What was this? A game to distract him? Was Romeo trying to pull his attention away?

"Not attacked," Romeo whispered. "She murdered them."

His hand formed a white-knuckled fist.

"No," Romeo continued, speaking to himself now. He studied one of his hands. A knuckle had broken open, staining his skin like the cherries they'd eaten in boyhood. He stared at it, dazed. "She annihilated them. They screamed. They asked me what to do. How this had happened. Now their blood is on my hands. All of those landowners . . ."

He trailed off, pale. The way his hands shook eased Mateo's skepticism. Had his brother gone mad?

"She?" Mateo asked carefully.

Romeo shook his head. His voice lost all power as he lifted his chin. "Mateo, I have wronged you all my life." He swallowed, expression dull. "And now I will pay for it. Now I will pay for everything. And I'm sorry. I'm sorry for the burden of what I've kept from you all these years. I wanted her all to myself. And now? Now she's made a fool of me, too."

"Who is *she*?" Mateo snapped.

"Balta!" Romeo called. He spun to peer through the flames. "I surrender."

The flames winked out.

An astonished sea of faces stared at them when Romeo held up both hands. He stepped back.

"I surrender the throne to Mateo," he shouted. "I surrender! Did you hear that? Can you accept my failure?"

No one said a word.

"Can you live with him on the throne instead of me?"

Mateo tensed. The hair on the back of his neck stood up. Something wasn't right.

Romeo wasn't yelling at the landowners, but he was yelling at someone. He had broken. He bent over now, screaming into the sand, hands threading through his hair as if he wanted to rip it out.

Cool wind rushed past them, sending a chill down Mateo's skin. Vittoria, astonished, blinked several times. Everyone shared the same look of confusion. Even Balta opened his mouth to say something, but closed it again.

"Romeo." Mateo stepped forward. "What are you talking about?"

His brother fell silent.

Several witches gasped. Mateo sensed something shift.

"Mateo!" Benat shouted from the edge of the ring. "Behind you."

Benat grabbed a short sword from his belt and tossed it. Mateo snatched the hilt before it hit the sand and whirled around just as a glint of silver flashed at the corner of his vision. He swung, intercepting a swinging blade headed for his back.

A reverberating *thud* traveled down his arm as his sword clashed with the other blade. He parried a second stroke. He caught a glimpse of black hair and the edge of a whirling dress. Mateo stabilized himself, blocked another attempt, and then stopped cold.

A familiar pair of hazel eyes glared at him.

The words choked in his throat as he fell to a knee, powerless under that gaze.

"Mere?"

The woman pulled herself up, shoulders back. Tilted her head.

Esperanza.

Wrinkles lined her face. Her lips were thin, her cheeks gaunt instead of full. Her skin was pale, so pale. But it was her. Undeniably her. For the longest time, he stared at her. She studied him, inscrutable.

No matter how hard his mind tried to tell him it wasn't possible, he knew it was true the moment she spoke in her quiet, smoky voice.

"Mateo."

His mere was alive. He stumbled back. "What is . . ."

Words failed him. Had he been killed and sent to the afterlife? No. The astonishment and confusion on the faces around him meant he hadn't died. He could feel the cool sand between his toes. Smell the stench of smoke from the oval.

Could this actually be Esperanza?

"Mere? I . . ."

Romeo gained his feet. Fury radiated through him. "You promised to spare the landowners," he cried. "You swore to me that not a single one of them had to die if I helped you!"

Esperanza raised a thin brow. "I told you the Guardians would turn on them. But you've never wanted to hear what you don't want to face. Don't be a fool, Romeo. Of course landowners would die. There must be bloodshed if there will ever be change. You've always known this. Besides, what does it matter if the landowners die? Workers have died for decades. It's time to even the playing field."

"What else have you lied to me about?" he demanded, his voice shrill. "The throne? Were you really going to give me the throne?"

She spread her hands. "Do I not stand before you, as I promised? Were you not the one who was to win the Law of Rights?"

"What else?" he shouted, a wild glint in his eye.

Esperanza's gaze narrowed.

Mateo wanted to throw up. Only the rough sand beneath him kept him centered. He struggled to pull himself back together until he felt a hand on his shoulder. Vittoria crouched at his side. The dusky scent of magnolias washed over him.

"Mateo," she whispered while Romeo shouted something else at Mere, "this is real. It *is* your mere. I don't know how or why, but we'll figure it out later. Remember why you are here. You are now the High Priest. You are strong enough for whatever this situation demands of you. You owe her nothing."

"I can't." Shock rendered his brain almost mute. "She . . ."

"You can." Vittoria squeezed his shoulder. "You will know what to do. The answers will come out eventually. You are strong enough, Mateo."

Jolted out of his stupor, Mateo slowly stood. Vittoria stepped back, close to Benat. Mateo straightened. Still, he reeled. Mere alive.

And Romeo had known.

The pieces fell together like the ashes blowing off the boats. Romeo's comment at the Test of Courage. *I owe you something.* His frustration at Mateo's affection for him. Had guilt turned Romeo away from Mateo?

Hodei's dying words, the assassination attempts he wouldn't claim.

I was not your enemy.

Had it been Mere all along?

"I suppose there is one thing I didn't tell you," Esperanza said to Romeo, although her voice still rang over the crowd. It drew Mateo back to the present.

Romeo's fist clenched as Esperanza closed the distance between them. "What?" he spat. His left hand closed over a knife hilt as Esperanza approached. Romeo tightened his grip on it, knuckles white.

She leaned forward, her face a breath away. "I never really believed you could kill Mateo."

Esperanza slid her sword into Romeo's ribs with a violent jab. Romeo gasped, mouth agape. Mateo shouted, but it was too late.

She withdrew the bloody blade. Romeo staggered back, into Mateo's arms. A witch in the crowd screamed.

"No!" Mateo cried.

He clutched Romeo to him, gently lowering him onto the sand. Wide-eyed, Romeo stared past Mateo, gaze fixed on the lightening sky. Pale pink and violet clouds veiled the sunrise. His lips moved, mouth stained with blood. Tears blurred Mateo's eyes.

"Brother." He put a hand on Romeo's bloody chest in trembling disbelief. The crimson stain spread in a circle. "I'm sorry. I couldn't save you either time. I'm sorry."

Romeo's body bucked. "Kill her," he whispered. His body slackened, and his eyes rolled back in his head. For a full minute, Mateo's body froze. He couldn't move. The shocked silence of the crowd meant he wasn't the only one stunned into silence.

Finally, Mateo straightened, Romeo's blood on his hands. Esperanza stood only a few paces away, chin high.

Anguish strengthened his cry.

"Why?"

"Because he surrendered." She scowled. "I have not hidden in those catacombs for over a decade just for him to give up as we reached the goal. He swore me a blood oath when he was eleven that he would help me get our revenge, and he broke it. If I didn't kill him, the magic would have." She waved a dismissive hand. "This was a merciful death."

The words spun through Mateo's head with ruthless abandon. Blood oath. Eleven years. Romeo had been tied to her by a blood oath since she'd supposedly died.

He had *always* known.

"Catacombs?" he whispered. "That's where you've been? You faked your death and hid in the catacombs?"

"It's easy to die when no one wants you alive."

"I wanted you alive!"

"And yet," she said primly, "you survived without me, didn't you? Mateo, we never saw eye-to-eye. You lacked nothing that you didn't find from other witches. You were always the stronger one."

No remorse showed on her face, which was as cold as glass. The same expression Romeo had given him when he'd tried to reach him. Mateo's thoughts stumbled over each other. Romeo. Mere. Death. Oaths.

"Why?" he asked again. "Why hide for eleven years? Why kill your son?"

A flicker of emotion disturbed her icy countenance. "Hodei," she said through clenched teeth. "It was the only way I could make him as miserable as he had made me. The only way to truly fight him. He had controlled me all of our marriage, then stupidly allowed me to live after he found out the truth, and that was his mistake."

"So you faked your death to hide underground and make him as miserable as possible?"

"No. I faked my death and assumed my place as leader of the rebels. Xavier was dead, and all we had built was falling apart. I had to do it, Mateo, or everything would have been for nothing." She gestured around them. "The ultimate plan never changed: we have always wanted to bring equality to the Network. The Castaneda line is tired. They are mad. We need a new leader. A new start. A new chance!"

A distant crash came from Necce. She grinned as if the collapsing catacombs were conspiring with her.

"There is no saving the Eastern Network, Mateo. There is too much hatred. Too much history. We must start over. Burn it down so we can all begin with the same thing: nothing. The landowners will know how it feels to be a worker, and there will be no inequality among us. How can you fight over belongings when there are none to cause trouble?"

"And winter?" Mateo rasped. "How did you plan to survive the cold season without shelter?"

"We shall rebuild!" she cried, her eyes alight with fevered passion. "With landowners and workers together, we will have shelters put together in time."

"Winter begins in two weeks! The temperatures are already dropping."

"We'll figure it out, Mateo!" She threw her arms wide. "As equals. And I will be the High Priestess to lead us through it. I will create the equality the workers have longed for. And *I* will destroy Hodei's dark regime and all he stood for. For what could discomfit Hodei even more than death? Me taking over his throne. It is," she whispered with a sly smile, "the ultimate revenge. I shall destroy all he made, and he will be forgotten. Stricken from history. As if he never existed."

"You set your rebels to kill the landowners," he managed. "To *slaughter* them. This wasn't about equality, this was about revenge. Now you expect to lead witches whose families you've murdered?"

"And what has Hodei done all these years?" she cried. "The landowners deserve to know what we've gone through, and if they must give their lives to understand, I accept that!"

"This is about the future! This isn't about what you feel you are owed. One dark deed doesn't deserve another. There are other ways to hold them accountable."

She scoffed. "Trials, you mean? Like the trials your sweet Vittoria would have faced if Romeo won? He would have drowned her in the ocean, Mateo! It was his plan. So would all of those landowners. They will destroy you if you don't get rid of them. We'll kill the men," she said firmly. "The women may live."

A ripple of shock tore through the crowd. Tension gripped the landowners, whose gazes darted from Romeo's body to Mateo.

Mateo bit back his response. Mere was right. Vittoria would have died if he'd lost and Benat couldn't get them away fast enough. No landowner would have shown mercy to any rebel. Any insubordinate.

Even if the landowners had to kill them all and lose their creature comforts for a while, he imagined they would have.

"You created more anarchy, Mere." Mateo advanced on her. "You lied to and cheated these witches for *years*! And you think you can rule them? You think you deserve that calling?"

He shouted now. Used magic to amplify his voice. Wanted every single witch to know exactly what they were up against.

"I earned it," she hissed. "I earned it for every day that I sat in those catacombs and made Hodei's life miserable. For sacrificing my son to him! I gave him Romeo to try to twist and turn into something else, but it didn't work. As always, Romeo was loyal to me."

Mateo could hardly comprehend what this meant. What Romeo had endured, pulled between two of the most evil witches he'd ever met. His parents.

Perhaps fate had served Mateo by removing him from their reach.

"I've earned this throne for everything I have given to my Network," Esperanza screeched. She pointed her sword at him, the edge glinting in the dawn. "And now I will rebuild it the way it should be. Without a single Castaneda on the throne. For the sake of peace, Mateo, you must join your brother. Now is the time of the worker. The time for a new regime! For equality!"

Mateo scoffed, unable to bear these wrathful words from her lips. Romeo's plea for Mateo to kill him whispered back to him now. *Kill me now, Mateo! Or you will never win this throne. Prove yourself worthy!*

Now he had to kill his mere.

His resurrected, maniacal mere.

"Equality." He shook his head. "No. You are building a world of hatred. You want to revenge yourself on Hodei, not take care of the Network. If you truly cared about equality, you would never have abandoned me."

Her voice was cold. "I did what I must. I have given my entire life to take Hodei's throne. To avenge myself for what he took from me! My freedom. My life. My son. My home. I'm not about to give it up now, Mateo."

"The assassins?" he asked, but he already knew.

She shifted. Her gaze dropped for half a second. "You stood in my way, Mateo. You always stood in my way. You stole the wealth I would have used to support the rebels. It took years to replace that wealth! We searched everywhere for it," she hissed, "but could never find it because of you."

"I was fourteen!"

"And strong! Determined as any boy I'd ever seen, and obsessed with magic. You had power already! How would Romeo or I have ever compared to you unless you lost everything? The Law of Rights was always going to be invoked, but I knew Romeo wouldn't be able to beat you. He cared too much. So I had to take care of you before Romeo could invoke it. Obviously," she muttered, "you're a hard man to kill."

"Forgive me," he replied icily, "for staying alive."

"You taking the wealth I had so carefully grown forced us to slowly build up the rebel force instead of acting right away. So I did. I strove to make Hodei as miserable and uncomfortable as possible with our attacks, and we waited for him to die so that I could stand in his place and do what always needed to be done for this Network. Fire. Destruction. Rebirth from the ashes."

"You're mad," he whispered.

She laughed. "I'm not mad, Mateo. I'm the new High Priestess, and you will bow to me."

Mateo gestured to Benat, who unsheathed his long sword and tossed it to him. Mateo caught the hilt, spun, and faced his mere.

"Romeo surrendered, and Hodei is dead," he called, amplifying his voice. "The rule of the Network is mine by right and by law, and I accept my throne. You are a usurper, a threat to all my witches, and you will die for your insurrection and your crimes against workers and landowners alike." He fell into a fighting stance, sword glinting. "If you want the East, you'll have to kill me first."

Esperanza stepped forward, black silk dress sighing in the wind.

"Gladly."

35

VITTORIA

Fear gripped Vittoria the moment Esperanza swung her sword.

Mateo easily blocked her strike and danced to the right, Benat's longer sword tight in his right hand. Esperanza advanced again, but Mateo staved her off. Despite all those years in the catacombs, she'd clearly prepared for this day.

Vittoria's heart ached for him, but swelled with pride for the way he held himself together. Today, Mateo would lose his entire family in one fell swoop.

"Will he win?" Sannara whispered. She stared at Mateo. At the crowd. At the sky. At anything but Romeo's body on the sand. Tears trickled down her cheeks, as if acknowledging his death would break something inside her.

"He must," Vittoria replied, grateful for Sannara at her side, grateful for the knowledge that Eneko was safe with Mere and Pere.

Esperanza pressed a chance to gain the offensive upper hand, but Mateo's defense came too quickly, and he pushed the advantage he had in size. Although she danced out of his way with smooth footwork, he took up more room than she did. His arm reached longer. She ducked out of the way with a grunt more than once.

When Mateo slashed at her neck, she slipped back. Her balance off, she dropped a hand to the sand and caught herself. Taking advantage of her open chest, Mateo swiped. She caught his blade with hers and tossed a handful of sand. He recoiled with a shout, sand in his eyes. With a hiss, Esperanza lunged for his thigh, but he knocked her away.

Vittoria shuddered when a slash of red appeared on Mateo's arm, but he didn't seem to notice. Esperanza tried to hide it, but she'd already begun to tire. Mateo spun and kicked up sand, but Esperanza blocked it with a spell and sent it back at him. Mateo seemed to test her, swinging high, then low, as if he didn't really mean to hit her.

Neither of them spoke.

No one in the crowd made a sound. Esperanza moved fast, her breaths coming in quick pants, until Mateo closed the distance. She tried to shove her sword into his ribs, but he anticipated her. Then he barreled at her like a ship.

There was no hesitation in his face. No fear in his eyes. No concern in the way he handled the sword as if it were an extension of himself.

Sweat beaded on Esperanza's brow as she blocked his advances, but her feet tangled in her dress. The sand gave out beneath her feet, and she fell. Mateo leaped and cracked the edge of her sword, slicing her wrist. She cried out, blood spurting from the injury. Her blade fell to the sand. Mateo kicked it away.

"For Romeo," he hissed.

His sword plunged into her chest.

Esperanza's body jerked with the sudden, violent thrust. She gasped, eyes wide as the force pulled her up, and then dropped her back. Wordlessly, her lips moved. She kept her gaze on Mateo, lips twisted in pain.

"You destroyed my brother," he whispered, tears in his eyes. "Now I have destroyed you. You will not exist in the annals of history. No one will remember your name. The Castaneda line will continue, and I will right the wrongs you and Pere have brought upon us. Let that be your dying awareness. I will never be like you, and that is the legacy I will always carry. That is the promise I make. May honor obliterate you."

The pale light of dawn caressed her startled expression. Her eyes flittered to Romeo before she choked on her own blood. A crimson stain tinged her lips as her breaths sputtered, then died away in a drawn-out sigh. Her muscles slackened.

For a long, long pause, Mateo stood there. Vittoria wanted to reach out to him. To remind him that he wasn't alone. That he wasn't his mere or his pere. That he was the High Priest and he had earned it. But she didn't. She remained quiet while he regarded his mere—truly dead before his eyes this time—as if for the first time.

There would be months of trying to understand what he had discovered today. Years of putting the pieces together. Years of mourning the family he should have had. Of regret for the atrocious things they had done.

But perhaps there was one thing he'd never question: that he was the one meant to do this.

Seconds later, Mateo yanked his sword free. A sucking sound came from Esperanza's chest as blood bubbled onto the sand. He stood over her with a snarl, dripping sword held in front of him. When no one else advanced, he stuck his sword in the sand. The sun rose overhead, ascending above the shimmering ocean. In the distance, another reverberating crash sounded. A slight tremor shuddered the sand at Vittoria's feet.

She stepped forward until she stood in front of him. His body trembled. He stared at the sand.

"Mateo." She put her trembling hands over his cheeks. Tears thickened her throat. "Look at me."

He blinked, absently putting a hand over hers. When their eyes met, she saw shock. Pain. A glazed sort of disbelief.

"You did it," she whispered. "You are the High Priest. The civil war is quelled. At least, so far. You have given us a chance to redeem the mistakes of the past and a reason to unite. You are the goodness from a broken family, and you are made to lead. The time to step up is now."

"No, *masuna*," he whispered, his fingers tightening around hers. "*We* have done it."

Mateo gathered Vittoria into his arms and held her close. She ignored all the eyes staring at them. The unbroken tension ready to ignite. Instead, she lost herself in the feeling of her heart pounding against his.

He was alive.

Mateo gripped Vittoria for a moment longer, as if he could physically draw strength from her. Then he slowly released her, but kept their hands tangled together. He moved in a slow circle to face all the witches around them.

"I am Mateo!" he called. Magic carried his voice over the crowd with a slight echo. *Mateo. Mateo. Mateo.* "I am the High Priest of the Eastern Network, and I will command your allegiance. If you don't wish to give it, that is your choice. You may leave for the wilds of the North. We will have an escort for you. My first order of business is to get everyone off this peninsula and somewhere safe."

Another rumble sounded from Necce, and dust billowed upward. Vittoria felt a surge of pride, and love. There was still tension in the air. Landowners warily eyed snarling workers. The hostility would run deep for a long time. Decades of servitude and oppression could not be rectified overnight, nor by a single leader. But Mateo seemed to instinctively sense that all witches in the Eastern Network had to know he *was* here for them.

"My second order of business will be to establish a new Council to make a plan to move forward into a new life. A better life. A fair life, where everyone is heard no matter their status and we all have a chance. Is there anyone who wants to challenge me?"

A territorial growl had replaced his usual diplomacy. Blood and bruises stained him, and he looked as haggard as the rest of them. The unusual appearance gave him a wild look, befitting a leader who had been through so much.

Silence hovered over the crowd in response.

Of course, witches would challenge him, Vittoria imagined. Give the landowners a few days to process the enormity of what had happened—all the Guardians turning to murder them, for one—and they would be spitting mad. An unbearable number of problems were going to pour into Mateo's lap for months and years. Workers would rightly want compensation and restitution. All witches would want an idea of what all this meant. Mateo wouldn't be able to do everything for everyone, but at least he was willing to start.

Right then, all Mateo needed was a chance to unveil his plan without a civil war breaking out. Without the terror of the night reaching a new fever pitch in the light of day and exploding like the powder that had nearly destroyed Magnolia Castle.

Another crash and rumble came from behind them. The ground shivered.

"It's time to clear the peninsula," he called. "The catacombs are collapsing underneath Necce as we speak, and no one is safe here. If you can transport, do so now. Those of you who can't, remain. I will find someone to transport you to safety."

The ground shook, but no one disappeared. Instead, all Necce's witches seemed to hold their breaths. Then the crowd parted behind Mateo, and Vittoria gasped. A few exclamations came from Mateo's right, and he whirled around, Vittoria still in hand. Weary, bloodied Balta, with his missing tooth and scorched hair, stumbled toward them through the sand. Once he stood a few paces away, he dropped to one knee. Tears brimmed in his eyes.

"To my High Priest and High Priestess." He put a hand over his left shoulder and bowed his head. "I pledge my life."

A ripple moved through the crowd. Vittoria whirled around, tucked close to Mateo's side, as workers began to kneel behind her. First Benat and his men and the workers behind them. A wave of rebels fell to their knees next, hands over their left shoulders. The movement spread outward until everyone—landowners, workers, and rebels—paid homage to their new leaders, even if some tight expressions hinted at reluctance.

Mateo's grip on Vittoria tightened, and she felt glad for the extra support. Relief made her dizzy, her thoughts blunted in the aftermath of so much fear and violence. What must Mateo feel like in comparison? She squeezed his hand.

"This has been a difficult and bloody night," Mateo continued. "But as it always does, daylight has come. I am the leader you need. I have prepared for this. I have plans for peace and safety. Plans to forge our new path. We will hear *all* witches. We will unite as one Network. Together, we can right wrongs and forge a new path forward. We will unite from within and create a new and better world."

Witches took up the cry, chanting, *Together! Together!* Waves crashed on the shore, washing away the blood in sheets of pink foam. Beams of sunlight burst overhead, banishing the gray clouds to the distant horizon.

Vittoria tilted her head back to look deep into Mateo's weary but exultant eyes.

"Together," she whispered.

36

"As always," Mere whispered, her voice thick with emotion, "you are perfect, *Principessa*."

With a trembling smile, Vittoria wrapped Mere in a warm hug. She closed her eyes, savoring the feel of Mere against her. Of *life*. Of presence, warmth, and existence. They were here, and that was all that mattered.

"Thank you, Mere."

Sunlight flooded her apartment in Magnolia Castle and filled her with warmth all the way to her soul. The tile floor felt cool beneath her bare feet as she pulled away, giving Mere one last grin. Her satin dress slipped over the tiles as she scuttled over to her bed to grab her cloth shoes.

Pere appeared from around the corner, perched proudly in his rolling chair and wearing a new blazer of emerald green. He stopped as soon as he saw Vittoria sliding into her slippers. Tears filled his eyes as he lifted a trembling hand to his mouth.

"*Masuna*," he murmured. "You are so lovely."

Vittoria reached for him and clasped both of his hands in hers. "Thank you, Pere. I am . . . so happy."

She reached up to touch her hair and make sure it hadn't fallen. Mere had brushed it, then coiffed it into a simple, elegant bun at the back of her head. Nothing dazzling. Today would stand on its own beauty. No need for anything elaborate.

"On this day of all days," Pere said with a little wink, "you should be the happiest woman in all of Alkarra."

Mere reached into a bowl, plucked a magnolia from it, and slipped it into Vittoria's hair with a little smile.

"La Principessa deserves her flower on her day."

"Thank you, Mere."

Mere stopped, put both her hands on Vittoria's shoulders, and pulled her close again. Their foreheads touched, eyes closing. "Thank you, *masuna*. You risked all to give us all. The Givers have blessed you. Now we no longer need them. They are retreating to their own paradise and awaiting us. I can feel the peace they have left behind." She pressed a hand to her heart. "You have freed your witches, and your Givers."

Before Vittoria could respond, a voice screeched from around the corner. Eneko appeared, nearly colliding with Pere's chair.

Sannara called out after him. "I told you!" she chided. "You go too fast. You're going to hurt someone."

With his adorable grin, Eneko skidded to a stop, eyes wide. The haphazard cloth tied around his neck was charmingly lopsided, and his once-combed hair was already disheveled. The lightest hint of sugar dusted his upper lip.

"Tori!" Eneko called. "You look really pretty!"

Sannara came up behind him with a weary but warm smile. She wrapped her arms around him. "Indeed," she murmured. "You are lovely, Vittoria."

"Thank you." Vittoria bent down to press a kiss to the top of Eneko's head. "I don't think Mateo will ever be as handsome as you, however. Don't tell him I told you that."

"He won't." Eneko grinned.

Vittoria laughed and bopped him on the nose. "Someone has found the hidden treat jar. Hmm?"

Eneko shrugged, affecting a bright, innocent smile.

"Nor as humble as Mateo," she added with a laugh. "Tell me, is Mateo ready?"

Eneko's head bobbed up and down.

"They're all ready, Tori," Sannara said, gesturing toward the hallway. A flutter of nerves overcame Vittoria's stomach, and she let out a long, slow breath.

"Is he waiting?"

Eneko's head bobbed again.

"Are there a lot of people in the room waiting, also?"

"They said I should tell you that it's ready to begin but they can't 'cause you're not there." He held up his hands. "You gotta hurry!"

Vittoria grinned. "Good. Tell Mateo I'm on my way, and then you can have another treat from the jar." She held up a finger. "*After* the ceremony."

With a whoop, he disappeared around the corner. Sannara followed sedately after, muttering something about busy boys. Vittoria smiled at her parents, gave them one last kiss, and watched them leave the room ahead of her. When Pere cast a look over his shoulder in question, she said, "I'll be right there."

Mere smiled warmly, took Pere's hand, and together they disappeared.

Another attack of nerves in her stomach prevented her from leaving. She paused to glance around the room with a sense of undisguised awe that hadn't gone away yet. Three weeks of living in the unburnt half of Magnolia Castle, and her wonder still hadn't abated. When a nervous tremor shivered through her stomach, she ran a hand down the simple satin and let out a long breath. Time to get this over with.

In, Mateo had instructed her, *and out.*

Two months ago, Mateo had ascended the throne as High Priest of the Eastern Network. Less than a day later, a peace agreement had been signed with the Central Network. Two days after that, refugee camps had been established in the orchards for landowners and workers—collectively referred to as *witches,* for now—while the damage to Necce was assessed. It appeared to be extensive. Plans to create new foundations and level the ground had been underway within a day.

A week after his ascension, a new Council had been instituted with new representatives—a mix of landowners and workers—with progressive ideals. Changes included a Restoration Committee, appointees to represent the rights of the workers through the transition, and a new Head of Education.

With diligent and steady work, Magnolia Castle's west wing had been restored enough for the High Priest to move back in.

Today, the entire Network closed the final door on their old lives.

With a deep breath, Vittoria approached a marble sculpture that stood on a shelf built into the wall. La Principessa. She reached out with a soft smile and put her other hand over her heart. "Thank you," she whispered.

Then she slipped out of the room and into the hallway with the quiet *hush* of her dress on the floor.

Sunbeams escorted her through marble halls and past paintings of previous High Priestesses. Esperanza's was not among them. Vittoria's shoulders were back, her head held high. The skin on her knuckles prickled as she passed the portraits. She remembered her life of hot cauldrons. Caustic potions. *Andreas* shouting at her.

She thought of the mobs of the desperate, the needy. Of the rage of the rebels, the fear of the landowners. They were still afraid, all of them. But a tenuous peace had settled on the land for now, which paved the path forward for negotiation and concession. Leaders had arisen from all areas. Education had started up immediately, so that workers would be able to represent themselves. Until they could represent themselves, Vittoria would be their voice.

She continued walking the path to her new life. Her mind was clear, her heart full.

I am, she thought, *the High Priestess.*

Mateo stood alone at a pair of double doors, clearly lost in thought. His hair was down, and it framed his stubbled face with long, shiny locks. He wore a freshly pressed white shirt under an emerald jacket, with black pants and dress shoes. Lines had appeared on his face from the stress of the last two months. He frowned too much these days, lost in the many cares and complexities of stabilizing his Network.

Regardless, he was elegance in male form if she had anything to say about it.

Mateo looked up when he heard her approach. A dazzling smile illuminated his handsome face. A new light burned in him now. The light of success. Of dreams realized. Of work accomplished.

A flush of warmth spread from the top of her head all the way to her toes when he looked at her like that. She slowed as she neared him and stopped a few paces away, a half smile lingering on her face.

Mateo would have none of that.

He strode to her, whisked her off her feet, and twirled her around. With a giggle, she clung to his strong shoulders. A tendril of hair escaped her bun and trailed across her cheek as he set her down. With gentle fingers, he brushed the hair from her eyes and tucked it behind her ear.

"Are you ready, *masuna*?" he whispered.

"Yes."

"You cannot go back after this."

She smiled, tilting her head back. He held her hands in his, swallowing her small fingers in his capable hands.

"I would never want to go back. Only forward. With you."

Mateo pressed his lips to hers in a stolen kiss that sent heat all the way back to her toes. She leaned into him until his fingers slid into her hair. Seconds later, he pulled away with a raspy breath.

"Later, my love. Now is not the time, or we'll make all of them jealous."

She laughed and put some space between them. His eyes sparkled when he winked at her, then held out a hand. "Shall we, Lady?"

"Yes, Majesty."

Mateo walked her to the double doors. Together, they peered into the room. Landowners sat on the left. Most of them were younger, forced to fill their peres' positions after so many deaths in the uprising. Workers filled the room on the right. Their faces were scrubbed. Clothes clean. Vittoria's parents sat in the front row. So did Sannara. Benat. Joska. Balta, newly appointed Head of Guardians. And Eneko, sitting on his mere's lap with a goofy grin.

Some of the landowners averted their eyes, unable to look at Vittoria. She ignored their fear and uncertainty. They would not bring their prejudices to this day, nor this moment. She wouldn't allow them that power, not when they had taken it from workers for so long. Today was about taking a step forward.

Leaving that behind.

Vittoria focused on what sat in front of her: her future, represented by two elegant golden chairs, equal in size. The one on the left was inlaid with glimmering pearls of various widths and tones, and the one on the right boasted emeralds.

"Mine is the one on the right," Mateo whispered with a roguish wink.

Vittoria suppressed a laugh. He was convinced that their handfasting two weeks ago at the rubble of the *eliza* of the Giver La Principessa had made him funnier. She couldn't deny him his humor now that it had space to emerge in a brighter world.

"And mine," she murmured, "is right next to yours."

He gripped her hand. "Where you always will be."

Together, Vittoria and Mateo walked to the thrones. They turned, faced their audience, and sat down. Zaldar approached with a circlet of rose gold, carved with magnolia flowers, and knelt before Vittoria with a warm smile.

"To our Lady," he said. "May we always call you *Majesty*."

Mateo reached over, took the crown, and carefully laid it on Vittoria's head. He stopped, pulled in a breath as he regarded her, then reached down and pressed a kiss to her hand.

"I don't deserve you," he murmured, "my High Priestess."

In all her life, Vittoria had never felt so light. So determined. So ready. With Mateo and her family at her side, she could do anything.

From the back of the room, Balta called, "Presenting Her Majesty, the *lavanda* maid Lady Vittoria Nerea Antoinetta Guita of the Mayfair Coven. Your High Priestess!"

THE END

ALSO BY KATIE CROSS

The Network Series

Mildred's Resistance (prequel)

Miss Mabel's School for Girls

Alkarra Awakening

The High Priest's Daughter

War of the Networks

The Network Series Complete Collection

The Isadora Interviews (novella)

Short Stories from Miss Mabel's

Short Stories from the Network Series

The Dragonmaster Trilogy

FLAME

Chronicles of the Dragonmasters (short stories)

FLIGHT

The Ronan Scrolls (novella)

FREEDOM

The Dragonmaster Trilogy Collection

The Historical Collection

The High Priestess

The Network Saga

The Lost Magic (coming September 3, 2021)

ABOUT KATIE

I write fantasy books so you can seize the light. Hold magic in your finger-tips. Command dragons. Throw yourself at the mercy of an attractive stranger. You'll forget the shadows of real life to live your wildest adventure.

And remember that you are the hero of your own story.